JOURN
TO THE
GREAT
WHITE THRONE
JUDGMENT

JUDY KAY SCOTT

Todd,
Throughout the years you have become a son to me.
Love, Judy Kay Scott

OakTara

Waterford, Virginia

Journey to The Great White Throne Judgment

Published in the U.S. by:
OakTara Publishers
P.O. Box 8, Waterford, VA 20197
www.oaktara.com

Cover design by Yvonne Parks at www.pearcreative.ca
Cover images © iStockphoto.com: girl in white dress/contrastaddict; www.shutterstock.com/blurred action from car at high speed/timy; stairs in sky/LilKar

Copyright © 2011 by Judy Kay Scott. All rights reserved.

Unless otherwise noted, Scripture verses are taken from the New King James Version®. Copyright © 1982 by Thomas Nelson, Inc. Used by permission. All rights reserved.

Other Scriptures taken from *The Living Bible,* copyright © 1971. Used by permission of Tyndale House Publishers, Inc., Wheaton, IL 60189. All rights reserved.

ISBN: 978-1-60290-274-9

Journey to The Great White Throne Judgment is a work of fiction. References to real people, events, establishments, organizations, or locales are intended only to provide a sense of authenticity and are used fictitiously. All other characters, incidents, and dialogue are drawn from the author's imagination.

Printed in the U.S.A.

⌘ ⌘ ⌘

First, I want to dedicate this novel TO GOD.
I could not have done it without His divine inspiration.

I would also like to dedicate it TO MY HUSBAND, RUSSELL SCOTT.
He has worked beside me, enduring long hours as I created this story.
Russell was my toughest critic and also my amateur editor.

Next, I want to thank MY DAUGHTER, SHERYL PERYSIAN,
for her encouragement and editing.

Last of all, a big thanks goes out TO ALL MY FRIENDS AND FAMILY
who helped and encouraged me along the way.

1

As I was twisting and moaning, I faintly heard a voice saying, "Please, sweetheart, wake up. Come back to me."

Struggling to open my eyes, I could see a blurred vision of a man in front of me. My eyes opened more and I cried out, "Tommy, Tommy."

"Yes, Lorraine, I'm right here!" Tears were flowing down his face and he laughed a little under his breath. "You haven't called me that in years. I thought I lost you, my darling."

In confusion I whispered, "What are you doing here? Did God send you to save me?"

"Honey, you were..."

Blurting out, I cried, "Oh, dear Lord, now I remember!"

Then my mind raced on as I recalled the horrifying ordeal I had just gone through. I remembered waking up in terror to the blast of a car horn, and the glare of headlights. I screamed, "Scotty, they're going to hit us!"

The next thing I remembered was being in a state of confusion. My mind was rushing for answers. *Where am I? Where's the car....the kids?*

Coming to my senses, I felt the car behind me. As I turned toward the car, I was horrified when I saw Linda all twisted up in the back seat. "Linda, Linda! Talk to me, baby. Are you all right?"

She didn't answer, so I shook her limp body. She didn't respond to that either.

"Scotty! They hit us, son, they hit us!" I yelled for him again, but still no answer. I leaned over the front seat to get a better look. He was slumped over the steering wheel, unconscious and bleeding. I buried my head in the back of the front seat and cried like a baby.

When I raised my head and started wiping away my tears, I noticed a woman hanging out the passenger side. She was covered in blood. I was hysterical and ran screaming from the car, "Somebody help me!"

Then I saw the car that hit us. It looked demolished. I hoped someone would still be alive who could help. I reached the other car and looked inside. A man with tears streaming down his face was holding a woman's bleeding head in his lap, as she lay motionless on the seat. Pounding on the window, I begged, "Please, Mister, can you help me?" He didn't answer. I thought, *He must be in shock. Why didn't he hear me?*

The wail of a siren startled me as I looked to see the lights from a patrol car. That sound was music to my ears. Help had come at last!

A black-and-white patrol car pulled up, and two policemen got out. They walked over to an elderly couple. My mind raced. *Where did they come from? I didn't notice them before.*

"Sir, are either of you hurt?" one of the officers asked.

"Oh no," I heard the old gent say. "No, we weren't in the accident. We saw it and stopped. My wife is a retired nurse and thought we could help."

"Yes," said the lady. "I suggest you get an ambulance here in a hurry."

"We have ambulances en route, ma'am. How about the people in this car," he said, pointing to the car where I was standing. "Do you know what condition they are in?"

"Yes, this is the only car we had time to check out. We were on our way over to the other one when you arrived. It's my opinion that the man will make it, but it may be too late for the woman."

"Thanks, ma'am."

I was getting upset. I wanted them to stop talking and go check on my kids. "Never mind this car," I yelled. "My kids are in the other car and they're hurt bad!"

The policemen completely ignored me, like I didn't exist. Instead, one of the officers tapped the hood of the car and said to his partner, "Bill, you stay here and help these people, while I check out the other car."

"About time," I mumbled under my breath.

The retired nurse shook her head. "Looking at the condition of that car, it doesn't look good for those folks either."

Her husband gave her a little nudge. "Come on, Ma, maybe we can help." The elderly couple struggled to keep up with the policeman. Even with my three-inch heels, I didn't have any problem keeping up with the officer. The only thing that mattered was getting help for my kids. On the way there I tried to tell him how bad my kids were hurt, but he kept ignoring me. I knew my kids were going to be taken care of now, but it still made me furious that he wouldn't say one word to me.

The ambulances pulled in about the same time we got back to my car. I was so relieved to know they would soon be working on my kids.

The police officer went directly to the open door, which was buried in the ground. He noticed a purse lying beside the car and picked it up. Then he looked inside at the woman covered in blood. I was curious, too, and took another look at her. *Who the heck is she? Was I that drunk when we left the party that someone could have rode with us? Had Scotty brought a girlfriend home with him? Why can't I remember! I can see that she went through the windshield; her face is all cut up. She sure is a mystery.*

The officer looked inside the purse. Among the cosmetics, he located a wallet. He opened it and read out loud, "Lorraine Patterson."

The old couple heard him say the name as they walked up. The woman asked, "Did I hear you right, Officer? Did you say that the ID is Lorraine Patterson's?"

"Yes, ma'am, I did. Do you know her?"

"Well, yes, I guess. If she is the same Lorraine I knew several years ago."

"Now, Mother," the old gent said, "it's been a lot of years. If she had been married, then her name wouldn't be Patterson anymore."

"You're probably right, but there is a possibility that it could be her. Some women take back their maiden name when they get divorced. Maybe she never got married. Look at that beautiful long black hair. In spite of how cut up she is, you can tell she is a very lovely woman. It could very well be her."

"I'm afraid…was, lady," one of the paramedics said. "I just took her pulse. I believe she is gone."

"Oh no, George, it can't be Lorraine!"

"Well, it's been at least twenty years since we saw her last, Ma."

"Yes, dear, when we tried to help her."

"Yeah, we ran into her outside that awful, God-forsaken abortion clinic."

"Yes, dear, she listened to us, and came to our alternative counseling sessions."

"Thank the Lord for that! She was a real mess when she came to us, wasn't she?"

"Yes, she was so upset."

"At least we tried, Ruth, to follow up on her like we did the other girls, but somehow we lost contact with her."

"Oh, George, look—those two youngsters…they're about the right age to be Lorraine's children."

"I hope not! This car reeks of alcohol. I can't imagine a mother being in a car with her kids that smells like this car does."

"And look at the way she's dressed; it's shameful!"

"I only hope she made peace with God before she died," her husband added.

"At least you told her about the good news of the Gospel of Jesus Christ. It was up to her to make the right decision. Either she accepted Jesus, or she didn't."

⌘⌘⌘

Tears began flowing from my eyes as I remembered. I did know them from many years ago! They had been good, caring people. They had really touched my heart in a big way. I wanted to give my heart to the Lord back then, but somehow I couldn't let go of the reckless life I was living. In the years to follow it only got worse.

Now, as I watched this tragic ordeal unfold, I felt so ashamed. I questioned myself: *What kind of a mother am I who goes out drinking with her kids? One who goes along to a party with her eighteen-year-old son and drags her fourteen-year-old daughter along? Why did I let Scotty take the keys and let him drive in that condition! If I hadn't, we wouldn't have had this disastrous accident….*

You stupid fool! I scolded myself. *What are you thinking? I was too drunk to drive, too! It's all my fault! I've hurt my kids, maybe even killed them!*

As I fought back the tears, I turned to Mrs. Bloomington and said, "That's not me. I'm all right!" I tried to get her to understand. "That is my ID, but it isn't me laying there dead. My purse must have flown out of the car like I did." I pointed my finger at me and said, "See it's me, Lorraine Patterson, I'm alive!"

I gestured to the dead woman's body. "That's not me….it….it's someone we must have picked up. It's someone who looks like me, that's all!" But, I still wondered, who was she, and where did she come from?

Then a strange chill came over my body. The paramedics were working hard to save my kids. I heard one say, "I don't think we'll make it to the hospital in time for either of these two."

I glanced over at the dead woman again, and suddenly I knew who she was. At the realization of knowing, I screamed, "It's ME!"

In spite of my struggle to survive, I felt myself fading further and further away from the scene of the accident. I was whirling through a dark tunnel. In the distance I saw a point of light. As I reached the end of the light, I was in a new dimension. Something like smoke appeared all around me, and I had to squint. I could barely make out anything in front of me. I heard horrible moaning and groaning. Several people dressed in hooded dark robes reached out to me.

"No, no!" I cried out. "I don't want to go!"

In spite of my pleas, I was ushered forward. My body seemed to have no control; I was forced to move on. Over my left shoulder, in the far distance, I saw a tremendous lake of fire. I could feel its raging heat, but I still had that awful chill.

Suddenly one of the hooded beings turned his head and stared at me. His face was full of anguish and pain. That tormented soul was my very own father, who had died from committing suicide a few years back! The horror in his face made him ugly; he was a fragment of a shattered man. No longer that tall, proud, handsome attorney he once was.

"Father," I called, "where are we? Are we in hell?"

He shrugged and motioned for me to follow.

Then another hooded being turned his head. I knew this agonizing soul as well. "Dan," I cried out, "it's me, Lorraine. Scotty's mom."

Dan Hill had been my son's best friend. He spent more time at our house than at his own. I was totally devastated when I heard on the news that Dan's murder may have been cult related. My son and Danny did everything together. I had been afraid that Scotty would be next.

Now I had to get Danny to help me. I pleaded with him, "Danny, please, you've got to help me. Where am I? Can you help me get back? The kids and I were in a terrible accident, and they're both hurt really bad. I need to get back so I can help them. Please, Danny, help me!"

He didn't say a word, only summoned me to follow.

A third tormented soul turned a hooded head toward me. I fell on the ground and began to weep when I saw it was my closest friend, Kathy. When I was able to compose myself, I studied her face. She was no longer that fun-loving, cute, spunky girl I'd known since high school. That woman did not exist anymore. She looked as destitute as my father and Danny had. A few months back I received the news that she went to a party and overdosed on drugs. I had mourned over my friend. I swore to myself that I wouldn't do any more drugs, but it was a struggle.

Kathy sadly summoned me to follow like the other two had.

No matter how hard I tried to turn back, an irresistible force pulled me forward. Finally, the tormented souls stopped. They motioned for me to continue on, while they lingered behind. I was out of my mind with fear as I continued my horrifying journey. That's when I was drawn to a bright light. The light became unearthly brilliant, and I seemed to float toward it. As I got closer I felt that it was a being—the most powerful, ultimate being in the universe.

Like thunder out of the sky, the being spoke to me: "LORRAINE, DO YOU KNOW WHO I AM?"

"God is that you?" Immediately, I knew it was Him! I fell to my knees and buried my head in shame. "Am I really dead? Are you God?"

"YES, LORRAINE, I AM THE LIGHT OF THE WORLD, THE TRUTH, THE WAY, AND THE LIGHT. I AM THE ALPHA AND THE OMEGA, THE FIRST AND THE LAST, THE BEGINNING AND THE END. I AM THE CREATOR OF THE UNIVERSE, AND THE LAMB OF GOD.

"THE BOOK IS OPENED. NEXT THERE WILL BE ANOTHER BOOK OPENED, WHICH IS THE BOOK OF LIFE. THE DEAD ARE WRITTEN IN THE BOOKS. THEY ARE JUDGED, EACH ONE ACCORDING TO HIS WORKS. EVERYONE THAT IS NOT FOUND WRITTEN IN THE BOOK OF LIFE WILL BE CAST INTO THE LAKE OF FIRE."

I begged, "Please, forgive me! Give me one more chance! Give my children another chance. Linda's only fourteen. Scotty has had a rough life, because of me. I know I've done wrong. I rejected you and lived a terrible, sinful life. I was the worst mother in the world, but I love my kids. Please, they're too young to die. Let them live, and somehow let them open their hearts to you!"

"LORRAINE, YOUR NAME IS NOT WRITTEN DOWN IN THE BOOK OF LIFE. YOU HAVE DEFILED YOUR GARMENTS. YOUR SINS WERE NOT COVERED BY MY BLOOD. YOU ARE NOT WORTHY OF ME. I HAVE BLOTTED YOUR NAME OUT OF the Book of Life. You would not accept the gift of eternal life that I offered you—the blood that I shed on the cross for your sins. I have stood at your heart's door several times and knocked. You refused to let me in. Now I will show you the journey you took in life that brought you to The Great White Throne Judgment."

2

My past life began to unfold before my eyes as I witnessed it. Every image I saw was associated with emotion. I felt joy, sorrow, and pain. Each event felt as real as my life had been. On my first journey, I found myself in a busy New York hospital. The Lord Jesus had taken me back to the day I was born, thirty-five years earlier....

There were a few nurses gathered around me, admiring what a cute baby I was. One of the nurses said, "What a beautiful little girl, and look at all that hair!"

Another nurse said, "She sure does have a lot of hair." She grabbed a baby brush and a pink ribbon, and soon I had a lovely pink bow holding up a ponytail on top of my head. It pulled a little, but I liked being fussed over...although the soft, warm, pink nightie she put on me felt better.

"There," said the second nurse. "All ready to see Mom."

The nurse walked into my mother's room and laid me in my mother's arms, but Mom didn't seem very happy.

The nurse asked, "Mrs. Patterson, have you been able to get in touch with your husband?"

Mom wiped tears from her eyes. "No, not yet."

"Well, you sure have a beautiful baby. Everyone in the nursery has been admiring her. She has the most gorgeous, big, blue eyes, and that hair. I see a lot of babies in here, but she sure is the cutest one I've ever seen. You must be really proud."

"Yeah, sure," Mom said in a unconvincing tone.

Just then a tall man walked into the room. As he approached our bed he said, "Hi, Marge, how are you doing? Looks like this time you got serious about having your baby."

Mom had a really angry expression as she told him, "I'm fine, no thanks to you. And yes, I had *our* baby! Where have you been? I tried and tried to reach you, but I couldn't."

"I was working on an important case."

"You weren't at the office. I called!"

"I didn't want any interruptions, so I turned the phone off."

"Did your new secretary stay all night working, too?"

"Most of the night. I needed her help."

"I know. Remember, I was your secretary before I became pregnant, and you made me quit. I know how you work, all right!"

"Then you can also remember how you let yourself get pregnant when I was already engaged to someone else. You knew I was to be married in a few weeks."

"For the last time, Jim, I didn't get pregnant on purpose."

"You can't deny how infatuated you were with me."

"You know you wanted me as much as I wanted you."

"Yeah, Marge, you were fun, but Silvia's dad was a senior partner in the law firm I was about to work for. You blew that for me by getting pregnant."

"Just stop it! I'm sick of hearing that over and over again. The realization is that we are married now and have a beautiful little girl."

"A girl?" He frowned. "I wanted a son...a boy to carry on the name of James Patterson."

"Well, get over it. You have a girl, and she looks a lot like you. Look at her black hair and blue eyes. You can't deny she's yours."

Jim gave a quick look ."Yeah, I guess she is kind of cute."

Our homecoming wasn't any better either. My father yelled at mother, "Why are you so depressed, woman? You've got the world by the tail. Before you came to New York and landed a job with my firm, you were a farmer's daughter. Now look at you—married to a successful attorney, living in a spacious penthouse, and a new baby to boot. What more could a farm girl from Michigan want?"

"A husband who loves me. One who doesn't cheat on me with his secretary, when I'm in the hospital having his baby."

"Stop. I don't want to talk about that subject anymore. It's done, finished!"

"Okay! I guess I'm tired. Let me get the baby settled, then I'll be fine."

I watched my mother carry me into the nursery. She laid me down in a beautiful canopy crib and kissed me on the forehead. There was another woman in my nursery. Mother said to her, "Do you have all the instructions I gave you for the baby's care when I hired you?"

"Yes, ma'am, I do."

"Kim, you came very highly recommended as a good nanny, and therefore I've put a lot of trust in you. You'll have full responsibility of this child, since I have a lot of other things around here to do. The baby has a very large comfortable room, as you can see. You have an adjoining bedroom with a bathroom in-between. There's everything in here you'll need to take care of her. Also, there's a back entrance off your room so you can take her out for walks in her stroller. You are to prepare meals for the two of you in the kitchen. There is a small dinette table in there."

"Don't worry, Mrs. Patterson, I would be honored to take full charge of this darling little baby. She is so adorable."

In those early years, nannies came and went. My parents couldn't seem to keep them. It wasn't because of me, though. The nannies all liked me. But my mother drank too much and could get very hateful. When a nanny would bring me into the main part of the house, mother would yell at them. She didn't want a child messing up her spotless, immaculate penthouse. Then there was my father, who would stop to visit me, but he always seemed more interested in the nannies than me.

I had everything in that charming, storybook bedroom that any little girl could possibly want. I had every type of toy imaginable. But I felt neglected and unloved. My parents lavished me with material things, but left out what really meant the most to me—their love and time. I was terribly lonely and unhappy. I was confined to my room most of the time. My parent's visits were becoming more and more scarce. Mom was always out somewhere, or making sure everything was perfect, in hopes that Father would be pleased with her. That didn't help much, though; they continued to fight. Father was at the office most of the time, and Mom was always accusing him of having a girlfriend.

When I was seven, my dad came home with a big bouquet of red roses. He swung my mom around and gave her a big kiss. With a big smile on his handsome face he said, "Break out a bottle of our best champagne. We're going to celebrate tonight!"

Mom was overwhelmed and liked the burst of attention. "What is this all about, Jim? Did you win a big case or something?"

With a arrogant smile he said, "Better than that. I've been asked to become a junior partner in the firm! That, of course, means more prestige and considerably more money."

When they empted the bottle of champagne, Father opened another. Then he said, "Call a job service and get a full-time maid, because you're going to be too busy entertaining clients with me." He got all mushy. "You are a beautiful woman, Marge; you will be a great asset to me. We could really become a great team!"

Mother slurred, "And you, James, are tall, dark, and handsome. On top of that, you're the most intelligent man I have ever known."

"And you, my beautiful wife, have been blessed with looks, charm, and grace. I can't possibly see how we could go wrong!"

That was a happy night for my parents. Mother was finally feeling loved and appreciated.

However, from that time on, I saw even less of my parents. They were gone most of the time entertaining. As time went on they soon began to drift in different directions. Mother spent a lot of time going to high-society events and luncheons, while Father did most of his entertaining over drinks.

At six o'clock each evening my nanny took me down to the kitchen to eat dinner. If my parents happened to be home for dinner, the maid served them dinner in the formal dining room. Mom would sit down at the table promptly at six-thirty, wearing a fancy dress. Unfortunately, Father didn't always make it home for dinner. There were nights he didn't make it home at all. Mother would wait for him impatiently, while the maid kept her wine glass full.

There was one particular night that Father arrived home late, and Mom had way too many glasses of wine. She was so mad that she was shaking. Her nerves had been becoming increasingly worse lately, and this night was no exception.

My mother yelled at my father, "Where have you been?"

One of Mom's hands accidentally hit her glass, and wine spilled all over the white linen tablecloth.

I was in the kitchen having a late snack with the nanny and heard my parents arguing. I hated it when they fought.

"What in the world is wrong with you, woman?" Father yelled. "Can't you even drink a glass of wine anymore without spilling it?"

"I'm sorry, Jim, but if you would get home when you are expected, maybe I wouldn't get so worked up and spill my drink."

Dad yelled back at her, "When I'm expected? Excuse me, but have you forgotten I'm the one around here who makes the living—and a darn good one, I might add. You can expect me home when I get here, not a moment sooner. I don't have any nine-to-five job, you know!"

"You can't tell me that it's office business all the time," Mom fired back. "It's monkey business, that's what it is. You monkey around with other women. I know you; you can't keep your eyes off other women."

"Knock it off, Marge. Jealousy does not become you. I don't fool around. I don't know how you come up with these stupid ideas."

Mom was really shaking as she reached down in her skirt pocket, pulled out a pill box, and took a couple pills.

Dad gave her a nasty look. "Sure, go ahead and take your drugs. No wonder you are so messed up! Between those prescription drugs and all the booze you drink, you are in your own little world. They are prescribed, aren't they?"

"You arrogant jerk! Of course they're prescription."

"Yeah, but how many doctors did it take to get that good of a supply? I don't know how you do it, Marge. When we are out in public, you manage to keep control of yourself. You missed your calling; you should have been an actress. It's a good thing others can't see what an empty, exhausted woman you are at home. Poor little Lorraine doesn't have a mother. Good thing we can get reliable nannies. However, if we aren't careful, we'll run out of them. You can't seem to keep them. They can't stand your drunkenness."

"My drunkenness? It's not me who chases the nannies away, it's you! The way you always flirt and tease them, no wonder they won't stay. Furthermore, these pills and booze are the only way I can cope with the long nights I have to put up with being alone."

"You're not alone. You have a daughter, for Pete's sake!"

"She is just a child. I need a man's company. I can't stand it anymore. I want a divorce!"

"You pathetic witch," he yelled, "you would end up a bag woman on the street if I divorced you. Remember, I'm the best divorce lawyer in New York!"

With every nasty word my parents slammed at each other, I became so distressed that I finally screamed at the top of my lungs, "Stop, stop! Mother and Father, stop fighting!" I shook my head from side to side, holding the palms of my hands over my ears. Then I ran crying hysterically to my room.

⌘ ⌘ ⌘

After witnessing this part of my life I stood again before Jesus at The Great White Throne Judgment. "Oh, it hurt so much to relive my early childhood," I told him. "I was such a miserable, lonely child. I had almost forgotten how wealthy my parents had been. It seems like so long ago. I didn't want for the material things then; I only wanted love from my parents. But they were always arguing. Even with all that money they still couldn't be happy."

"NO, LORRAINE, MONEY CANNOT MAKE PEOPLE HAPPY. MONEY IS THE ROOT OF ALL EVIL. DO YOU KNOW THAT IT IS EASIER FOR A CAMEL TO GO THROUGH THE EYE OF A NEEDLE, THAN FOR A RICH MAN TO ENTER INTO THE KINGDOM OF GOD?"

"Are you saying, God, that no matter what I did, because I came from a wealthy family, I was doomed?"

"NO. MANY MEN WHO ARE RICH HAVE A LOVE FOR THEIR MONEY AND WILL DO EVIL THINGS FOR THE SAKE OF MONEY. MONEY IS THEIR GOD. I HAVE COMMANDED THAT YOU ARE TO HAVE NO OTHER GODS BEFORE ME. A RICH MAN CAN ENTER INTO THE KINGDOM OF GOD IF I AM HIS GOD. IT IS IMPOSSIBLE WITHOUT ME, BUT WITH ME, ALL THINGS ARE POSSIBLE. WHEN YOU BECAME OF THE AGE OF ACCOUNTABILITY, IT WAS THEN YOUR RESPONSIBILITY TO ACCEPT MY GIFT OF SALVATION AND FOLLOW ME. IF YOU WOULD HAVE DONE THIS, YOU WOULD HAVE INHERITED EVERLASTING LIFE.

"NOW I AM GOING TO SHOW YOU WHEN YOU FIRST STARTED TO REJECT ME AND TURN FROM ME."

3

In this leg of my journey, God showed me my life at nine years old. Sadly I was telling another nanny good-bye. I pleaded with her, "It isn't fair! I don't want another nanny; I want you to stay."

Jill sat down beside me on the bed and put her arms around me. "I'm going to miss you too, sweetie. I know we've been together now for almost a year, but I need to move on. I've saved some money for college; I'm starting next month."

"Please, Jill, don't go!"

"I've already given your mother my resignation. I should have told you before today, but I kept putting it off. It was so hard to tell you. I'll be leaving soon. In fact, your mother is interviewing another nanny as we speak."

Mom was in the living room interviewing a young lady named Connie Nelson. "Your résumé sounds impeccable, and you have good references. Have you ever worked with a child who has some emotional problems?"

"Yes, Mrs. Patterson, I once cared for a boy who was mentally impaired."

"Great, however, Lorraine isn't mentally impaired. She's just very withdrawn and insecure. If I decide to hire you, it probably will take awhile for her to warm up to you. She is very shy."

"How is she around other children?"

"We don't socialize with other families, so Lorraine doesn't get that much of an opportunity to play with other kids. My husband is a very busy attorney, and I'm loaded down with a full calendar of social events. I make sure that the nanny takes Lorraine to the park as often as possible. She never mentioned if Lorraine plays with other children, or not."

"What about at school?"

"Reports back from her teacher say that Lorraine has a problem getting involved with other children. She is even too scared to read out loud or answer questions that she is asked by the teacher. Consequently her grades suffer because of it. That makes her father angry. He really came down hard on the last nanny we had. Jim insisted that she needed to do more to help Lorraine with her studies. No matter how hard she tried to drill it into her head, it didn't help."

"Mrs. Patterson, children learn faster when they learn by playing. If you hire me, I'll help her with homework by making it fun. I have some wonderful educational toys I can bring along."

"Connie, I don't know, nothing seems to work. There's still the social problem at school."

"Do you think that she might be a little slow?"

"Absolutely not! Her father and I are intelligent people. Mr. Patterson is a successful attorney, and I have a degree in business. There is no reason that our daughter wouldn't be smart, too. I can't understand why she is shy and reserved. Jim and I are both outgoing. Lorraine gets everything she could possibly want. You should see her room—it's full of all the latest toys. We get her the very best nannies that we can find. What more could a child want?"

"Yes ma'am, but with respect, ma'am, nannies are only hired help. We can't take the place of a child's mother's or father's love and attention."

"Excuse me, young lady, we do love our child. But we are busy people. We don't have the privilege to always be there for her; that's why we pay so dearly for good help."

"Yes, ma'am."

Mom was not happy over Connie's bold remark, but she had the best references, so she hired her to be my new nanny.

It didn't take me long to become close to Connie, because she was so sweet and full of love. Each morning I could wake up to her happy, smiling face. Connie spent more time with me than anyone else had. She actually acted like she was happy to be playing with me. We took turns every night reading to each other.

In spite of my new relationship I had with my nanny, one day I felt very sad and depressed. When Connie wanted to know why I was so sad, I said, "Please don't take this Sunday off! Stay home with me."

"Oh come on, Lorraine, you can get along without me for one day, can't you? That's the day I leave in the morning to visit my family and go to church."

"You go to church?"

"Yes, faithfully every Sunday. Why is this Sunday different? Why do you want me to stay?"

"Because it's my tenth birthday, and I don't want to be alone on my birthday."

"But you won't be alone. Your mother and father will be with you. I would think that you would like to spend the day with them. You don't get to see them much throughout the week."

"Oh whoopee. Maybe they will take me to a swanky restaurant where I have to be on my best behavior. Then we will go home, and I will spend the rest of the day in my room all alone."

"Yeah, but Sunday is different; it's your birthday! I'm sure they are planning a big surprise for you."

"Don't count on it; they don't always remember my birthdays."

"They are very busy people, Lorraine, but I'm quite sure they wouldn't miss something as important as your tenth birthday."

"Yes they will! I hear them fighting sometimes. I know it's about me. I heard Father tell Mother she trapped him into marrying her. They wish I never was born!"

"That's not true, honey. Your parents love you. Parents sometimes have a lot of pressures to deal with and say things they don't always mean. I know they are happy to have you as a daughter." Connie giggled. "After all, how could they resist those big dimples?"

That made me smile a little. I looked up at her. "Take me to church with you Sunday? I don't want to be alone on my birthday."

"No, I couldn't. Besides, I know your parents will have something planned."

"No, Connie, I swear, they won't. Try it. Ask Mother. I bet she won't even remember it's my birthday. Go ask her now…please?"

"Oh, all right! You stay here, and I'll go see if I can find her."

Connie found my mother in my parents' bedroom sitting on her overstuffed chair drinking a glass of wine. I didn't stay in my room, because I wanted to hear for myself if Mother would remember. Connie didn't see me following her.

Connie reluctantly walked into the bedroom. "Mrs. Patterson, I'm very sorry to disturb you, but I need to talk to you about Lorraine."

"What has that child done now?"

"Oh, she has been a perfect angel. She is even doing better in school. That's not what I wanted to talk to you about, though. I wanted to ask you if it was all right to take Lorraine to church with me Sunday. I could have her home by twelve-thirty. I know it's her birthday, but she really wants to go."

My mother looked puzzled. "What date is this Sunday?"

"August third, ma'am."

"I completely lost track of time. Last month went so fast. I'm so glad that you reminded me about Lorraine's birthday. I'll get the maid to bake her a cake. I could call about that ad for a clown that I saw in the paper. Maybe he could get a laugh out of her; she is always so moody.... Now what's this about church?"

"It's a small church that I have attended almost all my life. It's called The Gospel Grace Church."

"Gospel Grace Church!" Mom said with a nasty grin. "What kind of a denomination is that?"

"It's not; it's undenominational, but it is really a good, God-fearing church. Lorraine could learn a lot there. They have a wonderful Sunday school program."

"If it isn't a well-known denominational church, I don't want anything to do with it. I don't want my daughter getting mixed up in a cult."

"I assure you, ma'am, it is not a cult!"

I could see Connie was beginning to get upset.

"As for taking Lorraine to church, the answer is no."

I could tell Connie was trying very hard not to show her anger. She asked my mother, "How long has it been since you took Lorraine to church?"

"To tell the truth, Connie, Lorraine has not been to church as yet. She is too young to understand, anyway. When I feel she is old enough, I'll send her."

"May I ask, ma'am, when was the last time you went to church?"

"That is none of your business, young lady. However, let me think. It was ...it has to be over twenty years ago, I guess. I stopped going when I was a freshman in high school. My parents were very strict, but I got very independent at that time and refused to go anymore."

"How about Mr. Patterson?"

My mother laughed out loud. "Jim? You got to be kidding. I don't know if he even believes in God or not. He would never go, and I would not be comfortable going to church with just my child."

"Please, do not think I mean to intrude here, but I really believe Lorraine needs to go to church. Forgive me if I'm being too bold, but perhaps your whole family does."

"How dare you to be so intrusive!"

Connie was lost for words for a few seconds. Then she reluctantly said, "I mean, Mrs. Patterson, it could help your husband meet new people. It could make his law firm grow. People look up to men who take their families to church."

"All right, all right. Get out of here—I'm tired of hearing about church. Just go. I have to get ready. Jim should be getting home soon."

I jumped up from my hiding place and ran back to my room, crying hysterically. When Connie got there, I was yelling, "I hate her! I hate her!"

"Lorraine, honey, please calm down."

"I told you she wouldn't remember my birthday! It will be a stupid day! I don't want some stupid old clown around trying to make me laugh. I hate my father, too. He never remembers my birthdays either."

"Lorraine, you don't really mean that. In the Bible, it tells us to honor our father and mother."

"I don't care what it tells us to do in the Bible. How can I honor a mother and father who don't care about me? Besides, I don't believe in God anyway!"

"Lorraine, please, don't say that. Jesus loves you very much."

"Jesus doesn't even know me, and I don't know Him. My father doesn't believe in God, and I don't either!"

"Oh, Lorraine, it hurts me to hear you talk that way. God is real! He created you. He created everything. It is because of His shed blood on the cross that we can live with Him for all eternity; where there will never be any more tears."

Connie, softly wiped the teardrops away that were falling from my eyes. "God loves us so much that He sent His only son, Jesus, down on the Earth to die on the cross as a sacrifice for our sins. We need to realize that we are sinners, lost and headed for hell. The only way we can be saved is through the shed blood of Jesus Christ. Jesus is the only way to be saved. We are washed pure by the blood of Christ. All you have to do to receive this wonderful gift is to accept it. Then the Holy Spirit will fill your heart with love and righteousness. When we accept God, we know right from wrong. Jesus really wants us to have a personal relationship with Him."

"How can we do that if He died on the cross?"

"Three days after He was crucified on the cross, He came out from the grave alive. After a few days He ascended up to Heaven, where He is sitting at the right hand of God. The Lord Jesus left His Holy Spirit in the hearts of all those who will receive Him. Lorraine, people may let you down, but God never will. You will never be alone if you have the Lord Jesus in your heart."

"Connie, if God is real, how could I ever get to know Him?"

"By reading his Word in the Bible. It is divinely inspired by God. Jesus, the Son of God, walked the Earth for thirty-three years. His glorious words are written down in the Bible. Christ said, *'If you know me you know the Father.'* God is a Trinity made up of the Father, Son, and Holy Ghost." She looked at me gently. "Lorraine, do you want to open your heart, and let Jesus in it today?"

Although I felt a strong conviction in my heart that day, I refused to come to the Lord. I angrily lashed back at her, "No, I can't do it now."

"Wouldn't you at least like to go to church so you could learn more?"

"You know I can't, Connie! Mother told you that you could not take me. You know my parents won't go to church, even though you tried to convince Mother it could help them make more money!"

"Oh, Lorraine, I'm sorry you heard that. I am really ashamed for saying that. The most important thing for me right then was finding a way to get you to church. Building up your father's law practice is not a good reason to attend church. It's hypocritical."

⌘⌘⌘

From The Great White Throne Judgment God spoke again to me. "I SENT CONNIE TO YOU AS A MESSENGER. SHE TOLD YOU ABOUT MY GIFT OF SALVATION, BUT YOU REJECTED IT. I ALSO SENT CONNIE AS A MESSENGER TO YOUR MOTHER, SO SHE WOULD OPEN HER HEART TO MY GOSPEL. CONNIE

SUGGESTED IT WOULD BE BENEFICIAL FOR YOUR FAMILY TO GO TO CHURCH. YOUR MOTHER HEARD HOW IT COULD BENEFIT THEM FINANCIALLY, NOT WHAT IT COULD DO FOR THEIR SOULS. PEOPLE SOMETIMES TAKE GOOD THINGS AND MAKE THEM BAD...AN EXAMPLE OF HOW MONEY CAN BE THE ROOT OF ALL EVIL.

"NOW, WATCH AS YOUR MOTHER CONSPIRED WITH YOUR FATHER, BY USING THE CHURCH FOR EVIL TO GAIN RICHES."

4

Mother was extremely beautiful that evening when Father got home from the office. She had been planning what she would say to him all afternoon. After a few glasses of wine, my mother said, "Darling, I had an interesting conversation with Connie today. It started out by her asking to take Lorraine to church with her this Sunday. By the way, this Sunday is Lorraine's birthday."

"Oh really? I forgot. That's your job to keep track of birthdays. Did you get her anything yet?"

"No, I'm as bad as you. I forgot, too. Thanks to Connie, she reminded me. I have been so busy planning for that charity ball, I simply forgot. Anyway, that's not what I wanted to talk to you about. Connie brought up an interesting topic. It's something we haven't explored. It could really boost your clientele."

"Tell me more. I'm always interested in expanding my client list."

"Well, you are a very distinguished successful attorney, but if you could improve your image in the community, wouldn't that make your practice grow even more?"

"It probably would. How do you propose I do that?"

"By attending a large, wealthy church!"

"Be serious!"

"No, Jim, I am serious. These churches have thousands of people attending. There are doctors, real-estate tycoons, people from all walks of life. They all need a good lawyer once in a while. Think about it, Jim, we could become tremendously wealthy by just going to church. Think of all the people we could meet!"

"You might have a good argument—but me in church? No way!"

Mother continued in her own special conniving way over dinner and into the evening. Finally, my father threw up his arms and yelled, "Okay, you win. I'll try it for a month, but only one hour a week. If I don't see it working, that's it, no more church!"

For the rest of the week Mother checked out all the churches in a radius of fifteen miles until she located the largest church, in the wealthiest section of New York City.

That Sunday morning Connie laid out a beautiful pink dress, a pair of shiny white shoes, and pink lacy socks. The outfit was part of my birthday presents from my parents. When I put them on, I felt like a princess!

"Here, Lorraine, I have a special present for you."

Connie gave me a small box wrapped and tied with a bow on top. When I opened it, I found a necklace with a gold cross. "Oh, Connie, that is beautiful! I love it. Thank you."

Connie had tears in her eyes as she gave me a big hug. "I am so happy that you are finally going to church."

"Me, too. Thank you so much for talking my mother into it. This will be the first time I can ever remember both of my parents taking me anywhere. This Sunday will be such a special birthday for me."

"Come on, honey, it's getting late. Let's get you out in the living room so your parents know you are ready!"

We waited and waited in mother's immaculate living room for my parents to come in. When they came in, they were arguing. "I told you, Marge, you were going to make us late! Look at the clock. Let's go."

"Jim, if you would have gotten up when I called you, we wouldn't be having this conversation. I had to call you three different times before you finally got up. How do you expect me to get ready when I have to cater to you?"

"That's it, Marge, I'm not going! I didn't want to go in the first place. I knew it was a bad idea."

They argued and argued until Mother decided she better give in. "Jim, calm down. I'm sorry, I didn't mean it. That dinner party lasted way too long last night. We both had too much to drink. Let's just go and get this thing over with, okay?"

"Yeah, I guess so."

"Don't just stand there gawking," Mother barked at Connie. "Get Lorraine's coat on. It's late!"

The church parking lot was huge, and we had to walk about a block to get to the church. When we got in front of the church, I was overwhelmed. I had never seen anything like it in all my life. We stood at the bottom of what seemed to me a mountain of steps. Toward the top I could see a few people still walking in. At least we weren't the only one's late. After we climbed the steps, we opened the door to a large reception area. Across from there was another set of doors.

As we walked through the second set of doors, we saw a huge congregation singing like a choir of angels. It was easy for us to slip in and take a seat way in the back. Then a man in a robe stood up and started talking. He talked too long and I didn't understand a word he said, except *"Love one another...love your neighbor as yourself...feel good about yourself by helping those less fortunate."* Other than that, I didn't get anything out of it. Father's eyes kept going open and shut. It made me so tired that I could feel myself nodding off to sleep.

We were all wide awake, though, when the pastor introduced a loud four-piece band. They called the music "Christian Rock." My parents didn't like it, but I did. After that the pastor said a prayer and then closed the service.

The following Sundays all were about the same way. The mornings would start out with my parents at each other's throats.

Soon a month had gone by. We were on our way home from church that Sunday, and my father said to my mother, "That's it; I'm done. I will not waste my time one minute longer in that coliseum, listening to a boring man and some hard rock group sing!"

"Jim, remember our plan! We need these people."

"What for? We haven't talked to one person since we started going! Next you'll want to be putting flyers in the reception room."

"Don't be silly. We have to figure out how to meet these people."

"It's too big of a church! To tell you the truth, I don't think anyone even noticed that we are new. Most everyone seems to rush out as soon as it's over. I guess we aren't the only ones who can only take one hour of church a week."

"Wait, maybe I've got something. Remember when Lorraine needed to go to the bathroom? Well, I noticed that there was another large room where others were gathering. They were having coffee and cookies. That's when I realized that not all people go home right after church. There are quite a few who stay and socialize. We are going to have to stay long enough for that. That's where we will meet your potential clients!"

Father thought that Mother had a pretty good idea, so they continued their Sunday ritual, along with that additional half-hour social time. As for me, I began to resent going to church. I soon found out that it wasn't a family day together; it was strictly business for my parents. I still felt unloved and neglected. Sunday mornings at home were even more hectic. I hated the fighting.

Poor Connie, I was even giving her a hard time when she tried to get me ready to go. Social hour at the church was even worse. I always tagged behind my parents as they talked to various people. I didn't see any other kids in there. No one seemed to pay any attention to me, except on one particular Sunday. A very pretty young woman came up to my mother and introduced herself. "Good morning," she said. "I'm Jenny Bowers."

"Hello, Miss Bowers. I'm Marge Patterson, nice to meet you. Miss Bowers, this is my husband, James Patterson."

Miss Bowers held out her hand to my father and said, "Glad to meet you."

"Likewise, Miss Bowers, the pleasure is all mine."

"I wanted to welcome your family to our church. Sorry it took so long. This is a really big church. I'm ashamed to admit that I don't know half of the people who attend. However, I am one of the Sunday school teachers. I'd like to invite your family to stay for Sunday school. We have several adult classes to choose from. Our children are dismissed for junior church just before the pastor starts his sermon. Then they have Sunday school class during social time and adult Sunday school. The kids have a great time. We have lots of activities for them to do."

I peeked my head out from behind my mother. Miss Bowers saw me, and said, "Oh, this must be your daughter?"

Mother took me by the hand, pulled me in front of her, and answered back, "Yes, this is our daughter, Lorraine."

Miss Bowers held out her hand for me to shake. I felt proud and gave her my hand. As she shook my hand, she said, "I am so happy to meet you. I know you will enjoy our youth group. There are classes for every age group. There will be lots of kids in your class."

That sounded good to me—anything to get away from that boring preacher and that dreadful social time. However, I wasn't sure I wanted to go off to some big class where I didn't know anyone. It sounded as bad as school. I was scared.

I didn't have to say a word. Father was quick to say, "No, Miss Bowers, I'm afraid that Lorraine will not be able to attend class today." He handed her a business card and told her, " I am a very busy attorney, and I have a lot of papers to go over this afternoon, so we can't stay. If you need any legal work, you've got my card."

"Thank you. Maybe next week?"

Dad gave a polite smile. "Perhaps."

Every Sunday was the same way. Our home was full of hate and discontent. My parents disliked church just as much as I did. I argued with them that I didn't want to go, but they insisted we go as a family. After all, we had an image to uphold; and my father's law business was beginning to increase.

⌘ ⌘ ⌘

As Jesus and I watched from The Great White Throne Judgment, I cried, "Lord, can't you see? It wasn't my fault! My parents were nasty, scheming, conniving people. They wouldn't even let me go to Sunday school. If they had, I would have learned about the Bible. I would have had a chance to know You. It's their fault!"

"NOW I WILL SHOW YOU THE NEXT FEW YEARS. THESE YEARS YOU WERE REACHING ACCOUNTABILITY. THE DECISION TO FOLLOW ME WOULD BE YOURS AND YOURS ALONE. DURING THIS TIME, I SENT TWO VERY SPECIAL CHRISTIANS INTO YOUR LIFE AS MESSENGERS OF MY GOSPEL. I WANTED CHRISTINE WILLIAMS AND THOMAS PERKINS TO SHOW YOU HOW TO WALK A CHRISTIAN LIFE. I GAVE THOMAS THE CALLING TO BE A MINISTER OF MY WORD. I CHOSE YOU TO BE HIS HELPMATE. YOU WERE GIVEN A FREE WILL. IT WAS YOUR CHOICE TO LISTEN TO YOUR HEART AND FOLLOW MY WILL. THE FINAL DECISION WAS TO BE YOURS...."

5

My mother's scheme of attending New York's finest church worked out very well. The affluent law firm where my father worked flourished, due to their new activity. The senior partner of the firm was so pleased with his performance, he made Father a full-pledged partner. Father's net worth doubled, along with special perks.

Things at church remained the same for our family. People got tired of Father's excuses and stopped asking us to stay for Sunday school. I was shy and stayed with my parents during the pastor's message, instead of joining the kids in junior church. Our whole family hated to go to church, but Father made a lot of good contacts so we stayed on; that is, until he felt that he had exhausted all possible leads.

Our family life hadn't changed much…if anything it got worse. I was now approaching thirteen, and becoming even more lonely and withdrawn. My mother fired Connie about a year earlier. She was too outspoken to suit my mother. Mom didn't want to hear what she had to say. Connie tried to tell her that she needed to spend more time with me, but that made Mother mad. She also wanted Mother to get more involved with my school, working with my teacher. Mother wouldn't listen to anything she had to say.

My new nanny did just the essential things she had to do. She watched a lot of television and read. I never got close to her.

One evening Father said to my mother, "How would you like to move out of the city?"

"What? Why would you even consider something like that? Your law firm is here. You were just made a senior partner in the firm. Why would you want to move?"

"Marge, I'm only talking about moving somewhere within an hour's drive. I can transit, no big deal."

"But I love this penthouse. I don't want to move."

"This penthouse doesn't fit my image anymore. Apparently I have larger expectations than you do. I'm talking about a huge estate that would make this penthouse look like the projects."

"Oh, really, can we afford something like that?"

"Of course! I have already been talking to a realtor about it." He grabbed his briefcase. "As a matter of fact, I have some pictures of a couple estates right here."

Mother was shocked when she started looking at the pictures. She gulped. "They are mansions! Are you serious? Can we really afford an estate like one of these?"

"We can, and we will."

Father was a very determined man; once he made up his mind to do something, nothing could stand in the way. Two months later we moved into an old stately mansion forty-five minutes from the city. The grounds were beautiful, but to me it seemed big and cold. I was granted a whole wing of the mansion right off the kitchen, where I ate. Mother and Father ate their meals on a massive Victorian dining table and were served by our new maid. My parents also hired a cook and a groundskeeper.

At first Mother was hysterically happy and thrilled about her new lifestyle but soon felt lonely and neglected by Dad. He kept a small apartment back in the city. He told Mother he needed it for long nights at the office. He spent a lot of nights in that apartment, while Mother grew more depressed and drank even more. She was impossible to be around, so I kept my distance. She didn't want to be bothered with me anyway.

I turned fourteen that August. For a birthday present my parents gave me a computer. My father was more excited about it than I was. I didn't know anything about how to operate the thing. Father was too busy to show me. Mother wouldn't be bothered with it. The hired help never touched one before. So there it sat.

In addition, in honor of me turning fourteen, I was told I could have my dinner in the formal dining room from then on. At first I was thrilled. Did this mean that I was now old enough for my parents to want to spend time with me? Could we possibly have a happy family time together?

Sitting at the mammoth dining room table that night made me feel uncomfortable. It was too formal and rigid. There wasn't even any conversation until Father took his last bite. Then Mother said, "Lorraine, your father and I have decided that now that you are fourteen, you no longer need a nanny. However, we will have the cook look after you."

"Mother, I'm fourteen years old now. I don't need a babysitter!"

Father glared at me. "Young lady, apologize to your mother! No child of mine will be so disrespectful. It's not like the cook will be your babysitter, but you do need some guidance. It's for your own safety. I'm gone a lot and your mother, well…it's final the cook will look after you. Now apologize!"

I stared down at my plate. "Yes, sir. Mother, I'm sorry."

Gloria, the cook, was all right. I liked her. She was a middle-aged, chubby woman with a warm heart. Gloria was much better than the nanny was anyway. I had a lot of fun when I used to eat in the kitchen with her and the rest of the hired help. There had been the five of us: Gloria, Rachael the maid, Bruce the gardener, the nanny, Alice, and me. We were always laughing and talking at the table. How bad could it be to have her watch over me? I'd been taking care of my personal needs ever since Connie left. I didn't need anyone to watch me!

A few days later Gloria asked me, "So, missy, how does it feel eating with the grown-ups?"

I wrinkled my nose. "I liked it a lot better when I had dinner in here with you guys."

"Oh come on—eating with your parents in that elegant dining room, with silver candlesticks gracing the table? Why, I'd give anything to be in your shoes."

"It's no big deal. I had a lot more fun with you guys; at least we talked and laughed together. I don't think my parents know how to do that."

"I thought you wanted to spend more time with your family."

"Family! You call us a family? My parents are so cold and shallow. When we used to go to church in New York, they had everyone fooled into thinking we were the all-American family—that my father was the pillar of the community! What a joke that was. The only reason they went to church was for one thing, money! They're phonies. Besides, there is no love in this family. My parents fight all the time, and they certainly don't have any time for me. I hate it here. I wish I could run away!"

When September rolled around, I was sick at the thought of starting at a new school. It was bad enough going to school in the city, but getting used to having so many different teachers scared me to death. Now, not only was I facing a new school, but as a freshman I would have a different teacher for each of my classes. As for friends, I didn't have any. It wasn't because I didn't want one—I did with all my heart. I was just too shy and thought I wasn't worthy of anyone's friendship.

Mother called a taxi to pick me up on my first morning of school. I was literally sick, knowing what I had to face. At school I was so scared! I sat in the back at all my morning classes. I either kept my eyes frozen on the teachers or down at my desk.

At lunchtime I found the cafeteria, stood in line, got my food, and found a table in a corner. I glanced around, envying others for laughing and talking with friends. I hated being there. Then, out of nowhere, a pretty, lighthaired girl stopped at my table and asked, "Do you have this table saved?"

I felt my face get red. "No, no one else is sitting here."

"Mind if I sit down?"

"Of course not. Please, have a seat."

The girl put her tray down and said, "My name is Christina Williams. You were in my science class first hour."

"I'm sorry I didn't see you."

"Oh, that's okay. You're new at this school; that's why I noticed you. I've gone to school with most of these kids forever. Maybe we will have another class together. Next hour I've got Miss Davis for English, second hour Thompson for gym, and Pindergass for Algebra, last hour."

"Yeah! We'll have Algebra together."

"Great! We can sit together in that class. That is, if you want to?"

My face lit up and I said, "Yes, I'd love to!"

"Okay, meet me by the lockers before you go to Algebra, and we'll walk to class together."

We talked the rest of the lunch period. I was so happy to have someone to share my lunch with. Christina was smart, witty, and cute—just the type of person I would love to have as a friend. She was so nice that she reminded me of Connie, whom I missed so much.

Christina met me by the lockers just as she promised. She acted happy to see me. For the first time in my life, I was happy to walk into a class room. Christina picked our seats close to the front. That is something I never would have done on my own. Somehow having a friend next to me gave me confidence.

Then a boy sat down next to Christina and said hi to her.

Christina smiled widely. "Hey, Tommy, I didn't know we had Algebra together. This is great! You can help me. You're a brain in math." She turned toward me and said, "Tommy, meet Lorraine. She's new."

"Yeah, I know, Christina. I've attended this school as long as you have. How could I miss a girl as pretty as Lorraine?"

My face got as red as Dorothy's red shoes in *The Wizard of Oz*. I was so embarrassed. No boy ever paid attention to me before, let alone called me pretty.

"Tommy cut it out; you made her blush. Don't pay any attention to him; he's harmless. Tommy and I are good friends. We also live in the same neighborhood."

"Nice to meet you, Tommy," I said softly.

After class, Christina and Tommy walked me out of the school. For the first time I felt that I belonged, maybe even had friends. Tommy kept us in stitches, he was so funny. I thought he was kinda cute, too. There was something awful special about him…maybe it was his awesome personality. Whatever it was, I felt very happy that day.

All that week Christina and I hung out together. Occasionally Tommy would join us. I met a few of her other friends as well. At lunch that following Thursday, Christina asked me, "Would you like to go to Teen Meet with me tomorrow night?"

I didn't know what to say. I never had a friend to go anywhere with. I asked her, "What is Teen Meet?"

"It's sponsored through our church. We meet at church each Friday night to have fellowship and make plans for our monthly events."

"I don't think so, Christina."

"Why not? I'm sure it would be all right with your parents; it's at church."

"It's not that, it's…I hate going to church! I'm sorry, but I hate it. We went to this really big church in the city. The only reason we went was so my father could get potential clients for his law firm."

"Didn't you have a good time at Sunday school?"

"Sunday school?" I rolled my eyes. "My father wouldn't stay for that. As soon as social time was over, he was out the door."

"I'm sorry, I'm sure you would have enjoyed it."

"I'm not! It probably would be just as boring as the rest of it."

Tommy walked up to our table and sat down. "What's boring?"

"Going to church. Christina asked me to go to Teen Meet with her."

"Lorraine had a bad experience while going to a big church in New York," Christina explained.

Tommy leaned over Christina and touched my hand. "I'm sorry you had a bad experience. Please, don't let one church make you bitter about all churches. We love our church, don't we, Christina?"

"Of course, Tommy."

"You two go to the same church, too?" I asked.

Tommy laughed. "Yeah, we do. You see, my family moved here five years ago, right next door to Christina; our families became close friends. Christina's parents invited my folks to church, and we've been going ever since. They have a wonderful youth program there. I don't know what I'd have done without it. It's made a positive impact on my life."

"For me, too, Lorraine. I love the fellowship we have with our Christian families, especially with the kids in our youth group."

"I'm sorry, you guys, but the idea of church really turns me off. Maybe we could go to a movie or something?"

⌘ ⌘ ⌘

As I looked down from The Great White Throne Judgment, I saw my new friends working hard to convince me to go to their youth group at church. I could see inside their hearts, which were full of Christian love.

Then Jesus spoke these words to me: "THE HOUSE OF GOD IS THE CHURCH OF THE LIVING GOD, THE PILLAR AND GROUND OF THE TRUTH. I SPOKE ABOUT THE SEVEN CHURCHES IN THE BOOK OF REVELATION. YOUR CHURCH IN NEW YORK CITY WAS LIKE THE CHURCH OF LAODICEANS. THEIR WORKS WERE NEITHER COLD NOR HOT, SO THEN, BECAUSE THEY WERE LUKEWARM, I SPEWED THEM OUT OF MY MOUTH.

"MY BELOVED CHILDREN CHRISTINA AND THOMAS'S CHURCH WAS LIKE THAT OF THE CHURCH OF PHILADELPHIA. IT WAS HOLY AND TRUE. I PUT BEFORE THEM AN OPEN DOOR, WHICH NO ONE COULD SHUT. FOR THEY HAD STRENGTH TO KEEP MY WORD, AND HAVE NOT DENIED MY NAME. FOR THEM I HAVE KEPT MY COMMAND TO PRESERVE. I ALSO WILL KEEP THEM FROM THE HOUR OF TRIAL WHICH SHALL COME UPON THE WHOLE WORLD TO TEST THOSE WHO DWELL ON THE EARTH."

6

During the next few weeks, it seemed all Christina and Tommy talked about was their Teen Meet at church. I felt somewhat jealous and left out, but I was determined that no one was getting me to go to church. However, I loved my friends, and I loved school.

My favorite class was gym. It was like someone who had a stutter, who could sing great in spite of it. I was terribly shy, but when it came to competing in sports, I shined. I especially liked volleyball. I was playing my heart out one morning when one of my classmates slapped me on the back and said, "Good save. You're really good at this game."

"Thanks," I said proudly.

"You're Christina's new friend, aren't you?"

"Yes, we have become friends. I met her my first day of school. I came from the city."

"Cool! My name is Sarah; what's yours?"

"Lorraine. Lorraine Patterson."

"Christina and I don't have any classes together this year, but we are really good friends, too. We go to the same Church. By the way, has Christina invited you to our Teen Meet yet?"

"Yes, she has, but I'm not interested in going."

"Bummer! This Saturday night we are going to start our annual volleyball tournament. Last year we came in third place. We could really use a good player like you."

"I wish I could help, but I really don't want anything to do with church. It's a long story."

"I'm sorry you feel that way. I love going to Teen Meet."

When I saw Christina and Tommy in Algebra that afternoon, I told them about meeting Sarah. "Can you believe it," I said, "she wanted me to go to your Teen Meet, just to help you guys win a volleyball tournament."

"Wow!" Tommy said. "You must be pretty good, huh?"

"Yeah, I guess. I do all right."

Tommy grinned. "Holding out on us, huh? You've got the talent we need to win the tournament this year, and you didn't tell us?"

"Well, you're going to play, aren't you?" Christina spoke up.

"No! You know I've told you guys that I don't want to go to church!"

"Well," Christina said with a mischievous smile, "it really won't be like going to church. It's only a special event put on by our church group. It's in the church's gym, but it still wouldn't be going to church."

"Yeah," Tommy spoke up again. "It's more like a sports event. We even have fans there. Of course that only amounts to a couple of friends and our families. I bet your folks would love to see you play in a tournament, wouldn't they?"

"You've got to be kidding me…my parents?"

Just then the bell rang, and we settled down to the dreaded Algebra.

After class my two friends wouldn't give up trying to talk me into joining their team. They were so convincing, I finally gave in.

That Saturday night I was in the middle of a very competitive volleyball game. We ended up losing that night, but you would never know it. Everyone was so happy to see the members from the opposing team, they could care less who actually won.

The coach on the opposing side said, "You all did such a great job, tonight the ice cream is on me."

"You can go, can't you?" Christina asked me.

"What? Go where?"

"After all our games, most of the kids go over to the grill a couple blocks from here. We either get a bite to eat or have some ice cream. How about it? Do you want to go?"

"It sounds fun, but I'm not sure if I can get a taxi to wait for me."

"Forget the taxi. My mom and dad can take you home. In fact, if I knew you had to take a taxi, I would have suggested picking you up before. Plan on it every Saturday night, okay?"

"Sure, that will be great!"

We saw Tommy when we were getting ready to leave the church. Christina called out to him, "Guess what? I talked Lorraine into going for ice cream with us."

"Cool! You better give your parents a call. It might be past your curfew."

"My folks didn't say anything about a curfew; besides, they went to the city. They'll be staying at the apartment tonight. I suppose I could let Gloria know, though."

It was so much fun going to a small restaurant with a bunch of kids and some adults. We packed the small grill. After I was served my dish of ice cream, I almost started right in eating it. However, lucky for me I noticed that no one started eating until the waitress had everyone served. Then our coach stood up and said, "Let's pray."

I was so embarrassed. I'd never prayed in a public place before. In fact, I really never prayed, only went through the motions at church. I bowed my head a little, but my eyes scanned around the room. To my amazement, all eyes were shut tight. Most had their heads bowed and their hands folded. Other than the coach saying the prayer, you could have heard a pin drop.

For the next three months I looked forward to Saturday nights. I loved playing volleyball with all those neat kids. We had so much fun together. I got a little tired of everyone asking me to start going to Teen Meet on Fridays. After they wore me down, I finally relented and said yes.

The youth minister at Teen Meet was an energetic thirtysome-year-old man by the name of Floyd Ressma. He made us laugh a lot. However, when he talked about receiving Christ in our hearts, and giving our lives over to him, I felt awful uncomfortable. I tried to think of other things during those times. After the sermon, we would have our choice of several activities that were planned for us. I always tried to get with the group that Christina, Sarah, and Tommy were in. I especially enjoyed playing games with Tommy. Everyone thought he was special, including me. He was so smart and so considerate of others.

After the games we were served a small lunch that some of the women from the church made. I was even getting used to the prayer before we ate. Of course I was invited by several people, including the youth minister, to come to church on Sunday, but that was just not going to happen.

On one Friday night at Teen Meet the youth minister's sermon piqued my interest. "Tonight my talk will be on choosing close friends who are equally yoked to you. It is based on the Scripture from 2 Corinthians 6:14. What does it mean to be equally yoked?"

One girl raised her hand. "To have someone who has the same interest as you."

"Yes, that's right, but what else?"

Another kid raised his hand. "Someone who likes to go to the same places you like to."

"Yes, that also is a part of it. Anything else?"

Still another tried his luck. "Someone you care deeply for."

"That's important too. But can anyone tell me what they believe God meant by it?"

Tommy raised his hand then. "A Christian should only make close relationships with fellow Christians."

"That's the answer I was looking for."

I was so proud of Tommy for getting the right answer. He was so smart. I thought to myself, *Maybe destiny will bring Tommy and me together. We do like the same things. We both love volleyball, and we do have a lot of fun at Teen Meet together. I'm really not sure about this equally yoked thing, though. He is a bit too religious to suit me.*

The youth minister continued, "As young Christians (and I pray that you all are), it is extremely important that you pick friends who are on the same spiritual level as yourself. God wants us to have Christian love towards everyone, but when it comes to our personal lives, he wants us to be equally yoked. God wants you to hang out with other Christians. If you hang out with unbelievers, it could influence you in unrighteous behavior. It is so important to have Christian friends to help support you in this corrupt world. We must live in this world, but we do not need to be a part of the corruption and sins of this world.

"You might say, 'I'm strong in my Christian faith. If I become a close friend to a nonbeliever, maybe I could help them become saved.' Trust me, it doesn't work that way. Chances are, the nonbeliever will bring you down instead of you bringing him to Christ. I'm not saying that you shouldn't associate with nonbelievers. The Bible tells us to go and spread His Word. God merely says not to yoke yourselves to them. Not to become closely involved, like a friend you spend your time with. I realize that some of you aren't dating yet, but nevertheless you should start preparing now for your future. The type of friends you pick now will be the same type of kids you will date later. It's a chain reaction; the person you decide to date could be a candidate for marriage some day. Now, wouldn't you say that is pretty important?"

The pastor stopped for a moment, then said, "Let me tell you about two of my Christian friends from college, Carol and Robert. One of them got married to another Christian, and the other one to a nonbeliever. The first one, Carol, who married the Christian man is a very happy woman today. Matter of fact, she and her husband are members of this church. Their children are being brought up to love the Lord.

"Robert, on the other hand, is a very brokenhearted man. He married an unbeliever and now he is divorced. They were unequally yoked. His wife took their three children and moved far away. She moved in with a very abusive man. Robert is sick about it. He only gets his kids once a month because they live so far away. He is concerned about their welfare. As well, he should.

"So which scenario would you like to live in? I'm not saying that Christian people don't get divorced, but I'm saying you have a lot better chance if you do have a Christian partner. God has spelled out in the Bible how we are to live. If you and your future spouse study the Bible and then apply God's teachings to your life, then I could guarantee you would not have to go through a divorce."

The pastor held his arm up toward the ceiling. "I praise the Lord every night that I married a wonderful Christian woman like my Sandy. I am so fortunate that I met her at college. I was saved only two years before. I'm so thankful that I attended that particular Christian concert, because that's where I met the love of my life. We have a marriage I know was ordained by God."

⌘ ⌘ ⌘

From The Great White Throne Judgment I looked down at that church service where I heard each and every word the youth minister had to say that night. I said to the Lord, "Why didn't I pay attention to the minister's words? They were so important to me. They would have made a big impact on my life. Things would have turned out differently!"

"IT WAS YOUR DECISION. I WAS AT YOUR HEART'S DOOR AGAIN THAT NIGHT, BUT YOU WOULD NOT OPEN YOUR HEART TO ME.

"I SENT FLOYD RESSMA, THE YOUTH PASTOR, TO YOU, SO YOU WOULD

HAVE THE OPPORTUNITY TO BECOME A CHRISTIAN. IF YOU HAD BEEN SAVED, YOU WOULD HAVE UNDERSTAND WHAT HE WAS TELLING YOU ABOUT NOT BEING UNEQUALLY YOKED TOGETHER WITH UNBELIEVERS. YOU WOULD HAVE LEARNED NOT TO BE TEAMED UP WITH THOSE WHO DO NOT LOVE THE LORD, FOR WHAT DO THE PEOPLE OF GOD HAVE IN COMMON WITH THE PEOPLE OF SIN? HOW CAN LIGHT LIVE WITH DARKNESS?[1]

"FOR CHRISTIANS ARE MY TEMPLE. I DWELL IN THEM, AND WALK IN THEM. I WILL BE THEIR GOD, AND THEY SHALL BE MY PEOPLE. THEREFORE, I WANTED YOU TO COME OUT AMONG THEM, AND BE SEPARATE AND TOUCH NOT THE UNCLEAN THINGS, AND THEN I WOULD HAVE RECEIVED YOU. I WOULD HAVE BECOME YOUR FATHER AND YOU MY CHILD."

7

That school year was the most wonderful time of my whole life. It was liberating; I was finally coming out of my shell. I now had friends I had always dreamed about. No longer did I have to go to class alone or eat lunch by myself. With these new friends I no longer felt like that introverted person that I had been all my life.

Teen Meet was also a big part of what made that year special. For the first time in my entire life I felt loved and happy. I learned to socialize and have a great time doing it. I even began to find out that I did have a good sense of humor after all.

Like all great things, the school year was coming to an end. The last day of school five of us were having lunch in the cafeteria together. Everyone was excited about the summer break, and what great plans they had for summer. Everyone except me. I didn't want the school year to end. I had loved it.

"Lorraine, why are you so quiet?" Christina asked me.

"Oh, I'm just a little sad that school's over. Summers are so boring for me. I'll miss all of you."

Tommy spoke up. "Hey, blue eyes, there's still Friday and Saturday night Teen Meet."

"Oh, I didn't know that."

"Yeah," he answered. "That's when we really have fun outings. We go on trips to the beach, horseback riding, camping in the mountains…all sorts of great things."

"Yeah," Sarah said, "and don't forget in the early autumn, the hayride and picnic. They are a blast!"

"Cool. Maybe summer will be great after all."

I was really getting excited about the eventful upcoming summer. I wanted to contribute, so I asked, "Maybe you guys could come out to my house. We have this really large pool on our estate. I won't use it by myself…I hate doing anything alone. Also, we have a tennis court! You guys are more than welcome. I'd love it if you came over. It would be a blast!"

Christina looked a little skeptical. "Do you think your parents would want to have a bunch of kids around? Besides, they probably will want to use it themselves."

"They are talking about entertaining, having some pool parties this summer, but that would only be on the weekends. We could have our parties during the week. Gloria, our cook, is cool. I know she would fix us refreshments. My folks wouldn't say anything. Besides, they probably wouldn't even know. As long as we stay out of the house and let my mother alone, she'll be okay. My dad is always in the city till late. They leave Gloria to watch over things."

"That sounds like a lot of fun," Christina said. "Also, if you are interested, Lorraine, my folks take us on a lot of day trips in the summer. My sister thinks she is too grown up to go with the family anymore, and my little brother is a bore. I'm sure my mother would let me take you along. After all, you are my best friend."

It was such an honor to hear Christina say that. I was bursting with pride. I wasn't aware that she considered me her best friend.

Tommy got a fake hurt expression and said in a whiny voice, "I'm hurt, Christina. I thought I was your best friend!"

"You silly boy! You're my best friend too, but Lorraine is my closest girlfriend."

"Okay, I guess, as long as I'm your best-est guy buddy."

Everyone laughed, and we hustled to finish our lunches before it was time to leave for our next class.

At the end of our Algebra class Mr. Pendergass gave us our final grade. I was devastated!

When class was excused, I ran out of the room as I fought back tears. When Christina and Tommy caught up with me, Christina asked, "What's the matter?"

"I don't know what I'm going to do. I can't go home with this grade. My dad will be *so* angry with me!"

"Let's see, Lorraine. How bad is it?" Christina asked me.

Shamefully I let her take a glimpse of my awful grade.

"That's not so bad. My grade was only slightly above yours, and I was happy. Besides, you aced everything else! My parents would take me out and celebrate if I brought home a report like that."

"How did you do in Algebra?" I asked Tommy.

"Well...I aced it. I would have helped you if you would have asked. I didn't realize you were struggling with it."

My fears were well placed. My dad was furious with me when he learned about my Algebra grade. He threatened to ground me from all Teen Meets and told my mother to hire me a tutor for the summer. That's when I thought about what Tommy had said. If I would have asked for help, he would have given it to me.

When Mother and I were alone, I mentioned to her that I had a friend at school who had a four point grade average, and Algebra was his favorite subject. I lied a little and told her that he wanted to do tutoring this summer. She agreed, so I called Tommy.

I was so nervous! I normally would never call a boy on the phone, but I was desperate this time. I didn't want some old stiff neck trying to teach me Algebra. I didn't need another Mr. Pendergass. Now Tommy, that was a different subject. I thought about how much fun it would be working with him on a one to one basis. I could have him all to myself. I hoped I wouldn't embarrass myself and look like a dummy. I was shaking when I held the receiver to my ear and said, "Hello, may I speak with Tommy?"

A pleasant lady's voice said, "Yes, you may. Who may I say is calling?"

"It's Lorraine Patterson. I'm a friend from school."

"Sure, dear, Thomas has mentioned you often. I'll call him."

I was sure sweat was coming out of every pore of my body, I was so nervous. Then I heard his warm voice on the phone. "Well, hi there. I'm surprised to hear from you so soon. What's up?"

I took a big breath of air. "Tommy, I need your help."

"Sure, Lorraine, anything! What's the matter?"

"Well, you know I told you how mad my dad would be with me because of my Algebra?"

"Yeah."

"Well, he was furious. He might even ground me. He told my mother to find me a tutor. The idea of some boring tutor coming to my home makes me ill. I thought about you, Tommy. I know how good you are at it. Do you suppose you might be interested in the job?"

"Like I said, Lorraine, I would do anything to help you. I would love helping you with your Algebra. While I'm there, if you want, I'll show you how to use that computer you were telling me about."

"Oh thank you, that makes me so happy! It will be fun with you for a teacher, and after the lessons we can play tennis or take a swim in the pool. It will be great! Besides, I know my dad will pay you really well for helping me."

"Yeah, it sounds like fun, but I don't want any pay for it. We're friends! I can't think of anything better than to hang out with you all summer."

"Thanks, Tommy! You don't know how much this means to me."

Father didn't ground me, and he did let Mother hire Tommy. I didn't let on what close friends Tommy and I really were.

For the most part, the summer turned out to be really great. Tommy came over three times a week to tutor me. Sometimes I would call Christina and Sarah to come over after the lesson to swim, play tennis, or just take a walk around the huge estate. As much as I enjoyed Christina and Sarah, I had more fun when it was just Tommy and me.

Also, that summer Christina's family invited me to go on one of their weekend trips. I got a taste of how loving a family could be.

Toward the end of the summer Mother began spying on Tommy and me. We weren't doing anything wrong, but her alcoholism clouded her perspective. She misconstrued our friendship and thought the worst.

One August evening at the dinner table, my dear mother took a large sip of her glass of wine and announced that they were sending me to a private high school. I felt like dying, I was so angry.

Father backed her up. "We feel this is the best thing for you. It is a very prestigious school. Only the most influential people send their kids there. I'm sure you will find a better class of young people attending. It's known for a more advanced curriculum, so you will really need to buckle down on your studies. You need to keep your grades up. If not, I will be forced to ground you from all activities, including your Teen Meet."

I cried out, "But why, Father? Why are you punishing me this way?"

He frowned. "I'm not punishing you. It's for your own good. We should have sent you there last year. It is extremely important that you go to the right school, so you can be accepted by the best colleges. In fact, it would mean a great deal to me if you choose to go to Harvard. I would be extremely proud of you if you followed in my footsteps."

"You want me to become an attorney like you? I don't know, Father, if I could do that or not, but I promise I'll get a four point this year. Please, just let me go to Hillsdale High with my friends!"

Mother had put down another drink by this time. "Young lady, it is for your own good. You have way too many friends at Hillsdale. They distract you from getting good grades and concentrating on college. Especially that so-called tutor!" Then she told my father, "Do you know, this tutor wouldn't even accept any money when I tried to pay him. He said that he and our daughter were too good of friends!"

My father fixed his piercing blue eyes on me. "Do you mean that this study program was just a fake so you could hang out with your friends?"

"No, Father, not at all. Tommy is the best at Algebra. He has even taught me how to work the computer. I like Algebra now. I'm very good at it. There's no question in my mind that I'll ace it this year. Please, let me stay at Hillsdale."

My father sat back in his chair. "Well, if you can promise."

Mother jumped in. "No! Don't you dare give in to that girl. We need to separate her and that boy. They have been getting too chummy this summer."

"That's not true," I said in a rather loud voice. "Tommy and I are only friends. That's all!"

"Ladies, ladies, calm down. Marge, you know you are always quick to jump to conclusions. Have you actually seen anything to substantiate your claims?"

"Well, I know they spend a lot of time together, too much. I've watched them when they were alone in the pool, always hanging on to each other. They take long walks together on the estate. Once I saw them holding hands. I didn't follow them, but I didn't like it one bit. They see each other at least five times a week. Lorraine needs a break from that boy!"

My father gave my mom a disgusting look. "They're kids. Give them a break."

"Kids, my foot! They're both fifteen! What kind of a lawyer are you, anyway? The evidence is right before your eyes, if you only open them and see." Mother turned to me. "Don't listen, Lorraine." She turned back to my father and continued talking to him. "Our daughter is becoming a very attractive young lady. I can remember back to the time I was fifteen. I'm sure, if you remember the things that ran through your mind, Jim, back then, it would scare the pants off you. Of course, you haven't really changed that much, have you?"

"Excuse me, Marge! Besides, this is not about me. It's Lorraine's future we need to be concerned with here. You're around the house a lot more now, so why haven't you gotten a better control of things?"

"And I don't have things to do around here? Who entertains at the drop of a hat? And…and who keeps up a community front by heading several charity events? I could go on and on. Just because you're never home anymore, don't blame me for everything."

"It might help if you were ever sober. What about Gloria? Wasn't she supposed to watch over her?"

Mom smirked. "Yeah! Gloria was supposed to look after her. We pay her extra for it. However, Gloria has been too interested in that new gardener we hired to pay attention to Lorraine."

I couldn't take any more of their bickering. "Just stop it!" I screamed. "Stop your fighting! This is my life, not yours. Can't you for just one day think about what makes me happy, or what's good for me?"

My father jumped up from his chair and pointed his finger at me. "That's it, young lady. For the last time you don't raise your voice at me, or your mother. Maybe your mother is right. Maybe you are getting out of control. You are going to that private school!"

⌘⌘⌘

As I watched from The Great White Throne Judgment my heart was torn in half by the pain I felt as I watched myself run from the dinner table that night. I didn't get any sleep that entire night because I couldn't stop crying. The couple of weeks building up to the transfer were driving me crazy. It was really hard on my friends too. We had talked and made all sorts of plans for starting high school this year. Now it was all in vain. From the Throne I could see how my friends' hearts were bleeding in pain over my parents' decision.

Again I begged God for answers. "Why, God? Why were my parents so cruel to me? Why couldn't they see the innocence between Tommy and me? Why wouldn't they let me stay and go to high school with my dear friends? Lord, I know my life would have turned out better, if only they would have let me stayed with my wonderful Christian friends."

"Yes, Lorraine, you're right. Your life could have been different if your parents would have let you stay at the same school with your Christian friends. However, your life would have been different if only you would have accepted me as your personal Saviour.

"As was done to you, I knocked at the heart of each of your parents, but they would not open their hearts to me.

"Either man is with me, or is with the evil one, being sons of Satan.

"Your parents thought they were doing the right thing for you, but they were as fools. You see, their minds were full of evil, so their words were evil. They could only see evil instead of your innocence.

" How could they, being evil, speak good things? For out of the abundance of the heart the mouth speaks. A good man out of the good treasure of his heart brings forth good things, and an evil man out of the evil treasure brings forth evil things. But I say to you, every idle word men may speak, they will give account of it in the day of judgment. For by your words, you will be justified, and by your words, you will be condemned."

8

The night before attending my new high school, I was broken hearted. When I went to bed, I soaked my pillow with tears. It wasn't supposed to be this way. I was supposed to be happy, starting high school with all of my friends. Now I was all alone, with no friends again.

At seven that next morning Gloria was pounding at my bedroom door, yelling at me, "Come on, missy, you're going to be late for your first day of school."

Slowly I rolled out of bed and went to the door to let Gloria in.

"Good morning, missy! Where's that big sunshine smile I normally see from you?"

"You know I can't smile, Gloria. You know how much I wanted to start high school with my friends. Last year I was scared about starting a new school, but at least I wasn't leaving any friends behind. I love my friends, and we all were looking forward to starting this year together. You don't know what an empty feeling it is to go to school without even one friend."

"I know, Missy. If it were up to me, you would be staying with your friends, but it's not. Now come on, get ready, I'll start your breakfast. Also, your mother has given me permission to drive you to school and pick you up in her swanky new car."

Twirling my finger I said, "Whoopee...oh, I'm sorry, Gloria, that will be great. Thanks."

As I had expected, the new school was a nightmare. I truly hated that school. The teachers were all prim and proper, not to mention very strict. Everyone seemed to come equipped with friends—everybody except me, that is. All my friends were back at Hillsdale. I felt like I was invisible; no one seemed to even notice me. I felt so alone.

The first two weeks were very hard. I couldn't even concentrate on my studies, I was so miserable. Then I bumped into a girl in the hall. Our books flew all over. By the time we got them all sorted out we were laughing. She said, "Hi, I'm Amy Regalon. Sorry I bumped into you."

"Oh no," I said. "It was my fault. I guess I wasn't thinking. By the way, my name is Lorraine Patterson."

Amy gave me a weird look. "You're in a couple of my classes. I came in late a few times and sat next to you in the back row."

"Oh, yes! I remember you now."

"Cool! Maybe we could sit together in class, if you don't mind?"

"Mind! I'd love it."

"Yeah, Lorraine, I'm new at this school, so I don't know anybody."

"Me too!"

"Oh, yeah? I hate this school! The kids are all snobs, and they are so cliquish."

"Why are you going here?" I asked her.

"Because I got into some trouble. My parents wanted me to get away from my friends...like that will help. It just makes me more rebellious."

"I'm here for the same thing, too. I went to Hillsdale last year and I have some really good friends from there. We planned all summer about what fun we would have at high school this year."

"No! You went to Hillsdale? So did I."

"Really!" I said. "It was a very large school, and I only knew a handful of kids."

"Yeah, it was big. I hung out with a small bunch of kids that I had to leave behind. My parents just don't care about my feelings."

"Mine either. They couldn't care less about what I want. Making money is their only concern."

"Mine too. My mother works as a editor in New York, and my dad owns a recording studio. I never see them, but they can lay out some heavy rules. I can get around most of them, but I couldn't get out of this dumb school."

"My father's a lawyer out of New York. My folks are always too busy. They have our cook, Gloria, look after me. She's okay, and leaves me alone most of the time."

Amy and I became instant friends. It felt so good to finally have a friend at school.

Toward the end of the week Amy asked me, "Hey, Lorraine, how about coming to a little party Saturday night? My parents are spending the weekend in the city. I have the house all to myself."

"I'd love too, but I can't."

"What? You can't? Come on! You'll get a chance to meet all my friends. They're really awesome. I'm even having some dudes over I met at my dad's recording studio. They can play some really screaming guitars."

"Wow, Amy, that sounds fabulous, but really, I've already made plans with my friends from Hillsdale High. I couldn't break my plans. We've been planning this hayride for a long time." I was too embarrassed to tell her that it was a youth group from church.

"That's cool, but I wish you could have. Not to worry, my parents are out of town a lot; there'll be more parties. As a matter of fact, my buddy Greg is throwing a party next Saturday night. His parents will be gone; they are in a band and travel a lot. Greg has his own little three-piece band; he's pretty good. He always throws a blowout of a party!"

Saturday evening didn't seem as exciting as it had before, as I started getting ready for the hayride. My mind was on Amy's party; I wondered what I was missing. There was something intriguing and suspenseful about going to a house party that had a live band and a houseful of nothing but kids.

I slipped into my jeans and red sweatshirt. Then I looked in the mirror, admiring my image. My confidence was soaring. For the first time in my life, I liked what I saw in the mirror. I was proud of my tall, slender, curvaceous body. My long black wavy hair hung over my shoulders and halfway down my back. I gave a quick smile to my image as I admired the deep dimples in my checks. It felt good to finally feel good about myself.

When I got to the hayride I couldn't help but be happy and excited. The air was full of excitement. It was even more exciting when I spotted Christina and Sarah. They ran up when they saw me, and the three of us walked toward the hay wagon.

While we were walking, Christina said to me, "You're going to think I'm crazy, but for some reason I thought something happened to you. When you were a little late, I thought something bad happened!"

"Silly, do you think you are a psychic or something?"

"NO! I don't believe in that stuff, but I had an uneasy feeling about you, that's all."

"Christina, you know I'd let you know if something came up and I couldn't make it, don't you?"

"Yes, but it was so weird."

In a low, apologetic voice I said, "Oh, that does remind me. I won't be going to our end-of-the-season picnic."

"What? Why not? It's the most important event of the year. Are you grounded or something?"

"No, nothing like that. It's just...I'm going to a dance with a girl from my new school. I thought you would be happy that I made a friend at school. You know how I can't stand being alone."

"Yeah, but why make plans on the same day of an important Teen Meet event?"

"She asked me to go this Saturday night, and I turned her down because of the hayride. When she asked me out for the next Saturday night, I couldn't tell her no again. She'd think I didn't want to be friends with her. I can't lose her friendship, Christina. I could never replace the friendship that we have, but I do need to have a friend at school! You can understand, can't you?"

"Yeah, I guess. That's okay, Lorraine." Her eyes twinkled. "If you're not going to be there, I'll make it a romantic picnic with just Tommy and me sitting together. After all, we both have a huge crush on him. Maybe, I'll be the one to win Tommy's heart!"

I laughed at her. "A romantic picnic will never happen. Tommy's not the romantic type."

"Who is this girl, anyway?" Christina asked, switching topics.

"Maybe you guys know her. She went to Hillsdale last year. Her name is Amy Regalon."

Sarah's mouth dropped open. "Oh yeah, I've heard about her. Christina, you have, too. Doesn't she hang out with that really bad bunch of kids who are always getting in trouble?"

Christina turned to me. "Unfortunately, I do remember her! Lorraine, promise me you won't go out with her. She is really bad. If you hang out with her, you will get a bad reputation."

I was grateful when we reached the hay wagon, since it saved me from having to answer her. Tommy was already in the wagon. When he saw us, he held out his hand and helped us in. What a wonderful time we were having, riding in a horse-drawn hay wagon on this crisp autumn night. We played hard that evening, and when we were all exhausted, we sang gospel songs. It was so neat. I really enjoyed the singing. After singing, Christina, Tommy, and I lay back, quietly staring up at the stars. Christina was the first to break the silence as she said, "Tommy did Lorraine tell you that she isn't going to be at our picnic next week?"

"No! Why not?"

"I'm sorry, but I made plans with my new friend from school. I forgot about the picnic. Besides she asked me to go to a dance with her this week, and I had to turn her down. I wouldn't have missed this for anything."

"Well, the picnic is a lot of fun, too," Tommy said. "You can't miss it. We all want you to be there. Right, Christina?"

"Yes, we do! Lorraine, tell Tommy who your new friend is."

"It's Amy Regalon. Do you know her?"

"Do I know her? Not personally, only by reputation! She's bad news. I'd look for a new friend if it were me."

"Sorry, guys, I don't make friends that easy! What in the world would it hurt to go to a simple little dance with her?"

Tommy looked hurt. "A dance? Why a dance?"

"I like music." I frowned. "Tommy, you're acting like I'm about to commit a crime, or something. It's only a dance!"

Tommy's face grew red. "Well, I kinda thought that if you wanted to go to a school dance that I would be the one taking you."

"I didn't even know that you knew how to dance, or even would want to! That is so sweet, Tommy, you wanting to take me to a dance."

Christina broke into the conversation. "Have you forgot some months ago when the youth pastor spoke on finding friends that are equally yoked?"

"Kind of. I know I have the same interest in things that you guys do, but I'm also interested in doing other things, too. I want to see what it's like to go to a party with a band and lots of kids."

"What?" Christina said in a loud voice. "You're not even going to a high school dance, you're going to a house party?"

"Well, so what?"

"So what! Listen to me, Lorraine. Amy and her bunch have the worst reputations around. If you start hanging out with them, you might as well kiss your good reputation good-bye! No decent kids will want to hang out with you if you party with those lowlifes! If you go out with them, you are asking for trouble."

Now I was getting upset, so I lashed out at her, "You know, Christina, you're just jealous. You should be happy for me, that Amy wants to be my friend. I know she is different than you guys, but she is the only one who has offered friendship, and I need that badly! All the other kids are snobs; they have their own little cliques. All I know is that she is really nice to me and a whole lot of fun! Don't you know how desperately I need that right now?"

Christina was boiling mad. "That is being desperate; it's scraping the bottom of the barrel! You could hold off until you meet a decent girl to be friends with. With a friend like Amy, you don't need enemies. Come on, Tommy, let's go sit with someone else. I'm not even sure if Lorraine is equally yoked to us."

"Come on, Christina," Tommy said in a calming way. "Lorraine just doesn't realize the dangers of hanging out with that type of individual."

"Fine! Stay if you want. I'm going to find Sarah."

I was so hurt by my best friends' words, I began to cry. Tommy comforted me by putting his arms around me. "She didn't mean it, Lorraine. Christina was just really upset with your decision. She is really concerned about you. To tell you the truth, so am I. You don't know what goes on at those parties. If you want to go to a dance, I'll take you to one of our school dances. You'll need to teach me how to dance; but if it means that much to you, I'll learn."

"Thanks, that's sweet of you. Maybe some time we can go to a school dance, but I really want to go to Amy's party Saturday night. Tommy, are you really sure you know what goes on at those kinds of parties? Have you ever gone to a house party?"

"No...but..."

I interrupted him and pleaded, "Go with me, Tommy. Please, go with me. I'm sure Amy won't mind. If you're with me, nothing will happen!"

"No, Lorraine. I would never put myself in that type of a situation. I might not have been to one, but I've heard plenty. They brag all over school about it. There's drinking, smoking marijuana, and who knows what else. A lot of older kids hang out at those parties and are always looking for young, innocent girls. Especially beautiful girls like you. Neither one of us should go. I don't know how you could even ask me, or want to go yourself. On top of that, it really bothers me to think of you dancing with other boys. You can't trust them, Lorraine, especially the college guys that go to those kinds of parties."

"Why, Tommy, I didn't know you cared so much."

Tommy reached down and gave me the most tender, sweet, loving kiss.

Smiling up at him, I said, "Oh, Tommy, I didn't know you felt this way about me!"

"I hope you aren't mad at me for kissing you, but I've wanted to kiss you for a long time. I wasn't sure if I should or not. I was afraid it might hurt our friendship; we've been friends for so long that the last thing I want to do is lose it. I really care a lot for you, Lorraine. I've never kissed a girl before."

"This was my first kiss too. I could never get mad at you, To be honest, I care deeply for you. I've tried to tell myself that I just liked you as a friend, but those feelings have definitely changed. I'm not real sure what these feelings are, but they are getting stronger."

Tommy smiled. "That's why I had to let you know how I feel now, before you start going out and dating different boys. Lorraine, will you go steady with me?"

"Oh, Tommy! Yes, yes, Tommy, I will!"

"Will you give up the stupid idea of going out with Amy Regalon and that bunch of kids?"

"Going steady does not give you the right to tell me what friends to choose. It isn't fair to put strings on our relationship. You should trust me to choose my own friends and trust me to make my own decisions."

"It's not that I don't trust you; it's them I don't trust. They are too wild for you."

"Don't worry about it. Besides, I haven't made up my mind yet. If I do, you don't have to worry; you know I have a good head on my shoulders. I won't do anything stupid. As for dancing with other boys, you've got to be kidding. You know I'd be too shy to talk to a boy I don't know, let alone dance with one! And besides, we are going steady."

"Good, because I can't stand to think of you in the arms of another guy."

"Oh, you silly boy! Now that we are going steady, I wouldn't dream of dancing with anybody but you. Please, believe me, Tommy. I will always be true to you."

"Well, I guess I can't do anything else but trust you, 'cause you'll do what you want anyway. I still don't like it; but you're right, the decision is yours to make. I know one thing for sure. I don't ever want to do anything to lose our friendship! No matter what, I'll always be here for you."

Tommy then took me in his arms again and kissed me for the second time. This was a much more passionate kiss, one I dreamed about the rest of the night.

⌘⌘⌘

My tears were flowing as I watched from The Great White Throne Judgment. "None of this would have happened if it weren't for that Amy. She caused all my problems. If only I wouldn't have met her!"

"IF YOU WOULD HAVE TRUSTED IN ME FOR YOUR SALVATION, YOU MIGHT HAVE BEEN ABLE TO RESIST THE TEMPTATION. IT WAS AS IN THE DAYS OF ADAM AND EVE. I FORMED MAN OF THE DUST OF THE GROUND AND BREATHED INTO HIS NOSTRILS THE BREATH OF LIFE; AND MAN BECAME A LIVING BEING. I PUT HIM IN THE GARDEN OF EDEN TO TEND AND KEEP IT. I GAVE A COMMANDMENT TO THE MAN, THAT OF EVERY TREE OF THE GARDEN HE MAY EAT FREELY; BUT OF THE TREE OF THE KNOWLEDGE OF GOOD AND EVIL, HE SHALL NOT EAT OF IT OR HE WOULD SURELY DIE.

"FROM ADAM'S RIB I MADE IT INTO A WOMAN. I CALLED HER EVE. I BROUGHT EVE TO ADAM TO BE HIS WIFE.

"NOW THE SERPENT WAS MORE CUNNING THAN ANY BEAST OF THE FIELD WHICH I HAD MADE. HE TEMPTED HER TO EAT OF THE TREE OF THE KNOWLEDGE OF GOOD AND EVIL. HE TRICKED THE WOMAN BY GIVING HER FALSE ASSURANCE. HE TOLD HER THAT SHE WOULD SURELY NOT DIE. HE TOLD HER THAT I KNEW THAT THE DAY SHE ATE OF THE FORBIDDEN FRUIT, HER EYES WOULD BE OPENED, AND SHE WOULD BE AS GOD, KNOWING GOOD FROM EVIL.

"LORRAINE, YOU WERE LIKE UNTO EVE. YOU WERE CURIOUS AND WANTED TO TASTE THE FORBIDDEN FRUIT. AMY TEMPTED YOU. YOU TOOK A BITE AND THEN OFFERED TO TOMMY. UNLIKE ADAM, TOMMY WAS ABLE TO RESIST TEMPTATION. YOUR ADVERSARY THE DEVIL IS LIKE A ROARING LION, WALKING ABOUT, SEEKING WHOM HE MAY DEVOUR."

9

My mind was made up. I was going to tell Amy that I wouldn't be going to the party with her—or anywhere with her, for that matter. However, when I got to school, Amy was waiting for me on the steps. I just couldn't bring myself to tell her. She acted so happy to see me, how could I possibly tell her I didn't want to hang out with her anymore?

Amy couldn't stop talking about the fabulous party she had at her place Saturday night. She told me, "Don't feel bad, Lorraine, the really fun party will be at Greg's this next Saturday night. You simply can't miss that party. Greg is so much fun, and he is a pretty good musician. Most of the kids who were at my party said they were coming. It will be a total blast!"

"I don't know, Amy. You'd be the only one there I'd know."

"Don't worry. My friends will love you. I can't wait for you to meet them. They are a riot. I'm quite sure you will like them, too!"

"They don't sound boring, that's for sure."

"No way!"

"I don't have the slightest idea what to wear."

"That's no problem. Got a credit card?"

"Well, no, but I'm sure I can get one."

"Cool! I'll take you to my favorite stores at the mall. To tell the truth, Lorraine, you do dress a little conservative. You're a sophomore now; it's time to give your wardrobe an uplift."

I was a bit embarrassed by Amy's bold statement, but I somewhat agreed. "You're right, Amy, it's time I did my own shopping. My mother buys for me like I'm still in elementary school. I like the things that you wear, but don't you get in trouble for wearing them here at school?"

"I did when I went to Hillsdale. I got suspended twice for wearing my skirts too short. This school has more class and is up to date. They aren't very strict here at all when it comes to dress codes."

"Super! I won't be able to replace my wardrobe all at once, because my mother would notice that. But if I buy a little at a time, she probably wouldn't even know it."

"Great! We better get to class. I've already gotten three warnings about being late."

That week Amy and I made a plan on how I could get out of the house Saturday afternoon to go to the mall. From the mall we would be able to go straight to the party.

Saturday finally arrived. Now to orchestrate my plan. As usual, mother didn't show her face until noon. When she did come out of her bedroom, I knew enough to leave her alone for at least two hours. It took that long for her to get over her hangover. I waited for the right moment to approach her. It was two-thirty in the afternoon. She was curled up on the sofa with a glass of wine in her hand.

As I sat down in a chair next to her, I cleared my throat. "Mother, I've made a new friend at school."

"Fabulous, darling! See, I knew you would. Does she come from a good background?"

"Yes, Mother, she does."

"Well then, tell me something about her parents. What type of work is her father in?"

"He owns a recording studio in the city."

"That sounds good. How about her mother?"

"I believe Amy told me that she was an editor at a publishing house in New York City. I don't know—why does it matter?"

"Lorraine! Don't you remember that your father and I wanted to send you to this school because there was a better class of children that attended there? Of course it matters what social class you pick for friends. Your future could depend on it."

"I thought the main purpose was to keep me away from Tommy?"

"Well, that, too. His family is only middle-class. You spent too much time with that boy, and you are too young to handle something like that. Believe me, child, you'll thank me someday."

"Sure, Mom, whatever."

"Don't take that tone with me!"

"I'm sorry, Mother."

"Tell me more about this young lady you've become friends with."

"She invited me to a movie tonight. Her mother will take us and bring me home. Please, Mother, may I go?"

"That might work out. Your father and I are having dinner with clients tonight, and Gloria wanted to have the night off. That way I won't have to worry about you. It sounds like Amy has upstanding parents. Sure, Lorraine, you can go, but be home by eleven."

"But, Mom, we're going to a double feature, and then Amy's mom is taking us to get a bite to eat afterwards."

"Oh, okay. You be back by midnight, you hear?"

"Yes, Mother, thank you. One other thing. I really need a new outfit for tonight."

"Don't be silly. You have lots of clothes—some I don't think you've even worn. Besides, Lorraine, I don't have time to take you shopping now. Your father is picking me up at seven. I barely have enough time now to make myself presentable for tonight."

"Mom, I really think I should have a nice new outfit for meeting Amy's mother tonight. Amy really dresses nice. And, you don't have to worry, I can grab a taxi. Amy said she would meet me at the mall and help me pick out something. She has such good taste in clothes."

"Lorraine, I don't have any extra cash on me right now."

"That's okay. Why don't you let me use your credit card? You won't need it anyway. You'll be with Father."

"Well, I guess so."

"You know, Mom, Amy has her own credit card. So do most of the kids who go to this high school. Don't you think I should have one now that I'm fifteen?"

"Well…that's a subject I'll have to take up with your father."

Mom got up and grabbed her purse. She got out her credit card and reluctantly handed it to me as she said, "Here, don't go crazy. Now leave me alone so I can get ready!"

My plan had worked, I was meeting Amy on the west side of the mall at four o'clock. I was there right on time. Amy was there waiting for me. It was my first trip to the mall without my mother or Gloria. The mall had a whole different meaning now. It was fun and exciting! I was free, liberated!

As we hurried down the corridor Amy told me, "My friend Kathy is going to join us on our shopping spree. That's all right with you, isn't it?"

"Sure, of course."

"Cool! She is so neat! What's even better, she's got wheels."

"She has a car?"

"Yeah, it's an old clunker, but it's wheels!"

"I thought she was a sophomore?"

"Yeah, she is. Kathy was held back last year. She's sixteen."

"How neat to own a car."

"Yeah, my dad told me that if I don't get in any more trouble, he will buy me a brand-new car this summer."

"Oh, my gosh! That means we'll be getting driver's training this spring!"

"Duh, yeah!"

"That also means I'm going to have to work on my parents. I'm sure they will want me to drive a new car, too. They have this status thing, you know. Besides, I'd love to have my very own new car."

Amy started waving her hand as she said, "Here comes Kathy now."

Kathy was a small, slender-framed girl with fiery red hair. It was easy to see she was bursting with energy. When she got close to us, she was waving vigorously and calling out, "Hey, Amy, good to see you. I'm glad you called. You know how I love shopping at the mall."

"Kathy, this is my new friend, Lorraine. Lorraine, meet one of my best buds, Kathy."

"Hi, Kathy. You look a little familiar. Where have I seen you before?"

Amy spoke up. "She was cheerleader last year at Hillsdale High."

"Oh, yes! That's where I saw you. You're a great cheerleader."

"Thanks, but not good enough. They kicked me off the team."

"Yeah," said Amy, "not because she wasn't good enough. It was because she was caught smoking."

Kathy slapped her on the shoulder. "You don't have to rub it in. I didn't need cheerleading anyway. Too many rules to suit me!"

I smiled. "Do you still attend Hillsdale?"

"Yeah, unfortunately."

"Oh well," I said, "let's go hit the shops and then we'll all feel better."

That certainly did help! It was a ball shopping, trying on all sorts of clothes. Kathy was such a nut, I could tell right away we were going to be good friends. Kathy and Amy helped me pick out my new fabulous outfit. Amy found me a black leather skirt. It was short and had an alluring slit way up the side. Then Kathy picked out a blue, off-the-shoulder sweater. I sure didn't have anything like that in my closet.

Amy pushed, "Go on, Lorraine! Go in the dressing room and try them on."

I felt embarrassed. "I don't know. I'd feel sleazy in something like this."

Kathy said, "Don't be silly, it's the latest style! You'll look great in it. Come on, go try them on."

"Okay, you guys, but if I feel uncomfortable, I'm not buying them."

I went to the dressing room and tried on the provocative outfit. I stood before the mirror trying to decide if I loved or hated it. The girl in the mirror didn't even look like me. I kind of thought that I looked like one of those stunning ladies out of a James Bond movie. I was really nervous before I walked out of the dressing room.

Amy and Kathy squealed with delight as I stepped out.

Amy spoke first. "I can't believe it! You look so hot! I wish I had your looks and body! We have got to keep Greg away from her tonight."

"You got that right," Kathy said. "Lorraine, you look like a rock star. The blue in the sweater matches your blue eyes perfectly!"

I took another look at myself in the mirror. "But don't you think the sweater is a bit…too low. And maybe the skirt a little…too short?"

"Are you kidding?" Kathy asked. "That outfit was made for you!"

"I totally agree," said Amy. "You look absolutely gorgeous in it." She laughed. "I'm jealous of you. All the guys will be after you tonight."

"Well, you don't have to worry about me. I'm going steady."

Amy looked surprised. "You never told me! Besides, how great can he be? If he is so great, you would be out with him tonight instead of us. Just wait, there are so many gorgeous hunks that go to our parties. You'll be like a kid in a candy store."

Kathy laughed. "I'll tell you what! Those tennis shoes on your feet do nothing for that outfit. Come on, Lorraine, you need to buy some groovy high-heel boots to make this outfit complete. Next door there's a really cool shoe store."

I paid for my clothes, took the tags off, and then wore them out of the shop. We went into the shoe store, where Amy spotted a really cool pair of black leather boots. "Look at these honeys. They match your skirt perfectly."

I slipped them on and paraded in front of the mirror.

"It's WONDER WOMAN!" Kathy said loudly.

I got embarrassed. "Are they…too much?"

"No, I'm only kidding. They make the outfit. Now all you need is your hair teased and feathered. A good makeup job and you'll be good to go."

Amy suggested, "Let's go to the ladies' room. If you want, I'm really good at makeup. I can do it for you. And Kathy's good with hair."

"Yeah, that will be great, you guys!"

When they were all done primping me, I glanced in the mirror. I couldn't believe my eyes. I looked nineteen or twenty. The girls kept going on about how much I resembled a movie star. Amy said I was a young version of Jacquelyn Smith, and Kathy agreed with her.

We left the mall and went to Kathy's car. We all had to get in on the driver's side because the passenger side handle was broken. It was an old car, but I was having the time of my life, laughing and kidding around with my two new friends.

⌘ ⌘ ⌘

Looking down from The Great White Throne Judgment, I felt guilt as I faced the Lord. I said to Him, "It didn't bother me to lie to my mother back then, but now I feel great guilt because of my lies."

"A FAITHFUL WITNESS DOES NOT LIE, BUT A FALSE WITNESS WILL UTTER LIES. A FALSE WITNESS WILL NOT GO UNPUNISHED.

"YOUR TONGUE WAS LIE UNTO A BOX. YOU HAVE BENT YOUR TONGUE FOR LIES. FOR YOU PROCEEDED FROM EVIL TO EVIL, BECAUSE YOU DID NOT KNOW ME. HE WHO SPEAKS LIES WILL NOT ESCAPE.

"A RIGHTEOUS MAN HATES LYING, BUT A WICKED MAN IS LOATHSOME AND COMES TO SHAME. NOW YOU FEEL SHAMEFUL, BECAUSE YOU STAND BEFORE THE SPOTLESS LAMB OF GOD. I CAME INTO THE WORLD TO TAKE AWAY MAN'S SINS. I WAS SLAIN ON THE CROSS OF CALVARY TO COVER THE SINS OF MAN. ALL THEY HAD TO DO IS ACCEPT MY GIFT OF SALVATION.

"LORRAINE, YOU CONTINUED TO REJECT MY GIFT. THAT IS THE REASON THAT YOU FELT SO LITTLE SHAME ON EARTH."

10

After Kathy, Amy, and I left the mall, we stopped at a fast-food restaurant and had dinner. I was having such a wonderful time. I was quite sure that if I went straight home after this, it still would be the best day of my life. But there was more to come—the party!

As we drove out of town, I noticed how rundown the neighborhood looked. We drove past a small junky house that Kathy pointed to and said, "That's where I live, so we're almost there! Greg's place is only about a mile from my house."

Sarcastically, I thought to myself, *Oh great, I've never been in such a rundown neighborhood before. I wonder if it's even safe to drive in.*

It was about eight-fifteen when we pulled into the long driveway at Greg's house. Cars were parked all over, even on the grass. Greg lived in a long, ranch-style house.

When we walked through the door, we saw an arrow pointing down to the basement. Amy and Kathy led the way. I could tell that they had been there before. I was totally amazed as I stepped into the basement. It was like magic. What I thought would be a dingy old basement was completely transformed into a nightclub. I had never been in a nightclub before but had seen a lot of them on television. There was so much atmosphere, I couldn't believe it! Except for the bathroom and small kitchen, the whole basement was one big open party room. It was dimly lit by strings of lights and candles on the tables. Loud rock music blasted in my ears. A three-piece band was playing on a small stage, where flashing colored lights were dancing about. At the opposite side of the room there was a long bar with bar stools in front of it. The place was packed with people. Some were standing around talking; some were sitting at small tables or at the bar. A few couples were dancing in front of the bandstand. If I didn't know any better, I'd have sworn I was in a real nightclub.

I was overwhelmed at my surroundings. I loved music, but I'd never really heard hard rock, not that loud, anyway. I was taken in by the whole scene. I was totally engulfed as I watched the band members playing their instruments and singing. I asked Amy, "Who is that gorgeous lead guitarist?"

"That's Greg!"

"You've got to be kidding?"

"No, it's Greg. Quite a hunk, isn't he?"

"Well, yeah!"

Greg was a tall, slender guy with dark hair that hung almost to the middle of his back. He was very handsome in a rugged sort of way. He wore a fringed leather vest, and a pair of holey jeans that were so tight, I don't know how he got into them. He sure looked good, though.

"I'll introduce you when they get done with their set," Amy assured me.

"That's okay. I was just wondering, that's all. I have a boyfriend, remember?"

Kathy laughed. "Yeah, sure. The way you are eyeing him up, I wonder."

We were only there fifteen minutes when this big brute of a guy who was standing a few feet from us looked over and pointed his finger in our direction. Then he motioned his head toward the dance floor. I asked Kathy and Amy, "I wonder what he wants?"

Kathy said, "He's motioning to you. It's his way of asking you to dance."

"Yeah," Amy said. That's Ralph Sidfield. He's one of the college guys and captain of the football team. He thinks he's God's gift to women. He usually gets any girl he wants. He is kind of cute in a rough way."

I turned my face away from him. I certainly didn't want to dance with someone that rude. Besides, I promised Tommy.

Next thing I knew, he was standing in front of me. "Didn't you see me ask you to dance?"

I answered him, "I didn't know that you meant me."

Sarcastically he said, "Well, yeah, why do you think I pointed at you? Well, you going to dance or not?"

"No thank you. I don't care to dance right now."

He grabbed my wrist. "Come on, baby! I don't take no for an answer!" He started pulling me by the wrist, saying, "Come on, chick, we're going to dance."

He reeked of alcohol. There was no way I was going to dance with this obnoxious drunk. I was trying hard to get away from his grip.

When Greg saw what was happening, he put his guitar down and jumped off the stage. He came over and grabbed Ralph by the shoulder, whirled him around, and got in his face. "She said she didn't want to dance! Now go find someone else who does want to dance with you, or I'll throw you out on your ear!"

"Okay, okay, it's cool. I didn't know the chick belonged to you, but if I was you, I'd keep better tabs on her. She's the foxiest chick in here tonight." Greg gave him another nasty look, and Ralph said, "Okay, man, you don't have to worry about me. I'm out of here."

My face was beet red when Greg smiled at me and said, "Does *my* chick have a name?"

Amy spoke up. "Yeah, Greg, this is my new friend I was telling you about—Lorraine."

Greg smiled. "Well, hi there, Lorraine. Welcome to my little party shack."

Kathy corrected, "You mean your parents' party shack?"

"Hey, you don't see my parents, do you? When they're gone, the party shack is mine!"

"I guess I can't argue about that." Kathy laughed.

I smiled at Greg. "Hi, it's nice to meet you."

"It's great meeting you too. I haven't been a very good host; why don't you girls come over and join the guys and me at the band's table?"

We followed him over to a big table beside the bandstand. After he got us all settled around his table, Greg said he'd go to the bar and get us each a draft. He left so quickly, I didn't have time to tell him no, that I didn't want any alcohol of any kind. After all, I had promised Tommy I wouldn't drink.

Greg brought back three glasses of beer. He put one down in front of each of us. I didn't know what to say. Greg had a special way about him; he had charisma. It was too embarrassing to tell him no. Besides, after all, he had come to my aid and saved me from that conceited Neanderthal. How could I insult him by refusing a drink? After all, how bad could one little glass of beer be?

Greg smiled at me. "I have to get back to my band. Feel free to help yourself. There's all sorts of booze, wine, or anything else you might want.

I'll play a set, and then the guys and I will join you ladies. Maybe, Lorraine, you'll save me a dance?"

My face felt so red. How could I dance with Greg, when I promised Tommy that I would only dance with him? Without thinking, I took a big gulp of beer. I about spit it out! I didn't want to complain to my friends, but it was terrible. I kept sipping it, hoping it would be gone soon.

Amy and Kathy knew a lot of guys there and were dancing most of the time. I had a few guys come over and ask me to dance, but I always refused. I probably would have refused even if I wasn't going steady with Tommy. The only time I've ever danced before was at home in front of my mirror. I convinced myself I'd be too embarrassed to dance anyway.

Greg finally got done with his set and came over to our table. Before he sat down, he said, "Wow, am I ever thirsty. I'm going to get me a brew." He looked down at my glass. "Where's my manners? You're empty. I'll pick you up one, too."

"Oh no, I ..."

"I'm sorry, Lorraine, I didn't think to ask you, I just brought you beer. I'll bring you back something special. You'll love it." Before I could say no, he was off again.

When Greg got back from the bar, he sat down next to me. He put a tall champagne glass with rosy pink wine in front of me. I took a sip and was surprised at how good it tasted. Greg asked, "Is that better?"

"Much better."

The other two members of the band joined us at the table. Greg introduced them to me. Just then Kathy and Amy came back and said, "Hi, guys, you're sounding good tonight!"

"Man, Greg must have a crush on you, bringing out his parent's fine crystal," Kathy commented.

I blushed again.

Greg put his arm around me. "Nothing too good for my date." Everyone laughed and then took a big swallow of their drinks. Of course, I had to follow the rest of them and take a big drink, too. Besides, it tasted like a fruit drink—how bad could that be? And, after all, I was having so much fun; I didn't want to be a drag.

During the time that the band was on break there was a disc jockey playing music. When he put a slow romantic song on, Greg stood up and gently put his hand on my shoulder. He asked, "Come on, you gorgeous woman, would you please dance with me?"

I had never been called a woman before, let alone *gorgeous!* Before I could think straight, I said, "Yes, I'd love to."

As we started to dance, Greg said, "You know, it's important that we dance. That way everyone will think you're with me. No one will bother you—that is, if you don't want to dance with anyone else. I noticed when I was playing that you turned down every guy who asked."

I felt safe with Greg. After all, he was quick to save me from that nasty drunk. I looked into his eyes. "You are absolutely right. I don't want to dance with anyone but you."

I didn't even think about Tommy as Greg drew me closer. When the song ended, Greg continued holding me until the music began again. We danced close the entire song. When it finished, Greg bent down and gave me a lingering kiss on my cheek. I had chills all over my body. Then he brushed my hair away from my ear and put his lips close to my ear as he whispered, "I need to get back to the bandstand. Will you be here for the next break?" I whispered back, "Yes, I'll be here."

When I got back to my table, there was a full glass of wine waiting for me. Amy had filled my drink when she got one for herself.

Back on the stage Greg and the boys began really rocking. Amy stood up in a hurry and motioned to Kathy and me to get up and dance. I shook my head no and said, "I don't know how!"

"Don't be silly," Amy said. "Just let the music move you. Come on, it's fun!"

Reluctantly, I joined them on the dance floor. They were dancing and having so much fun, so I joined them doing my thing. I had watched *American Bandstand* and *Soul Train*, so I had a fairly good idea about what moves to make. I was having the time of my life dancing. However, the more I danced, the more wine I consumed. It went down like soda pop. Before I could finish a glass, there would be another full one sitting in front of me. While others had to buy their drinks at the bar, Greg was having drinks delivered to me.

When Greg's set was done, he joined our table again. We all had a great time together laughing, drinking, and making small talk. Greg and I even danced a couple more slow songs. I felt like we were one soul as he held me even closer to him.

Soon Greg was back on the stage again, and the three of us girls were tearing up the dance floor. I don't know how many glasses of wine I had, but I really was getting tipsy. Kathy was the first to notice that I was getting drunk. She went up to the stage and whispered to Greg, "Hey, Greg, we have got to get Lorraine home; she is really getting drunk."

"Wait, Kathy," Greg said. "You and Amy have both been drinking heavily. Besides, it's getting late. I need to clear this place out for the night. Let me drive you girls home. I don't want anything to happen to you guys. Besides, I think I'm falling in love!"

Greg's next song was his typical closing song of the evening, "The Party's Over." When he finished it, Greg said, "Drink up, guys and gals. The party is over for tonight. See you at the same time and place next week."

Greg hurried off the stage and assisted Amy and Kathy as they were trying to help me out of my seat. I tried to talk to Greg and a big hiccup came out instead. I giggled. "Whoops. They want me to go home, Greggy, but I'm having too much fun. Tell them we should stay a little longer, okay, Greggy-Pooh?"

"Honey, you could stay longer, but the party is over for tonight. They'll bring you to the next party, won't you, girls?"

"Sure," they both echoed.

I couldn't walk on my own. Greg put my arm around him on one side and Amy was on the other. "Why did you girls let her drink so much?" Greg asked. "She is really in bad shape."

Amy felt bad. "I guess it's my fault, I don't think Lorraine has ever drunk before. She can't handle it. She's a big girl, though. She could have said no."

As soon as they got me outside, I threw up all over. Good thing I waited to get outdoors. That sobered me up a little. I was so embarrassed. Especially in front of Greg, who seemed to be very infatuated with me.

Greg helped me get in the back of his VW van, where he had an air mattress. That was the last thing I remembered until we got to the mall. Amy was shaking me, trying to wake me up. Finally I started to come around.

"Lorraine," Amy pleaded, "you've got to get with it. I don't know where you live from here."

"Okay, okay," I said as I managed to sit up. "I took a taxi to the mall, but I'm pretty sure I know the way."

"Great," Kathy said sarcastically.

We went the wrong way a few times, but somehow I managed to find my house. As we pulled up to the gate, Greg said, "Oh my gosh, get a load of this place."

"You never told me you were this rich." Amy sounded shocked.

Kathy's mouth flew open. "Oh my goodness! You live in a mansion!"

I struggled in my pocket to get the sensor to the gate. When I got it out and started punching in the numbers, I said, "It's no big deal, you guys. I'd trade Greg's party house for this any old day."

The gate opened and we drove down our long drive.

"We better let Lorraine off as soon as possible," Greg said. "Her parents will kill us."

"Don't worry so much," I said with a giggle. "Let me out and I'll look in the garage and see if they're home yet." I couldn't reach the window, so Greg got out and looked in the garage. "There's a Cadillac in there," Greg said.

"Only one car?" I asked.

"Yeah, only the Cadillac."

"Cool! Then Marge and James aren't home yet," I said in a stiff manner.

Greg helped me to the massive double doors in the front of my house and waited as I fumbled for the keys. I finally got the right key in the lock and opened the door.

"I'm going to split before your parents get home and catch us. Can you make it from here okay?"

I slurred out, "Sure, Greggy-Pooh."

It wasn't as easy as I thought. I had to practically crawl up the stairs to get to my room. I threw my soiled clothes down the laundry chute and then fell into bed.

My friends must have just missed my parents. It wasn't more than ten minutes later when I heard my parents in the hall. They were obviously continuing an argument they had on the way home. I could hear my mother screaming at my dad, "I am sick and tired of this affair with your so-called secretary. Shelly was throwing herself at you all night! It's one thing behind closed doors at your office, but it's a whole different thing out in public. I feel so humiliated. How can you do that to me! James, I mean it this time: I want a divorce!"

"Will you shut up, Marge! I don't think you want a divorce. Why, you have it made. You couldn't even pay your booze bill on your own! Don't worry about Shelly. She told me tonight that she is dating a clown by the name of Richard Memons. So it looks like you don't have anything to worry about."

"Well, she has probably seen you as the two-timer that you really are, but don't worry. I'm sure you will have another tramp on the side before long. You always do. Remember, dear, I know how you work!"

"Will you be quiet. Quit your shouting. You're going to wake up Lorraine. By the way, didn't you say she went out tonight?"

"Yes, she did. Maybe I should go check on her. Gloria had the night off. Maybe she's still out. You know what they say, like father, like daughter. She looks just like you; she probably will take after you, too."

My mother staggered into my room. She glanced over to my bed and saw me lying in it. She couldn't smell the vomit or the alcohol on me. After all, her own drinking covered it up.

⌘ ⌘ ⌘

Looking down at this scene from The Great White Throne Judgment, I was so ashamed of that night. I cried to God, "I had such good intentions that night. I was going to be true to Tommy. I had planned not to take a drop of alcohol. It was pushed on me, Lord. I wouldn't have taken it on my own. It was Amy and Kathy's fault for taking me to that stupid party.

"And that Greg! That guy sure was my downfall in life! If only I wouldn't have met him, my life would have been so much better. I wish I would have listened to Christina and Tommy and not become Amy's friend. Why did I do that? Why?"

"YOU WERE THE ONLY ONE WHO COULD MAKE YOUR DECISIONS. WHEN YOU MAKE WRONG DECISIONS, THERE ARE ALWAYS CONSEQUENCES. IF YOU WOULD HAVE BEEN A CHILD OF THE LIGHT, YOU WOULD HAVE BEEN WISE AND NOT HAVE MIXED WITH THE CHILDREN OF DARKNESS. WITH MY SPIRIT WITHIN YOU, YOU COULD HAVE RESISTED THE TEMPTATION OF DRUNKENNESS AND WOULD NOT KEEP COMPANY WITH THOSE THAT DO.

"FOR THOSE WHO SLEEP, SLEEP AT NIGHT, AND THOSE WHO GET DRUNK ARE DRUNK AT NIGHT. BUT LET US WHO ARE OF THE DAY BE SOBER, PUTTING on the breastplate of faith and love, and as a helmet the hope of salvation.

"Excessive drinking harms the body, with error of vision, causing vomiting, and causes people to stumble in judgment. Drunkenness produces bondage in the life of the one it has ensnared. Woe to those who rise early in the morning, that they may follow intoxicating drink; who continue until night, till wine inflames them! Drunkenness can destroy the heart, causing rebellion and addiction. They drink through their music and have alcohol in their feasts; but they do not regard the work I have done, nor consider the operation of my hands.

"Being drunk is a stumbling block and a bad example to those around you. It is good neither to eat meat nor drink wine nor do anything by which your brother stumbles or is offended or is made weak. Drinking intoxicating beverages affects you spiritually and morally.

"When I walked the earth, I told the people to take heed to themselves, lest they be weighed down with carousing, drunkenness, and cares of this life; for the day will come on you unexpectedly. For it will come as a snare on all those who dwell on the face of the whole earth. Watch, therefore, and pray always that you may be counted worthy to escape all these things that will come to pass, and to stand before the Son of Man."

11

The next morning when I woke up, I thought I was going to die. With the addition of my head pounding, someone was pounding on my bedroom door. I got to the door and opened it just enough to see Gloria's smiling face. "What do you want?"

"Well, when you didn't come down for breakfast, I thought something might be wrong."

"Yeah, Gloria, I don't feel good. The flu or something."

"Would you like me to bring a tray up to you?"

"No! I couldn't eat a thing."

"Well, if you get hungry later, give me a call on my extension."

I nearly closed the door in poor Gloria's face, as I turned and headed straight back to bed.

I didn't come out of my room until six that evening, just in time to join my parents at the dinner table. I was only able to eat a little dinner.

After dinner I went back to my room. As soon as my head hit the pillow, I got a call on my phone. Guilt filled my head when I heard Tommy on the other end. "Hi, Lorraine, how's it going?"

"Great, Tommy."

"I was wondering, did you have fun at Amy's party?"

"Well, yes, thank you for asking."

"I bet there were a lot of kids there, right."

"Yeah, a lot."

"Were there any adults there?"

Trying not to lie to him, I thought about the college boys and said, "Oh, yeah, there were about three or four adults."

"Well, that's good. So it wasn't any wild drinking party, then?"

I laughed nervously. "They served fruit drinks." It wasn't exactly the truth, but the wine was made from fruit.

"Did you dance with anyone?"

"I danced with a group of girls to some rock songs."

"Did you dance with any boys?"

"What's with the third degree? Don't you trust me?"

"I'm sorry, Lorraine, but I need to know. After all, we are going steady, so don't I have the right to know?"

He caught me; there was no way out, I had to lie. "No! Are you happy now? I didn't dance with any boys!"

"Great! I feel much better. I was so worried."

"Tommy, remember I promised you that I wouldn't dance with any other boy, and I meant it!"

"Okay, I feel so much better now. I'll be able to sleep tonight. Oh, don't forget about Teen Meet Friday night. The topic will be on the 'Myths of Dinosaurs.'"

"What? What in the world would that have to do with church?"

"I'm not sure, but it's got my curiosity up. We'll find out Friday."

"Yeah, it's got my curiosity up, too. Hey, I've got some homework to finish. I'll see you Friday. Good night, Tommy."

The next morning I felt ashamed of myself when Amy walked up to me. Scrambling for words, I said, "I'm so sorry that I made such a fool of myself at the party Saturday night!"

"What are you talking about?"

"You know, getting drunk, throwing up, the whole thing."

"Oh that! That was funny. Hey, don't think anything of it. All my friends loved you. At least they know you're not a 'Miss Goody Two Shoes.' You're full of fun like the rest of us!"

"You aren't mad at me then?"

"Of course not. We all drink too much now and then. Did you get in trouble with your parents?"

"No, I lucked out. My parents got home just a few minutes after I hit the bed. They thought I was sound asleep. I was so sick the next day."

"Yeah, those hangovers can be nasty. I've had my share. So could you cover that up?"

"I told them I had the flu."

"Good for you. You're getting the hang of it."

The week dragged. I thought the weekend would never get here. I missed Tommy and couldn't wait to see him. He called me a few times during the week, but it wasn't the same as seeing him in person. I felt so proud to be his girlfriend. He was so well liked and respected by all the kids and adults at Teen Meet, and I was going steady with him! By now everyone would know that Tommy and I were going steady.

I really thought I was in love with Tommy; however, every time I thought about Greg, I got excited and it gave me chills. I tried to stop thinking about Greg, but he was always in the shadow of my mind. I would remember the intimate romantic dances we shared. The warmth of his lips that kissed my check. I still remembered how his breath felt as he whispered in my ear. I wondered if I would ever get the chance to be held in his arms again. Amy and Kathy told me how popular he was with the girls. Maybe he was only being nice to me because I was new to his parties. Maybe next Saturday night he'd choose to dance with someone else....

Why was I so concerned about Greg? After all, I was going steady with the best guy in the world!

Thursday night I was looking in the mirror, brushing my long, dark hair. It was becoming evident, even to me, that I was becoming a young woman. Then the phone rang, and I picked it up.

"Hi, Lorraine. It's me, Christina."

"Hello, Christina. I thought you were mad at me?"

"I am, or I mean I was. Did you have fun going out with Amy?"

"It was different. I guess I had some fun."

"Are you going to go out with her again?"

"I'm not sure yet."

"Well you can't miss Teen Meet Friday night. It is going to be very interesting. It's all about dinosaurs."

"Yeah, I know. Tommy called me and told me. I thought dinosaurs were strictly a science thing or stories in kids' books."

"Yeah, me too, but I hear we will have a big awakening about them."

"Sounds cool."

"Yeah. Would you like my mom and me to swing over and pick you up Friday night?"

"Oh that would be too much trouble. I can call a taxi."

"That's silly. Why take a taxi when you can ride with me? Besides, it will be fun. Afterwards we can stop at the restaurant. Everyone from the meeting will be there."

"Sure, sounds like fun! Thanks."

The meeting Friday night was mind-boggling. It was against everything that I had been taught in school. When the meeting was over, most of the kids, the youth minister, and a few parents went to the restaurant. The waitress helped us arrange several tables so we could all sit together. There must have been around twenty of us.

There was a lot of excitement in the air as the earlier meeting's hot topic poured over into our social time at the restaurant. With a big smile on his face, Tommy was the first to comment. "I can't believe it! I was totally brainwashed! I never believed in that Evolution theory junk, that man came from monkey; but I never questioned it when they said that dinosaurs were around for 150 million years."

"Yeah," spoke up Christina. "Remember when our class went to the museum for a field trip? We were in awe of the dinosaur exhibit. Read all the scientific facts about them, and now to find out that it was all lies!"

"It was interesting for me to learn that the famous Evolutionary Geological Column Theory is completely a hoax," Pastor David said.

"Yeah," laughed Tommy. "The Evolutionists claimed that, of all things found on the bottom of the fictional geologic column, it was the 'simple life form' that evolved first. They figured birds evolved last, because they were on top."

"Did it ever occur to them that maybe a clam shell was at the bottom, because it was already on the bottom?" said another boy.

"Besides, a clam shell weighs more than a bird's feather, so it would be buried first."

Another boy said, "Yeah, and a heavy dinosaur would naturally be on the bottom!"

"That's exactly right!" Pastor David said. "It's easier for us to understand this because we are Christians, and we understand the Creation Theory. We believe in what the Bible tells us about Noah and the Flood. We know that God created and designed the world approximately 6,000 years ago…consequently there was no life form before that."

"Just the fact that trillions of fossils were found in all parts of the world prove that there had to be a worldwide flood," said Tommy. Animals and plants that die today do not become fossils unless they are buried rapidly under layers of mud. He looked sheepish. "I used to think that maybe God had created another world on Earth before, and after that He created the one we know now. I thought maybe the dinosaurs came from the first Earth." Everyone laughed and Tommy continued. "I see how silly that is now. I guess I was trying to rationalize how the dinosaurs were so old, yet God created the Earth only approximately 6000 years ago. When you look at the Creation Theory, it all makes sense."

"What about the Absolute Time Theory?" I asked. "I remember studying that last year in Science. The text said that the carbon dating and other radio-metric dating is accurate."

"That involves only unprovable assumptions," Tommy answered.

"Yes, the tests were always contradicting each other," the Pastor said. "One part of a mammoth carbon dated at 29,500 years and another part of it at 44,000. There was a frozen baby mammoth—one part of it was dated 40,000 years, another part was 26,000. The wood that was around its carcass was 9-10,000. I don't know about you, but it sure sounds like a contradiction to me."

"But what about the Big Bang Theory?" I asked.

"The Big Bang Theory would have the same chance as a tornado blowing through a junkyard and assembling an auto or a jet plane." Christina laughed. "There are so many different intricate and complex forms of life that there is only one who could do it. It was designed and created by our Lord!"

Tommy said, "I liked the story he told about finding a tooth."

"Yeah," laughed one of the boys, "they made a whole new species of man out of it, with a wife to boot! Then they found out it was actually a pig's tooth."

⌘⌘⌘

As the Lord and I listened to the conversation at the restaurant, I looked up at him. "Lord, were my friends right? Was everything that I learned out of my science textbooks about Evolution a lie?"

"YES, LORRAINE, IT WAS A LIE MADE UP BY THE DEVIL AND PLACED IN THE HEARTS OF MAN. I SAID IT WOULD COME TO PASS IN 2 PETER. IT READ THAT IN THE LAST DAYS THERE WOULD BE SCOFFERS. THESE SCOFFERS SCOFF AT THE BIBLE BECAUSE OF THEIR LUSTS, NOT THEIR SCIENCE. THEY WILL teach Uniformitarianism (theory of geologic processes). All things continue as they were from the beginning of creation.

"It is up to each man and woman to make a conscious decision to accept or reject creation. People of the world can be so foolish. The evidence of Creation is overwhelming."

12

Last night I'd had a wonderful time with Tommy, but now it was Saturday, and all my thoughts were aimed at Greg and the party tonight. This past week I couldn't get Greg out of my mind. I asked myself, *Why should I be thinking about him when I have a great guy like Tommy?* I tried hard to push Greg from my thoughts, but I was so intrigued by him.

"What's all the commotion?" my mother said as she walked into my bedroom.

"I'm just rummaging through my closet. I can't find one thing that is suitable to wear tonight." *I've got to find something that will get Greg's attention!* "Mother, I'm going to the movies with Amy tonight, and I don't have anything to wear."

"Didn't you buy a new outfit last weekend?"

"Well yeah, but you don't expect me to wear the same thing I wore last time we went out, do you?"

"There must be something in your closet."

"Mom, they're all school clothes. I can't wear the same thing I wear to school, when I go out."

"Point well taken." My mother laughed. "Surely, I couldn't expect you to wear school clothes to a movie, now could I?" With a canny expression, she said, "I have a surprise for you."

"Cool. What is it?"

Mom reached in her pocket, pulled out a shiny gold card, and handed it to me. "I talked to your father, and he agreed that it would be good for you to have your own credit card."

My mouth flew open and I squealed, "Thank you, thank you!"

"I'm going into the city tonight to meet your father, so I won't see you before I leave. I never had a chance to see what you bought last week. I'm hoping you're using good judgment."

"Oh, yes, Mother, I did, and I will." I hugged her and thanked her again.

I couldn't wait to use my new credit card. As soon as I got to the mall, I bought Amy and Kathy each a new top. I bought myself another real hot outfit, which my friends assured me would get noticed. Then I treated us all to dinner.

After dinner Kathy said, "Why don't we stop at my house to get ready, seeing it's on the way?"

"Great idea," Amy said.

As we drove up and stopped at Kathy's house, I really felt sorry for her. I had never known anybody before that lived in poverty. Her front steps were broken, and the house needed a paint job. We walked into a tiny messy living room where Kathy's mother was sitting on an old sofa, watching a small TV set.

As we walked past her, Kathy said, "Hey, Ma."

She just grunted something at her.

"Did your mother see us?" I asked.

"Probably, but her soaps are on, and nothing can interrupt them. We don't see much of each other, which is the way I like it. She works at a convenient store from nine at night until five in the morning. Then she sleeps until her soaps come on."

When we went into Kathy's bedroom, she asked me, "Lorraine, please let me do your hair, okay? I love your hair! I'd kill to have long hair like yours."

"Yeah," Amy said. "It's so pretty and bouncy. Is it naturally curly?"

"Yes, and I hate it! I wish I had straight hair."

"I'd trade you any day," Amy said.

I let Kathy fix my hair and then put on my new tight designer jeans and off-the-shoulder blouse. When I finished putting on tons of makeup, Amy told me, "Lorraine, I swear you look like a movie star!"

"You should try out for a modeling job. I know you would get it." Kathy remarked.

"Yeah, sure! You girls look better than me any day."

Kathy put the last touches on her makeup. "Okay, this gorgeous trio of lovely ladies is ready to party!"

We arrived at Greg's at about nine-thirty. I was even more nervous tonight than I was last week. *Would Greg be glad to see me, or would he be pursuing some other girl?* I felt awkward and insecure, even though

Kathy and Amy assured me I looked gorgeous.

"Do you think it will be all right coming in this late?" I asked.

Kathy laughed. "We're just fashionably late, that's all."

We walked down the basement steps. The place was packed and Greg's band had everybody rocking.

As soon as Greg spotted us, he let his guitar strap slide off his shoulder and put his guitar in its stand. He then jumped off the stage and hurried over to us. "Lorraine, glad you could make it again!"

"Thanks, Greg, I've really been looking forward to being here."

"So what are we?" Amy said. "Chopped meat?"

"No, of course not. It's good to see all you gals tonight. Come on over to the band's table. I left it open in case you came."

"Hey, Amy," Kathy said. "I guess we know the right VIP to hang out with."

"No doubt!" Amy laughed.

Greg escorted us to the band's table and asked me, "Lorraine, do you remember the guys in the band?" Greg pointed to one and said, "That weird-looking one is Jeffery. The drummer is Eddy."

Smiling at the two musicians, I said, "Yes, of course. You guys sound great tonight."

They both nodded and thanked me.

"Come on, guys, help me get some drinks for these lovely young ladies."

After they served the drinks, Jeffery sat down next to Amy, Eddy by Kathy, and Greg sat next to me. Greg set a tall champagne glass in front of me, filled with that sweet tasty wine that I had enjoyed too much of last week.

"Oh Greg, I shouldn't!"

"Why?"

"I made such a fool out of myself last week, by drinking too much."

"You're in good hands. We'll watch out for you, so enjoy yourself!"

That I did! I was having even more fun than I had the week before. I never laughed so much in my whole life. When Greg was on stage, I danced with Amy and Kathy. Several boys were looking at me, but they could tell that Greg was interested in me. Greg and I danced at least one slow song each break. There was always a fresh glass of wine in front of me. Even before I had one finished, there would be another one waiting.

The last time Greg went up on stage, I said to the girls, "I should stop drinking 'cause I'm really starting to feel it."

"Remember, Greg said not to worry. You're in good hands," Amy reminded me.

"Yes, but I really had a terrible hangover last week. I don't know if I want to live through that again!"

Both Amy and Kathy laughed. "We don't have any problem with that, do we Kathy?"

"Why? What do you mean?"

"Shall we tell her, Kat?"

"What! Tell her how we have fun and stay high without having a hangover the next day?"

"What are you girls talking about? You're not talking about smoking marijuana, are you?"

"You're a very smart girl, Lorraine," Amy said. "That's exactly what I'm talk'n."

"But that's a drug, and illegal."

"Yeah, sure. So what's your point?"

"Isn't it hard to get?"

The girls laughed again and Kathy said, "No! If you are interested, just say the word."

"But, I don't even smoke!"

"No big deal," Kathy said. "We can teach you; it's easy. Well, maybe not the first couple of times; but you'll get the hang of it fast enough."

"What would Greg say about me smoking p-pot?"

Laughing again, Amy said, "Greg deals the stuff! Kathy, let's take her upstairs and show her where the real partiers are."

Kathy looked at me reluctantly. "Lorraine, it's a top secret for only those that Greg trusts. You have to swear you won't tell anyone."

"I promise I won't say a word, but I'm not sure if I should or not."

The band went on break, and the boys joined us again. Kathy told Greg, "I hope you don't mind, but we told Lorraine about upstairs."

Greg looked nervous at first. "So, Lorraine, do you smoke weed?"

"No, but I swear I won't say anything."

"Well, I guess seeing you already know, you might as well join us."

"I didn't know what to say, so I just agreed.

"Hey, you are my girl, right?"

"Yeah, I guess, if that's what you want."

"If that's what I want? I couldn't get you out of my mind all week. I've never met a more exciting, gorgeous girl in all my life. Yes, I want you to be my girl!" He put his arm around me and gave me a hug and then a big, romantic kiss on my lips. I felt the passion rising up within me. Tommy had kissed me several times, but I never felt the passion I felt with Greg.

After the kiss he asked me, "Now that you are my girl, I can trust you, can't I?"

"Of course, Greg."

"Okay, then all of us will go up and have a joint. If you want to take a hit, you're welcome. No pressure, okay?"

"Okay, Greg."

It was a big surprise to me that there were so many kids upstairs. I had no idea before that anyone even used the upstairs during the party. We stood in a large circle with several other kids. A small cigarette was passed from one kid to another. When it got to me, the peer pressure was more than I could handle. I had gained too many new friends not to participate. I took a drag like I saw the others do, but I coughed as the harsh smoke went down my throat. Everyone chuckled a little. Someone said, "We have a virgin smoker tonight." Then they all laughed.

⌘ ⌘ ⌘

I was full of rage as I looked down from The Great White Throne Judgment. "Lord, it was their fault. They introduced me to alcohol and drugs. I couldn't tell them no; I needed their friendship so badly. I was so desperate to have friends, I gave into their peer pressure. Because of them, my life was ruined. I didn't know any better. I was young and naïve. Surely you can't hold me responsible for the path they pushed me down?"

"LORRAINE, YOU WERE AT THE AGE OF ACCOUNTABILITY. THEREFORE, YOU HAVE NO EXCUSE WHEN YOU STAND BEFORE THE LAMB OF GOD. ONLY YOU CAN MAKE THE DECISION THAT WILL LEAD YOU DOWN THE PATH OF DARKNESS.

"I LET YOUR EARS HEAR THE MESSAGE THAT YOU MUST CHOOSE FRIENDS THAT YOU ARE EQUALLY YOKED TO. IF YOU WALK WITH THE UNRIGHTEOUS, you will become one with them. Even though you saw the darkness in these people, you did not turn and seek after the righteous for fellowship. Because you were too impatient to find friendship, you chose friends that were unrighteous.

"When the devil brought you to temptation, you were unable to resist. If you would have been saved by my grace, you could have prayed that you were not led into temptation, for the spirit is willing, but the flesh is weak. I taught my disciples to pray: Forgive us our sins for we also shall forgive everyone that is indebted to us, and lead us not into temptation, but deliver us from evil.[2]

"It is not wise to go where you might be tempted. The wrong desires that came into your life were not anything new or different. Many others have faced exactly the same problems that you did. If you would have trusted in Me, I would have kept the temptation from becoming so strong. You would have been able to stand against it. I am faithful and would have showed you how to escape temptation's power so that you could have stood against it."

13

Just like last Sunday morning I was sick—not only from what I consumed the night before, but from guilt and shame. Lying in my bed, I sorted out the hazy details of what had transpired the night before. All sorts of feelings raged through my mind. Anger was the strongest emotion. I was angry at Amy and Kathy, because they drew me into their little drug world. I was angry at them because they allowed Greg to drive me home, just the two of us. I was outraged at Greg for taking advantage of me, but mostly I was mad at myself for not saying no. The whole ordeal was a fog, but I knew what I had done. I thought the shower would take the dirtiness I felt away, but after scrubbing and crying for forty-five minutes, I finally gave up.

Still in bed at two in the afternoon, I got a phone call from Kathy.

"Hey, gal," she said in her perky way, "looks like you and Greg are really an item now, the way you two were making out on the dance floor. Did he get you home before your parents caught you?"

"Yes," I whispered. "We beat my parents home."

"Tell me about you and Greg! I'm dying to know."

"I really don't want to talk about it, okay!"

"You sound mad. You sure were happy last night. What's wrong?"

I started crying again. "Everything! What do you think, Kathy?"

"I don't know, but I'm sure you're going to tell me, aren't you?"

"Why did you and Amy feel it was so important to take me upstairs? It was bad enough that I was drinking, let alone smoking pot!"

"Wow! We were only trying to help you. It works for us, so we thought it might for you, that's all. Besides, we didn't twist your arm; you did it willingly."

"What could I do? Everyone else, including Greg, was doing it. I would have looked like a square nerd if I didn't take a drag."

"Whatever! It was your choice to do it. You have to admit, though, you sure were a lot of fun afterwards!"

"Yeah, that's what I mean. I had too much fun afterwards!"

Kathy giggled a little. "No! You didn't, did you? Did you and Greg...?"

"Yes! And it is not the least bit funny! I'm so upset about it, I don't know what to do."

"Just calm down, Lorraine. The main thing is that you make sure you're not pregnant. I have some of my morning-after pills left, so meet me at the mall, and I'll bring you a couple. That will take care of last night. Then we have to get you to the clinic for some birth-control pills."

"Wait! Maybe one for last night, but I don't want that to happen ever again."

"Oh, come on, Lorraine, it wasn't that bad, was it?"

"No, but I know it was wrong. I feel so dirty."

"It's only natural to feel that way the first time. After a few more times, you'll think nothing of it."

"How can you say that? I wanted to wait until I was married, or at least was older, or was in love with the guy."

Kathy laughed. "You had me fooled last night, then. The way the two of you were dancing and kissing after visiting upstairs, why, I was sure you guys were in love."

"Greg took advantage! He knew I was too stoned to stop him."

"I don't think Greg would have done it if he knew you were a virgin. Amy and I didn't even know. Most of the kids who hang out with us aren't. Greg really likes you, Lorraine. He must have thought it was what you wanted, too."

"Well, it won't happen again!"

Kathy was quiet for a minute. "Lorraine, I know what you're going through. However, you really like Greg, right?"

"Well, yeah."

"I despised the dirty old man who took my virginity away."

"Why, what happened? Were you raped?"

"Well, sort of. He was one of my uncles."

"Your own uncle?"

"Not really an uncle. My ma had me call all her boyfriends that. I was only twelve when he talked me into smoking some pot with him. We had a few beers before that, and you know how the stuff takes away all your inhibition. With only a little struggle, I gave in to him."

"Did you tell your mother?"

"Yeah, but she blamed me. She said that I wore too skimpy of clothes around him, that I enticed him. She blamed me for the whole thing!"

"Did he keep raping you?"

"For three more months, until he left my ma for another meal ticket."

"That's terrible, Kat. I'm really sorry."

"I'm all right now. I pick who I want, or don't want! That's why you shouldn't be upset with Greg—the two of you make a great couple."

"I still think it's wrong!"

"If you want to keep Greg as your boyfriend, I'd suggest that you think about it. Do you know how many girls wish they were in your shoes? Greg is very popular with the girls. He only dates girls who like to have a good time, or he dumps them."

Throughout the following school year, I took Kathy's advice about Greg and continued our intimate dating. It made me very popular at Greg's parties that I was Greg's girlfriend. My newfound popularity also spilled over at school. Many of the kids who attended the parties also went to my school. Going from a shy, timid girl with no friends to Miss Popularity was more than I had dreamed of. It made me extremely happy.

Somehow I managed to date Greg and still make Tommy think I was going steady with him. How I was able to keep it from either boy was a mystery even to myself.

At this point everyone at Teen Meet thought I was true to Tommy, except for Christina, that is. She was suspicious. I didn't hang out with her anymore, so she guessed I was still friends with Amy.

My popularity at Teen Meet was also growing. My newfound confidence was showing. Everyone knew that Tommy and I were an item, which was fine with me. After all, he was the most popular boy in our church group.

When school was out for the summer, both Tommy and Greg wanted more of my time. And as for my parents, I didn't have any trouble getting out of the house. My father was spending more time at his New York apartment than at home. Mother drank herself to sleep every night by at least eight o'clock. All my mother seemed to care about was the fact that I seemed happy and was a social butterfly. What possible problems could her teenage daughter have?

Now my only problem was juggling my two social lives. Greg was the most demanding. He felt I should be out with him every night. I convinced him that my parents demanded family time at least three times a week. Those nights I devoted to Tommy.

I still cared very deeply for Tommy, and he made no bones about it: he was falling deeply in love with me. I saw Tommy on Monday, Wednesday, and Friday nights. We spent a lot of our time together doing sports activities such as swimming, volleyball, walks in the park, and horseback riding. I loved the time we spent together and didn't want to give it up. Even though Greg and I were in a more intimate relationship, I loved the sweet, innocent love that Tommy and I shared.

When school started up that fall, I dropped out of Teen Meet. That freed up a night for Greg. However, Tommy was very unhappy about it and wanted answers. He asked me, "You've been making a lot of excuses about not going to Teen Meet lately, why?"

"Tommy, it's just that I don't feel comfortable there anymore."

"But why? I really miss our time there together."

"Don't you think we're getting a little old for a church teen club? We're juniors in high school, for Pete's sake! Besides, everything the youth pastor talks about, he calls 'a sin'!"

"Well, there is an awful lot of sinning out there, Lorraine. He wants us to be aware of the problems in the world."

"I don't need him pounding it down my throat all the time."

He was quiet for a minute. "I didn't know you felt that way. But, maybe you're right: we are much older than most of the kids who go there now. Maybe it's a good time to become a helper or assistant. I'll talk to the youth pastor about being his assistant; maybe you can help."

"No thanks!"

After being with Greg, I knew the passionate desire for a man. When I kissed Tommy, I would sometimes lose control, leaving me with a burning desire. Tommy would always take control of the situation and gently push me away. He said to me one evening, "Remember what the Bible teaches us. It tells us that we must restrain until we are married. It would be against God's will if we continued."

"But, Tommy, I don't want to wait that long, do you?"

"Yes, I do. I want to please God in everything I do. I plan on being in the ministry. After high school, I plan on going to Bible College."

I was flabbergasted. "You mean you want to become a pastor of a church?"

"I'm not sure yet. All I know right now is that God has called me into the ministry. That's why it is so important for me to stay holy. I want you to be in my future, Lorraine. After I graduate from college, if I feel the same as I do now, I want us to get married."

"Oh my gosh! Tommy, are you proposing to me?"

"I know I have strong feelings toward you, and I love being with you. I realize we are too young to think about anything so serious right now, but maybe someday."

I was happy to know that Tommy cared so much for me, but there was no way I could see myself as a pastor's wife. I had been putting on an act, and Tommy had fallen for it. I had lied to him and told him that I had let Jesus into my heart, that I was a Christian.

My conscience was tugging at my heart to let Tommy go, but I just couldn't. I couldn't give up my Tommy, not yet. I thought, *Maybe he'll grow up, and forget all this religion stuff.*

⌘ ⌘ ⌘

I fell to the ground in front of the Lord Jesus, hysterically crying. I managed to stop long enough to say, "I was a rotten person! How could I continue leading a sweet and loving boy like Tommy on, while all the time I was being intimate with Greg. I didn't deserve to have a boy like Tommy loving me. He was too young and naive to see the lack of spirituality in me." The guilt and pain I felt was so overwhelming.

"YOU COMMITTED THE SIN OF FORNICATION—SEX WITHOUT MARRIAGE. OUT OF MAN'S HEART COMES EVIL THOUGHTS OF LUST, THEFT, MURDER, ADULTERY, WANTING WHAT BELONGS TO OTHERS, WICKEDNESS, DECEIT, LEWDNESS, ENVY, SLANDER, AND PRIDE. ALL THESE VILE THINGS COME FROM WITHIN; THEY ARE WHAT POLLUTE YOU AND MAKE YOU UNFIT FOR GOD.

"YOU WERE FULL OF WICKEDNESS AND SIN. YOU WERE PROUD, CARING NOT THAT YOU BROKE YOUR PROMISES. YOU WERE HEARTLESS WITHOUT PITY, PLEASING YOUR OWN LUSTS, AND DISOBEDIENT TO YOUR PARENTS. YOU were fully aware of God's death penalty for these crimes, yet you went right ahead and did them anyway.

In the Book of Corinthians, it talks about fornication. It says you should run from sexual sin. No other sin affects the body as this one does. When you sin this sin, it is against your own body. If you are of God, your body is the home of the Holy Spirit God gave you, and He lives within you. For I have bought you with a great price. So if you would have received My gift, every part of your body was meant to give back glory to Me, your God. A Christian's body is a temple of the Holy Spirit."

14

It was a beautiful fall day, and school had just let out. Greg drove up outside the school and picked me up in his old VW van.

"Hey, gorgeous woman, get in."

"Greg, what are you doing here? I didn't think you'd want to get within a hundred yards of a school since you dropped out."

"Hey, I just needed to see my baby. There's no law against that, is there?"

I laughed a little until I could see that Greg wasn't laughing at all. "What's the matter, honey? Is something wrong?"

"Just get in the van, will yah?"

"Sure, I'll give my mother a call and tell her I'm going to the gym with Amy and Kat."

We drove out of town, down our favorite two-track without Greg saying anything except an occasional grunt now and then. When he pulled into our secluded hideaway, he stopped the van and hung his head.

"Greg, you're scaring me. What's wrong?" My mind was racing. *Did he find out about Tommy? Or did he find someone else, and is he going to break up with me?* "You know, Greg, we can talk about anything. I'm sure whatever is bothering you, we can work it out."

With his fingertips, Greg brushed a teardrop from his eye.

"I'm sorry if I've done something to make you mad," I said, "but don't break up with me!"

Greg finally smiled a little. He put his arm around me and gave me a hug. "I ain't going to break it off with you."

"You're not?"

"Of course not! But what do you have to be sorry about?"

"Oh, nothing. I just thought I did something to make you mad at me, that's all."

"No, beautiful, it's not you or us. It's my parents."

"Oh no! They weren't in a car wreck, were they?"

"Nothing like that. My ma's coming back home."

"Is their tour over? What about your dad?"

"The old man's not coming back. Least not for a very long time."

"What are you saying, Greg?"

"My dad was jamming with the guys in the band, and they got busted with Coke."

"Oh, my gosh! What about your mother?"

"She got lucky. She was out with the drummer's girlfriend."

"That's good, huh?"

"Yeah, but my old man's looking at least twenty years."

"Was this his first offense?"

"No. He's been busted a couple times for pot and assault. He's going to do some serious hard time."

"Oh, baby, I'm so sorry!"

"That's not the half of it. My ma told me on the phone that when she gets into town, we're going to have to find a cheap apartment. Seems they haven't been getting enough gigs lately, and our house is in foreclosure. We have to vacate in two weeks."

"That's awful! Your party shack! What about your band?"

"All gone, just like that. Nothing's left."

"There'll be other places for you guys to play."

"There ain't no band!"

"What?"

Greg cussed. "There ain't no more band! As soon as the boys heard about the house, they quit me and got hired by other bands."

"But they're your closest friends…"

"Hey, not no more! There is no such thing as loyalty when it comes to money. I'm tired of those lazy jerks anyway."

From that night forward Greg changed. He was no longer that small-town rock star with his own nightclub. His popularity took a nosedive.

He complained to me one night, "I've hit bottom. Why don't you break up with me? You know you can do better. Find yourself some rich guy. Someone your parents will approve of."

"I don't want some rich guy, I want you. Besides, you'll be back on your feet in no time."

Greg smirked. "Yeah, sure! How am I supposed to do anything living in a small apartment with my old lady? There's no way I can even practice my music anymore."

"Well, there are other parties. Maybe you can play at a bar?"

Greg swore. "How many times do I have to tell you? I ain't got a band left!"

"Put an ad in the paper."

He swore again. "That takes money!"

"I could pay for it."

"I ain't takin' charity from any woman. So drop it!"

"We could go Dutch treat on dates."

"I sell enough to cover our habits, but my old lady is constantly nagging me about getting a job to help out with the bills. If I can't take care of you, Lorraine, some other guy will!"

"That's crazy."

"No, it ain't. I see how guys are always talking to you, and I see how you flirt back."

My mouth flew open. "Greg! I'm only being friendly. I never said anything to you when girls threw themselves at you when you were playing in the band. You never stopped them. I could tell you liked it!"

A whole slew of profanity rolled out of Greg's mouth. "Excuse me. That's what women do to guys in a band! They're my fans. How do you expect me to get fans if I'm not nice to them?"

As Greg's popularity dwindled, mine was on fire. I even became a cheerleader. He became more irritable and jealous over me each day. His temper was raging out of control. No matter where we went, he was always accusing me of flirting. It was typical for us to break up at least once a month. When that happened, there were always guys waiting in line to take me out. The only reason I went out with them was to show Greg that I didn't need him. But along with showing Greg, it also gave me a bad reputation.

Christina called me on the phone and begged, "Please, Lorraine, why don't you break up with Tommy? You would be doing him a favor to let him go. What do you need him for, when you are already dating half the boys in town?"

"How dare you! And why should you care?"

"Because I love him!"

"Well, so do I. It's Tommy's business if he wants to date me or not."

"If you love him, how can you hurt him so bad, by being so sleazy?"

"Listen, Miss Goody Two Shoes, I'm not a sleaze."

"Oh come on, Lorraine. It's all over town that you've slept with lots of boys."

"I go out with a few different boys once in a while, but what Tommy doesn't know won't hurt him. I'd advise you to keep your big mouth shut."

"You're even beginning to talk like street trash. I don't have to say a word. Tommy hears the rumors."

"If Tommy heard something about me, he would have said so!"

"Tommy's just too loyal to you. He hears things but refuses to accept them as truth. I know he's hurt by the rumors, and deep down he knows they're true."

"For your information, Tommy has asked me to marry him when he gets out of college."

There was a brief silence. Then, "You have got to be kidding me. Marry you? At least that is years away. That will give him plenty of time to see what a little tramp you really are."

"If you think he'll want a boring Miss Goody Two Shoes like you, think again. There's no way he would marry someone like you."

"I would make a wonderful pastor's wife. I would go anywhere in the world with him. I'd love to be a missionary. Forget Tommy, and go be a lawyer like your father. Somehow I can't see the two of you complementing each other."

Christina made me so mad that I hung up on her. I had to talk to someone, so I called Kathy and made arrangements to meet her at our favorite coffee shop. If anyone could cheer me up, it was Kathy. I had shared most of my big dark secrets with her, but now I was telling her my deepest, darkest secret. I admitted that while I had been dating Greg, I was also dating Tommy. It made me feel so good to be finally sharing my secret. Kathy's advice was to drop both boys and replace them with a guy from my own social status.

Later that year, Kathy and I sat on the steps of the school as we opened our midterm report cards. I sat there dumbfounded until I could get the words out of my mouth. "I can't believe this. Not only am I not on the honor roll, but I'm failing Calculus. This is devastating!"

Kathy threw her card down on the ground. "You're upset because you didn't make the honor roll? I won't even pass this year if I don't get these lousy grades up."

"Well, Kathy, looks like our party life has finally caught up with us."

"Heck no! However, maybe we need to spend a little more time studying."

"You think? Hey, I got to go. Of all the nights, I believe my father's going to be home tonight."

After showing my report card to my father, I hurried to the phone and called Kathy. "Hey, Kat, you're never going to believe this one."

"What? Are you grounded till you're thirty?"

"No, I'm not even grounded. My father made threats of pulling my credit card if I didn't shape up, that's all."

"Cool! What's up with that?"

"I don't know, except he has other things on his mind. At least he doesn't have time to worry about me. I barely see him anymore. He's always been so determined that I keep my grade point up. Wants me to go to Harvard University, where he went. He has always wanted me to follow in his footprints. I do too! I can't imagine why he is taking my grades so lightly."

"Wow, is that what you really want to do, be a lawyer?"

"Yes, with all my heart. My dad would be so proud of me. I have to buckle down and study harder."

"Lorraine, I really admire you for wanting such a great career. I don't even plan on going to college. Sometimes I think about dropping out of high school."

"Don't talk that way."

"Let's face it: I'm not rich and smart like you."

"Oh, that's baloney! You are very smart, and you can get grants to help you through college."

"With my grades?"

"No, and I won't get to law school with my grades either, but we can if we hit the books. We can get our grades up by the end of the year."

"Yeah, maybe you're right. Now let's stop talking doom and gloom. Let's talk about fun things, like the Junior and Senior Prom that's only a few months away. I asked Eddy, the dude from Greg's old band, and he said yes. Who are you taking—Greg or Tommy?"

"I've been trying not to think about it. I don't know which one to take. My parents wouldn't approve of either of them. What am I going to do, Kat?"

"To tell you the truth, if it were me, I'd drop them both. You know guys are standing in line waiting for you. Ask one of those high-society guys. I'm sure your parents would approve of somebody like that handsome hunk, Randle Anderson."

"The football captain?"

"The one and only."

"You're having me aim awful high, aren't you? I'd have to fight half the cheerleading squad."

"Hey, you're a cheerleader. You have a better chance than any of them."

"I don't know. Besides, I think he's dating someone now."

"So?"

"His parents belong to the same country club that mine do. His dad's a doctor. I believe my mother mentioned that his mom worked on some charity event with her. What do I do? Come on, Kat, help me out. Which boy should I ask?"

"Well, I wouldn't ask Tommy if I were you, because he's a nerd."

"Tommy's not a nerd!"

"Well, he's square, and you don't have a real romantic time with him. From how you talk, you guys are more like best friends."

"He is my best friend, and I love him dearly, but you're right: he isn't my most romantic choice."

"Besides, he doesn't fit in with your friends. We'll want to party after the prom, and Tommy won't go for that."

"That's for sure!"

"Yeah, and you know how jealous Greg gets. If you went to the prom with Tommy, I can see Greg storming onto the dance floor and starting a fight with him."

"You don't think he would do that, do you?"

"Come on, Lorraine, it's not like he hasn't picked a fight with other guys over you."

"Yeah, it's happened a couple of times when I broke up with him, and I went out with someone else. He hasn't been the same since his dad got arrested and lost the house. When Greg lost his party shack, there was no place for his band to play anymore. His popularity went down fast, without a band."

"Yeah, that was when he really started getting jealous of you. He no longer was the most popular of the two of you, you were! You need to get away from that dude. He seems to be getting violent lately. I thought he was going to hit you last week when you guys had that fight."

"I know. I want to break it off with him, too. I think he's been using crack. He just started working at a foundry, and he has changed a lot. He told me that a bunch of guys at work are on crack. He asked if I wanted to experiment with some. Said he hasn't tried any yet, but I think he has."

"I'm sure he has. It would explain his new violent temper. Since he hasn't been in a band lately, nobody even wants to be around him anymore. Even Eddy doesn't want to hang out with him. Greg's a loser, Lorraine. You need to upgrade to someone like Randle. He's the most popular boy in his senior class. I hear talk around school that you're a candidate for homecoming queen. Randle is captain of the football team—handsome, popular, comes from money, he's a shoe in for king! You two sure would make a handsome couple as king and queen of the homecoming court."

"Wow, that would be a dream come true."

After several nights of struggling, I made the decision to break up with Tommy. I couldn't take him to my prom. Besides, it wasn't fair to him to keep him on the string when I knew there wasn't any future for the two of us. It was true what Amy had said: we were more like friends than lovers. We were growing apart, going down separate paths. There was no way I'd ever be a pastor's wife or some kind of a missionary.

I couldn't see Greg in my future either. We had fun together (when we weren't fighting), but I wanted a man with great career goals, like myself. My first task was to break it off with Tommy; after that I'd work on Greg's demise.

The next time I went out with Tommy proved to be one of the hardest nights I'd ever went through. When I explained to him that we had grown apart and I needed to move on, tears fell down his checks.

"Lorraine, I love you so much. I don't know if I can live without you.

I thought you loved me, too. I laid my heart out to you! I even asked you to marry me, when I was finished with college. You let me believe that you would. Was it just that I wanted it so much, or did you really deceive me?"

"Tommy, I'm so sorry. I didn't mean to hurt you. These past years we were together were beautiful, but we've grown up into different types of people. We want a different kind of lifestyle. The most important thing to me is becoming an attorney. I'm sorry, but I'm just not cut out to be a pastor's wife, or a missionary! If that's what you want to do, I don't want to hold you back. It's best this way, Tommy, before we get any more involved. I don't want to hurt you more than I have already."

"Is it true then, Lorraine: are you really deeply involved with Amy and her bunch?"

"Yes, Tommy, it's true. They're really not that bad of kids. I've got some nice, close friends."

"They say you've been dating someone else. Is that correct?"

I felt so guilty I started to cry. "Yes, yes, Tommy, if you must know; I've been dating a boy named Greg for the last year."

"How could I have not known? I was so stupid! Christina has told me over and over again you were cheating on me. I wouldn't believe her. My buddies told me, and I got mad at them. I owe them all an apology. I was wrong about you. I wasn't always sure if you were a Christian or not, but I thought if you stuck with me, you would come to have a personal relationship with God, but I guess I was wrong. I allowed my feelings to override and blind me to the importance of choosing you. I believed that you were a person who believed and loved the Lord. Oh, how wrong I've been."

I broke down and cried even more.

Tommy put his arm around me. "Lorraine, I still care for you. If you ever need a friend, I'll be here for you."

⌘ ⌘ ⌘

I cried even harder at The Great White Throne Judgment Seat, as I relived those emotional moments with Tommy. I said to the Lord, "I can't believe that, after what I told him, he still cared for me and wanted to be my friend. I rejected him, and he still cared for me."

"Tommy was following My example. He read in the Book of Hebrews that I would never fail nor forsake My children. Tommy loved you with a Christian love, one that would never fail nor forsake you. He was loving of others, for love comes from God, and those who are loving and kind show that they are My children.

"God showed His love by sending Me, His only Son into a wicked world to bring to them eternal life through My death. It was My Father's great love toward mankind. If He loves you that much, should you not love one another?

"Tommy knew how much I loved him, because he could feel My love. I am Love, and anyone who lives in love is living with Me in their hearts. As Tommy lived and walked with Me, his love was growing perfect and complete. Those who do love Me will not be ashamed at their day of judgment, as you are here today."

15

Friday nights were fast becoming my favorite night of the week, because of the football games. Cheerleading added so much excitement to my life. It was also a break from Greg. When I had been dating Tommy, he never came to our games either because of Teen Meet. Greg didn't want anything to do with high school, so he never went to games. Most of the kids were aware that I was dating Greg, but I still had a feeling of freedom at those games. This Friday night was going to be an even more special night; I had an agenda.

Our school was playing one of the New York City schools. They were a hard team to beat, but we had a good pep rally last hour, so our football team was ready! It was an out-of-town game, so after school I jumped on our school bus. I looked around and didn't see Shelly, one of the cheerleaders. She wasn't just one of the cheerleaders; she was the lucky one who was dating Randle. He always sat with her on the bus, but Shelly was nowhere in sight.

I walked up to him and said, "Hi, Randle, where's Shelly?"

"Hey, Lorraine. Shelly wasn't feeling good, so she went home."

"Oh, the poor dear. Do you mind if I sit in her place tonight?"

Randle was sitting on the aisle seat so he moved his long muscular legs and motioned for me to sit down. "It would be my pleasure."

We discussed our football team, and how good they were. So far we had lost only two games. Tonight would be our real challenge—the other team hadn't lost a game yet. We talked for about fifteen minutes, and then he asked me, "Are you still dating that long-haired guy who plays in a band?"

For the first time I felt rather embarrassed to admit I was dating him. "Greg. Yeah, off and on. When we haven't broken up, that is."

"You guys fight a lot?"

"Yeah, lately we do. His temper is getting bad. He's very jealous."

"Do you cheat on him?"

"No! When we break up, I go out with other guys, but only when we break up."

Randle smiled. "I know all about jealousy. Shelly is the most jealous girl I've ever met."

"She doesn't lack confidence," I said in a catty way.

"That she doesn't." He laughed. "Her family comes from old money, and she thinks she really is somebody. My parents aren't hurting, and neither are yours, but we don't put on airs like she does. She' very high maintenance."

"It sounds like you aren't very happy with her."

"That's putting it mildly. We've been fighting a lot lately. I think I'm going to break up with her. If you weren't so stuck on that hippie you go out with, maybe you and I could go out sometime."

"Really? That's interesting, because I've been thinking a lot about you, too. As far as Greg, I don't feel anything for him anymore. I was just trying to find the right time to drop him."

"So you will go out with me?"

"Sure. Just give me a little time to break the news to him, and I'll be free."

"Great! I'll need a couple of days to let Shelly down, too."

I did my best cheering that night, because I was so happy at the thought I would be dating the team captain—a guy I could take home to my parents, and the hottest guy in school!

Monday morning when I woke up, I was so excited and happy about going to school. I wondered if Randle had broken up with Shelly over the weekend. I hadn't had a chance to break it off with Greg. He had been so nice the past weekend, I didn't have the heart to.

As I sat in my first hour class dreaming of Randle and the upcoming prom, I pictured us riding in a convertible around the football field as king and queen of the court. The prom! How romantic it will be to dance with the handsomest, most popular boy in school...not to mention, the captain of the football team. And we would be the king and queen of the junior/senior prom.

Then, out of nowhere, I got an excruciating pain in my stomach. It was so bad that when the teacher saw the intense pain on my face, she told me to go to the nurse's office. I slowly got up on my feet and started walking toward the door. When I collapsed onto the floor. I was out cold.

The teacher yelled, "Stacy, get the nurse!"

Within minutes the school nurse was in the classroom checking on me. She said, "We need to call an ambulance. Lorraine needs to be checked out at the hospital."

When I came to, a few minutes later, everyone was hovering around me. Soon I heard a siren outside the school's window. Minutes later a couple of medics came into the room and put me on a stretcher, and I was rushed to the hospital. They did a few tests on me, and then it seemed like hours as I waited for the doctor to return. In the meantime the principal had called my mother. She arrived soon after I'd been admitted. She actually seemed concerned and worried about me. This was the most attention I had from her since I could remember.

After a couple of hours my mother said, "Honey, I'm going down to get a cup of coffee at the cafeteria. Have the doctor page me when he comes back."

About a half hour later the doctor walked in and frowned.

Imagining all sorts of things, I asked, "Doctor, what's wrong? What's wrong with me?"

The doctor cocked his eyebrow. "You are all right, Miss Patterson. You are healthy, anyway."

"Then what happened to me?"

"You just need to slow down for a couple of months and to take better care of yourself. You are pregnant."

It felt like the bottom had just fallen out from under me. "No!" I said. "I can't be! You must be wrong. Take another test. I'm on the pill, so I can't be. No way!"

"Lorraine, do you take one each day, without missing any?"

"I don't know...I mean, I guess once in a while I might miss a day or two. Not often, though. I didn't think a pill or two would make any difference."

"You were wrong, young lady, it does. The pill is only 95 percent safe, and if you don't take the proper dosage, your odds of getting pregnant increase substantially. Look at you; you are living proof of it. There is no doubt, Lorraine. You are pregnant."

I broke down crying. "I can't be pregnant! What can I do? I can't have a baby. I'm a junior in high school. This was the happiest year I ever had! I want to be homecoming queen and go to the prom with a special boy, who will be crowned the king. Then there's college. I want to make my father proud of me. I want to become a successful lawyer, just like him!"

"You have a lot of big decisions to make. With every action, there is consequence to deal with. You'll need to talk this out with your parents."

"No, I can't!"

"What about that special boy? Is he the baby's father? Do you plan on telling him?"

"No! He isn't the father. We haven't even started dating yet, but we were going to as soon as I break up with Greg."

"Then is Greg the father?"

"Yeah."

"Will you tell him?"

"No! I don't want anything more to do with him!"

"Why?"

"I told you, I'm breaking up with him. I can't stand him anymore. I don't want to get married. I'm just a kid! Besides, Greg has nothing to offer me or a baby. He's just a dirty foundry worker. My parents would never approve of me dating him…let alone marrying him."

The doctor cocked his head. "Well, it doesn't matter if he's good enough for you or your family. He has a moral right to know you are carrying his baby."

Mother walked into the room just then and screamed, "Baby!"

"Lorraine," the doctor said, "you need your family at a time like this to help you with the important, life-changing decisions you have to make now. I'll leave the two of you alone so you can talk."

We both sat there a few minutes staring into each other's tearful eyes.

She was the first to speak. "Lorraine! How could you let something like this happen? How could you be so stupid?"

"Stupid? You're one to talk, Mother! Did you forget? You made the same *stupid* mistake nearly seventeen years ago."

"What? What in the world are talking about?"

"Don't play innocent, Mother. I figured it out! I've known for a long time I was born five months after your wedding, so don't you call me stupid!"

"That was quite different, young lady. Your father and I were much older and out of college. Your father was already a fairly successful attorney, and I had a career as a legal secretary. You are merely a child. You haven't even finished high school, let alone college!" Mother caught her breath. "Is the boy you're involved with a junior, too?"

"No, Mother, he's out of school."

"Then he's in college. Hopefully he's in his last year. I suppose we could support the three of you until he gets out and gets a good job. What is his career choice?"

"Will you shut up, Mother? First of all, his name is Greg. Second of all, I don't want to marry him!"

Her mother stiffened. "What do you mean? Of course you want to marry him. He's the father of this baby, right?"

"Yes, but I don't love him!"

"Quit being selfish," her mother hissed. "You should have thought about that before you let yourself get involved that way. You made your bed, and now you have to lie in it. You owe that much to your unborn child. A child needs a father to support it and to give it his name." My mother took another deep breath and then continued drilling me. "Now, what did you say Greg is going to college to be?"

"Mother, I didn't say he was going to college. You assumed that. He dropped out of high school in his senior year."

"A high school dropout? I can't believe you could get yourself mixed up with someone like that! Well, it's done, so we'll have to figure out what to do. If he gets his GED, and his parents are willing to help, we could help support you while he's going through college."

I started laughing. "Mother, you are so out of touch. Greg's dad is in jail, and his old lady has just lost their home. I don't think they will be helping put their son through college, because he's a burnout! Besides, he wouldn't go if he could. He does have a job."

"A job, that's good! Doing what?"

"He works in a foundry."

"Like a factory?"

"Yes, Mother, like a factory. Calm down, I told you I wasn't going to marry him. I don't want to live my life in poverty either. Trust me, he wouldn't make a good husband, let alone a daddy."

"Are you sure the baby is his?"

"Yes, Mother, of course it's his." *At least I'm fairly sure.*

"I'd think that if you were going to mess around, you'd at least have been with someone from your own background. Oh well, it's done now. Get dressed so we can get home and figure this out before your father gets there. I dread telling him. He'll be so angry and disappointed in you."

"What's new? There's no way I could ever measure up to what he wants, anyway, so why should I even try now?"

As soon as we got home I ran upstairs to my room and cried until I couldn't cry another drop. I was so totally wiped out and depressed. I couldn't imagine how I had got myself in such a mess. That morning I had been the happiest I could have possibly been, and then just hours later I was devastated. I thought back to when things were simple, when I dated only Tommy.

I thought to myself, *That was a beautiful, wholesome love. I was really happy then. Why didn't I stay away from Amy and her friends? Maybe if I had, I would still be friends with Christina and Tommy. I wouldn't be in the boat I'm in now. I wonder what they are doing tonight. Are they now dating and in love, now that I'm out of the picture? I want so desperately to call Tommy, but how can I explain to him that I let myself get pregnant? He would never approve.*

Then, between the tears and memories, I heard the maid calling. My father was there, and dinner was being served.

The mood at the dinner table was silent and distant as I sat down. My mother and father kept their eyes down, staring into their plates as they ate. They never uttered a word for the first fifteen minutes.

Father was the first to break the silence. "So I hear you went and got yourself pregnant, right?"

Meekly I answered, "Yes, sir, but I never meant for it to happen."

My father turned to Mother with a condemning look. "Hasn't anyone heard of the birth-control pill? Why didn't you have her on the pill, Marge?"

"Don't you dare blame me for this one!" she threw back at him. "I had no idea our daughter was involved in that type of activity." Mother then turned to me. "You are far too young to be involved in this type of behavior. Just look at the mess you have gotten us into. Why in the world didn't you come talk to me when you felt you couldn't restrain yourself from such reckless behavior?"

"You have your own problems, Mother. I couldn't talk to you. You have no idea what I've even been doing this last year or who I've been with. I don't think either of you care anymore. I've been on the stupid pill for a year! I messed up and forgot to take one; that's how I got pregnant."

Mother guzzled down her glass of wine and ordered the cook to bring her another. She stared at me for what seemed like a long time, then said, "You mean to tell me you've been displaying this kind of behavior since you were a mere child?" She dropped her head into her hands and murmured, "I had no idea."

"Of course not, Mother," I yelled. "You were either too busy, or depressed, or just plain drunk! How would you be able to know what I'm doing in that condition? And you, Father, you've been like a ghost in this house. You don't even stay here much anymore; you live at your cozy little pad in the city. Do you have a girlfriend too? Mom says you do."

My father's face was red with anger. Had I gone too far?

"That's enough!" he shouted. "This is not about your mother and me; it's about this problem you've made for yourself. You did it; you have to pay the consequences. I will not have you talk that way to us! You show us some respect, do you hear me?"

I yelled back, "Respect? How about ME? You two have never given me any respect! The only time you pay attention to me is when I do something to embarrass you!...Mother, you're always accusing Father of running around on you. And, Father, it's probably true, 'cause you aren't home much anymore. So don't talk to me about respect! Neither of you have any respect for each other, or me."

My father slammed his fist down on the table. "This conversation is about you, not us! It's not about your mother, nor is it about me; it's about an unwanted pregnancy."

Mother spoke up. "The boy that got her in this condition is a useless, high school dropout, whose dad is in prison and whose mom has been kicked out of her house."

"Is that true, Lorraine?"

"Well, yes, sir. I mean, no! It's true that he dropped out of high school, and it's true what she said about his parents, but he's not all bad. He has some good traits. He's got a full-time job."

"Doing what?"

"He works really hard at a foundry."

"Do you want to marry this loser? I've raised you with a silver spoon in your mouth. You have never wanted for anything! For the life of me, I can't see why you were messing around with a lowlife like him. You could have had the cream of the crop, for heaven's sake! You are a beautiful, intelligent young woman with a brilliant career ahead of you. Why in God's name would you lower yourself to be with someone like that?"

I started to cry again. Then I looked up at my father and said, "I don't know why, Father. I am so sorry! Believe me, the last thing I want to do is be married to him."

Father patted me on the back. "Good girl! There's no reason in the world that you should be saddled with someone like that. He's probably a gold digger, after my money."

"No! Greg's not like that. When I started at the new high school, he was the first boy to pay attention to me. When I first met him, he never knew I came from a wealthy family. I've even tried to pay for a few dates, and he wouldn't hear of it. We've been dating a long time; he really cares a lot about me."

My father gave me a dirty look. "Too long, if you ask me. Now we have to clean up the mess. Lorraine, you did tell me that you don't want to marry this bum, right?"

"Absolutely! No way do I want to be married to anyone right now."

"Okay, then, what would you like to do about this mess you've gotten yourself into?"

"I don't know, Father. I only know I want this all to go away. I was so happy at school before all this came crashing down on me. I've gotten really, really popular in school now. A bunch of my friends said I was a shoe in for homecoming queen. There is this really special boy I wanted to date. I planned on breaking up with Greg. Randle has already told me he wants to date me. He is so cool! The captain of the football team."

My father listened intently, then said, "So he's not a lowlife like the one that got you pregnant?"

"Not at all! I'm sure you and Mom know his parents from the country club."

"What's their names?"

"His dad is Dr. Robert Anderson."

"Good family. I know him and Lillian very well."

"Yes," my mother commented, "Lillian worked on a charity event with me. Nice lady."

"Yes, and there's college. I want to become an attorney, just like you, Father. My life was going so great before this terrible thing happened."

"Calm down, honey. Everything can still go on just like it is."

"How, Father, how?"

"With just a simple little operation, things can go right on like they did before. The best part is, no one never needs to know besides the three of us, and the doctor and nurses at the clinic, and they are very discreet."

Mother slammed her glass of wine down on the table, spilling a portion of it. "Sure, Jim, that's always your solution about everything, isn't it? Just get rid of it, and it will all go away." Sarcastically she said, "Lorraine, honey, Daddy will take care of your problem. Just have this little abortion, and everything will be just fine! Just get rid of the kid, Lorraine. That was your father's idea when I was pregnant with you, too."

"Marge, this is the best and only solution we have right now. As soon as we get it done, Lorraine can go about her business like nothing happened. She can drop the bum and start dating Bob's kid."

"There is another solution, Jim! She can go to this place up north that I heard about for unwed mothers. They take care of everything. They even have in-house schooling. Just before Lorraine starts to show we can send her there. They take care of the adoption and everything. She can adopt it out and then come home and start over with a clean slate. No one will know the difference. We'll tell everyone that we sent her to Europe to finish her high school at some distinguished school."

"No, Mother, I want to graduate with my friends. Do you know what it is like for me to finally be popular? I want Randle Anderson and me to be crowned king and queen of the prom. Mother, I really like him and want to be his girlfriend. Maybe even go to college with him. And who knows, maybe we'll get married. I'll have a career as a lawyer, and Randle a doctor. We could have a wonderful life together. Please, Mother, I don't want to go away and have a baby!"

"That settles it," my father said in a deep, stern voice. The kind of voice Mother never dared to stand up to. "You have made up your mind that you want an abortion, right?"

"Yes! Yes, Father, I do!"

"Then don't worry about it anymore. It's a done deal. I'll make all the arrangements. My secretary had an abortion a few months ago, so she can give me all the information I need."

After setting down her empty wine glass, Mother gave Father a nasty look and said, "Another one of yours?"

"Don't be stupid, Marge." The subject was dropped fast when my father's face flashed her the most evil expression I'd ever seen.

With tears flowing down my cheeks, I screamed, "Mother just shut up and leave Father alone. He knows what's best for me. You should have listened to him when you got pregnant with me, and then we wouldn't be in this awful situation now. Why didn't you abort me like he wanted you to? Neither one of you ever wanted me anyway! You both would have been a lot happier if I had never been born. And I wish I hadn't!"

My father was quiet for a minute; then he put his hand on mine. "Lorraine, never doubt that your mother and I love you. We do. It's just that life can get so complicated at times. We don't always take time to show you, but we do love you. In spite of the consequences, we are glad that we decided to have you. You're my little girl. And I am so proud that you want to take after me and become a lawyer. Honey, I want to give you all the best things in life that I can. I've worked hard all these years to provide my family with a luxurious lifestyle. I guess I've neglected you in the process, but the intentions were good."

"James, I still can't see her killing that innocent baby, just because she couldn't behave herself!"

"Father," I begged, "please don't let Mother force me to go away and have the baby. It was hard enough when you guys made me change high schools. I hated starting high school without my friends, but Mother was so afraid of Tommy and me getting too close. What a laugh that is. Tommy is the most decent boy I know. You sure could have trusted me with him, but you didn't! I can't go through this again, Mother. I can't lose my newfound popularity. I won't!"

"Lorraine is right, Marge. She has made up her mind, and so have I. She is going to have that abortion!"

As Mother pointed her finger at me, she spilled her full glass of wine that the maid had just poured for her. She yelled, "God's going to punish you, Lorraine! I will have no part in killing my grandchild!"

"Don't worry, Mother, I don't need your help or support. I can do this thing by myself. After all, I've had to learn to be independent. I had to, because you were never there for me. I can do it without you. I hate you, Mother." My eyes filled with tears again, and I ran out of the room crying.

❈ ❈ ❈

"Why did you let me get pregnant and ruin my life?" I cried to the Lord as I stood before him at The Great White Throne Judgment Seat.

"It was your decisions that caused the consequences that happened in your life. The consequence of sin is death. For the wages of sin is death, but the gift of God is Eternal Life in Me.

"You reaped what you sowed. Your wrong desires led you to plant seeds of evil, and it caused you to reap a harvest of spiritual decay and death. If you would have planted good things of the Spirit, you would have reaped Everlasting Life, which the Holy Spirit gives you.

"Sin separated you from God. Without Me in your heart, you accumulated a lot of sin. Sin led you to drunkenness, telling lies, a wild lifestyle, and to an unwanted child. When you followed your own wrong thoughts, your life produced evil results: impure thoughts, eagerness for lustful pleasure, hatred and fighting, jealousy and anger, constant effort to get the best for yourself, complaints and criticism, the feeling that everyone else was wrong except those in your own little circle of friends, wild parties, and your final rejection of Me.

"You could not hide from Me. I am all-knowing. Because you lived like that, you now cannot inherit the Kingdom of God. If you would have accepted Me, I would have been there for you, helping you to resist sin.

"When the Holy Spirit lives in people's lives, it produces these types of fruit: love, joy, peace, patience, kindness, goodness, faithfulness, gentleness, and self-control. Those who belong to Me have nailed their natural desires to My cross and have crucified them there. If My children are living by the Holy Spirit's power, then they would follow the Holy Spirit's power in every part of their lives. They won't need to look for their own evil pleasures, and the wrong type of popularity, which leads to terrible consequences."

16

The following day Greg ran into one of my classmates from school. He told Greg all about what had happened to me at school the day before. He told him how I had passed out in the classroom, and that paramedics came in and rushed me to the hospital.

Greg went straight home and waited by the phone for a call from me. He even lost a day's work, hoping I'd call. When I didn't, he became even more anxious to find out what had happened. He got in his van and drove straight to my house, determined to see me. As always, when he arrived, the iron gate was locked. With a shaking finger, he pressed the intercom.

Gloria, the maid, answered. "Hello, welcome to the Pattersons. Who may I say is calling?"

"Uh, this is Greg, Lorraine's boyfriend. I want to see her!"

"I'm sorry, but she is unable to come to the door right now. However, Lorraine's father said if you stopped in, he wanted to see you."

My father had taken a few days off to help me deal with my problem. The situation I was in was awful, but at least I was getting to spend some time with my father.

Greg told me later he felt like running, but he was too concerned about me. The gate automatically opened, and he drove through and down the long drive, then got out of his van. He walked through the arbor, which led to the heavy wooden doors of the mansion. As he was about to knock, the doors swung open. Inside stood a short, plump, middle-aged woman in a maid's uniform. She looked him up and down and said, "Welcome, sir. Mr. Patterson is waiting for you in his study. Follow me, please."

This was the first time Greg had been inside my house, and he was overwhelmed. As he followed the maid, he noticed the elegant foyer, with a set of curved staircases gracing both sides. He was in awe of the black marble floors and the gigantic crystal chandelier.

The maid opened a door and announced him. He felt intimidated as he stared at the distinguished man across the room from him.

My father didn't bother to move out from behind his massive desk. He ordered, "Come in, come in! Don't just stand there. If you want some answers about Lorraine, get over here!" My father could be very intimidating when he wanted to be.

Greg walked over to him and stood shaking in front of his desk. He felt like a little boy who was called to his teacher's desk because he had done something very bad.

My father stared at Greg for a couple seconds, then said, "So you are the one my daughter has been wasting her time with!"

"Yes, sir, I'm Greg Williams, your daughter's boyfriend."

"You've got to be kidding! Right?"

Greg did look a little pathetic as he stood in front of my well-groomed father. Greg had his favorite old holey jeans and a T-shirt on. Not to mention, he hadn't washed his hair in over a week.

"No, sir! Lorraine and I have been together for over a year now. I really love your daughter, Mr. Patterson. When I get a raise at the foundry, I'm going to ask her to marry me."

My father could only shake his head and laugh. Then his expression turned serious. "Over my dead body, boy. Lorraine is through with you."

"I won't believe it until I see her, and she tells me!" Greg fired back.

"Don't get impertinent with me, boy! Lorraine told me she wants nothing more to do with you."

"What happened to her? Why did an ambulance take her to the hospital? I have to know, please, sir, what's wrong with Lorraine?"

"It's none of your business anymore, but there's nothing wrong with her. She's just a little exhausted, that's all. Too much running around with wild scum bags, like you."

"I wouldn't talk that way to me, sir. Someday I'll be your son-in-law!"

My father jumped up from his chair and pointed a finger in Greg's face, shouting, "I'm telling you, you hippie, no good bum; you are never going to see my daughter again. Do you hear me? If you try to persist, I'll have a restraining order served against you so fast, it will make your head spin! You get near her, and I'll have your butt thrown in jail!"

Father came out from around his desk and shoved Greg toward the door. "Now get out of my house before I call the police!"

On the way out Greg yelled back at my father, "Not you, or anyone, is going to keep Lorraine and me apart! I don't believe she doesn't want to see me anymore! We'll be together again—mark my word!" He was convinced it wasn't my idea to break up with him; he was sure it was all my father's doing.

My father called out the door after him, "Give it up, you long-haired hippie, or else you will live to regret it! I never want to see your ugly face around here ever again, do you hear me?"

In spite of my father's threats, Greg was not about to give up on the girl he loved. The next day he sat outside the school waiting for me to get out. I was still at home, but when he saw Amy and Kathy, he stopped them and asked, "Where's Lorraine?"

Kathy wasn't her normal jovial self. "We don't know, Greg. Lorraine hasn't been back to school since they took her away in the ambulance last Wednesday. We've really been worried about her."

Amy said, "Yeah, we've both been trying to call her but can't get past the maid. Thought she'd call one of us by now. You haven't heard anything either?"

"Not really! Just had an unfriendly visit with the high and mighty Mr. Patterson. I went to Lorraine's house to see her and got her old man instead. All I got from him was threats to leave Lorraine alone. I think he's hiding something."

"Yeah," Kathy said. "If she's still out of school, that means something must be really wrong."

Greg hung his head. "Yeah, you're probably right."

Amy hesitated a couple of minutes, then said, "Greg, there's been some rumors floating around school about Lorraine."

"Such as?" he said in a protective way.

"Well...is it possible...? I mean, Greg, could Lorraine be pregnant?"

"No! Of course not! Who's been spreading those kinds of rumors? I'll bash their heads in!"

Kathy looked into his eyes. "Now don't get mad, Greg, but is there a chance that she could have had a miscarriage?"

He stiffened. "No. She would have told me if she was pregnant. You know how close we are. It's just a stupid rumor; don't listen to it."

My father decided that it would be better if I went back to school the following day. He told me to tell everyone that I just had the flu, but I was fine now. After school Greg was waiting in hopes he would see me. I tried to avoid him, but he saw me anyway and ran toward me.

"Lorraine, how you doing?" He put his arms around me. "I've been so worried about you. Did your father tell you that I was at your house? He's sure a pain in the...!"

"Greg, calm down, I'm all right now. I just had a silly bug. I'm fine!"

"Did your old man tell you I was there?"

"Yes."

"He had the nerve to kick me out. Said I was to stay away from you, or he would have me thrown in jail."

"Listen, Greg, he would have you arrested. He's dead serious about us not seeing each other anymore."

"That ain't fair, baby. We love each other too much. I can't live without you! We can just keep sneaking around like we always have. He won't find out."

"Greg, I got the flu from being overtired. I have to get my strength built back up—that's why my father isn't allowing me to go out for a while."

"Well, can I call each day to see how you are, or see you after school?"

"No! I'm sorry, but if you call, my father will be informed about it and you know what he'll do. We can't meet after school because I have to be home directly after school each day. Please, Greg, don't make this any harder on me than it already is!"

"Your old man is such a jerk! He thinks I'm not good enough for you. Baby, I'm the best thing for you. We're happy together."

"Yes, when you don't lose your temper, and we get into an argument."

"Come on, babe. Jump in my van for a few minutes; we need to talk."

"No, I don't think so. I told you my father wants me coming straight home from school."

"Baby, please! We need to talk. I need to know that you still want me as much as I want you. I've got a couple of joints to relax you."

The invitation was tempting, I hadn't had a hit in almost a week. I really needed to get high. I felt like I was ready to explode inside. I needed something to calm me down, so I said, "Okay, Greg, just this once."

At our familiar parking place down a two-track road we shared one of the hand-rolled cigarettes. As always I was mellowed out by the drug. When he began to kiss me passionately, I didn't resist. I'm not sure if it was from force of habit, or because marijuana always made me uninhibited. I guess it was probably a combination of both. I was giving Greg wrong signals, but it felt good at the moment, and that's all that mattered right then.

When we finished the last joint, Greg asked, "Babe, is there a chance that you could be pregnant?"

"Greg! What gave you a stupid idea like that?"

"It's all over school. Some people have said that you might have had a miscarriage at the hospital."

"Oh, that's ridiculous. I didn't have a miscarriage."

"What do you mean, you didn't have a miscarriage? Does that mean you could still be carrying my baby?"

"Will you please drop it, Greg? I'm not pregnant!" I shouted.

"Don't lie to me, Lorraine!"

I began to cry. "All right, all right," I said between the sobs. "Yes! Yes, I'm pregnant, but you don't have to worry about anything. In the very near future there will be no problem. My father's taking care of everything."

"What's that supposed to mean? I don't want your old man doing anything! This baby is my responsibility, too. Let's get married! I really do love you, and I've been wanting to ask you to marry me for a long time. I was waiting until you got out of school, and I got a better job. Now would be the perfect time. We're going to have a baby, and I'm getting a raise at the foundry. It will all work out just great, you'll see."

"I'm touched you feel that way, but forget it. There's no way I'm going to have a kid now."

"You aren't going along with your old man's plan and have our baby killed, are you?"

"Get real, Greg. It's not a baby; it's only a seed, a fetus. If I was further along, it might be different, but now it's nothing. Shut up about this. I don't want to have a baby!"

"Doll, you're wrong. It's not just a fetus; it's a living, breathing baby. Before I dropped out of high school in my Sex Ed Class, they showed us slides of different stages of pregnancies. When the baby is only eight weeks old, its head becomes large, its little brain is developing. You can even tell if it's a boy or a girl, a real little kid! Come on, Lorraine, how could you kill your own little baby?"

Tears streamed down. "What do you expect from me? I can't take care of a kid now. As for school, I love it. I don't want to quit! You know my dreams and goals, Greg. I want to become a lawyer like my father. There is no way it would ever work out for me to go to college with a kid to take care of. We'd never be able to afford it. There's no way, Greg. My father would never let me keep a baby. He's dead set against it."

"Man, your father is a real jerk! I bet the abortion was his idea, wasn't it?"

"Yes, but I totally agree with him. Just a simple procedure and I'll be on my way to continuing a happy life. My father is only trying to help me."

"Yeah, he wants to help all right...help kill my baby. If one of those rich snobs were the father, he probably would want you to marry him. He thinks I'm not good enough to be your husband or daddy to your baby." He snorted. "What does your old lady have to say about it?"

"She's against abortions. Her idea is for me to go upstate to a home for unwed mothers. They handle all the adoption procedures. I don't want to do that, because I don't want to give up graduating with my class. I'm having too much fun with cheerleading and everything."

"Oh this is just great! Your old man wants you to kill the kid. Your old lady wants you to give our baby away. And you! You just want to have fun, and forget about all your responsibilities. Got to tell you, Lorraine, I'm real disappointed in you."

"Yeah, well, what do you care? It's not you who has to carry this...this kid in your stomach for almost five and a half months. You're not the one giving up all your dreams and goals. And for what? To support a baby I don't even want? Greg, you are being awful unfair to try to put a burden on me like that!"

"Babe, you haven't been listening, I'm not putting the whole burden on you. I'm offering to share it. I told you, Lorraine, I want to marry you. Next month I'm getting a raise at the foundry, and I will work hard to take care of you and that little child in there," he said as he patted my stomach. "In a few years, maybe I will be able to put you through college."

"Get real, Greg. Do you know how expensive law schools are?"

"No."

"I didn't think so. Greg, I can't marry you. I mean, I can't marry anybody right now. I'm just too young! I have my whole life ahead of me."

"We can have a wonderful life together with our little kid."

"No!" I said vehemently. "I can't, because I don't love you, Greg!"

"Fine, you spoiled little brat, don't marry me; but let me have the kid. I don't want you killing him, and I don't want someone else raising my son or daughter."

"Don't be stupid. You couldn't take care of a little baby. Besides, my father would never allow it."

"I don't believe that you don't love me anymore. I think you're too upset to know how you feel. This kid is our responsibility, not your father's. Run away with me, Lorraine! Your old man won't find you at my ma's place. When you turn eighteen, we will get married. Come on, Lorraine, say yes! Otherwise you'll have to live your whole life feeling guilty about killing your baby."

My tears were flowing even more as I said, "Yeah yeah, I'll think about it. Would you please take me home now? My father is going to be furious with me for getting home so late."

We didn't talk on the way home. When we got close, as usual Greg dropped me a couple blocks from my house, so no one would see him. When I stepped out of the van, I turned toward Greg. "I need a little space, Greg. I'm not going to see you for a while, okay? I'll give you a call sometime."

Greg looked angry and sarcastically said, "Yeah sure, babe."

I no sooner got the door shut, and Greg put his van in drive and sped away.

⌘⌘⌘

As I looked at Jesus on His Great Throne, I asked, "Greg was right, wasn't he? It is wrong to abort a child, isn't it?"

"YES, LORRAINE, IT IS WRONG TO MURDER AN UNBORN CHILD IN A MOTHER'S WOMB. BEFORE THEY WERE FORMED IN THEIR MOTHER'S WOMB, I KNEW EACH OF THEM. LIFE BEGINS AT CONCEPTION, BECAUSE THE SOUL BEGINS AT CONCEPTION.

"The Holy Scriptures in Genesis 25:22 refer to Isaac and Rebekah's unborn babies as children.

"After Moses led the children of Israel out of bondage, he received the Ten Commandments from the Lord God on Mount Sinai. God also gave Moses many laws to govern his people by. Among the laws there was one referring to the unborn child. The law is in Exodus 21:22-23: If men fight, and hurt a woman with child, so that she gives birth prematurely, yet no harm follows, he shall surely be punished accordingly as the woman's husband imposes on him; and he shall pay as the judges determine. But if any harm follows, then you shall give life for life.

"If God made a law specifically referring to the rights of the unborn child, then surely the unborn must mean something to God!

"My Father has personally made each child that is in a mother's womb. Each of them are individually created. They are each an individual person. None of these creations should be torn apart by tongs and forceps, or poisoned drugs. For whatever you do to the least of them, you do to Me.

"An abortion is killing a child. Thou must not murder! Those who do will be in danger of the judgment where you, Lorraine, stand in front of me today."

17

Just as I thought, my father was furious with me when I walked through the door. He had been home since this whole mess started. For once I was the most important issue in his life. Maybe it was because I would be an embarrassment to him, if anybody found out. Whatever the case, he was angry with me.

He shouted, "Where have you been, young lady? I've been worried sick about you!"

I couldn't look him in the eye. "I walked home. I needed to think."

"Well, it's too late for that. I've got all your arrangements made. I have an appointment for you at the abortion clinic at four-thirty, two weeks from this Friday." My father handed me a business card.

As I took the card, my father said, "Only two and a half weeks and life will be back to normal, Lorraine. You can go out into the world and make your father proud of you!"

"Yeah that's great, Father, but I'll be almost three months along by then. Couldn't we do it any sooner?"

"I tried, honey, but that was the first opening they've got. I tried to slip them an extra hundred bucks, but they were firm. Believe me, I want this whole mess cleaned up as much as you do!"

I put my hand on my stomach and sadly said, "Okay, Father, thank you."

The day I had been agonizing about had finally come. When I got out of school, I flagged down a taxi to take me to the clinic. On the long trip over there I felt like that lonely little girl I once had been. I wondered how was I going to do this terrible thing all by myself. I wished my mother would have been there for me. Why did she have to be so stubborn and not give me the support I needed so badly? *Why does she have to be so set in her way about this abortion thing? And what's with her telling me "God will punish you"?*

I wasn't even aware that she believed there was a God. You could never prove it by her actions. I wondered, maybe she was right! I believed there was a God. I sure didn't believe in all that Evolution junk. Would God really punish me if I aborted this fetus? I convinced myself that if there was a God, he would understand. *He knows how much I have been through, and how happy I am now. Besides, God is love, and I really don't believe there is a hell.*

Can I really go through with this? I asked myself. *I wish my father would have taken the time to be with me. He planned to be here, but at the last minute backed out. Said he had too much of a backlog.* I felt that if he would have been here for me, I would have had no problem going through with this. But there I sat, scrunched down in the back seat of a taxi fighting back tears.

I had thought that I didn't need Greg anymore, but I sure could have used him now. Why couldn't he have supported me on this? He was as bad as my mother was. Those things that he told me about the growth of a tiny baby haunted me. I wondered how my baby looked at that very moment. Was it really formed into a real, living, little baby now? I reached down and felt my tummy. For the first time I felt like there was a baby growing inside me.

If only I would have shared this with Kathy or Amy, I knew they would have been here to support me. But my father had made me promise not to tell anyone, so I kept the awful secret. Now, as I slowly opened the cab door and stepped out onto the sidewalk, it was only me and the child I carried inside me.

The clinic's office was drab and cold looking as I walked through the door. I passed a row of chairs with a couple other girls sitting in them and went up to the window.

"Your name," the receptionist asked.

"Lorraine Patterson."

She fumbled with a couple of files. "Oh, yes, you are thinking about an abortion. Is that correct?"

"Yes. I mean, I've come here today for an abortion, yes."

"Well, have a seat and the doctor will be with you soon."

The time dragged as I sat there for almost two hours. The girls sitting in the waiting room were called and went. A few more came in after me. Some were crying, and others just looked mad. None of us girls talked to each other; we all had our own demons to deal with.

For some reason I found myself thinking of Tommy. I told myself if I would have listened to him, I wouldn't be in this predicament. I remembered that one time after Teen Meet we discussed the message that we had heard. Everyone, especially Tommy, was talking about the Judgment. Could it be true? *Will God punish me for aborting this child? Will I end up at The Great White Throne Judgment?* All I knew at that point was that I wanted to jump up and get out of there!

It was too late. The receptionist called my name.

Surprisingly, the doctor was a woman, which for some strange reason gave me a little more comfort. I told myself that I was there now and had no choice but to go through with it.

The doctor must have read the anxiety on my face, so she said, "Try to relax, Lorraine. Do I see some reluctance in your eyes?"

"No! Doctor, I just need to get this thing done. Sure, I've had my doubts, but doesn't everyone who comes here?"

The doctor smiled. "Not everyone, Lorraine."

"Well, my father and I have put a lot of thought in this, and it's the only thing that makes sense."

"You may very well be right, but I always have this counseling session first and then set a date for the actual abortion."

"No, Doctor, please! I need it done now. The baby is getting bigger each day."

"There won't be much change in another week or two, Lorraine. It will still be merely tissue, a fetus."

"But, Doctor, I can feel it growing in me."

"I'm sure you feel some activity in there; your body is adjusting. There won't be any significant changes in only a week or two."

"I want it done now!"

"I am very sorry, young lady, but I have other patients scheduled for today. You are just going to have to wait, or find another clinic. It's your choice. If you want the appointment, stop at the window and make one."

I knew my father had called all over trying to find a clinic. This was definitely the quickest clinic I was going to get in, so I set up an appointment. To my disgust, it was in another two weeks.

When I got out of the clinic I wanted to get as far away from that awful place as I could. My vision was blurred by tears as I hurried down the sidewalk, bumping into a man and woman who were in my path. The man had some papers in his hands that fell to the ground. I felt terrible for bumping into them, so I stopped and picked the papers up for him. "I'm really sorry, mister."

The man smiled. "That's okay, Miss. You look like you've been crying. Did you just come from that clinic?"

I felt guilty and hesitated for a moment. Then, in between sobs, I said, "A...yes."

The woman put her arms around me. "You poor child, did you have an abortion?"

"No, not yet. I wanted to, but the stupid doctor wanted to counsel me first and give me time to think about it. I don't have to think about it! I know what I want, and it's not a baby! I can't get the abortion for another two weeks. I don't know how I can wait that long..."

The kind, middle-aged woman looked directly in my teary eyes. "I know you are going through a tremendous crises in your life right now. Will you let my husband and me help you?"

I looked back in her eyes. "Thanks for caring, but there's nothing anybody can do for me. The only solution to my problem is an abortion."

The woman asked me my name, and I told her. Then she said, "Our names are Ruth and George Bloomingdale. We have an organization that helps young girls with their unwanted pregnancies and gives them an alternative to having an abortion. We'll be meeting an hour from now."

Mr. Bloomingdale handed me one of the flyers I'd knocked from his hands earlier. "Here—the address is on the top. Only three blocks from here."

"I'm sorry, but I don't see any sense to it. I've made up my mind."

"Oh come on, Lorraine." He smiled. "You don't have anything to lose by attending. Oops, that is nothing, but that little baby you are carrying."

I gave him a dirty look and stormed away. However, something kept gnawing in my soul, and I couldn't put my finger on it. Something in my heart kept telling me I should go to that meeting. Maybe it was only curiosity, but it weighed heavily on my heart. I finally gave in and went to the address written on the flyer Mr. Bloomingdale had given me.

Mrs. Bloomingdale greeted me at the door with a huge smile on her round, pudgy face. "Come on in, Lorraine, we are about to start."

I followed her into a room where six young girls were sitting in a half circle. In front of them was a movie screen.

Mr. Bloomingdale walked up and stood in front of the screen and introduced himself and his wife, Ruth. "I am so delighted that each and every one of you young ladies have made the decision to be here tonight. This will probably be the most important meeting you will ever attend in your lifetime. The decision on each of your minds will be a lifetime decision that will always live in your hearts and minds.

"My lovely wife and I are involved in this Christian outreach program. Its goal is to save babies from being slaughtered. God creates life, and no one has the right to take it. An unborn child is a real human little person, and it was from the time of conception. Each child has a right to be born. I know each of you believe that you have an overwhelming problem right now, but the decision you are considering is murder. It is murder to abort your child! There are alternatives. Before I point those out, please watch with me these startling slides."

In front of my eyes the screen showed pictures of a fetus in all of its different stages. I was shocked when I saw one at three months, about the same stage as mine. I saw the changes that it would be going through, in the two remaining weeks before the abortion. I was stunned! The fetus looked like a real little baby! Greg had described how it would look, but seeing it on the big screen in living color was much more graphic and real.

Mr. Bloomingdale continued, "You see, the word *fetus* is a Greek word for a young child. Abortion clinics like to use the Greek word so people won't associate the word with the true meaning. Most of us don't know the Greek language. The clinics don't want you to know what the true meaning really is; but in fact, it does mean 'young child.'"

Mrs. Bloomingdale turned on the projector, and Mr. Bloomingdale pointed to a slide that appeared. "Take a look at this slide. You see, from the second month to the third month makes a lot of difference."

The other girls and I gasped at what we saw. "As you can see, the little fingers and toes are becoming more pronounced, and you can even tell this baby is a boy. There are even centers of ossification appearing in most of his bones. That's the process of bone formation. Look here at this slide. The child is in his three-and-a-half-month stage." I was in awe as I peered at this slide. It was a precious tiny little baby boy with a head, arms, fingers, legs, and toes. He was a complete darling little baby!

Mr. Bloomingdale continued showing all the stages throughout the nine-month pregnancy. Then the horrifying slides began. The slides were of terrible procedures used in removing the poor little babies from their mother's wombs. There were several slides showing various ways to abort a child. Everything from using suction to cutting up the unborn child. The graphic color made the bloody procedures even more gory. The slides showed babies with blood all over their tiny little bodies. They showed the horror and the pain on their little faces as they were snatched from their mother's womb and brutally killed.

One of the girls in the group jumped to her feet, covering her mouth as she choked, and headed for the bathroom.

Mr. Bloomingdale hung his head as he sadly said, "I realize how awfully painful it is to witness these horrifying slides, but it was essential that you do. You need to understand that those little ones you are carrying are God's own living children. Performing abortion is murder! You are a part of that murder when you allow it to happen."

Mr. Bloomingdale called a fifteen-minute break. Most of us, including myself, were in shock. There were some refreshments on a table, but I wasn't able to eat or drink anything.

When we were all seated again, Mr. Bloomingdale talked about alternatives. He concluded his presentation by telling us about Jesus and his salvation.

One of the girls broke in and asked, "This wasn't my first pregnancy. I had another one, and I had it aborted. Does that mean I'm going to hell?"

"Maria, God doesn't want any of His children to perish or go to hell. All He asks is that you let Him into your heart. God will then give you eternal life with Him and will forgive all of your sins. All you need to do is say a simple prayer, and ask Jesus to be your Lord and Savior as you yield your life to Him. If you truly believe that Jesus Christ shed His blood on the cross to wash away your sins, then you will be saved. To have a relationship with Him you need to walk a godly life, and live your life for Jesus. Once you are saved, you will want to be pleasing to our Holy God."

With tears flowing down her eyes, Maria asked, "So God will forgive me for killing my baby?"

"Yes, Maria! All you have to do is receive Him in your heart, and repent by asking His forgiveness of your sins."

"I want that," Maria cried. "Will you help me? I've never prayed before."

Mr. Bloomingdale prayed a salvation prayer to the whole group. Maria accepted Jesus as her Savior that night as well as three other girls. It was a glorious closing of the meeting, everybody was hugging and crying (mostly tears of joy), but my heart still was heavy. I had wanted to ask Jesus into my heart, but I still couldn't give up the life that I thought was so great. So again I rejected the Lord.

But one good thing happened. Because of that meeting, I decided there was no way I could have that baby inside me killed. I didn't have the slightest idea what I was going to do, but I knew I could not kill that precious little baby.

When I got back home that evening, it was nearly ten o'clock. My parents had been worried to death about me. With great stress and emotion my father asked, "Did something go wrong with the abortion? Did they have trouble stopping the bleeding, or what?"

"No, Father. I'm sorry! I was too upset to come home right away, so I stopped at a diner. I hadn't had anything to eat since noon."

"You could have gotten something at home," my mother snapped.

"Yeah, I know, but I wanted to be alone for a while. I'm sorry I worried you guys."

"Yes, you do worry us, but we understand. We know this was going to be hard on you. Well, tell us, how did it go?"

"Well, Father, it didn't. I mean, the doctor would only give me counseling at this visit. I have an appointment for two weeks."

I didn't know what to say to my father, I couldn't get myself to tell him the truth. The truth that the baby inside me was not going to be aborted, it was going to be born!

Father pounded his fist on the table. "Two weeks! I thought this terrible mistake would be all over by tonight. Now it has to hang over our heads for another two weeks!"

"I was mad too, Father, but they said they didn't do abortions until they counsel first. They want each girl to be completely sure before they go through with the procedure. They were filled up for two weeks."

My mother gasped. "You could be showing by then. Everyone will know! We can't let that happen. Lorraine, it's still not too late to get you to that special home up north. They will adopt the baby out to parents who will love it."

Father angrily shouted, "Will you shut up, Marge? Lorraine does not want to give birth to this kid!"

I said sheepishly and quietly, "Maybe Mother's got a point."

"Don't be ridiculous," Father snapped back. "You have too much going on for you right now. Why should you throw away the happiest time of your youth? No! I'll call tomorrow and try to speed it up."

⌘⌘⌘

"Jesus, doesn't that mean something: I made the right decision not to abort my child? I'm not a murderer! I believed that there was a God, too! Why am I here?" I cried.

"Just knowing that there is a God does not give you eternal life. Satan even knows that God exists. Knowledge does not give you salvation. Not everyone who says to Me, 'Lord, Lord, shall enter the kingdom of Heaven, but he who does the will of My Father in Heaven.'"[3]

"You cannot get to the Father without first coming to Me. As My Word reads in John 3:16-17: 'For God so loved the world that He gave His only begotten Son, that whoever believes in Him shall not perish but have Everlasting Life. For God did not send His Son into the world to condemn the world, but that the world through Him might be saved. Therefore, if one has been justified by faith, they will have peace with God through Me."

"In the Holy Bible it is written in Romans 6:23: 'For the wages of sin is death, but the gift of God is Eternal Life in Christ Jesus our Lord.' Also in 1 Thessalonians 5:9: 'For God did not appoint us to wrath, but to obtain salvation through our Lord Jesus Christ.'

"When I walked this earth, I told a man named Nicodemus that: Unless one is born again, he cannot see the kingdom of God.[4] I explained to him that being born again of the Spirit means to have a new spiritual birth.

"The first and greatest commandment is in Matthew 22:21: 'You shall love the Lord your God with all your heart, with all your soul, and with all your mind.'"

18

The date for my abortion was fast approaching, but it would not be an appointment that I was going to keep. I didn't want to be pregnant, but I couldn't face the emotional consequences of killing a child. Keeping a secret like that was driving me crazy. I wanted so badly to share this with Kathy and Amy; we had always shared everything before. I came close a few times to spilling the beans but caught myself in time. My parents had drilled into my head not to tell a soul.

Greg was the only other person I had confided in. Of course, my parents didn't know that I told him; they'd have killed me! I was going nuts. I had to talk to someone, so I called Greg.

Greg sounded shocked when he received my call. "Lorraine, honey, is that really you? I have missed you so much, baby!"

"Yeah, and I missed you too."

"If you missed me, why didn't you call sooner?"

"I've had a lot on my mind, Greg."

"Well yeah, me too! I would have called you, but I'm sure your old man would make certain that I couldn't get through to you."

"You're probably right."

"Why are you calling now?"

"I'm going nuts here, Greg, trying to keep this big dark secret!"

"What—the abortion?"

"Well, sort of. That's what I need to talk to you about. I've decided not to have the abortion."

"You're not having the abortion? Wow, that's great, baby! What made you change your mind?"

I told Greg all about meeting the Bloomingdales and the slides that I had seen. I could see his smile in his voice as he said, "Told you so."

"Yeah, you did. It's just terrible how they slaughter those tiny helpless babies. I couldn't let them do that to my baby. I saw a baby in the same stage as mine. It was so cute. I can't believe how developed it was.

How can anyone kill a baby like that?"

"Lorraine, I'm picking you up as fast as I can get there. Be ready!"

"No! I can't leave the house now; my parents will see me. They don't let me do anything lately."

"Is your old man bent out of shape because you aren't getting the abortion?"

"No! 'Cause I haven't told my parents yet. I don't know how I'm going to tell them. My father will be furious with me."

"Babe, I've got to talk to you in person; this is too important! Slip out the back door; they'll never notice. I'll pick you up at the back gate."

Somehow I managed to sneak out of the fortress that evening. I had to get out of there. My problem was driving me crazy. Greg was right—my parents never noticed. They were too involved in one of their arguments to notice me. It was a piece of cake slipping out the back door.

When I jumped into Greg's van, I was smoking a cigarette. He swore at me and said, "Put that thing out! Do you know how much damage it could do to our baby?"

"Well, Doctor Greg, to tell you the truth, it's the other kind of cigarette that I need right now. I haven't had a buzz in three weeks!"

"Forget it—they're a lot worse for the baby than the regular cigarettes are."

After we arrived at our special getaway in the woods, I was able to persuade him to give me a few hits from his reefer. I knew what it took to persuade Greg to do whatever I wanted. I knew he couldn't resist me.

I took a few hits and then my nerves chilled. I became mellow once again. Now life's problems seemed less severe. At least it was a temporary fix.

After a romantic escapade, Greg got serious and said, "Babe, we really need to talk!"

Flippantly I said, "So talk!"

"Yeah, okay," he said a bit distraught. "We need to be serious about our situation."

"What situation?"

"The baby! We can raise this kid ourselves."

"You got to be kidding me!"

"No, I'm serious as a heart attack. It's our kid; we should raise it!"

"We can't, silly. How can we afford a baby? Besides, my father would never allow it."

"You can move in with me and my old lady. When you turn eighteen, we can get married. There ain't a darn thing he can do about it! I'll take good care of you and the baby. I realize I can't give you the lifestyle that you were raised in, but I can give you and the kid love. I'll make a better daddy than your old man ever thought about being."

"Greg, do you know how much the hospital bill alone will be? My mother's right—the only thing I can do now is go away and adopt the baby out."

"No, Lorraine! There's got to be a way we can do this. What about your old man? Maybe when he finds out how serious we are, he'll at least pay for the hospital bills."

"Babies require a lot of stuff like cribs, car seats, diapers, clothes, all sorts of things. And all that before it's even born!"

"Well, yeah. If your old man can help us out until we get on our feet, I'll pay him back every penny."

"He wouldn't miss the money, Greg. It's just that he's so set against me keeping the baby, no matter what."

"If I came from one of those rich families, I bet he wouldn't have any problem with it, would he? Heck no! It's because I'm a high school dropout, and I work in a foundry. My parents weren't trash either, you know! They were doing pretty good for a while, until my old man got on hard drugs. He even had a CD made at a studio. My parents had big dreams of becoming famous. And they were good, too. They could have made it."

"Weren't they a little old for rock stars?"

"Yeah, but they had this dream for a lot of years. The gigs kept getting farther and farther apart. I didn't know how bad it was until my old man was arrested. Like you, Lorraine, my parents left me alone a lot. When I was small, I had to stay with my grandma. She never cared where I was or what I was doing. I was fourteen when she died. My parents thought I was old enough to stay alone by that time (as if anything had changed).

"You see, babe, I never had a good family life either. That is why this kid is so important to me. We can have a family together with all the love we didn't get when we were kids. It will be different with our baby; I'll always find time for him."

I nodded slowly. "I've got to admit that sounds good. I've always wanted to be in a loving family. Maybe my parents will help us a little. Maybe they will even sign for us to get married, so we can be married before the baby is born. That should take some of their embarrassment away."

Greg threw his arms around me. "Then you'll do it?"

"Yes, Greg! Yes! It would be a good idea to get my clothes and things out first, and then talk to my parents. That way it will be quick and easy when they give their permission."

"Great idea! When do you want me to come over and help you get your things?"

"Tomorrow is as good as anytime. My mother will be leaving for some committee meeting at three and my father shouldn't be home until six. That way we can have the van all loaded before they get home. We can wait until they get home and then tell them our plans."

"Great. I'll go home tonight and let my old lady know that you're moving in, and that she's going to be a grandma!"

"Sounds like a plan."

"Yeah, I just hope your old man doesn't kill me, or throw me in jail!"

We had a good laugh over that. Then we had another joint to celebrate our new life together.

The next day Greg pulled his van up to the back entrance at 3:30. I was out there eager to let him in. "You just missed my mother!"

"Yeah, I know. I was waiting down the street for her to leave. I thought she would never go."

"That's my mother...never on time for anything. That leaves us only two and half hours before my father gets home."

"What time will your old lady get home?"

"Who knows with her! It depends if the meeting is wet or dry."

We headed up the stairs with boxes Greg had brought. I kept packing as Greg carried boxes down the stairs to his van. Before we knew it, two hours had raced by.

Greg came up the stairs huffing and puffing and saying, "Uncle!"

"What do you mean, uncle!" I whined. "I'm not done yet, Greg. I've got things I can't leave!"

"Babe, you've got more stuff than twenty girls would need. Now come on: the van's packed solid. Besides, your old man will be home in a half hour. Your old lady could walk in any time."

"Okay, just take this box. I have one little box I need, and then I'll come back for the rest."

"All right, but it will have to be after we get our own crib. My ma's two-bedroom apartment won't hold it all. I'm not sure if we can get all this stuff in."

When Greg got to the bottom of the stairway, there was my mother staring him in the face. She was as startled as him. They both screamed, and Greg dropped the box. My mother threw her hands up in the air and yelled, "Don't hurt me. Take what you want, but don't hurt me!"

When I heard the commotion downstairs, I ran to the landing to see what was the matter. I couldn't help but laugh when I saw Mother with her arms up in the air. "Mother," I called, "Greg's not a robber. He's going to be my husband!"

That's when she fainted. I ran down the steps and got a cold cloth to put on her face. When she came to, she said, "Your what?"

"Mother, I have decided to do the right thing and marry the father of my baby. Mother, this is my boyfriend, Greg. He loves me and wants to make a home for the baby and me."

"Lorraine, you haven't thought all this out clearly. Your father will never allow this!"

"But, Mother, it's the only solution. I thought maybe Father could help us a little until we can get on our feet. Mother, you're going to be a grandmother! Isn't that cool?"

My mother sputtered, "No, it isn't cool! I'm way too young to be a grandmother!"

Greg, trying to be polite, said, "I know you look much too young to be a grandma, but we'll let you spoil him."

"Listen, young man, if I were you, I would get my buns out of here before Lorraine's father gets home, or I'm afraid you will be one sorry boy!"

We heard the huge solid wood door open and shut.

"Too late," I announced.

Father walked up to us and slammed his briefcase on the glass foyer table. "What in the world is going on here?"

"Father, I can't go through with the abortion. I can't kill my baby!"

"That is absurd, Lorraine. You were all for it! What happened? Did this hippie talk you out of it?"

Greg pushed past me. "Sir, I want to marry Lorraine. I'll make a home for her and the baby."

"Over my dead body, you will!"

I stood next to Greg and took his hand, "Father, we love each other. We can be married way before the baby is born; no one will notice."

"I don't give a cat's rat who will notice or not. You are not going to marry this lowlife! Is that clear?"

Tears trickled down my check as I said, "No, Father, it isn't clear! I'm still going to marry Greg when I turn eighteen, if I get your approval or not!"

It was evident my father was trying very hard to control his anger, trying hard to be the competent lawyer he was. "Lorraine, for a graduation gift I was going to buy you a brand-new car! I'll even take you shopping to get the exact car of your dreams. You can have the best year of your life! You can keep on cheerleading, be queen of the prom, graduate with all your friends, and drive around in a fabulous car. What about college, becoming a lawyer? All you have to do is have that simple little abortion. It's that simple!"

My heart was breaking; these were all the things that I wanted more than anything. But something inside of me could not bring myself to kill my baby, not after I saw how developed it was already. How could I do that?

I put my arms around my father's neck and in a low voice said, "Thank you, Father. As much as I sincerely want all of that, there is no way that I can kill this baby."

My father pushed me away. "Well, then, at least go where your mother wanted you to, and adopt the kid out!"

Greg stepped up again and angrily said, "No way, old man. That's my baby, too. Come on, Lorraine; we're leaving now!"

My father grabbed Greg's arm and twisted it around his back. He looked like a mad man. "Does this feel like an old man to you? Don't you ever call me old man again, or I'll break you in half!"

"Father," I screamed, "let him go!"

My father let him go with a little shove. He glared at me. "Go to your room!"

"No! I'm leaving with Greg, with or without your permission."

I never saw my father as mad as he was that night. He picked up the box that had fallen on the floor and tossed it at me. "Okay, you spoiled little brat, that's it! If you walk out of this house with that lowlife, you will never get one penny of support from me. I swear, Lorraine, if you do, you're dead to me. You'll no longer be my daughter. I'll disown you!"

Greg grabbed up the box from the floor, took my hand, and led me out of the house. I couldn't have done it on my own. My eyes were too blurred from tears, and my mind was in a daze. How could my parents throw me out of their lives forever? How could I live without all the luxuries I'd enjoyed all my life? I realized then how I had taken them all for granted. How could I have thrown it all away?

⌘⌘⌘

After watching that part of my life from The Great White Throne Judgment, I said to the Lord, "I can feel the terrible pain in my heart from that day. I couldn't believe my own father would disown me! And to think how I could give up all those luxuries. I could have had anything I wanted for the rest of my life. How could I have given it up just for a little baby?"

"IF YOU TRUST IN MONEY, YOU WILL PERISH, BUT IF YOU WOULD HAVE TRUSTED IN ME, YOU WOULD HAVE FLOURISHED LIKE A TREE. IT IS BETTER TO HAVE LITTLE AND BE GODLY THAN TO OWN AN EVIL MAN'S WEALTH; FOR THE STRENGTH OF EVIL MEN SHALL BE BROKEN, BUT THE LORD TAKES CARE OF THOSE HE HAS FORGIVEN.

"THE SADNESS YOU ARE FEELING FROM THE TIME YOUR EARTHLY FATHER CUT OUT YOUR RICHES WILL SEEM LIKE JOY COMPARED TO THE HORROR YOU WILL FEEL WHEN YOUR HEAVENLY FATHER CUTS YOU OFF FROM HIS RICHES IN HEAVEN. INSTEAD, YOU WILL BE CAST INTO A FURNACE OF FIRE, WHERE YOU WILL WAIL AND GNASH YOUR TEETH."

19

It was a nasty winter day as snow pounded on the windshield, only worsening the torment in my soul. Was I really leaving my luxurious life behind to live in poverty? I was being torn from my parents to live with a guy I recently wanted to dump. My parents had their faults, but now that I was leaving, my heart was aching. I couldn't imagine taking care of myself, let alone a tiny little baby.

I looked over at Greg as he drove the van further and further away from my parents' luxurious estate. He had a big smile like he was the happiest guy in the world. He was used to living a modest life, but how could I ever adapt to it?

He looked over at me. "Hey, baby, wipe those tears. This is going to be great! Now we can be together all the time. No more sneaking around to see each other. No more lies!"

"Yeah, Greg, it's just great," I said with little enthusiasm. "Isn't it taking us too long to get to your mom's place? We should have been there before now. We never took the expressway to your house, either."

"Well—ah, there's been a sight change of plans. My old lady only had welfare for a short time, until I turned eighteen. She couldn't locate any work around here. So my uncle who lives in the city knew this neighborhood bar that was looking for a daytime manager. He told my ma about it, and she took the job. The job came with a two-bedroom apartment upstairs over the bar. We moved into it a couple of weeks ago. It's small, but hey, it's a place to stay until I can get us our own place."

In a whiny voice I said, "You're moving me back to New York City? I hated living there! And live above a tavern? You've got to be kidding! I lived in New York most of my life, but in a spacious penthouse. Now you expect me to live with you and your mother in a tiny apartment above a smelly old bar?"

"Baby, it's not that bad! The bar is a friendly neighborhood place. They have the best burgers in all of New York City!"

The thought of a greasy hamburger made my pregnant stomach feel sick. The last thing I wanted to hear about was food right then. I wanted Greg to leave me alone while I tried to sort out the terrible decision I had made hours earlier. The traffic was getting busier, so Greg was content to devote all his attention to his driving anyway.

When we got to the City, Greg was driving down streets where I had never been before. I had thought that New York was all sparkle and glitter. My parents never allowed me to view this part of the city before. I never realized that there was such a diverse population. This was truly the slums of New York City. I wanted to die. How could I possibly adjust to this after the prosperous life I had always known?

Neon lights shone their bright reds, yellows, and blues lighting up the darkened street as Greg turned into a dark alley. He pulled into a parking spot in front of a sign that said *Smitty's Bar & Grill*. Greg looked at me with a slight smile. "We're here, baby. Welcome home."

With tears running down my cheeks and my eyes wide, I prayed, *If you really exist, God, please strike me dead!*

Greg was over at my side of the van opening the door. "Come on. My old lady should be getting out of work anytime now. I'll take you into the bar to meet her first. Besides, I bet you're hungry. I know I'm famished."

Greg led me into a dark dirty hallway as he began to give me the mini tour. "The door on the right leads up to our apartment. The door to your left is a beer cooler."

Straight ahead, through a windowed door, I could see the bar. I smelled the nasty aroma of stale beer and heard men laughing and pool balls hitting.

Greg opened the door and grabbed hold of my hand as he led me behind him into the tavern. He waved at the chubby middle-aged bartender and said, "Hi, Mac, make me two of those fantastic Smitty hamburgers, will yah?"

"Want a couple of beers with those?" Mac answered back.

"Only for me. My woman doesn't need any alcohol." Turning to me, he asked, "What you want with your burger, honey?"

I was so nervous, I could barely talk. I said in a low voice, "Milk, please."

The bartender gave me a sarcastic smile. "We ain't got no milk in here, missy. The dairy's down the street five blocks."

The four guys sitting at the bar laughed along with Mac. Greg even chuckled a little.

I was embarrassed, and a little angry as I said, "I don't care. I'll have a Coke—whatever you've got."

"Coke I got, missy."

Greg said, "Jake, this is Lorraine, my girl. She's going to be living here with my ma and me."

Mac shook my hand. "Nice to make your acquaintance. Not every day we get such a beautiful woman in here. Hope you didn't take offense of my kidding. I only kid around with those I like. If I quit kidding, then you better watch out, right, Greg?"

"Right on, Mac."

A tall, skinny, middle-aged woman who looked like she had been drawn through a mill walked up to the bar where we were standing and said, "Hey, Greg, this must be the girlfriend you've been telling me about, right?" She looked at me and said, "Hi, honey, I'm Greg's ma, Shirley."

Greg grinned widely. "Yeah, babe, this is my ma. Ma, this is my girl, Lorraine."

His mother smiled. "I kinda thought so, seeing you told me you were moving her in today." She turned to me and said, "I don't know how it's going to work out, honey. We don't have much, but what we got, you're welcome to. Hope you didn't bring much; there's not a whole lot of room in our tiny apartment. It's a roof over our heads, that's all."

I smiled back at her. "Thanks. I hope I haven't inconvenienced you."

Greg spoke out. "Yeah, ma, I really appreciate you letting Lorraine stay with us. I plan on getting us our own place before the baby gets here."

Shirley's face turned sober now. "Yeah, that's right: you two are going to make me a grandma. I wasn't expecting that so soon. To tell you the truth, I don't feel old enough to be a grandma."

Greg laughed. "It'll grow on you, Ma. We'll even let you help us take care of him; won't we, Lorraine?"

"Yeah, sure, even if he turns out to be a she."

Everyone in the small bar had a laugh about that one.

"Are you off work now, Ma?" Greg asked his mother.

"Yeah, I was just having my after-work drink."

"Good. Drink up, and I'll get our burgers to go, so we can show

Lorraine her new home. She's had a rough day. I'm sure she will want to lay down soon, huh, babe?"

"Yes, I'm exhausted."

When Greg gave me the grand tour of my new living quarters, I couldn't believe my eyes. Besides being small, it was filthy. It felt like I was condemned and put in jail. I could have put this whole apartment in my bedroom back home. Now this was going to be my home! How horrible I felt. Not just because of my living conditions, but I missed my family already. I remembered my father's words—that he didn't want anything to do with me anymore. I cried myself to sleep that night as I would the next several nights to follow.

The next morning I got up at ten o'clock. Greg was still sleeping. He had taken off from work to get me moved in last night, but he was used to sleeping in because of his second shift job. Shirley was busy getting ready to go down to the bar to start her day's work. She saw me and said, "There's food in the refrigerator and cupboards. Fix you and Greg whatever you want. I'll be home between seven or eight." She laughed and said, "Depends how many beers I get bought for me after work."

When Shirley left, I felt so alone. Greg was in the other room sleeping yet, but I was filled with despair and loneliness. *Well, there's no maids here to clean this mess up. If I don't want to live in filth, I guess it's up to me. That's the least I can do for imposing myself on Greg's mother.* Actually, when I role-played that this was just Greg's and my apartment, it was kinda fun playing Suzy Homemaker. By the time Greg dragged himself out of bed, I had the apartment tidied up.

The only thing he really noticed was that I had coffee waiting for him: that made him happy. After he thanked me for the coffee, he said, "I'm going to have to get something to eat and pack a lunch. I've only got a couple hours before I will need to leave for work."

I felt useless as I stood in front of the refrigerator holding the door open. I didn't know the first thing about cooking. My family always had the maid to cook for us. I'd never even opened a can of beans! I turned around and asked Greg if he wanted some eggs and toast.

He laughed. "Babe, I'm a hard-working foundry man. I need meat and potatoes to satisfy me! However, looks like you are kind of lost there,

Miss Lorraine. Let an old expert show you how."

He got the potatoes out of the bottom of the cupboard and showed me how to cut the skin and spots out. I cut my finger a couple of times, but finely got the things peeled. I watched carefully as Greg instructed me how to go about cooking him a meat and potato dinner. It tasted pretty good when we shared the meal around the small dinette table, which faced the open living room.

After dinner, Greg took a shower and soon was off to work, leaving me all alone in my new prison.

There was never a moment in my entire life that I felt more alone. I washed the dishes, made our bed, cleaned up the bathroom, then took a very long shower. I had brought a night bag filled with a change of clothes, so I could at least feel clean. The rest of my boxes remained in the van. Putting away my things would have to wait for another day. I looked around Greg's bedroom (which now was our bedroom) and couldn't imagine where my things could possibly fit.

It was eight o'clock, and Shirley hadn't made it upstairs from work yet. I was terribly bored but not anxious to be alone with this woman I'd met briefly downstairs. I wished I could get to know her better when Greg was here. When she finally unlocked the door at nine thirty, I was sort of relieved. I wouldn't admit it to anyone, but I was beginning to be afraid of being alone. When she staggered in, she said, "Sorry, honey, I meant to get up here earlier to visit with you, but some old friends came into the bar tonight and I couldn't get away."

She smelled like she brought the bar upstairs with her. I told her, "That's all right, Shirley, I've made myself at home."

"Well, isn't that nice," she said with a hiccup to follow. "I'm glad you did. Did Greg get off to work with a good dinner?"

"Yeah, we worked on it together."

"Good! How about his lunch? Did you pack him a lunch, honey (hiccup)?"

"Yeah, Greg showed me how he liked it."

"Good—that's something I won't have to worry about doing anymore. He's got you to do it. Hey, sweetie, if you don't mind, it's been a long day; I think I'll just turn in for the night."

"Sure, that's fine." *My pleasure! The last thing I need right now is to try to carry on a conversation with a drunk woman I don't even know. At least I won't have to miss my mother being drunk; looks like Greg's will take that place.* Even though Shirley was sound asleep in her bedroom, I didn't feel quite as scared. Someone else was in the apartment besides me.

The next day after Greg woke up he helped me bring in my boxes. Our bedroom was full of boxes to the ceiling. There was little room to walk around the already small room. Greg shoved his clothes as far back as possible in the closet so I could hang a few things. He also opened up one of his dresser drawers and stuffed his underclothes in the drawer below. "There," he said, "I made room for some of your things. Remember, this is temporary. I'll get us a bigger apartment of our own soon."

That took care of a couple of boxes. The rest of the clothes I would have to leave in boxes. Most of my clothes were getting too tight on me anyway.

My goal each night was to stay up to greet Greg when he got home from work. His hours at the foundry were from four in the afternoon until twelve midnight. It took him about forty-five minutes to get from work to our apartment he had told me. So I expected him home about a quarter to one. I curled up on the sofa watching television and had the greatest of intentions to be wide awake when he arrived home. By the time the eleven o'clock news came on, I was sound assleep on the sofa.

I had the door double locked by using the deadbolt lock (I felt much safer that way). I was sleeping soundly when I was abruptly awakened by the pounding on the door. With eyes half open I went to the door and called out, "Who is it?"

"It's me, Lorraine! It's me, Greg. Open the door."

I quickly unlocked the door and started apologizing. "I'm so sorry, Greg! I really am sorry that I fell asleep. I didn't mean to. I was going to unlock the door just before I thought you would be here. I didn't mean to lock you out, honest."

"No big deal! Don't worry about it, babe. Why don't you go to bed when you're tired? You need more sleep now because of the baby, don't you?"

"I guess I do, but I want to be up when you get home from work."

"That's sweet, babe. Well, to tell you the truth, I do get really hungry when I get home from work. How about those eggs you were going to serve me earlier today? You might even fry those leftover potatoes we had, if you don't mind?"

"Sure, Greg, I'll try." I tried to do a good job with the eggs, but I got them too hard, and I burned the fried potatoes. Greg gave me a couple of hints for the next time. When he was done eating I asked him, "Can we, please, go to bed now? I'm so tired."

"Babe, you go right ahead and go to bed. I can't sleep when I first get home from work. I usually watch an old movie, and after that I can sleep."

"No, that's okay, honey. I want to stay up with you." I snuggled up on the couch with him and was sleeping within fifteen minutes.

⌘ ⌘ ⌘

Pain ripped within my heart as I stood before Jesus at The Great White Throne Judgment. "I made a terrible mess out of my life. I knew it was a mistake to run off with Greg as soon as we drove away from my parents' home. I cried out for You, but You didn't answer! Why, Lord? Why didn't You answer me, or didn't You even hear me?"

"I HEARD YOUR DESPERATE CRIES, AND I WAS SADDENED BY THEM. YOU CALLED OUT AND SAID IF THERE WAS A GOD OUT THERE, SMITE YOUR LIFE. ANYONE WHO WANTS TO COME TO GOD MUST BELIEVE THAT THERE IS A GOD AND THAT HE REWARDS THOSE WHO SINCERELY LOOK FOR HIM.

"BECAUSE I AM A MERCIFUL GOD, I WOULD NOT TAKE YOUR LIFE UNTIL I GAVE YOU ANOTHER CHANCE TO RECEIVE FAITH. I AM THE WAY, THE TRUTH, AND THE LIGHT TO YOUR SALVATION. IF YOU WOULD HAVE HAD FAITH ONLY THE SIZE OF A MUSTARD SEED, THEN YOU COULD HAVE MOVED THE MOUNTAINS OF YOUR LIFE. WITH FAITH IN ME, YOU CAN LAY YOUR BURDENS AT MY FEET, AND I WILL GIVE YOU PEACE."

20

Midnight would mark our first month's anniversary of moving in together. I wanted everything to be special. I had planned a celebration, a midnight brunch in our cramped kitchen. I wanted this breakfast to be the best ever. Besides his normal eggs and toast, I had bought two steaks and hash browns at the grocery store. I'd even set aside some grocery money to buy two candles for the table. I had gotten myself in Greg's routine of sleeping, so I had no problem staying up late, waiting for him.

Even though I was starting to show, I put on the most flattering clothes that I could find. Some woman Shirley knew from the bar gave me some maternity clothes. Most of them were way too big for me. But they were better than my uncomfortable jeans that I no longer could zip up.

Shirley was in bed sound asleep. At least she wouldn't be any intrusion to our little celebration.

As the clock got closer and closer to 12:45, I got more and more excited. I couldn't wait to see Greg's face when he saw the special table I had prepared for us. The potatoes were fried, and I put the steak on to cook at 12:40. Everything should be ready for him when he walked through the door. *Oh, yes, one more thing*, I remembered. I had a beer in the freezer getting really cold. I took it out and set it out for him. He always wanted a beer as soon as he got home.

My eyes and ears were glued to the door. I listened, hoping to hear him walking up the stairs so I could get the door open before he started to unlock the door. I planned on throwing my arms around him, telling him about my romantic first month celebration I had planned.

When the clock struck 12:40, I didn't hear a sound. I continued waiting by the door until 1:00 a.m. Then I went to the window that overlooked the back alley, hoping to see his van pull up. I watched another half hour and nothing. *What could have happened to him? He's always home the same time every night. Maybe he was held up by an accident. Oh no, maybe he was in an accident!*

I paced from the window to the door, hoping he would get there any minute. I couldn't hold back the tears. I thought something terrible must have happened to him.

At 2:00 a.m., I was beginning to get angry. *If there had been an accident, someone would have contacted me by now. He could have called if he had to work late!*

The potatoes and the steak had burned and been turned off an hour before. Trying to calm myself, I turned the television on to some late, late old movie. Then finally at 2:30 I heard sounds coming up the stairs. I ran to the door and called, "Greg! Is that you, Greg?"

I heard him yell back in a slurred voice, "Who do you think it is: the Easter Bunny?"

When I got the door open, Greg stood there with a big smirk.

"Where have you been? I have been worried sick!...You're drunk, aren't you?"

"No, I'm not drunk," he slurred. "A bunch of the guys were going to stop at the bar to cash their checks, so I thought for once I would cash my check there, too."

"Why didn't you tell me that you were going to do that? You have always come straight home from work before, so why now?"

"The boys talked me into it tonight. They called me a wimp if I didn't stop at the bar with them. I couldn't have that now, could I, baby?"

"Don't you baby me! I thought you got into an accident and had to go to the hospital!" I grabbed his beer off the table and threw it at him.

Greg caught it as he glared at me. "Thanks, baby! I need another beer."

"You need another beer like you need a hole in the head."

Greg ripped off the tab on the can of beer and took a big slurp, then spit it out. "You know I can't stand my beer warm!"

"Well, how about a nice, cold, burned steak and potatoes, and candles that are all burned down?" I fired back defiantly.

Greg walked over to the stove. "When are you going to learn to cook? I don't want that mess. Besides, I had something to eat at the bar. Where'd you get money for a steak?"

In between my sobs I said, "I've been saving up my grocery money so I could make you a special breakfast for the first month's anniversary of our living together."

"What? That's ridiculous! If you wanted to plan a special meal, you should have let me know, so I would be here."

"But you've always come home each night after work. Why did you have to start tonight?"

"Hey, woman, if I want to stop off at the bar to unwind with the guys, I will! I work really hard, and I need to unwind!" Greg shoved me hard into the kitchen sink, hurting my stomach. When I cried out in pain, he snapped, "Quit acting like a baby and get this mess cleaned up."

That wasn't the last time that Greg didn't come directly home from work; there were plenty of times. Each time he became more aggressive. The larger my stomach grew, the less attention he paid to me. I started to go to bed before he got home from work. That would make him mad, because I wasn't up to make him breakfast (that is, if he didn't stop and eat at the bar).

Then we had fights about money; there was never enough. When I was eight months along, I said to him, "Greg, we have got to start buying things for our baby."

He scowled at me. "What kind of things?"

"You know—clothes, diapers, bottles, a car seat, and a bathtub. Oh yeah, a crib, crib sheets, and blankets. I don't know…they need a lot of things."

"Where do you think we're going to get the money to buy all those things?"

"For one thing you could cut down on going to the bar. That would save us a bundle."

"What do you want me to do, Lorraine? Go crazy? I've got to have a way to deal with all the pressure I'm under."

"You! What about all the pressure I'm under?"

"If you don't like it, baby, then get out!"

"You know I don't have any place to go," I cried.

That night when Greg was at work I called my parents' home. A voice answered that I didn't recognize. "Hello, Patterson residence, may I help you?"

"Yes, who is this?"

"I'm the maid. How may I direct your call?"

"This is Lorraine Patterson. I'm Marge's and James' daughter. Let me talk to Gloria, please."

"Gloria no longer works here, Miss. In fact, I'm her replacement."

"Gloria doesn't work for my parents anymore? Why?"

"I heard from the gardener that she was let go right after you left home. Seems she tried to stand up for you to your father, and he fired her."

"Oh, no! Poor Gloria; she really needed her job."

"Yeah, well so do I. Now what can I do for you?"

"Is my mother there?"

"Yes, Miss, she is; but I have strict orders from your father that if you called not to let you talk with your mother. He said to tell you that you made your bed, and now you must lay in it. He does not want anything to do with you."

I felt that my world had fallen out from under me. Greg was abusive, and my parents would not have anything to do with me. I was trapped with an abusive man I didn't even love.

That next weekend I convinced Greg to take me to J.C. Penney's to look at baby clothes and equipment. The prices blew Greg's socks off. So Greg suggested we try a Wal-Mart. I had never shopped at one before. I had always gone to the mall when I lived at home.

Greg shook his head when we started looking at prices. "There's no way, Lorraine, that I can afford these prices, either."

We left the store and went home, where we continued our argument. Greg yelled at me, "You are going to have to humble yourself, little rich girl, and go to a Goodwill store or the Salvation Army."

"What? You expect me to put my baby in used clothes and furniture?"

"Yeah, I do. If the kid's going to get anything, that's the only way I can do it."

"If you just stayed out of the bars, you could buy our baby the things it will need!"

Greg's response to that was doubling up his fist and hitting me. I grabbed the chair, or I would have been on the floor. My eye was black and blue for two weeks.

The baby was due in only a couple of weeks. I had to have something to bring my baby home in; besides, I was told that I couldn't take the baby out of the hospital until we had a car seat for it. Greg told me that he'd take me to the Goodwill Store and that was it. That was all he could afford. I had no choice so I agreed.

At the Goodwill store, Greg let me pick out a few sleepers, a couple of receiving blankets, one heavy blanket, crib sheets, bottles, some T-shirts, a plastic bathtub, a rubber ducky, and a car seat. I was totally amazed at how much we got for such a small price. However, Greg was complaining about every dime we spent. I saw a really nice crib, but he said we would have to wait a couple of weeks before he had enough money to buy it.

Two weeks came and went. Greg told me he still didn't have enough money to buy that crib at the Goodwill store. He made up a lousy excuse, but I knew that he had spent it at the bar. We were arguing about it when my water broke, and my labor pains started. I was glad that Greg hadn't left for work yet, and so was he. After throwing some things into a bag, we were off to the hospital. After eighteen hours of excruciating pain, my beautiful son was born.

When I held my boy for the first time, I felt so much love. I had never loved anybody or anything as much as I loved this sweet little child. I looked up at Greg and said, "Isn't he the most beautiful baby you've ever seen?"

Greg seemed awestricken and could barely get a word out of his mouth. "Wow, he's awesome!"

I named him Scott James Patterson. My father's name was James Scott Patterson. I hoped he would turn out as prosperous as his grandfather. Greg was proud of our little Scotty and insisted on signing his birth certificate as his father. He told me that he would adopt him and give him his name when we got married next year, when I turned eighteen.

After Greg left the hospital, I called my parent's home again. I was so full of joy over my new little boy. I wanted to share that joy with the ones I loved the most, my parents. To my surprise, my father answered the phone.

Hearing his voice again made me happy, and I couldn't wait to share my good news with him. So with excitement in my voice I answered back, "Father, it's Lorraine!"

His voice was stern as he said, "I thought the housekeeper told you that I didn't want you calling here anymore."

My spirit dropped. "Yes, Dad, but I thought you would like to hear the good news that you have a grandson."

There was silence at the other end of the phone. Then I heard my father clear his throat. "How can I have a grandson when I don't have a daughter anymore? I told you that if you left with that burnout, you would be dead to me!"

Tears welled in my eyes. "Daddy, I wanted to stay with you and mother, but there was no way I could!"

I could feel his anger as he said, "Oh yes there was, young lady! You could have gone through with that abortion, or gone away for a few months and had the baby adopted. But no, you took the cowardly way out and ran away with that boy!"

"You could have let me stayed home and have my baby."

"That was out of the question!"

"Oh, yeah, wouldn't want to tarnish our reputation, now would we? At least let me tell Mother about my baby."

"No, Lorraine, she's sleeping. Besides, she has been chronically depressed, thanks to you. She's been drinking more and lays around all day. I had about enough of it. About a month ago I walked out. I'm staying in my apartment full-time now."

I shouted at the receiver, "How could you, Father? How could you leave her when she needs you the most? Did your secretary move in with you?"

"How do you know about her?"

"You and Mother don't always keep your voices down when you argue. Besides, I'm not stupid. I could see what was going on with you."

"Why, you little hypocrite! You're living with a guy you aren't married to, and just had his baby. How dare you judge me. I'm your father! A grown man, not a seventeen-year-old kid like you! Now don't bother me, or your mother again. Do I make myself clear?"

I was crying too hard to answer, so I hung up the phone. The joy of little Scotty now was clouded by the hurt my father had lashed out on me.

⌘⌘⌘

At The Great White Throne Judgment Seat I felt the terrible pain that my father was thrusting upon me. I asked the Lord, "How could he have been so cold and mean to me? Was I really a hypocrite, Jesus? It was his fault that I'm here now, facing condemnation!"

"No, Lorraine, you are responsible for your own actions! Your parents set a bad example for you, but nevertheless, it was up to you to make your choices in life. I have given you a free will so you can make your own decisions.

"Your earthly father was an unrighteous, proud man. I, your Lord, hate cheating and delight in honesty. Proud men end in shame, but the meek become wise. His riches did not help him when he was judged; only righteousness counts then. The wicked shall fall beneath their load of sin. When an evil man dies, his hopes all perish, for they are based on this earthly life. I rescue good men from danger while letting the wicked fall into it. Evil words destroy.

"When I walked on the earth, I spoke these words: 'Judge not, that you be not judged. For with what judgment you judge, you will be judged; and with the measure you use, it will be measured back to you. And why do you look at the speck in your brother's eye, but do not consider the plank in your own eye? Or how can you say to your brother, Let me remove the speck from your eye; and look, a plank is in your own eye? Hypocrite! First remove the plank from your own eye, and then you will see clearly to remove the speck from your brother's eye.'"[5]

21

Two days after Scotty was born, we were released from the hospital. Greg and I didn't have any insurance so they rushed us out. Now we were forced to take our baby to a tiny, cramped apartment, shared with my mother-in-law.

As soon as we walked in the apartment, Shirley was there with her hands held out, saying, "Lorraine, let me take my precious little grandson. You must be worn out. Go sit down. I'll take care of him while you rest."

Reluctantly, I handed Shirley my baby. As she held him, a big smile broke out. "Oh, Greg, he looks just like you did when you were a baby!"

Greg smiled proudly. "Yeah, he's a handsome little fellow, all right. What do you think, Lorraine? Does he look like his old man?"

Hesitantly I answered, "Yeah, I guess there's some resemblance."

He looks just like my father. As long as he's got his looks and not his character, he'll be all right. The baby certainly has the same color hair as my father and me. I took my finger and gently stroked his hair.

Later that evening, after Shirley finally gave me back my baby, I cuddled him in my arms. I loved him so much! The last couple of days had made its mark on me. I was tired out! I sat on the sofa watching my sleeping baby until my head began nodding....

Waking up with a start, I looked over at Greg, who was engrossed in a football game on television. He had taken tonight off work so he could spend the first night home from the hospital with his new baby and me. Instead he was completely engulfed in the football game.

"Greg!" I called out.

I had to call a second time to get his attention. It was such a small living room you could hear a pin drop. My loud voice made Shirley jump, and she was sitting at the kitchen table. With his eyes still glued to the set, he said, "Not now, Lorraine. They're about to score a touchdown!"

Upset with him, I now yelled, "Is that football game more interesting than your new son? You've put off buying a crib. So now where am I supposed to put him to bed? He needs a place to sleep, Greg!"

Greg swore. "Can't this wait until a commercial break?"

My temper was really beginning to blaze now. I shouted at him, "No, Greg! It can't wait. I'm tired, and I need some sleep before he wakes up for his next feeding."

"Well, I don't know…make a bed for him on the sofa."

"On this worn-out, dirty old couch? No way! Besides, where are we all going to sit then—on the floor, Indian style? In a few weeks Scotty will roll over and join us on the floor. Think again, genius!"

"Darn it, Lorraine," Greg yelled back, "it's only going to be a couple of weeks, then I can go buy that crib you wanted at the Goodwill Store."

"What makes you think that it will still be there? It was almost like new, Greg. For what they were asking for it, I'm sure someone has bought it by now."

Greg's face got red. "If that stupid crib is gone, they'll get another one in. We haven't tried the Salvation Army yet; maybe they will have one."

"I'm sure not as nice as that one was! We'll just have to go back to a department store and buy a new one."

"I told you, I can't afford a new one. I'm not made out of money like your old man!"

"Well, maybe we can put one on layaway and make payments."

Greg slammed his clenched fist on the coffee table, waking up the baby. Scotty screamed his little lungs out.

"See what you did? You woke the baby up!" I accused.

Greg jumped up. "Shut that kid up! I can't take your complaining and that kids screaming!"

"You could have bought Scotty a brand-new crib with all the money you've spent at the bar recently!"

Greg's mother got into the act then. "You kids stop your fighting. What kind of parents are you? Baby's first night home from the hospital, and his parents are arguing like a pair of children! Babies can sense when someone's upset. When you fight, that affects him too. Now, Lorraine, if you will listen to me, I have a solution."

"What is it?"

"When Greg was born, me and his dad didn't have much to live on either. He was a struggling musician, so we had to compromise too. We had a dresser much like yours. I made a bed for him in the top drawer of that dresser. It worked really good for a couple of months." She laughed. "Until the little rascal tried to crawl out of it."

I didn't have a choice, so I threw my clothes out of the only drawer I had in the dresser and replaced them with a pillow, covered with Scotty's blankets. He looked so sweet and cuddly as he laid in his drawer bed.

After a few months I no longer waited up for Greg, because I wasn't getting very much sleep. Scotty wanted a bottle at least every four hours. There were some times that I would be up feeding the baby when Greg got home; other times I was sound asleep when he got home.

A few more months went by, and I still couldn't get Scotty on a good schedule. I figured if he woke up and cried, he was hungry, so I gave him a bottle.

One early morning I was slightly awakened by Scotty's little gurgles and cries. This had been the third time tonight that he was awake and crying. Half asleep and in a drowsy condition I said, "Go back to sleep, Scotty, Mommy's tired." Then I fell back to sleep....

All of a sudden I was fast awakened by screams and cries, coming from the floor. To my dismay, the baby must have raised himself up and tumbled out of the dresser.

I was horrified. I didn't think he was old enough to stand up by holding on to the edge of the drawer. Scotty was screaming as I jumped up and grabbed him. I held him tight in the dark bedroom, saying over and over again, "Mommy's sorry, Scotty. Momma's so sorry."

Shirley came running into the room, turning on the light. "Give me that child; let me see if he's all right!"

In a panic, I handed her my baby. We both examined him thoroughly. He had a huge bruise on his head and one on his arm. About that time Greg got home. He heard Scotty crying in the bedroom and shouted at me, "Lorraine, get that kid a bottle!"

We came out of the bedroom with Scotty in Shirley's arms.

"What's going on?" Greg asked, his breath stinking of alcohol.

I was crying as I explained to him what had happened. "We've got to get Scotty to the hospital! He fell out of the dresser drawer."

Greg slurred out, "What kind of a mother are you, anyway? Letting our little baby fall like that. Didn't you get up when he cried?"

"I'm all ready blaming myself," I said. "I don't need you to make me feel worse! Besides, if you would have gotten him a crib like you promised, this wouldn't have happened!"

The three of us spent several hours in the ER room, having X-rays and waiting for the doctors. We were relieved to find out that our baby didn't have a concussion or any broken bones. Thank goodness, he only had some nasty bruises.

When we got home from the hospital and got Scotty settled down in our bed, Greg told me he wanted to talk. I put Scotty in the middle of the bed with a pillow on each side of him, and then went in the living room with Greg. "Greg, can you make this quick? I'm really tired."

"Okay, Lorraine. I just want you to know that I feel really bad about the crib. In fact, I know there's a lot of things that Scotty needs, or will need. That's why I've decided to take a part-time job that Larry offered me."

"Who's Larry?"

"He owns the bar where I stop at. He said he could use another bartender."

"But you work a full-time job now! You're always exhausted. How could you possibly work another one?"

"You let me worry about it, okay? I can get some speed from a guy at work. He takes it all the time, and you should see him work. The guy's never tired! The kid needs things, Lorraine. How else can I afford to buy them?"

Greg took the part-time bartender job and, as he promised, in two weeks he bought Scotty a crib at the Goodwill Store. It wasn't as nice as the one I saw at first, but at least Scotty had a crib.

In spite of the part-time job, money seemed to be just as tight as always. I could see the toll that Greg's long hours were taking on him. He was more irritable and harder to talk to. I had to walk on eggshells to avoid an argument. When I asked him where the extra money from his new job went, he would get violent.

He didn't get home one morning until 6:30. I was already up with Scotty. Of course I was worried about him. I thought he'd been in an accident or something worse. When he walked in all in one piece, I began to question him. "Where have you been? Do you know what time it is?"

Greg looked at me with a strange expression. "What are you doing up this time of morning?"

"Greg, it's 6:30. I'm always up at this time with the baby."

"Wow, man, I didn't know it was so late."

"It's obvious you're high. I thought you were working last night."

"I did! I had a couple of shots when I was working; then I really got sleepy for some reason. One of my customers sold me some cocaine. He said it would stimulate me, and oh man, did it! After work I sat around with a couple of guys just to unwind."

I finished feeding the baby and went and laid him down. I was still steaming at Greg when I walked back into the living room. "How dare you spend our money on expensive drugs! No wonder there's never enough money for anything."

Greg's peace-loving mood changed in an instant. "Just one minute, you little witch! It's my money! I don't remember you going out there working your tail off like I do."

"Well, I work hard taking care of your baby and the apartment. I cook for you whenever you want me to. This is a partnership."

"Okay, little partner, go do your part. Fix me a big breakfast. Not just some eggs and toast, I want the works. I want some potatoes and steak with them too."

"But that steak is for dinner today. That's all the meat we have."

"I don't care. Fix it now!"

After breakfast Greg laid down and tried to sleep, but he couldn't. He got up and paced back and forth.

I didn't want to approach him in that condition, but I didn't have a choice. In as sweet a voice as I could muster, I said, "Greg, the baby is almost out of clothes, and you need some work uniforms washed. I need some money to go to the Laundromat today."

Greg gave me a sarcastic look. "I ain't got any money."

"But you know I always go to the Laundromat on Wednesdays. Maybe you shouldn't have spent all your money on drugs!"

Greg's face got bright red. Next thing I knew Greg's fist was coming right at my eye. As he hit me square in the eye, I fell backwards, and blood poured out of my nose.

Greg grabbed me. "I'm sorry baby, I'm sorry. I'll never do it again."

"You said that the last time you hit me," I cried.

"I know, but I'm so sorry. I promise, this will be the last time."

A couple hours later Greg was asleep and I was in the bathroom, trying to cover up my black eye with makeup.

Shirley walked in. "Let me see your eye, dear."

I tried to turn from her. "It's okay."

"Lorraine, you have to learn not to push Greg when he's high. You were asking for trouble."

"I wasn't pushing him, Shirley. He knows I always go to the Laundromat on Wednesdays. How does he expect me to wash his dirty work clothes if I don't go? Then he's got extra clothes that he needs for his bartending job. Not to mention our baby's clothes. What does he want me to do? Use rags for Scotty diapers?"

"All I'm saying is, when he's drunk is not a good time to bring up money to him."

"Or you mean when he's high on drugs?"

"My boy doesn't do drugs, does he?"

"Oh yes he does, Shirley!"

She looked surprised, but I knew that she knew. She had to know.

Shirley went and got her purse. She pulled out a five-dollar bill. "Here—will this do the washing you need?"

I took the money and thanked her.

⌘ ⌘ ⌘

At The Great White Throne Judgment I cried out to Jesus, "How could Greg have done that to me? He promised to love Scotty and me. If he loved our baby, he would have given him the things that he needed. And if he loved me so much, how could he physically abuse me?"

"GREG LOVED YOU AND SCOTTY, BUT IN AN EARTHLY WAY. HE WAS NOT A RIGHTEOUS MAN, SO HE WAS UNABLE TO LOVE YOU IN A CHRISTIAN MANNER. FOR A CHRISTIAN, THE BIBLE IS A GUIDE TO LIFE. IT GIVES A DETAILED PLAN ON HOW A MAN OR A WOMAN IS TO ACT TOWARDS THEIR LOVED ONES. WITH ME IN THEIR HEARTS, THEY CAN OBTAIN THESE GOALS.

"GREG WANTED TO TAKE CARE OF YOU AND YOUR BABY, BUT HE FELL SHORT. BECAUSE OF THIS, HE FELT GUILT. HE USED ALCOHOL TO COVER HIS

GUILT. HE WORKED TWO DEMANDING JOBS TO MAKE ENDS MEET. THE TWO JOBS PUT SUCH A STRAIN ON HIM THAT HE TURNED TO HEAVY DRUGS TO KEEP HIMSELF GOING. THE GUILT, ALCOHOL, AND DRUGS ALL WERE A FACTOR THAT LED HIM TO PHYSICALLY ABUSE. WHEN MAN LIVES IN SIN, ONE EVIL ACT FOLLOWS ANOTHER. FOR WHOSOEVER COMMITTETH SIN IS THE SERVANT OF SIN.

"I, YOUR GOD, AM AGAINST THOSE WHO ABUSE OTHERS. IN LEVITICUS 19:18 IT SAYS: 'YOU SHALL NOT TAKE VENGEANCE, NOR BEAR ANY GRUDGE AGAINST YOUR NEIGHBORS, BUT LOVE THEM AS YOURSELF; I AM THE LORD. MARRIAGE IS HONORABLE AMONG ALL, AND THE BED UNDEFILED; BUT FORNICATORS AND ADULTERERS GOD WILL JUDGE.[6]

"IT IS GOOD THAT A MAN AND WOMAN MARRY BECAUSE OF SEXUAL IMMORALITY. EACH MAN SHOULD HAVE HIS OWN WIFE, AND EACH WOMAN SHOULD HAVE HER OWN HUSBAND. IN THE HOLY SCRIPTURES IT TEACHES: HUSBANDS, LOVE YOUR WIVES, JUST AS CHRIST ALSO LOVED THE CHURCH AND GAVE HIMSELF FOR HER. SO HUSBANDS OUGHT TO LOVE THEIR OWN WIVES AS THEIR OWN BODIES; HE WHO LOVES HIS WIFE LOVES HIMSELF."[7]

22

With Scotty in one arm and the other loading clothes into a washer, I proceeded to do my most dreaded job—washing clothes at the Laundromat. I had lugged Scotty and the laundry four long blocks. My huge basket held four loads, and the baby rode on top of the pile. Now that was some juggling act, believe me. So here I was at the Laundromat, stinky diapers and all. Nothing was more embarrassing to me than to air my dirty laundry in public.

There was a black lady next to me that just finished loading her washing machine. She watched me struggle to manage my active baby in one hand and the dirty clothes in the other and smiled. "Hi, you look like you could use a third hand, girl."

"Yeah, that's for sure!"

"If you like, I could hold your baby while you finish loading," she said with a hesitant smile.

At first I didn't want to trust Scotty with this stranger, but her friendly expression appeared so sincere. I was touched by her generosity. "Sure, thanks," I said as I handed her my baby. As I was loading the machines, I could hear her talking and playing with Scotty. When I finished, I went and sat down beside her and reached for my baby.

"Thanks a lot!" I told her. "That was such a big help. You are really good with kids. Do you have any of your own?"

"Yes, I sure do. Mine are all growing up. I miss not having little babies anymore. God blessed me with six children. The youngest one is starting middle school already, and I have one starting college."

"Wow, no wonder you are so good with babies. By the way, my name is Lorraine."

"Lorraine, it is a pleasure meeting you! I'm Dina. You kind of remind me of my oldest girl; she's about your age. If I'm too nosy, tell me. But how did you get that big shiner?"

I'm sure she could tell I was embarrassed by her question. Apparently the makeup I put on earlier didn't do a very good job covering it up. Also, my hair that I brushed over that eye was not doing its job.

"That's okay, girl, you don't have to say. I've seen enough black eyes to know where they come from."

Glancing at her sheepishly, I asked, "Does your husband hit you?"

"Oh, honey, thank the Lord no! I made sure when I was picking my mister out that he was a good Christian man. That's a pretty good insurance that you will have a good stable life and a good daddy for your kids. No, I work as a clerk for Social Services. I see plenty of black eyes and worse that come through the door."

I hung my head. "I guess I had it coming. Greg is trying very hard to make a living for us, and I get too impatient with him."

"Honey, you're making excuses for your husband. No man has the right to hit his wife under any circumstances."

"Well, Greg really isn't my husband, so that's why I need to work harder on being more patient with him."

"No, you don't! You can break away from this abusive man easier because he's not your husband."

"But Scotty's his child, and when I turn eighteen, we're going to get married. We would have gotten married before, but my father wouldn't allow it."

"Sorry to say, child, but maybe your father was right. Maybe he could see that this was an abusive boy. Is Greg a Christian?"

"I don't know; we never talk about God."

"Are you?"

"I think there must be a higher power, like God. I went to church when I was younger, but I'm not sure if I believe everything that I heard or not. Besides, if there is a God, he's probably given up on me already."

"Lorraine, honey, God would never give up on you, so you must never give up on him."

I was relieved when I saw her washing stop. All this talk was making me really nervous.

About the time Dina's clothes were all loaded, my washing stopped. Again she offered to hold Scotty, and again I was happy for her help. When I sat down beside her again, she gave me a card. "When you have had enough of being abused, call this number. It's a home for abused women. They help you get on your feet so you can become self-sufficient."

I took the card. "Thanks, but I'm sure things will get better when we get married."

"Don't count on it. With an abuser, they usually get worse. If he will beat you up as a girlfriend, believe me, he will do it when you're his wife.! Then you will be more committed to this guy. Marriage vows are not to be taken lightly. Do your cute little baby and yourself a favor and call. Get out before it's too late."

In the weeks that followed Dina's words kept haunting me. Not only that I should leave Greg, but the question she asked me: was I a Christian? Did I really believe there was a God? Though the Holy Spirit was putting conviction in my heart, I pushed it aside, because my life felt so uncontrollable.

The next time Greg hit me, I fell down against our bed and scraped my back all up. Scotty's crib was in our small bedroom, so it woke him up. He was screaming at the top of his lungs when he saw me lying helplessly on the floor.

Greg of course picked me up and did his normal guilt thing again. "Oh, baby, please forgive me. I'm sorry! I didn't know I hit you so hard." He laid me on the bed, went to the bathroom, and got a cold cloth to put on my back. "I love you, baby! Why do you push me when you know I'm tired?"

I didn't answer him and rolled over and tried to sleep. I wished I would stop crying so I could get to sleep, but thoughts of the place that Dina told me about kept ringing in my ear. *How could I go on with my son witnessing my abuse? What might that do to him? Maybe Greg will even abuse Scotty when he gets older. Will the abuse get worse like Dina said...even more if I marry him?*

After Greg left for work the next night, I packed a couple of bags with mostly Scotty's things and walked out the door. Earlier I had called that number from the card Dina had given me, and my new life was waiting for me only a few miles away and a bus trip.

⌘ ⌘ ⌘

As I stood at The Great White Throne Judgment, I could see the fear and pain in my heart as I took the bus, out of Greg's life. I asked Jesus, "Was I wrong to leave, Greg? Should I have stayed and taken his physical abuse? What could I have done differently?"

"What you did wrong was not opening your heart up to the Holy Spirit when He was calling you. Dina was one of my dear children that I sent to you. She planted another seed in your heart. I was right there at your heart's door, but you turned me away again. You were more interested in the problems of the world, than to concern yourself with your eternity.

"You did the right thing by taking Dina's advice to leave a man who would physically abuse you. But you fell short when you did not open your heart to Me."

23

As I laid on a hard, lumpy mattress staring up at the ceiling, I felt alone and trapped. My baby boy and I were now living in a one-room residence. There was only enough room for a twin bed, a crib, and a few of our belongings. The facility also housed five other battered women and their children. We had a common lounge (with a television), a dining hall, and a kitchen for all of us to share. We also shared a bathroom that had a couple of private toilets and showers. On the wall of the kitchen was a list of our names, along with our cleaning assignments for the week.

After a few days of getting settled in, a woman by the name of Linda Morris invited me into her office. She said, "Please, Lorraine, have a seat. How has it been going for you? Did you get everything that you needed?"

"Yes, thank you very much. Thanks for all the toiletry and the disposable diapers. It seemed so good not to worry about washing all those cloth diapers!"

"Did those donated clothes fit you and Scotty?"

"Oh, yes, they were wonderful. Thank you!"

"There are some terrific Christians who sponsor this program. Is Scotty adjusting okay?"

"Yeah."

"How about you?"

"Well, yeah, I guess," I said in a low voice. "My baby and I are warm, getting fed good, and have a roof over our heads. I suppose that should be enough, right?"

"Lorraine, your happiness is the ultimate goal here. I realize that living here really can't do that for you. This home is not designed for that purpose. It is for the reasons you just mentioned: to keep you warm, fed, and safe. But there are other aspects that are just as important. We give you all your basic needs, leaving you time to reevaluate your life. We also like to discourage our guests from going back to an abusive lifestyle. No woman desires to be abused. Of course the decision is yours; you are a free agent here. However, we find that the abuser will continue to abuse, and in many cases the abuse will get worse. The only way I would recommend a reconciliation is if both parties are in counseling for at least six months before reuniting."

"You don't have to worry about that. It's definitely over for Greg and me. I've made up my mind that I never want to go back to him. It's just that I'm really confused and I don't know what direction to go in. I'm not even aware of the options I have."

"You don't have any regrets about leaving Greg then?"

"No!" My voice lowered. "I gave up everything when I ran away with Greg. I know now that I was only using him as a way out. I was pregnant and I didn't want an abortion—or to give my baby away. The only way that my parents would let me stay was to abort or adopt the baby out. When I ran away with Greg, my father disowned me. Greg promised me that he would be different than my dad. He was different all right…at least my father didn't beat me up. I can never forgive Greg for that.

"Before Greg came into my life, things weren't that great at home either, but at least I had all the luxuries that money could buy. I had my own credit card, and I had so many neat clothes. Some I had to leave at my parents' home; the rest I had to leave at Greg's. I also had a wonderful future planned. I was going to be a lawyer, like my father. He's very successful. I wanted so badly to make him proud of me. Now look at me, I'm nothing." I buried my head in my hands and cried.

Mrs. Morris put her hand on my shoulder. "Lorraine, look at me. You are still that same girl! You still have the same potential within you. Yes, you have made some wrong decisions along the way, but now is the time to start making the right ones. Think about your son, Scotty. You have your baby to consider now. The next thing you need to do is get your life in order and stand on your own two feet. Lorraine, you can make that happen for you, as well as for that adorable baby of yours."

"You are absolutely right, but how can I do it? Where do I start? I didn't even finish high school!"

"That would be a good start—getting your diploma. But first of all, we need to get you set up in your own home. Do you feel strong enough to work on that, Lorraine?"

"Yes, but I can't understand how. If there is a way, I'll do it!"

"I'm going to make a few calls and then we will go from there. First of all, I'm going to call the Friend of the Court's office. I'll make an appointment for you to meet with them. They will help you get child support from Greg. His name is on the birth certificate, isn't it?"

"Yes, it is."

"Good! Then I'll call the ADC office to see how they can help. They give living expenses and food stamps."

When I heard ADC and food stamps, I thought I was going to die from humiliation. "That's welfare, isn't it?"

"Why, yes, does that bother you?"

"Well, yeah! It's so belittling. I mean, just a little over a year and a half ago I lived in an affluent family, and now you are suggesting I have to live on welfare. There has got to be another way!"

"Perhaps you could call your parents and beg them to forgive you and give you another chance. Perhaps if they know you are not with Greg any more, they will be happy to welcome you home."

"Not with Scotty! That's the whole point with them. I would be too much of an embarrassment for them having a baby out of wedlock. I'm quite sure they told all their acquaintances (and my friends) that I've gone to Europe to finish high school and college. My father said he doesn't want anything more to do with me; he's disowned me."

Mrs. Morris tried to console me as I broke out in tears again. She gave me a hug. "I am so sorry, dear."

"Don't be. I can get along in this world without my parents."

"Yes, you can," Mrs. Morris said in a determined way. "And remember that welfare is not a permanent situation. Once you get a place to live, you will get a job, and before you know it, you will be off welfare in no time."

I sighed. "I can see it now: high school dropout and no experience. All I'll be able to get is a minimum-wage job. Once I pay the babysitter, all my money will be gone. How am I supposed to support Scotty and me that way?"

"You just have to take one step at a time. You told me you didn't want to go back to being abused. You said there was no way your parents would help you, right?"

"Right."

"Okay, then you have to start somewhere. It's time you put your needs above your pride. Going on welfare is a starting point."

"You're right. I'm sorry, Mrs. Morris. I understand what you are saying. I'll do it, but it's not going to be easy. It certainly isn't easy going from a rich girl to a poor one. I hate being poor. Please, make those calls for me. I really do appreciate your help."

My visit to the Friend of the Court was a disappointment, a dead-end. The office had called the foundry and found out that Greg had been fired from his job. The bartender job didn't count because he got paid over the counter. They told me I could come back when he began to work again.

As I sat in the waiting room full of people at the Welfare Department, I felt so out of place. I wanted to get up and run out. *Man, there's a bunch of losers in here. But if they're losers, what does that make me?*

It was so difficult to keep Scotty occupied, and I had to wait over two hours before I could get in to see a caseworker. When the receptionist called my name, I put Scotty on my hip and followed her down a maze of cubical offices.

Without looking up at me, the caseworker said, "Have a seat." She was busily looking though a stack of files. When she finally looked up, her glasses hung from the ridge of her nose. Her face stayed rigid as she handed me a booklet and gave me a three-minute tour on it. She gave me a quick explanation on how to fill it out. Then she said, "Take it home, fill it out. When you have it completed, mail it back into the department. If you qualify, I will send you a notice. Then you can call the office for another appointment."

With my mouth wide open, I stood in front of her. Then I said, "But, lady, my baby and I have been living in a shelter for three weeks now. We have to get out of there. Can't you make it any faster?"

The woman glared at me over the top of her glasses. "You should be grateful you have a roof over your head. Some of the people on my case load are living on the streets. You are not the only one in this city who needs help. You have to wait until all the proper paperwork is in." She closed my file with a bang and slapped it on top of the rest of the files. "You see this pile of files? We are all overworked and underpaid here at Social Services. You will have to be patient and wait your turn like the rest of the needy people. Now, anymore questions? If not, my next client is waiting."

I was so upset with that woman, I never wanted to go back to the welfare office again, but my need was too great. So I jumped through all the hoops and finally got my second appointment. This time I got smart and asked one of the mothers at the shelter to watch Scotty for me. That was good, because I had to wait just as long this time.

The receptionist explained as we walked down the hall that I would be seeing a different caseworker today. I thought, *Thank goodness for that!*

I sat down in the cubicle the receptionist pointed to. This time I was sitting across a small desk from a man. He held his hand out and shook mine as he said, "Ms. Patterson, I'm Mr. Endsley. I'm the educational specialist. Today we'll be running a battery of tests, if that is all right with you?"

"Sure, of course."

"Fine, then let's get started." After being tested for almost three hours, I felt drained. I was told to wait out in the lobby again while the tests were evaluated. After another hour I was called back to Mr. Endsley's cubicle.

He was sitting there shuffling through my test papers. He looked up at me. "Ms. Patterson, according to your test scores, you are a very intelligent young lady. I can see great potential here, but it will take a lot of hard work! Are you up to it? Are you willing to give it your best shot?"

"I guess so. What do I need to do?"

"We have an experimental program here at the Social Services department. It would be a golden opportunity for you. It is basically a training program. You will receive ADC funding as you go through the program. Upon completion, it will make you more marketable in the job market. It will open up opportunities in the clerical field, helping you to soon get off the welfare line."

I smiled causally at him. "That sounds great, but how can I participate in this program without a high school diploma?"

"That, my dear, is another advantage of this program. While you are training, we can also help you earn your GED, an equivalent of a high school diploma. We have two openings right now. Are you interested?"

"Of course I am! But did I hear right: I will be earning the money that welfare is going to give me? Like a real job?"

"You can say that, yes. You would be working and learning all at the same time, while receiving a check from the department."

"That sounds super, but I don't know how I could afford a babysitter for my baby."

"That's no problem either. We have a daycare center set up here for working mothers. As long as you are in this program, it will be one of your benefits."

"Great! When do I start? I can't think of any reason why I shouldn't go for it. Thanks, Mr. Endsley. I'm grateful for the opportunity!"

⌘ ⌘ ⌘

Now when I was standing before The Great White Throne Judgment I again had tears, but I wasn't feeling tears of sorrow or pain. They were tears of joy, because of the love and help that these people were giving me.

"Lord, why were these strangers—Linda Morris and the church people who sponsored the home for abused women—so willing to help people like me who are in need? I didn't know there were such caring people in this world. I thought everyone was only looking out for themselves."

"CHRISTIANS ARE THE LIGHT OF THE WORLD. WHEN I WALKED ON THIS EARTH, I TAUGHT MY FOLLOWERS:

LET YOUR LIGHT SO SHINE BEFORE MEN, THAT THEY MAY SEE YOUR GOOD WORKS AND GLORIFY YOUR FATHER IN HEAVEN.[8]

THIS IS MY COMMANDMENT THAT YOU LOVE ONE ANOTHER AS I HAVE LOVED YOU.[9]

LET BROTHERLY LOVE CONTINUE. DO NOT FORGET TO ENTERTAIN STRANGERS, FOR BY SO DOING SOME HAVE UNWITTINGLY ENTERTAINED ANGELS.[10]

WHEN THE SON OF MAN COMES IN HIS GLORY, AND ALL THE HOLY ANGELS WITH HIM, THEN HE WILL SIT ON THE THRONE OF HIS GLORY. ALL THE NATIONS WILL BE GATHERED BEFORE HIM, AND HE WILL SEPARATE THEM ONE FROM ANOTHER, AS A SHEPHERD

DIVIDES HIS SHEEP FROM THE GOATS. AND HE WILL SET THE SHEEP ON HIS RIGHT HAND, BUT THE GOATS ON THE LEFT. THEN THE KING WILL SAY TO THOSE ON HIS RIGHT HAND, 'COME, YOU BLESSED OF MY FATHER, INHERIT THE KINGDOM PREPARED FOR YOU FROM THE FOUNDATION OF THE WORLD: FOR I WAS HUNGRY AND YOU GAVE ME FOOD. I WAS THIRSTY, AND YOU GAVE ME DRINK. I WAS A STRANGER AND YOU TOOK ME IN. I WAS NAKED AND YOU CLOTHED ME. I WAS SICK AND YOU VISITED ME. I WAS IN PRISON AND YOU CAME TO ME.'

THEN THE RIGHTEOUS WILL ANSWER HIM SAYING, 'LORD, WHEN DID WE SEE YOU HUNGRY AND FEED YOU, OR THIRSTY AND GIVE YOU DRINK? WHEN DID WE SEE YOU A STRANGER AND TAKE YOU IN, OR NAKED AND CLOTHE YOU? OR WHEN DID WE SEE YOU SICK, OR IN PRISON, AND COME TO YOU?' AND THE KING WILL ANSWER AND SAY TO THEM, "ASSUREDLY, I SAY TO YOU, INASMUCH AS YOU DID IT TO ONE OF THE LEAST OF THESE, MY BRETHREN, YOU DID IT TO ME."'[11]

24

The weeks that followed were very challenging for me. It was a good thing that I was a fast learner. I had to work under stressful deadlines on the clerical duties, but I loved it. Sometimes while working on arranging case files, typing, or just doing the filing, I would make believe that I was an attorney gathering my research files for important law cases. At night I studied for my GED. That left the weekends to search for an apartment.

When I turned eighteen, I had been living at the shelter for two months and now was able to move Scotty and me into our very first apartment. It was far from the luxurious home I was raised in, but it was all mine! I did it on my own (well maybe with a little help). This was my first taste of independence, and I loved it.

The next week I was on cloud nine, telling everybody at the office about my good news, my new apartment. When I told Mr. Nickles, my supervisor (who was also my caseworker), he said, "That's great news Lorraine. I have some more good news for you: you have passed your GED. And that's not all. You passed it with a very high score!"

I let out a squeal of joy and clapped my hands.

"Do you know what that means?" he asked. "It means you have good enough grades from your old high school records and your GED scores that you could be accepted by a variety of colleges. All you have to do is pick a college of your choice, and if you are accepted, you can be starting as soon as this fall."

"That is so wonderful, Mr. Nickles. I can't believe it; I'll be starting college at eighteen, just as I had always planned! Mr. Nickles, you don't know how happy you have made me!"

I thought for a minute and then felt like the bottom dropped out from under me again.

Mr. Nickles must have picked up on my mood swing, for he asked, "What's the matter? Do you have a problem?"

"Yeah! How am I supposed to pay for college? Especially six years of it? That's how long it takes to become a lawyer. I have to scrape every penny I get now to pay my bills. How can I afford college?"

"Is that all you're worried about?" He laughed. "That's what I've been trying to tell you. You go out and pick the college of your choice, and your college tuition (including books and supplies) will all be taken care of through a special grant that the federal government is issuing right now. Along with that, you'll continue getting ADC, with extra for babysitting expenses!"

I jumped up and down in excitement and shouted, "Wow! I'm going to college! And I'm going to be a lawyer!" *Maybe then my father will forgive me and finally be proud of me.*

It took me another month to decide on the perfect college, and I had no problem getting accepted. Now with all that behind me, I was ready to let Mr. Nickles know that he could get my grant started.

When I walked into his office, I was so excited, I could barely talk. "Mr. Nickles, I've done it! I've got my college picked out and have already been accepted. On top of that, I can even get into a low-housing apartment just off from the campus. I am so psyched!"

Mr. Nickles sat at his desk with his fingers forming a tepee and leaning his chin on them, looking up at me with a blank expression. After a few seconds of silence, he cleared his throat. "Lorraine, I have some bad news for you. Please, have a seat."

My heart stopped as I braced myself with my hand on his desk. I slowly sunk into the chair across from his desk.

He cleared his throat again and spoke in a very soft tone, "A week ago I got a memo that said the government has put a freeze on all college grants right now. Perhaps in the near future they will open them up again, but for now, I'm sorry to say there is no money available at this time for you."

Boiling with rage, I said, "You knew this for a whole week, and you said nothing?"

"Lorraine, I was going to tell you last week, but I've been so swamped I didn't get a chance. I didn't hear you talk about it lately, so I wasn't sure you were still making plans. I'm really sorry about this."

"Sorry? How could you get my hopes so high and then dash them? Couldn't you have started the paperwork sooner, and then they would have had to acknowledge it?"

"Well, yes, but I've been making out paperwork for only the people who have everything in order. If I would have known you were so close to it, I would have. Lorraine, I'm not responsible for what the federal government does. When they get short on funding, they have to stop the grants."

"But you knew how much this meant to me! I'm not just one of your case loads, I work for you."

"Yes, Lorraine, and I'm truly sorry. But the good news is, you can continue working the program here at the department. When there is a clerical opening, you can put in for it."

I left his office crying and avoided him for the rest of the day. I couldn't wait until it was time to go home. I sure wasn't productive while I was there. When I got home, I was so angry, I even got upset with Scotty. That evening I couldn't stand sitting around my apartment. I was too mad.

I called my next-door neighbor and asked if her sixteen-year-old daughter could come over and watch Scotty for a while, and she agreed.

I walked several blocks and then spotted a red neon light blasting out the word *BAR* in big bold letters. The sign seemed to draw me in. I walked into the dark bar, and it was full of men. I could feel their eyes on me as I slid onto a bar stool. I was really nervous, because I had never been to a bar by myself before. I was about to order a Coke when some guy walked up and sat on the barstool next to me. "Give her a Strawberry Daiquiri on me. This lovely lady deserves the best drink you got, Jake."

The bartender looked at me blankly and asked, "Is that okay with you, lady?" *He's not even going to check to see if I'm old enough?*

"Yes...thank you."

The last thing I wanted that evening was to pick up some bozo in a bar. When he finally got the message, some other guy took his place trying to convince me that he was madly in love with me. At least, I didn't have to buy a drink all night. I shuddered to think how much a Strawberry Daiquiri would cost. It tasted really good, and it sure was making me giddy. The bartender suggested that I switch to Coke at about one o'clock. I noticed that he charged my admirers for a whiskey and Coke, rather than just a Coke. Either that, I thought, or the price of Coke was really high at that bar. It was getting late, and my last pursuer of the night gave up on me and went home to his wife. The place emptied out, and it was only Jake and me left.

Jake put another Strawberry Daiquiri in front of me and said, "One for the road, honey."

With a slur to my speech I said, "Thanks, Jake, you're a pretty good fellow. How long have you been bartending here?"

"I've been tending bar here for ten years. Last year I finally saved up enough money and bought out the owner. Now it's my joint. It's not so bad on the weekends; you should come in then. We have a three-piece band that plays and not a bad dance floor."

"Cool, I love to dance!"

"And I'd like to be the lucky guy dancing with you. On the weekends, I have more employees working. Maybe sometime I could get a dance?"

Jake wasn't too bad looking, but definitely not my type. Besides, he was at least thirty years older than me, at least as old as my father. The thought disgusted me, but I decided one dance wouldn't kill me.

"Sure Jake, if I stop in again. The only reason I'm here tonight is because I'm so bummed out and mad."

"What does a beautiful woman like you have to be mad about?"

I told him all about working at Social Services. I complained about all the hoops that the welfare department had put me though and the endless filing I had to do. I told him about the one thing that made me the most upset tonight, which was Mr. Nickles' promise that all my college would be paid! I poured my heart out to Jake about how much going to college meant to me, and how hard I had worked to find the perfect college. I even told him how hard it was to make a living for me and my baby.

Like a good bartender, Jake listened sympathetically to every word. When I was finished, he said, "You are right, gorgeous, you don't need all the hassle welfare puts you through. It was wrong getting all your hopes and dreams built up, just to crash them all in front of you."

"You're right," I said. A big hiccup followed, and I cupped my hands over my mouth and giggled.

Jake went on, "Why, those welfare people will tell you anything. They don't care about anything but their own hides. As long as they get their big paychecks, they could care less about the people they're supposed to be helping. You know something, pretty lady, you have got to look out for yourself in this world; because if you don't, no one else will!"

I took a big drink of my daiquiri, finishing it. Jake took my glass and replaced it with another he had been mixing while talking to me.

Slurring my words again, I said, "You are absolutely right, Jake! I'm so sick and tired of that stupid welfare system. All their red tape, not to mention all they put me through. One minute there's funding for college. Next minute, 'Oh I'm sorry.' I'm so sick of them having to know all about my business. When my ex-boyfriend gets another job and I can get child support from him, I'm going to tell that department what they can do with all their broken promises. I'll find a job, and then I can take care of me and my baby just fine!"

"That's the spirit, honey! Say, if you are serious, I could use another waitress/bartender around here. You'd be a natural. My locals sure loved you. You're captivating, charming, and witty. This place could use some class, and you are one classy lady. On top of that, you seem like a real smart gal. With all that going for you, the tips will be great. Besides, I can give you a fairly good salary. How about it? Do we have a deal?"

"How could I refuse such an offer? Now I can tell that old stuff shirt, Mr. Nickles, to take his welfare job and shove it!"

"Can you start tomorrow night at seven?"

"Sure, why not? I don't know how to thank you, Jake."

"You coming to work for me is all the thanks you can give me for now. But we do need to get this bar closed, before the liquor association closes me up."

"Got yah." I giggled. I tried to slide down off the barstool, but my legs felt like jelly.

Jake ran out from around the bar and grabbed me before I fell to the floor. That was the last thing I remembered until I woke up the next morning.

Pulling the pillow off my head, I finally realized that the noise I was trying to keep out was my baby crying. Scotty wasn't to be ignored any longer. He gave me his best roaring scream that the little tyke could give.

I sat up in a hurry and reached for the clock. *Oh my gosh, it's ten o'clock! No wonder Scotty is so upset. Oh no! I was supposed to be at work at eight! What am I going to do?*

"Don't cry, Scotty, Momma's coming." My head was throbbing in pain. When I grabbed my baby out of bed, his diaper almost fell off because it was so full. "Oh, you poor baby! Your mommy has been so naughty."

Scotty continued crying as I put him on my bed. I washed and powdered his behind and then put a new diaper on him. He continued to scream. I held him as I hurried into the kitchen to get his bottle. He was one starved little boy as he inhaled the milk. After I stripped the wet bedding from his crib and replaced it with clean ones, I laid my now contented baby down.

With my baby taken care of, I went into the bathroom and grabbed a couple aspirins out of the medicine cabinet. I threw them into my mouth and followed them down with two glasses of water. I was so thirsty! Then I went in the living room and looked at my watch again. *Oh no! Now it's 10:30 already! What am I going to do? Maybe I could call in sick. Tell them I was running a fever and just woke up. What happened to me? Didn't I set that alarm clock?*

I could only remember nearly falling off the barstool. From then on I had lost my memory. *Oh no, how did I get home, and undressed? I slightly remembered the bartender offering me a job and me saying yes, that I would take it. Oh no, the bartender!*

I rubbed my aching head, trying to figure out what to do. I wondered if Jake was really serious about the job offer, or if it was just a con. I called work and gave the receptionist a sob story about how sick I was and told her that I would be in tomorrow, or else I would call.

If Jake was serious about me working for him, I just won't show up for work tomorrow. Mr. Nickles doesn't deserve a notice after what he pulled on me. After the way I talked to him yesterday, I'm probably fired anyway. If I get that bar job, to heck with social services. Who needs it anyway? They're all a bunch of liars!

Starving, I went to the kitchen and opened the refrigerator. All I found was leftover pizza and a soda, so I made myself a breakfast out of them.

I went to the bar that evening to check out Jake's job offer.

He was there to welcome me with open arms and a big, cat-like smile as I walked in. "You were pretty loaded when you said you'd work for me. I hoped you wouldn't change your mind after I took you home, but I couldn't let you walk by yourself. You wouldn't have made it in your condition."

"Yeah, the drinks seemed to catch up with me all at once. Thanks for the ride." I was too embarrassed to mention what I surmised had happened, and I figured he was too. It was best not to say anything. I didn't want to jeopardize my new job with him.

"Hope you don't mind that I paid the sitter for you. She was a bit upset because it was so late. I overpaid her, but don't worry—it's on me. It made her smile again, anyway."

"Thanks."

⌘⌘⌘

Recalling this part of my life cut deep into my heart. I was so consumed in anger. I asked the Lord, "How could Mr. Nickles be so thoughtless to promise me something so important and then take it away again? I showed him. I showed that whole stupid welfare department that I didn't need them!"

"'Enter by the narrow gate; for wide is the gate and broad is the way that leads to destruction, and there are many who go in by it. Because narrow is the gate and difficult is the way which leads to life, and there are few who find it.'[12]

"Lorraine, the path you were taking at the social service department was a good, moral pathway for you to travel. Their office was offering you a great opportunity to improve yourself. If you would have been patient, they would have eventually made college obtainable for you.

"You took a spiral path down that led you to evil and immorality when you accepted the job at the bar. Working in an environment such as that led you to the wide path that leads to further sin and hell."

25

The job at Jake's seemed pretty exciting and glamorous. I was able to talk and joke with the customers and have fun along with them. But there were some parts of the job that weren't so glamorous. There isn't anything more stinky than a tavern at closing time. Scotty's diapers weren't even that bad! Like all the employees, I had to pitch in and do my share of cleaning. The bathrooms were the worst, especially the men's.

The weeks rolled on, and I soon became a very popular bartender. Jake's business steadily increased, and he said it was because of me. Jake's personal interest in me kept increasing. Then one night after closing, Jake poured me a drink and asked me to stay for a while, and unwind with him. He had a wife and two kids that he bragged to everybody in the bar about, but when he was there alone with me, his family never crossed his mind. At least he put them on the back burner. Unwinding with my boss became a habit. At least a couple times a week Jake and I sat around in the closed bar. We laughed, complained, and drank a lot of booze. There were even times when we would get carried away and turn to our lustful side.

During one of my shifts Steve, one of our regulars, asked me if I would like to join him at Dillon's when I got off from work. He explained that it was an after-hour bar. Steve had been trying to take me out for a long time. It sounded like fun, so I told him I'd go. It was a slow night, so I got out of there early. Jake looked rather jealous as I left the bar with Steve.

I loved the bar that Steve took me to. They had a three-piece band and a little dance floor. Now I could have fun and have a waitress wait on me. It became my favorite place to go after work. I stopped in there a couple times a week.

After a few weeks of stopping at my new after-hours spot, I was sitting at a table with some friends when a woman came up from behind me and shouted, "Lorraine! Is that you?"

I whirled around and about fell off my seat. "Yes! Kathy, tell me it's really you!" I jumped up, and we hugged.

"I thought you were still off to Europe, getting that big education."

"No, I'm afraid not. That's just the story my parents told everyone when I left."

"Where did you go?"

I told Kathy the whole story about how I got pregnant with Greg's baby, ran off with him, and what a jerk he had become. I also told her about my experience with welfare and explained that was the reason I was now a bartender at Jake's.

"Wow, that's some story! I never would have guessed. We all suspected you were pregnant at first, but your parents had us all convinced you went to Europe to study. So how are you doing, with a baby and all?"

"It's hard. I really love Scotty and wouldn't have changed having him for anything, but it has been a struggle. I make really good tips at Jake's, but it costs so much with rent, bills, and all the other household costs. And babies need a lot of stuff. Scotty's going to be two in a couple of months, and I can't keep that baby in clothes. He grows like a weed."

"Hey, I got an idea! My roommate, Dawn, and I live in this huge apartment here in New York, not too far from this neighborhood. It used to be a warehouse. It was converted into a loft. We love it, but it has really been a strain to keep up the rent, so we were thinking about getting another roommate. We don't want just anybody. It has to be someone we can have fun with, who likes to party! Dawn's got a ten-year-old daughter, so you guys could share babysitters when we go out. Matter of fact, what hours do you work?"

"From seven at night until closing."

"Super! You could save some on babysitters there too. Dawn has a day job. She leaves at 7:30 in the morning. You can watch each other's kids while the other one is working."

Kathy went on to tell me what my share of the rent and utilities would be. It was much cheaper then what I was paying; besides I loved the idea of living with my best friend. Of course I told her yes. I told her I would definitely move in with them, if it was okay with her roommate.

Within the week I was moving Scotty and me into our new loft with

Kathy and Dawn. I loved Dawn and her daughter, Rebecca, right from the start. We were like one big happy family. I was having the time of my life living with them. The three of us partied together a lot. There were times when Dawn and I couldn't find a babysitter, so Dawn felt confident that Rebecca was now old enough to watch over Scotty when we went out.

Even though I thought that this was the best time of my life, I was getting out of control. I started spiraling down the dark path of a destructive nightlife. I was consumed with neon lights, booze, and drugs. I still loved my little boy and took care of him the best I could, but when I was home with him I was drained from work and too much party life. Consequently, Scotty didn't get the attention he needed. My wants and needs always seemed to come before his.

Rebecca was a sweet girl, and I took way too much advantage of her. If she wasn't at school, I got her to watch Scotty while I caught up on my sleep. Scotty was a very active two-year-old and was into everything.

One night after work I stopped at Dillon's. I planned on only staying for a couple of drinks, but I met this really cool guy. Soon the sun was coming up before I knew it. I was flying pretty high and not only on lust. When I finally got back to my apartment, Rebecca was crying. I snapped at her, "What's the matter with you? Why are you crying?"

"Well, my momma had to leave to go to work, and Kathy didn't come home last night. You didn't come home either, so I couldn't leave Scotty and go to school. I can't be late for school again. My teacher told me I'd be suspended if I miss any more school."

I staggered over to her, put my arms around her, and slurred out, "I'm sorry, Rebecca, I didn't realize it was so late. I'll write you an excuse." When I finished the note I said, "Here you go, sweetie. I sure hope the teacher can read this. I can hardly read it myself."

After Rebecca stopped crying and was out the door to go to school, I turned on the television and put on a cartoon station. Then I placed Scotty in front of the set, hoping it would entertain him while I slept on the couch. It didn't take long before I heard him crying bloody murder. He had gone into the kitchen and had tried to get up to the table by climbing onto the chair. He didn't make it and received a terrible red egg on his forehead. I knew I had to keep both Scotty and me awake to make sure he didn't have a concussion.

Well, he lived through that one all right.

There was another morning that I pulled an all-nighter (unintentional of course). I got home about six that morning. Scotty was still sleeping, so I thought I'd catch a couple hours' sleep before he would wake me up. When I suddenly woke five hours later, it was eleven o'clock. I looked over at the crib, where I expected to see my baby, and he wasn't in it! He had never gotten out by himself before. I panicked and called for him. I went out in the living room, hoping maybe Kathy or Dawn was with him. Or maybe Rebecca stayed home from school and had him in her room. No one answered. I ran from one room to the other looking for my precious baby.

The last place I checked was the kitchen. There I found the poor little tyke. The refrigerator door was wide open, and he was sitting in front of it eating raw ground beef. It amazed me how he could get out of his crib without falling, then go to the kitchen and open the refrigerator door. Then he grabbed the meat and was able to bite off the plastic around it.

I sat down on the floor beside him and gently took the meat away from him. "You poor baby, you must be really hungry. Why didn't you come and get Mommy up?" I didn't really expect him to answer, but after what he had just done, I wouldn't count anything out.

All he could say was, "Mommy, Mommy, hungry."

"Yes, Scotty, Mommy knows." I picked him up under his arms and placed him carefully into his high chair. I didn't want his sagging full diaper getting on me. I wanted to get him fed before I did anything else. I threw some dry cereal on his tray and gave him a sippy cup with some milk in it and headed for the couch. I had just fallen off to sleep when Scotty began to scream.

I swore. "I guess there's just no rest for the wicked." *And I was very wicked last night,* I thought with a smile, recalling the new guy I'd met at Dillon's last night.

Most of Scotty's cereal and his sippy cup was lying on the floor. Half asleep I got him out of his high chair and took off his completely saturated, nasty diaper. I gave him a bath, fed him, and laid him down for a nap. I managed to get an hour nap before his crying woke me up again. I got him and placed him in front of the TV and turned on some kids' show. I flopped on the couch and was out like a light when I again was awakened by banging coming from the kitchen. Scotty was up to his favorite tricks, tearing the pots and pans out of the bottom cupboard. Just as I was about to retrieve our pots and pans, the phone rang.

"Yeah," I yelled in the phone.

"You're in your normal humor today, aren't you, Lorraine?"

"I'm not having a very good day. Who is this, and what do you want?"

"It's Greg's ma! I have some really bad news for you. Greg has been arrested for robbing a liquor store. He had a gun, Lorraine. They're talking about fifteen years in prison."

"So why are you calling me?"

"Why? For lands' sake, Lorraine, Greg is little Scotty's daddy. I thought you would want to know what has happened to him."

"Scotty's daddy…that's a laugh! He has only seen him once in this past year. And he hasn't paid one stinking penny for his support since I left him. You call that a daddy? To tell you the truth, Shirley, I could care less what happens to your son."

"You are a cruel, selfish girl! You know that this is all your fault, don't you?"

"*My* fault? What did I have to do with your son doing armed robbery?"

"You broke his heart when you ran off and took his son away. He really loved that kid. For some reason, God only knows why, he was heartbroken over you, too. If you would have stayed by him through the tough times, none of this would have happened."

I was so angry I lashed out. "Your son is nothing but a dope addict! He was too stoned all the time to keep any decent jobs. Of course he had to steal, so he could afford to support his habit. Don't try to blame your son's problems on me. The apple doesn't fall very far from the tree, does it, Shirley? His old man still is doing time, right?"

"Yeah, he will for a lot more years."

"Don't you think that the lifestyle you and your husband had may have a little bit to do with how he turned out?"

There wasn't any answer on the other end of the phone line…only heavy sobs and then a click of the receiver.

When Scotty was two and a half, I had to call 911, and the medics had to rush him to the hospital. He was burned severely over seventy percent of his body. After the doctor had him stabilized, he started drilling me as to what happened to my little boy. I was crying so hard, I could barely tell him.

"Doctor is he going to be okay?"

The doctor looked disgusted. "You are the boy's mother, aren't you?"

"Yes, of course I am."

"Your child has been through a terrible trauma, but with a few weeks of hospital stay, he should be fine. Perhaps he might need some skin grafting. Now I need some answers. How did this horrible thing happen?"

Between my sobs I said, "Well, I heard Scotty screaming in the kitchen. I jumped up and ran in there. I saw where he had pulled the coffee pot over on him. It was still steaming when I walked in. I didn't know what to do so I called 911. The ambulance got there in fifteen minutes and took him to the ER. It's all my roommate's fault! Dawn must have left the coffee pot plugged in. She always unplugs it before she leaves for work, because she knows how Scotty gets into everything. It's because of her that my poor baby is burned!"

"Who was watching your boy this morning?"

"I was, of course! I mean, I was there. I was in bed sleeping. Scotty was in his crib right next to me. He has learned to get out of it, but he's supposed to wake me when he gets up."

"He is only three, Ms. Patterson. According to the records, the incident happened at approximately 11:45 this morning. Surely your son wouldn't be sleeping that long. How do you take care of him when you are sleeping?"

"I usually always hear him when he gets up. I must have been extra tired this morning. I work until three in the morning, and I get very little sleep."

"If you need to sleep in the mornings, I suggest you bring in someone to watch over him during those hours. Next time it could be worse. You know, Ms. Patterson, I can still smell alcohol on your breath. I am thinking very seriously of turning this report into the proper authorities."

"No, please, Doctor, you can't do that. It was an accident! I'll never let anything like that happen again, I swear."

"I'll let it go now, even if it's against my better judgment. But if I ever see you and your son in here again because of your neglect or abuse, you can take it to the bank that I'm calling the authorities. If you love that little boy I suggest you take better care of him. A child is a very special gift from God."

⌘ ⌘ ⌘

After viewing these painful memories of my life, I fell down before the Lord, crying out with a broken heart, "Lord, I loved my little son so much. How could I have neglected him so? How could I put my own good times so much above his needs? I missed out on so much by not being a real mother to Scotty."

"I ALLOWED PAIN TO COME TO YOU THROUGH YOUR CHILD, SO YOU WOULD REALIZE YOUR SIN AND REPENT. THE DOCTOR WAS A SEED I GAVE YOU TO GRASP. HE TOLD YOU THAT A CHILD IS A PRECIOUS GIFT FROM GOD. MY HOLY SPIRIT WAS THERE ALSO, TUGGING AGAIN AT YOUR HEART. BUT ONCE AGAIN YOU WOULDN'T GIVE UP YOUR SELFISH, WICKED WAYS. IF YOU WOULD HAVE SURRENDERED TO THE HOLY SPIRIT, I WOULD HAVE SHOWED YOU MERCY AND ABUNDANTLY PARDONED YOUR SINS, FOR I AM A LOVING GOD.

"WHEN I WALKED WITH MY DISCIPLES AND PREACHED TO THE MULTITUDES, I BECAME ANGRY AT THE DISCIPLES WHEN THEY TRIED TO SEND A CHILD AWAY FROM ME. I TOLD THEM: 'LET THE CHILDREN COME TO ME, AND DO NOT FORBID THEM; FOR OF SUCH IS THE KINGDOM OF GOD.'[13]

"A CHILD IS THE MOST PRECIOUS GIFT I CAN GIVE A WOMAN. SHE IS TO NURTURE HER CHILDREN BY GIVING THEM CARE AND PROTECTION. BY HELPING THEM TO GROW AND DEVELOP THEIR LIFE. BY RAISING THEM UP SO THEY WILL RECEIVE THE KINGDOM OF HEAVEN."

"Please, Lord, let me go back and repent of my sins! I want to let my children know, before it is too late for them."

"THERE IS NO RETURN FROM THE GREAT WHITE THRONE JUDGMENT. YOU MADE YOUR DECISION WHILE YOU WERE YET ALIVE. NOW YOU MUST LIVE WITH IT FOR ALL ETERNITY."

26

It was a typical morning with Scotty watching cartoons, and me dozing on the sofa. I tried to sleep lightly but was unsuccessful. Instead of Scotty waking me up, the phone did. If it was another pesky telemarketer, I would give her or him a piece of my mind. I answered and on the other end heard a desperate voice.

"Lorraine, I need to see you."

"Who the heck is this?"

"It's your mother. Surely you haven't forgotten my voice, have you?"

"Now that you mention it, it has been a long time since I've talked to you. What's up? Why now?"

"You sound terrible, dear. Are you sick?"

"No, Mother, I'm not sick. You woke me up!"

"Why were you in bed at this hour? Do you still have your baby?"

"Of course I do! Scotty isn't exactly a baby anymore. He's three. He's right next to me watching cartoons. I was just dozing on the couch. At least I'm not sleeping until noon like you did when I was a little kid."

"You know perfectly well that I always had good nannies to watch over you. Three-year-olds are a handful; they take a lot of watching. I'm reasonably sure you can't afford a nanny, right?"

"No, I can't. Don't worry, Mother, I'm taking care of my son just fine. I don't need anyone else to help me raise my child."

"Can't you sleep at night when he is sleeping?"

"No, unfortunately I have to make a living. I work at a bar until closing."

"Oh, my land, my daughter is working in a bar?"

"Yes, Mother! I can't make that much anywhere else with my limited education. The tips are really great, and the customers love me."

"I can only imagine the clientele you run into there."

"All right, Mother, do you want me to hang up on you?"

"No, honey, I'm sorry. I didn't mean to upset you, or put you down. I still only want the best for you. It's a nasty world out there; you need to be so careful."

"How did you get my phone number?"

"I have employed a detective."

"Oh, I'm impressed! You've finally been missing me so much, you hired a detective. It would have been nice to hear from you sooner. I could have used the support."

"I'm sorry, honey, but your father forbid me to try to find you. Was it terribly hard on you?"

"Well, yeah! Greg became very abusive, so I had to move Scotty and me into a shelter for battered women."

"Oh, you poor thing! Did you get divorced from that bum?"

"Well, actually it worked out okay. I found out what he was like before I turned eighteen, so I never married him."

"That's good!"

Scotty was about to empty an ashtray out on the rug so I yelled, "No! Scotty! Bad boy." I grabbed him and set him down in front of the television again.

"Your son Scotty must be getting big now, right?"

"Yeah, your grandson is getting big. I can hardly keep him in clothes. He keeps me broke buying things for him. So why are you calling now? I haven't heard a single word from you in almost four years, since I was thrown out."

"Lorraine, I never wanted that to happen. It was all your father's doing. I wanted to call so many times, but he forbid me to do it. Besides, I've been a mess, a real basketcase, so your father says. I haven't been really good for anyone."

"I tried, Mother, to call several times. but the servants would only take messages. They wouldn't let me talk to anyone."

"That was orders from your father."

"Once when I called, I did get a hold of him. He assured me he still didn't want anything more to do with me. I thought he'd want to know he had a grandson. I asked to talk to you, but he wouldn't let me."

"Oh, my dear, I know. I have cried myself to sleep over this many a night, worrying about you and the fact that you were having a baby."

"Oh yeah! For all you knew I was dead, or maybe lost the baby! Father could care less, but how could you not want to know how I was?"

"I did want to see you, honey, but your father was so stubborn."

"I've been too busy to really miss him anyway!" I barked back. I wasn't sure who I was trying to convince—my mother or myself. I only know that I had a terrible gnawing in my heart.

"Lorraine, please, find it in your heart to forgive me. There's something I must tell you, but it can't be told over the phone. I must see you."

"You could come over here, but I'm sure you wouldn't be caught dead in this neighborhood."

"Lorraine, dear, can I get you to come over here, to the estate?"

"The great Patterson Estate? I thought I was never allowed to ever step one foot on that place again?"

"Dear, I'd never stop you from coming over here. Your father is gone on a business trip for a few days, so he'll never know you've been here. Please, Lorraine, will you come?"

"When I talked to him on the phone, he said he wasn't living at the estate anymore—that he lived full-time at his New York apartment. Has that changed?"

"Yes, Lorraine, that's part of what I need to talk to you about. But please, no more on the phone. Will you come?"

"If it is that important to you, Mother, then yes, I'll be there. I can be there within two hours. Is that okay?"

"Okay? That's great! Bring little Scotty. It's about time I got to know my grandson."

Driving up to my old, stately homestead brought back many memories in my mind. Some good, but most were unpleasant. My dread grew as I drew closer. I watched for the first glimpse of the old, massive, iron gate and its seemingly endless red brick fence. It was the one thing I always looked for as a child, to reassure me I was approaching the fortress. Now I was coming home again after almost four years, yet it really wasn't my home any longer. I was an outcast! A stranger in the home I grew up in. I wondered if my dream bedroom remained the same. Had my parents converted it into something else?

As I drove up to the gate, I was shocked to see a huge *For Sale* sign. I was shocked to think my parents would even consider selling their beloved estate.

I noticed that the gate was ajar, so I got out of the car and opened it manually. This was the first time I'd ever seen the gate unlocked. Could something be wrong?

When I parked and walked down the sidewalk and under the vine-covered arbor, I noticed that my mother was waiting at the open double doors. *I'm impressed, Mother. You're coming to the door to greet me instead of having one of the employees do it. Must be she misses me.*

Tears were running down my mother's cheeks as she opened her arms wide and gave me a big hug. "Come in, come in, my dear. Let me look at you. You are such a lovely, mature-looking woman now. You were a child when you left but now look at you. You're a beautiful woman! You sure are skinny, though. Do you get all the food you need? You aren't starving yourself, are you?"

"No, Mother!"

She reached for Scotty. "So, this must be Scotty". He was a bit reluctant, but after a little coaxing, he let her take him. "Oh boy, you are a big fellow, I can hardly hold you. I'm your grandmother, honey." He fussed a little, so she gave him right back to me.

"Come on into the dining room. I've prepared a special lunch for us."

"You've prepared?" I laughed. "Since when have you been doing any cooking?"

"I've had to, Lorraine. We had to let all of our employees go."

"You did what?"

"Yes, come sit at the table, and I'll tell you all about it over lunch."

Scotty and I sat down at mother's shiny, long Victorian table as she served and then joined us for lunch.

"Mother, I've been wanting to ask you, why is there a *For Sale* sign on the gate?"

"Well, dear, that in essence is the main reason I needed to talk with you today. However, it is a long story. I don't know where or how to begin."

"Just start at the beginning."

"Yes, I'll try. You were aware, I'm sure, that your father has had a lengthy affair with his secretary, Shelly."

"Yeah, I guess. I know the two of you fought about it all the time."

"Yes, and it was true! They did, in fact, have an adulterous relationship going on for years. Long story short, Shelly finally got tired of it and started dating another man. Jim wouldn't stop pursuing her, so she slapped him with a sexual harassment charge."

I sat, stunned. "What did he do about it?"

"You know how your father is: he was smug about it. Said Shelly didn't have a rat's chance against a top-notch lawyer like himself."

"Sounds like something he'd say. But he's right. He is a brilliant attorney, one of New York's best. I'm sure he got out of it, didn't he?"

"On the contrary! But in the meantime, he got all bent out of shape when she quit the firm and left him. I am of the opinion that he really missed the little tramp. However, it didn't take him long to find another secretary. He interviewed loads of them and ended up hiring a girl no older than you."

"Did you get a chance to meet her?"

"Yeah."

"Was she attractive?"

"Looked and acted like Marilyn Monroe."

"Oh, no! Could she even type?" I laughed.

"According to Jim, she was very qualified."

I laughed again. "Yeah, but at what?"

"Yeah, right! And you know, it didn't take your father long to be up to his old tricks again. After only three weeks on the job, Danielle socked him with another harassment charge."

"No!"

"She sure did. And with two harassment charges back to back, your father didn't have a chance. Why, it cost him a fortune in the lawsuit."

"Was he in trouble at the firm because of it?"

"What could they do? They had to fire him. That is a very prestigious firm with an outstanding reputation. They couldn't justify him staying, no matter how good of a lawyer he was."

"I'm sure he had no problem finding another position. He has an excellent reputation. He's won more cases than any other attorney in the city."

"Yes, but you have to remember, he has a new reputation now, as a supervisor with two sexual harassment charges hanging over his head."

"How long did it take him to get another position?"

"Over five months. The firm where he was hired is very small and not very reputable. His income has dropped substantially."

"You guys must have had to dip into the old nest egg, huh?"

"Nest egg? Don't I wish! There was no nest egg. Of course, the lawsuits put us back a lot, but we were living according to our means—basically from month to month. We lived a very high lifestyle, as you know. You never saw our yacht, did you?"

"No, I didn't, but I wasn't aware there was ever any money problem. I always pictured Father as being filthy rich and thought, if he wanted to, he could take off work for a year and sail around the world. I'm shocked!"

"You weren't the only one who was totally naive about the finances. Jim kept me completely in the dark. I never asked, because I never went without. I guess these last few years I've been out of touch with reality."

"Father must be devastated. He was so proud of his achievements."

"His pride has been shaken...but it's his own doing."

"Can't argue that."

"Even though this new firm is less than scrupulous, they insisted that he was to have no personal involvement with any employee, or he would be fired. That forced him to look elsewhere for his extramarital flings. He started going to strip joints and picking up the dancers."

"How do you know?"

"Because I didn't trust him and hired a private detective."

"I'm sure the strippers weren't cheap."

"No. Not like his freebees at the office were, that's for sure. He started drinking heavily and brought a lot of his clients to the strip joints. The detective said he threw around money like there was no tomorrow."

"How could he afford it?"

"He couldn't. The detective told me he was behind on all our bills. He also told me there was a rumor going around that he was dipping into the firm's profits...the firm, by the way, has connections to the Mafia."

I was stunned. "Ooh, you don't mess with those boys."

"No, you don't."

"If it's true, and they find him guilty, they could put Father away for a long, long time."

"You're right. That's why I needed to let you know ahead of time, to prepare you. I didn't want you to have to read it in the paper or see it on TV. But at this point, dear, it's only rumors, so don't dwell on it, okay?"

"He might be clever enough to get away with it," I said slowly, "and he's sure arrogant enough to think he can."

"That's true!"

"Oh, yes, one more thing. The detective found another tidbit of information. Jim has developed a gambling habit. According to the detective, he's going through a vicious cycle of winning and losing. Lately, he's been losing more than he's winning. I guess he keeps trying to recoup his losses. He still wins periodically; just enough to keep him baited."

"On top of everything else, Father is an impulsive gambler? I can't believe what he's doing to himself!"

My heart was crushed as I kissed my mother good night before I said good-bye. I still loved my father and hated what life had done to him. Mother and I promised each other that we would keep in touch, but it was not to be. I became too engrossed in my wild party life. And Mother, well, she slipped further into depression.

⌘⌘⌘

Sadly I stood before the Lord at The Great White Throne Judgment. My heart was crumbling as I felt my father's pain and humiliation. "Lord," I cried out, "my father had been such a successful man. He was full of pride over his accomplishments. Why did he have to be dragged down and degraded to such a low, despicable life? It's no wonder that I'm here now, with a father like mine! Why should I be punished for my father's sin?"

"BEHOLD, ALL SOULS ARE MINE TO JUDGE; THE SOUL OF THE FATHER AS WELL AS THE SOUL OF HIS CHILD IS MINE. A PERSON'S OWN SINS DETERMINE IF THEY LIVE OR DIE. IF A PERSON IS UNJUST AND DOES NOT DO WHAT IS LAWFUL AND RIGHT, AND COMMITS ADULTERY, MURDER, STEALING, WORSHIPS AND LOVES IDOLS (SUCH AS MONEY), I WILL JUDGE HIM HARSHLY.

"IN ORDER TO RECEIVE EVERLASTING LIFE A PERSON MUST BE LIKE A LITTLE CHILD AND BE BORN AGAIN. THEY MUST RECEIVE MY GIFT OF SALVATION IN THEIR HEART AND REPENT OF THEIR SINS.

"YOUR EARTHLY FATHER WAS FULL OF PRIDE, WHICH WAS ONE OF HIS MANY SINS. 'PRIDE GOES BEFORE DESTRUCTION, AND A HAUGHTY SPIRIT BEFORE A FALL.'[14] IT IS BETTER TO BE POOR AND HUMBLE THAN PROUD AND RICH. GOD BLESSES THOSE WHO OBEY HIM. HAPPY IS THE MAN WHO PUTS HIS TRUST IN THE LORD. FOR GOD RESISTS THE PROUD AND GIVES GRACE TO THE HUMBLE."

27

Six months passed by in my wild, out-of-control life. Scotty and I were still living with Kathy, Dawn and Rebecca.

Kathy and I were able to spend even more time together as we went out to clubs and parties. She now worked at a strip club where she was off at eight in the evening. Jake promoted me to day manager, because I had brought him a lot of new business. I thought I was having the time of my life, now that Kathy and I could go out any night of the week we wanted to.

I really thought I had the world by the tail until one very dark, depressing day. When I met up with Kathy at our favorite bar, I slammed my purse on the bar and rattled out a bunch of swear words. Kathy about fell off her bar stool. With a puzzled expression, she asked, "Are we having a bad day? I've never heard you cuss like a trooper before! What's up?"

"I'm pregnant!"

"You are what? Are you sure?"

"Yes, I'm sure," I said sharply. "I felt like I was, but I didn't want to believe it, so I stopped at the clinic to reassure myself. Now I know I am!"

"You didn't forget to take a couple of pills again, did you?"

"No! I learned my lesson from getting pregnant with Scotty. I must be one of the unlucky 5 percent."

"Bummer, Lorraine! What are you going to do about it?"

"I don't know. I don't have time to take care of Scotty like I should, let alone another baby!"

"Do you have any idea who the father is?"

"Do you know how many different guys I go out with?"

"Try to narrow it down. Who do you go out with the most?"

"Let me see. There's really only two I go out regularly with, and that's Andrew and Gary."

"Those are your only choices?" She looked thoughtful. "You could always get an abortion."

"Funny! But, no, that's out of the question. Remember, I was down that path before. I couldn't do it then, and I can't do it now."

"Hey, what about Jake?"

"I don't go out with him; besides, he's married."

"So? Come on, Lorraine, level with me. I know you and Jake have been together since you started working for him. It's obvious. Actually it's a big rumor around the bar. The way that Jake looks at you and acts around you, everybody can tell he wants you. Besides, I'm your best friend. Did you really think I wouldn't notice?"

"Busted! Okay, so maybe I am with him the most, but like I said, the guy's married."

"Duh. You haven't heard of divorce?"

"Yes, but he's got kids. It takes a year to get a divorce when you've got kids. I'm not so sure Jake would even be interested in divorcing his wife and marrying me."

"Of course he would. You have such a great personality, and you're gorgeous. The way that man looks at you, honey, he's in love!"

"Or lust."

"Whatever! You've seen his wife, right?"

"Yeah."

"Tell me he wouldn't want to trade that mousy plain Jane for you?"

"But there's still the fact that it takes a year to get the divorce."

"So, in the meantime, you and Jake can move in together. When it's over, you got yourself a husband. Make sure he signs the birth certificate."

"Mmm, I do his books now, and he isn't doing bad. More than likely, he is the father. Maybe I should go after the old boy after all."

That same night, I put my plan in place. I was out to snag a husband, my employer. I walked into the bar near closing and started picking dirty glasses up from the tables. Jake noticed me, and his expression turned sly. "Hey, doll face, what are you doing in this joint at closing?"

"Missed yah, Jake. Thought I'd come in and give you a hand closing up tonight."

"Is that right—a little lonesome tonight, huh?"

The place was empty, so I went over and put my arms around his neck and kissed him.

"Wow, I guess you really did miss me, didn't you? Just let me turn off the open sign, and I'm all yours."

"Great, Jake, because I have some wonderful news for you tonight."

"What is it, lovely lady?"

"Jake, sweetie, brace yourself. No, you better sit down."

"What, what? I hate surprises. Tell me!"

"You're going to be a father!"

"No! I didn't hear you right."

"Yes, honey, you heard me all right. You and I are having a baby!"

"Maybe you are, but I ain't! I'm already a father, remember? I have two great boys who depend on me."

"I know. I respect you for the way you take care of your sons. Having another child won't change that. I'm sure Mary will be fair with visitation rights."

"What? I'm not leaving my wife for you!"

"But, Jake, baby, we can get married when your divorce gets final. It will all work out, you'll see."

"No, I won't see. There is no way I'll ever divorce my wife, Lorraine! You can get that straight right now!"

I'd never seen Jake so mad before. His face was as red as a beet, and he was shaking in anger.

"What about your child that I am carrying?"

"If it even is! I'm not stupid, you know. I've got eyes and ears. You go out with every Tom, Dick, and Harry!"

"How can you talk to me that way? I thought you really cared for me. You are the only one I've been with, I swear."

"Look at you! You're a temptress—a seductive, gorgeous woman. With you right under my nose, I'd have been a fool not to be with you. You were there, convenient. An extramarital affair that the wife would never find out about. But it never was anything serious, and you were kidding yourself, if you thought it was. I love my wife. Her and those two boys are my whole life! I would kill anybody if they got in the way of me and my family. Do I make myself clear?" Jake hit the wall with his fist and put a hole in it. "Now get out of here! You're not welcome here any longer. You're fired!" I hustled out of there as soon as I could, for it was obvious that Jake meant every word of his threat.

⌘ ⌘ ⌘

I was so angry with Jake as I faced the Lord yet another time at The Great White Throne Judgment. "Lord, Jake was such a jerk! If he only would have left his wife and made a life with me and my children, I know things would have turned out differently for me. Maybe I would have gotten away from the party life. Maybe I would have even gone to church again."

"What you wanted from Jake was wrong. Adultery is a sin. I spoke to my disciples about this very thing. I said, 'Whoever divorces his wife for any reason except sexual immorality causes her to commit adultery; and whoever marries a woman who is divorced commits adultery.'"[15]

28

I found myself talking with Kathy about the previous night's fiasco. "I can't tell you how humiliated Jake made me feel. He had been only using me. He didn't care about me."

"Yeah, and it's a bummer that he fired you. What are you going to do? I guess you better hurry and choose one of the other bozos on your list."

"Oh, I can get another bartending job easy enough. I had several offers from other bar managers to leave Jake's, and come work for them. That's no problem. But getting married? Now that's a problem."

"Gary Barrows would marry you in a heartbeat. He's always telling me he wished he could have you all to himself. Did you know that he is really jealous of you dating other guys?"

"He doesn't have a right to. I'm a free agent, and you know I like it that way. Why in the world do I have to get married anyway? I had Scotty without a husband; why not this baby?"

"Because, dingbat, you need someone to support the baby. You can always divorce him and get child support."

"I could get child support anyway."

"Not as easy. And remember, he might not be the father. What if he gets a paternity test? You can't chance that, Lorraine. You need to get him to marry you."

"But he is so slow-witted!"

"No, he's not. Maybe he's a little strange, but at least he's fun to be with and has a steady job. Not bad to look at either. And best of all, he's available."

"You're right, Kathy. Let's make a plan."

After planning the perfect candlelight dinner, I then called Gary. I invited him to come over later that evening. He was thrilled at the invitation and agreed.

It would be just Gary and me in the romantic setting I had orchestrated. Dawn and Rebecca were gone for the weekend to visit with relatives. Kathy was taking Scotty and spending the night at her current boyfriend's place. Now there would be no interruptions in my plot to snag a husband.

Gary arrived right on time. He walked in carrying a dozen red roses in one arm and a bottle of wine in the other. He was full of smiles as he put down his gifts. He grabbed me in his arms and began passionately kissing me. I responded, and we exchanged kisses for a few more minutes. Then I lightly pushed him away, saying, "Darling, if we don't stop, your steak will be well done!" The delicious smells were as big a seduction as I was (for the minute anyway), and the steak won out.

The apartment was dim, and only candlelights danced about in a warm, romantic way. As we were enjoying the delicious dinner I had prepared, Gary looked up at me with love in his eyes and said, "You are the most beautiful woman in the world." He ran his fingertips down through my long, bunching curls. "The candlelight lights up your raven hair as if it were the night, and the light from the candles were stars. I've never seen you more beautiful than you are tonight."

We finished the meal and then went and sat on the sofa. After a few kisses, Gary whispered, "I love you, gorgeous lady." This was the first time he'd ever told me he loved me.

"Oh, Gary, I love you, too!" *This is going better than I planned.*

"Did I hear you right? You love me, too?"

"I thought you knew."

"I knew we've always had a lot of fun together, but I didn't think you were really that serious about me. After all, I know you date other guys. It makes me feel so jealous when I go into Jake's, and guys are falling all over you. I know you've got to be friendly, but I get so jealous. Maybe it's because I know you go out with a few of them."

"Well, baby, I'm a free woman; it's not like we are married. I assumed you were dating other girls, too."

"Lorraine, I swear, since I met you, I haven't been able to even look at another woman. I'm crazy about you!"

"I'm crazy about you too, but we aren't committed to each other."

"We can fix that. We can get married! Lorraine, will you marry me?"

"Marry you? Oh my gosh, Gary! Where did that come from?"

"If that's the only way I can have you all to myself, that's what I want.

Now that I think about it, I'd be the happiest man in the world if I could wake up with you lying next to me each morning."

"Wow, that does sound like a dream come true. But it's all so sudden. There are things to think about, like my little boy."

"Oh, yeah, I forgot you have a kid."

"But he's a great kid, Gary. You'd love him. I know you like to go fishing and hunting. You could teach Scotty all those things. It would be great!"

"I don't know. I've never been around kids too much. Kids and me don't really mix. How old is the kid?"

"He's four. Getting to be a big boy all ready. He's a hoot! I really love my son, Gary, so if you don't like kids, maybe this is not such a good idea after all."

"No, honey! It's not that I don't like kids. I mean, it would take a little getting used to, you know what I mean. I know he would come with the package. I can accept that, because I want you for my wife."

"Are you sure?"

"Yes, I promise. I'll be all right with your little rug rat."

"Cool! Maybe soon I can have your child. Our own baby. That would be great for Scotty. Maybe a little brother to play with, or a sister to tease."

"Not so fast there, lovely lady! Let me get used to having one kid. I'm not sure if we want any more. Think about it, baby. The way we like to party, how could we if we had a house full of rug rats?"

"I didn't say a house full, Gary. I meant just one sister or brother. It would keep Scotty happy and busy if he had a sibling."

"Don't get all bent out of shape, baby doll. I didn't say we wouldn't have a kid someday. It's just that we need to get adjusted to being married first."

Looks like I better keep my mouth shut about this pregnancy, if I want to pull it off. I wonder how I'm going to spring it on him later?

"Of course you're right, darling. We can wait to talk about those things. Let's not spoil our wonderful mood."

He took me in his arms and kissed my lips with hot passion. After the kiss, I pulled away a little from him, and with all the excitement I could muster up, said, "Why don't we run off to Vegas right now and get married in one of those little chapels? Just like in the movies! It would be great; we could fly out tonight. As soon as we get there, we could go straight to one of those Vegas chapels. We could have a mini honeymoon right there in the exciting city of neon lights, in sin city, Las Vegas!"

"Wow, slow down, beautiful! Sounds like a spectacular whirlwind, but we've got responsibilities. You got a kid. Remember him?"

"Of course, but Kathy has him at a friend's for tonight. I'm sure between Kathy and Dawn, they won't mind watching him for a few days, seeing it's my honeymoon and all. I'll write a note and call them tomorrow."

"But what about your job at Jake's? I don't think he can run that joint without you anymore."

"He already is, Gary. He and I had a big argument and mutually decided I wouldn't be working for him anymore."

"Good! I'm glad to hear that. Jake always acted like he owned you. If you asked me, even though he's married, I think the old boy had a thing for you."

"That's one reason I'm not there anymore. I don't ever want to step foot in that place again!"

"Don't worry, baby, we won't."

"Okay, then. I'll call the airport. I hear they have real good rates to Vegas. I've always wanted to go there with all the lights and casinos. Maybe we will get lucky at the slots."

"Yeah, I've never been there either. I like to play blackjack. I can show you how to win from the house."

"All right then, I'll call, and then grab a bag with a few essentials. We'll need our IDs and birth certificates."

"Hey, by the way, I never asked. How old is my bride-to-be?"

"I'm twenty."

"How do you get into all the bars?"

"Haven't you heard of fake IDs?'

He shook his head and laughed. "I hope you have a legal one to get married with. I'll have to stop off at my apartment and get my things too."

My plan worked. The next day I was Mrs. Gary Barrows. I could barely remember our Vegas wedding. We were intoxicated and high for the three days we were there, but I was quite sure we had a good time.

When we got home, my friends were a little put out that I dropped Scotty in their laps. They forgave me because they were happy that I was married, although, all three of us had mixed emotions. They thought that it was good for my sake, but sad because a part of them was leaving. We had shared so much fun together in this big old warehouse apartment. It was wonderful to have shared it with such good friends. Kathy and Dawn both said it would never be the same without me living there with them.

Even Rebecca cried when I was getting Scotty ready to leave. She'd probably spent more time with my little boy while I was living there than I had. I assured her I would bring him over to see her often.

The first two months were not too bad as a married woman, although I really missed my independence and the single life. Gary, on the other hand, couldn't get enough of his new bride. He was very controlling of me from the start. I didn't like it one bit but thought he would mellow after a while.

One night while we were lying in bed, he patted my stomach and said in a joking way, "Getting a little pudgy, aren't we? My beautiful, vivacious wife isn't going to turn into an ugly fat lady, is she?"

I was so mad that he would even say such a thing to me! I rolled over and wouldn't talk to him the rest of the night. When he heard me crying, he tried to make up with me, but I pushed him away.

The next morning he apologized all over the place. I finally forgave him but knew I had to think of something fast. I was now three months pregnant.

For another month I was able to hide my pregnancy, but then it was getting too obvious. I said to Gary, "I'm not sure, but I've missed a couple of periods and I've been getting sick in the mornings." In a sheepish voice I said, "Gary, I think I'm pregnant."

Gary lost his temper. "How did that happen? You told me you were on the pill!"

"They always worked for me before. I don't know why. The doctor told me they were 95 percent safe, so I thought that was good odds."

Gary was wringing his hands and walking the floor. There was panic in his voice when he said, "Now what are we supposed to do? Your kid gets on my nerves now. What will a crying baby do? I don't want this kid, Lorraine. You need to do something about it. Get rid of it!"

"Gary, I've done everything you've told me to do, but not this. I can't! There is no way I will get rid of one of my kids. I went through a lot to have Scotty, and I won't let anything happen to this child, either. If you can't handle it, I'll leave!"

"No! Don't get all crazy about this. I can't live without you now. I love you too much, Lorraine. But you'll probably need to go back to work after you have the kid. Our one-room apartment isn't big enough for the three of us now. With another baby, we'll need a bigger apartment, and I can't afford that on my own."

"Fine, that's no problem. I miss not working anyway."

Six months later I gave birth to a beautiful baby girl I named Linda. She was so beautiful, with plenty of dark, long hair. Gary said she looked just like her mother. I thought so. I hoped I was wrong, but I also thought that I could see some of Jake in her. I tried hard to push that thought deep down in my brain.

Right after my baby girl was born, I asked Gary if he would like to hold her.

Nervously he said, "Nah, she's too small and fragile. Shouldn't they have her in an incubator, or something? After all, she's a month too early, right?"

"Yes, she is, but she seems really healthy. She weighs six pounds and four ounces. If she would have been full-term, she would have been a whopper like Scotty."

"Yeah, I guess so."

During the next two years Gary started to have strong doubts about whether Linda was really his or not. He began to question when I got pregnant. When we were in the middle of an argument, he bought it up. He was trying to hurt me, and he held nothing back. "Linda's not my kid, is she?"

I was shocked he brought it up. I thought he was stupid enough to take my word. "How dare you! Of course she is!"

"Right. I think you were already pregnant before I asked you to marry me. You tricked me, Lorraine! Didn't you?"

"No! No, I didn't. How can you be so cruel? Linda is your baby!"

From then on, every time we got into an argument, Gary would bring up the same subject. All we ever did was fight.

When Linda was four, Gary looked at her and said to me, "You know, that kid reminds me of your old boss, Jake."

"That is the most ridiculous thing I have ever heard!"

"No, it's true. Look at her eyes and the shape of her face. She's a dead ringer of the old man. She's even chunky like him, not skinny like us."

I didn't make enough money at the bar where I had worked for the past three years, so I decided to change jobs. Kathy told me about an opening for a bartender where she danced. When I went in to interview, they hired me on the spot. They said with my experience and beauty, I'd fit in.

When I went home and told Gary about landing a job at the exotic bar, he was furious. He told me I couldn't take the job, but I took it anyway. I was determined he was not going to tell me what to do anymore. Of course, we had a big battle over it, but I won.

I loved working at the Kitty Cat Lounge. The tips were excellent. A lot of the customers came in because of me, not just to see the dancers. I had a lot of fun at work. It was also neat that Kathy worked there; we were able to see each other a lot. We even began going out after work together, or just hung around there after our shift was done.

Kathy and I sat at the bar one night talking about how unhappily married I was. Kathy asked, "Is Gary going to be upset with you when you get home late again?"

"To heck with Gary! I'm sick of him. I can't even stand to be around the dummy anymore. He's been kind of mean to the kids lately. I know it's his way of showing me that he doesn't approve of me working here, but he sure likes the money I bring in."

"How is he mean to the kids?"

"Linda cries whenever I leave, and Scotty begs me not to go. Gary's always hitting Scotty for something. I've noticed a few good-sized bruises on him, but he won't admit that Gary's been hitting him when I'm gone."

"Scotty's such a good kid, why would he hit him?"

"For one thing, he has always resented him. Another thing, Scotty is very protective of his little sister. If Linda does anything wrong, Gary gets after her. Scotty tries to stick up for her, and then he gets it! Gary is convinced that Linda is not his. I think he hates her. She looks more like Jake the older she gets. That doesn't help the situation any. I hate to leave the kids home alone with him."

"Then why do you?"

"Come on, Kathy, you know my circumstances better than anyone. Why pay a babysitter when he's home nights and can do it? Besides, Scotty takes care of his sister most of the time. If Scotty would just learn to keep his mouth shut. Gary is drunk most of the time."

"I still don't know, Lorraine. If I had kids, I don't think I'd leave them home with a guy I thought was abusing them."

"I told you, I don't have a choice! I've got a job. Besides, if I had to stay home more with the idiot, I'd go totally out of my ever-lovin' mind. If the kids stay clear of him when he's drinking, they'll be okay!"

"The kids are really getting big now. How old are they?"

"Scott's ten and Linda is six."

"Hey, I've got an idea. Dawn and I have decided to move to California. Why don't you pack up your kids and join us? Dawn's daughter, Rebecca, would make a good live-in babysitter."

"I don't think so, Kathy. It's too big of a move with the kids. We would be going out there with nothing but each other. I can't take that chance with my kids. I'd love to, but I better not."

⌘⌘⌘

As I watched Kathy and myself talking at the Kitty Cat Lounge, the Lord revealed to me what was happening with my family at home. I saw Scotty playing with Linda. Gary was sitting on the sofa drinking one beer after another. Then Scotty started teasing Linda. She screamed at him and then started crying. The noise disturbed Gary as he was watching a movie, and that made him mad! He slammed his beer can down on the coffee table and pulled his belt out of his pants. In a rage Gary whipped his belt across Scott's back a few times, and Scott fell to the floor.

Gary lifted the belt to hit Linda, and Scott cried out, "Please, Gary, please, don't hit her. We'll be quiet," he sobbed.

Gary stopped. "Okay, but I want you brats to go to your rooms, now!"

Both children lay in their separate bedrooms shaking. Linda was even more scared than Scotty. Lately, her abuse had become abusive in a much more horrifying way. To keep her from telling, Gary had told her that if she told anyone, he would lock her up in the kitchen pantry. He reminded her that rats visit the dark pantry. He also threatened to kill her and the rest of the family if she told.

With an aching heart, and tears flowing down my face I screamed out at the Lord as I stood before him at The Great White Throne Judgment, "Why, why, oh Lord? Why did I get stuck with an abusive man like Gary? How could he hurt my little girl so badly? I hate him with every painful breath I take!"

"You were living in an unrighteous lifestyle. You were embedded in sin. You were with several men who were not your husband. You were with Jake, who was a married man. He committed adultery with you, which caused you to be an adulteress. While being with child of another man, you deceived Gary into marriage. You chose him out of greed, not for kindness, love, or a good father for your children. Therefore, you picked another unrighteous man, also embedded in sin.

"I don't take pleasure in wickedness; I will destroy those who are deceitful and those who speak falsehoods.[16]

"Lorraine, your tongue devises destruction, like a sharp razor, working deceitfully. You deceived Gary with your charm and beauty, which was evil of you to do.

"'Charm is deceitful, and beauty is passing, but a woman who fears the Lord, she shall be praised.'"[17]

29

In the years to follow, not only did God let me view my own immoral life, he also let me see what misery my children were living as well. I had been too busy indulging in my own perverse pleasures that I wasn't aware of the pain my children were enduring. I didn't realize the deep scars that they had from my eight-year abusive marriage. Even after I divorced Gary, I had several other damaging affairs that affected my kids.

Linda withdrew within herself, and her self-esteem fell low. She was even more unpopular than I was in elementary school. Eating was her vice to ease the pain, and she put on thirty extra pounds. Most of the time I could find her in her bedroom reading a book, where she could escape from the world.

Scotty, on the other hand, took to the city's streets, getting mixed up in gangs and drugs. I wasn't much of a mother to either of my kids. I was too busy working and partying. I gave Scott way too much responsibility around the house. I trusted him to look after his sister, while I was gone, which was most of the time. He loved her, but when he started getting older he had better things to do than to hang out at home with his little sister. Maybe if I had been home more, I would have been able to keep some control over Scott. When I was there, I was too tired to fight over the control. Finally, I just gave up the struggle. I guess I wasn't surprised that he was out dealing drugs at the age of sixteen. I never tried to stop him from taking drugs. How could I, when I used them myself? He knew that I used drugs; it was just something we never talked about.

When I thought my life couldn't get any worse, I turned on the television and heard: "We interrupt our regular scheduled programming to bring you this special news-breaking story!" Then I saw my father's face flash on the set. "New York's once prominent lawyer, James Patterson, has been arrested for embezzlement. This took place in a small law firm, in which the once prestigious attorney worked. Patterson has been taken to the New York City jail, where he awaits his day in court. More details to come as this story unfolds."

I sat there in shock until Scott walked into the apartment, then I burst into tears. Scotty came rushing over to me. "What's wrong, Lorraine?" He had started calling me by my name soon after my divorce from Gary. I guess it made him feel older, more in control. I thought it was cute; besides, it made me feel younger.

"Scotty, my father's been arrested. He's in jail!"

"Your dad is in jail? Why? How come?"

"Several years ago my mother told me that there was some suspicion that Father was embezzling from the firm that he worked for. I hadn't heard a word from either of them since then until my mother called last year to tell me they had lost everything. They had to sell their precious estate and buy a small house a ways out of the city."

"That don't sound bad! I wish we could afford a house."

"Yeah, Scott, but your grandparents lived in luxury before that. The home I grew up in was a mansion. This place has got to be like a shack to my parents."

"Did she mention the embezzlement?"

"Yeah, she did say he was under investigation at that time. I figured it would go away like it did before. I thought he might have been guilty, but that he was too shrewd of a lawyer to get caught."

"Maybe you should go see him."

"Why should I do that? He disowned me! He wasn't there for us when we could have used his help."

"Right, Lorraine, but we were never in so much trouble as dear old granddad is in now. Maybe he would be happy to see you."

"I doubt it, but maybe I will get around to it, if I have time."

"Come on. I'll help you pack."

"No, Scott! I just can't see him right now!"

"Okay, but what about your mother? After all, she has made some effort to contact you through the years, right?"

"Yeah, maybe you are right. She must be devastated. My father has put her through hell. I hate him for what he has done to her." Then I added quietly, "And me."

"He's human, Ma, he made some mistakes."

"Yeah, but he was supposed to be so intelligent. How can someone that smart be so stupid to think he could get away with something like that?"

"I don't know. Maybe he's not as smart as he thought he was. But you really should go see him."

"I can't. I can't! How can I go see my distinguished father in an old dirty jail cell?"

I made plans the next day to go across the city to see my mother. I had her new address, so it was just the matter of locating it. When I couldn't, I stopped and phoned. When I didn't get an answer, I figured she was visiting Father in jail.

I finally located my parents' house and knocked on the door. There was no answer. I tried the back door...still no answer. Then from behind me I heard someone say, "There's no one home, Miss."

I turned sharply. "Apparently not, who are you?" I said to a young, attractive blond who was hanging over the fence.

"You're Jim's daughter, aren't you?"

"Yes, I'm James' and Marge's daughter. How did you know?"

"Your dad showed me your picture. It was an old picture, but I can still tell it's you."

"Have you seen my mother today?"

"No, but have you heard about your dad? The poor man! I'm sure he was framed. He has too much integrity to ever do anything like that."

"Yes, I did hear. That's why I'm here today. My mother must be devastated!"

"Yeah, and so is your poor dad. I couldn't believe it when they arrested him. He has been such a good neighbor—always willing to help when my husband was out of town."

I squinted my eyes at her. *Yeah, I bet. Especially if you wore that skimpy bikini around him.*

"Your father really is a great guy. I can't believe those charges against him."

I looked at her, thinking, *You don't know him as well as I do, lady.*

The woman chattered on. "I've been in shock ever since I heard about it. I don't believe a wonderful man like Jim could be guilty of such a terrible crime."

I was getting impatient with her slobbering over my father so I said to her, "I don't know, but right now I'm just interested in where my mother is. Do you have any idea?" *You dizzy blond!*

She gave me a pathetic look. "I've got bad news about your mother. The authorities came in three days ago and took her to a mental institution. A couple of us neighbors noticed she wasn't getting her mail, and newspapers were piling up. I called the police to check up on her. I thought she might have overdosed on all the meds she takes. That and the alcohol. When they found her, she was just sitting there in a daze. They said she hadn't eaten in days. I guess she couldn't handle losing a guy like your dad. I know if he was my husband, I'd probably go nuts, too!"

I gave her a nasty glare. *A man like my father. Lady, you are nuttier than my mother could ever be.* I wanted to slap her, but I said, "Thanks for all your information. I have to go now; I need to find my mother."

When I got to the institution where they took my mother, I was soon introduced to the staff psychiatrist. He warned me she probably wouldn't recognize me. He was right. She didn't even notice me as I tried to talk to her. When I looked into her face, it was like I was looking into the face of my grandma instead of my once beautiful mother. She had always been so proper and well groomed. Her hair was a mess. The once shiny blond hair that was never out of place was all frizzed up with gray hairs mixed through it. Before, she would never allow a gray hair to show on her head.

Mother wasn't even wearing makeup. Before, she wouldn't have been caught dead without her makeup on. I couldn't believe all her wrinkles. She looked so pathetic.

I mentioned it to the doctor and he said, "Your mother isn't aware of anything going on around her, let alone her appearance."

As I looked at my mother I remembered the past. *She was always so beautiful when she was about to go out and be among New York's finest. She was always so elegant. Now look at her! I hate Father for doing this to her. How could he? How could he have disowned me! I hate him, I hate him!*

I tried to talk to Mother again, but to no avail. She didn't even acknowledge I was in the room. She sat there staring straight ahead with a dazed expression. She was humming softly what seemed to be old love ballads. I wondered if they were special to her and Father in the early days. She seemed to have a yearning in her eyes. It was as if she wasn't really there, but back to a time when she was in love. I'm sure she loved my father at one time, although I doubt if he ever loved her. But then could the great James Patterson ever love anyone?

Wiping the tears from my face, I said to the doctor, "Well, I guess I should go. She doesn't know I'm here anyway."

"No, Miss Patterson, she doesn't. Leave your number at the front desk, and we'll call if there is any change."

Weeks passed, and I couldn't get myself to go visit my father in jail. His lawyer called and said that he wanted to see me, but I was having a hard time trying to convince myself to go. I tried to drown my thoughts of my father by going out and meeting new guys, drinking, getting high…anything I could do to forget him.

I was successful at purging my father from my mind until one day I turned on the television and saw the earth-shaking news. The glass of booze I was holding crashed to the floor as I heard the newscaster say, "Now for live-breaking news: James Patterson, a once famous trial attorney, has committed suicide while just days away from his own famous embezzlement trial. Patterson was found hanging in his cell at eight o'clock this morning. Efforts to revive him were of no avail."

I screamed, "No, Father! You can't do this to me!" I picked up a vase, threw it into the television, then fell on to the floor crying my heart out.

Linda heard the crash and came running from her room. She bent down beside me. "Mom, what's the matter?" Then Scott got out of bed and came running to my side. They both helped me back on the couch. They tried to comfort me as I told them what had happened.

"My father is dead!" I screamed. "I didn't even tell him good-bye. I should have gone to see him at the jail; he asked for me. He must have loved me if he wanted to see me, don't you think?"

Scott put his arm around me. "Sure, Mom, sure."

"It's too late, Scotty. Now I can never be the kind of daughter he wanted. He's gone!"

Linda took my hand. "You've got us, Mother."

"I know, honey. What would I ever do without my kids? You kids give me more love than my father ever thought of. How could he have gotten himself in so much trouble? How could he do this to Mother…and to me! All I ever wanted him to do was love me. Why, why couldn't he love me? Mother and I loved him so much. Why couldn't he love us back?"

Scott wiped the tears from my cheeks. "I'm sure he loved you in his own way. I'm a little surprised at how you are taking this. You've barely mentioned your dad."

"I doubt that he ever loved me! Nothing I did was ever good enough for him. No matter how hard I tried, I couldn't please him. Now I would give anything to have him back in my life. If I just hadn't been so stubborn...why didn't I go see him at the jail? If I had, maybe he would be alive now. If I only had a second chance to show my father how much I really loved him!"

⌘⌘⌘

I stood before the Lord at the Judgment seat and asked, "Lord, why did it hurt so badly when I found out my father was dead? I had made myself believe all those years that I hated him for disowning me, and then when I found out that he was dead, I was crushed."

"THERE'S A FINE LINE BETWEEN LOVE AND HATE. YOU HAD SUCH AN ABUNDANCE OF LOVE FOR YOUR FATHER THAT WHEN HE CUT YOU FROM HIS LIFE, THE ONLY WAY YOU COULD COPE WITH IT WAS TO TURN YOUR LOVE INTO HATE. YOU WERE ABLE TO FOOL YOUR HEART INTO BELIEVING THAT YOU HATED YOUR FATHER. IN REALITY, YOU LOVED HIM."

"OH, LORRAINE, IF ONLY YOU AND YOUR EARTHLY FATHER WOULD HAVE LOVED YOUR HEAVENLY FATHER, YOUR LIVES WOULD HAVE BEEN SO MUCH HAPPIER AND WOULD HAVE GONE EASIER. YOU WOULD NOT BE STANDING BEFORE ME AT THE GREAT WHITE THRONE JUDGMENT, TO BE SEPARATED FROM ME FOR ALL ETERNITY.

"THOSE WHO HAVE RECEIVED MY GIFT OF SALVATION ARE GOD'S CHOSEN. THE BIBLE SAYS: 'SINCE YOU HAVE BEEN CHOSEN BY GOD WHICH HAS GIVEN YOU THIS NEW KIND OF LIFE, AND BECAUSE OF HIS DEEP LOVE AND CONCERN FOR YOU, YOU SHOULD PRACTICE TENDERHEARTED MERCY AND KINDNESS TO OTHERS. DON'T WORRY ABOUT MAKING A GOOD IMPRESSION ON THEM, BUT BE READY TO SUFFER QUIETLY AND PATIENTLY. BE GENTLE AND READY TO FORGIVE, NEVER HOLD GRUDGES. REMEMBER, THE LORD FORGAVE YOU, SO YOU MUST FORGIVE OTHERS. MOST OF ALL, LET LOVE GUIDE YOUR LIFE, FOR THEN THE WHOLE CHURCH WILL STAY TOGETHER IN

PERFECT HARMONY.'[18]

"'STOP BEING MEAN, BAD TEMPERED AND ANGRY. QUARRELING, HARSH WORDS, AND DISLIKE OF OTHERS SHOULD HAVE NO PLACE IN YOUR LIVES. INSTEAD, BE KIND TO EACH OTHER, TENDERHEARTED, FORGIVING ONE ANOTHER, JUST AS GOD HAS FORGIVEN YOU BECAUSE YOU BELONG TO CHRIST.'"[19]

30

A small insurance policy took care of the funeral, but Father's lawyer let me know that nothing else was left. Even the house was going back to the mortgage broker.

It was a small funeral, to my surprise. Now that my father's wealth was gone, it seemed so were his friends. Of course, Mother was too sick to get out of the mental institution. However, I was thrilled to see two of my close friends walk in. I burst into tears when I saw Kathy and Dawn. They both put their arms around me and gave their condolences. I was almost speechless as I tried to talk. "When did you girls get back from California?"

"A couple of weeks ago," Kathy answered. "We meant to call you, but we have been so busy getting settled in."

"Yeah," Dawn said. "We heard about your father and dropped everything to be with you."

"I never heard from you gals since you left. What's it been, at least five years?"

Kathy looked down. "We really did mean to keep in touch, but if you think New York is wild, you should try California. It's some whirlwind out there."

"Yeah, I know, I keep busy here too. I don't know where time goes. But man, it sure is good to see you. I don't know when I have ever needed friends more than I do now."

"Are you married or seeing someone?" Dawn asked.

"No one particular guy. Most of the available men are bums. They're okay for a good time, but that's all."

Dawn laughed. "The same out in California."

"Dawn, how's Rebecca? She must be all grown up by now?"

Tears filled Dawn's eyes.

"She didn't stay out in California, did she?"

Kathy spoke up. "Rebecca is dead."

My mouth gaped. "What? What happened?"

The three of us collapsed into the chairs at the funeral parlor as Dawn told the tragic story of her daughter. "She started becoming rebellious toward me. She said I was always putting too much responsibility on her; that I never took care of her, and let her fend for herself. She told me that I had had fun all my life, and now it was her turn. She blamed me for everything. I had her babysit my friends' kids too much."

"Oh, Dawn that was my fault too. I was always shoving Scotty off on her to watch."

"Well, that was a long time ago. Out in California, I took advantage of her too much."

"I'm so sorry, Dawn. What happened?"

"She got out of control and started using heavy drugs. Kathy and I let her smoke a little pot with us when she became a teen, but I was shocked to see her turn to hard drugs. Rebecca was into crack really bad. Anything I would say to her, she'd blow up. It got so I couldn't even talk to her without her getting mad at me. I swear, Lorraine, sometimes I actually believed the girl hated me. She told me that plenty of times."

"Yeah." Kathy took over. "She started staying away from home for days on end. We were really worried about her. We knew there was some guy, but we didn't know who he was."

"We grew completely apart," Dawn said. "After not seeing her for weeks, a cop came to our door. He told me Rebecca was found dead and that her pimp was under investigation for her murder. I about died that day. It was a horrible shock finding out that she was dead. But, on top of that, to find out your daughter was a prostitute! Kathy and I have done a lot of exotic dancing, but never were we involved in prostitution. It kills me to think my baby was that messed up. Now she's gone forever."

"Oh, Dawn, I am so sorry!"

"Dawn and I couldn't have gotten through it, if it weren't for our new religion."

"Religion?" I laughed. "Come on. You're kidding me right?"

"No, we are involved in a new religion. It's not like church, or anything. It's more spiritual. We're involved in the New Age Movement."

"I've heard something, but I don't really know anything about it. What's it like?"

"It's wonderful." Dawn opened her purse and pulled out a necklace. "Here, we brought you this necklace to help you deal with your father's death. That's a crystal on the chain. It will give you the power to deal with life's tragedies and keep you strong."

"Thanks, you guys. It's beautiful!"

At the end of the funeral I walked up to the casket, bent down, and kissed my father on his cold, hard lips. I whispered, "Good-bye, Father. I love you. I'm sorry I failed you."

In the months to follow the three of us spent most of our time together. It was like the good old days. Kathy and Dawn got me saturated into their New Age Religion. Soon I was a strong believer in my faith. I told Kathy, "This new religion is wonderful. I like it because I don't have to change. I still can go out and party. It's not like most religions that make you give up everything. And I love the part that if I don't get things right in this life, I'll get another chance in a different life. I get as many chances as I need to get it right. It makes me feel better about my father. He even has another opportunity to make his life better in his next life. Thank you girls so much for turning me onto the New Age Movement."

"It helped me to cope with Rebecca's death. I knew it would help you too."

"It sure has, Dawn. It's assuring to know my father and Rebecca's souls will live on."

"Yes," Kathy said. "Karma is a balance of good and evil. It's a tool we use to choose the experience we have in our next life. We keep coming back in the world to reach perfection in our lives. It may take some of us only a few times, while others have thousands of reincarnations to get it right. When we get to that point, it will be a time of perfection."

I was glued to every word my friends had to say about this new religion. I asked, "You mean we can actually determine what we want to be when we come back?"

Dawn spoke up. "Yes! I truly believe Rebecca chose to die like she did. To die at an early age gave her the ability to help others know how very dangerous the life of prostitution really is."

"It's about forgiveness, too," Kathy said. "It's about every person paying in full for every failure, to achieve godhood. You can let go and forgive yourself; it's a learning process. The state of perfection is the final goal."

"Wow, man! That is really beautiful," I said as I passed around a joint.

"There's a chance for my old man and me too."

Night after night Kathy and Dawn filled my head with the New Age teaching. One evening while we were discussing it, Kathy said, "You know, Lorraine, there is no one god. We are all striving to be god within ourselves. We should strive to get in touch with our higher self. God is an it, an energy, a force, the complete consciousness of all living things. God is nothing more than creation itself. Humans are the gods who created the world. There is no good or no evil. It's all the same thing. Just like life and death, they're both the same. There's no heaven or hell. Only this world that we are to perfect."

"Yes!" Dawn said. "We have no limitations. We can do whatever we want to do, be what we want to be. We are divine, Lorraine, so we are under no law and accountability to anyone, but ourselves. Because we are divine, and we are our own creators, we are responsible for what happens to us and around us. By constantly improving by reincarnation, we can reach our divine nobility, giving us the ability to direct our future evolution for the betterment of humanity."

Kathy spoke up. "You see, a perfect world is just around the corner. A world where there will be a global transformation. Everyone will be enlightened and have social unity. It will be a golden age, without war, violence, racism, hunger, disease or even death. Humanity will truly be 'one,' with one language, one monetary system, one world government, with one mind and will."

I was very gullible at that time of my life, so I ate up all the garbage my friends were dishing out. The sad part was they really did believe in this stuff, too. I was to the point in my life that I was searching for some type of spirituality. I was fighting within myself to turn to God, but I felt like I couldn't give up my party life, so when the New Age Movement came into my life, I thought it fit just right.

⌘ ⌘ ⌘

I bowed down before Jesus at the Great White Throne and said to him, "I don't understand how blind I was to believe the stupid teaching of the New Age Movement. I guess I wasn't willing to give up my lifestyle. I was so embedded in the world's pleasures, I couldn't give them up."

"You could have repented of your sins and followed after Me, but you wouldn't. That's why you are facing an eternity in the lake of fire. The 'New Age Movement' is part of the end-time events that I talk about in the Bible. It is part of Satan's antichrist movements to deceive the nations. Thus, the end times of this age is close at hand.

"It is the last hour; and as you have heard that the antichrist is coming, even now many antichrists have come, by which we know that it is the last hour.'[20] Who is the greatest liar? The one who says that Jesus is not Christ. Such a person is antichrist, for he does not believe in God the Father and in His Son. For a person who doesn't believe in Christ, God's Son, can't have God the Father either. But he who has Christ, God' Son, has God the Father also.'[21]

"'For many deceivers have gone out into the world who do not confess Jesus Christ as coming in the flesh. This is a deceiver and an antichrist. If anyone comes to you and does not bring this doctrine, do not receive him into your house nor greet him; for he who greets him shares in his evil deeds.'[22]

"'I am the Lord your God, you shall have no other gods before Me. You shall worship no other God, for the Lord, whose name is Jealous, is a jealous God.'"[23]

31

My interest in the New Age Movement mounted. I went to as many lectures and seminars that I could on the subject. While skimming through a newspaper, I came across an interesting article. I said to Kathy, "Hey, get a load of this." I began reading, "Evangelist, Thomas Perkins, will be speaking on 'Prophecy Concerning the End of this Age.' The evangelist will be speaking at the North Holiday Inn, in New York, August 28."

"Sounds interesting," Kathy answered back. "Maybe he's lecturing on Nostradamus or perhaps Edgar Cayce."

"Yeah, it could be really interesting. On top of that, I might know the speaker."

"Oh, really?"

"Yeah! My first love's name was Tommy Perkins, but he was into Bible religion. Of course this could be Bible prophecy, I guess."

"Wow, Lorraine, I never knew you had any intellectual boyfriends."

I threw a sofa pillow at her. "You brat!"

"Was that the Tommy you were dating in high school? The one you broke up with, while you were dating Greg?"

"Yes, which I now know was a stupid mistake. He really was a great guy. Sometimes I wonder what my life would have been like if I had stayed with him...."

"Didn't he want to be a preacher, or something?"

"Yeah, thanks for reminding me. Reality check—me, married to a preacher?" We both rolled over in laughter.

When Kathy stopped giggling, she asked, "Have you seen anything of him since high school?"

"No, not at all. But you know, I wouldn't mind seeing him again. I'm kind of curious about what he's like now. Maybe he never became a preacher. Maybe he's into lecturing. I could handle that. I'm going, Kat! Do you want to go with me?"

"No. I'd love to, but I've got to work that night."

"Hey, no problem!" I said with a grin. "Maybe that would be for the best. If you know what I mean."

The night of the lecture I got to the conference hall a little late. The speaker had already started. I grabbed a seat in back where I could observe and not be seen. Besides, it was packed. Most of the seats were in the back.

There he was, right up in front of a mesmerized audience...my Tommy! Memories came floating back of the sweet, wonderful relationship I had with him. I really thought I loved him a lot back then. Tommy looked so handsome, I had to look twice to make sure it was him. His beautiful, warm personality shone through. There was no mistake. It was Tommy.

Tom woke me up from my daydream when he lit up a large visual on the stage in the darkened room. It was quite a dramatic spectacle. A large picture appeared behind him—a silhouette of what looked like a great warrior.

In a deep, loud voice Tom said, "It tells us in the Book of Daniel that the king, Nebuchadezzar, had many dreams that troubled him. He sent for his magicians, the astrologers, the sorcerers, and the Chaldeans so they could tell him his dream and give interpretation to it. The Chaldean told the king that there was no man alive who could do this. This made old Nebuchadnezzar very furious. He gave the command to destroy all the wise men of Babylon. Among these men, Daniel and his companions were rounded up to be killed.

"When Arioch, the chief executer, came to kill them, Daniel handled the situation by asking them, 'Why is the king so angry? What is the matter?'

"Then Arioch told him all that had happened. So Daniel went to the king. 'Give me a little time,' he said, 'and I will tell you the dream and what it means.' He went home and asked God to show him mercy by telling him the secret of the king's dream. That evening in a vision, God told Daniel what the king had dreamt. He blessed the name of God for giving him so much wisdom.

"Then Daniel went to Arioch, the one who was going to destroy the wise men of Babylon. He pleaded with him not to kill any more wise men and to take him before the king, and he would give the king the interpretation. When Daniel met with the king, he told him what his dream was about. 'You, O king, were watching; and behold, a great image! This great image, whose splendor was excellent, stood before you; and its form was awesome!'"

Then Tom pressed an electronic button that he held in his hand and the silhouette behind him lit up with brilliant colors. Tom used a laser beam and pointed to each part of the image as he talked. "'This image's head,' he told the king, 'is of fine gold, its chest and arms of silver, its belly and thighs of bronze, its legs of iron, its feet partly of iron and partly of clay.'

"Daniel went on to explain that the great image represented four world empires: The head represented King Nebuchadnezzar's kingdom of Babylon. Its breast and arms were silver, which represented the Medo-Persian empire. The belly and thighs of the figure were of brass, which stood for the empire of Greece. The fourth empire was symbolized by legs made of iron, which stood for the Roman Empire. The fifth was the feet with ten toes, which represented the New Roman Empire.

"The king watched as a stone struck the image on its feet of iron and clay and broke them into pieces. Then the iron, the clay, the bronze, the silver, and the gold were crushed together, and became like chaff from the summer threshing floors, and were carried away to be seen no more.

"This," Tom explained, "was King Nebuchadnezzar's kingdom, which was the most powerful of them all, but Babylon will fall by an inferior nation, Medo-Persia, which will then fall to Greece. Finally, Greece will be overthrown by the Roman Empire. All these kingdoms have come and gone. Only one remains and that is the New Roman Empire, the feet and toes.

"This is the part of the image that I believe is taking shape right now and is associated with the old Roman Empire. The toes represent ten kings who are to reign at the same time, who will form a confederacy on the ground of the ancient empire. Out of these ten nations the antiChrist will rise to power.

"There are several strong theories that this confederacy has already been forming. However, keep in mind that the Anti-Christ cannot take over until after the glorious rapture takes place. Many believe the Anti-Christ is the European Common Market, or otherwise known as the European Economic Community, or the European Union (EU). Others feel that the Anti-Christ could come out of The United Nations. When the Anti-Christ takes over, he will appear to give the nation of Israel peace and safety. But their peace and safety will last for only a short while, then he will bring chaos to the Jews and the new Christians who are saved in those days."

My mind started to drift away again from what Tom was teaching. I was daydreaming about how wonderful it would be to be the wife of this evidently successful speaker. One I just so happened to have a very loving past with.

Before I knew it, the lecture was over. I stayed in the background and watched this eager audience as they threw questions at him. I felt so proud of my old friend; the crowd couldn't get enough of his teachings. After the last person left, I stepped out of the shadows and walked up to him. I reached out and shook his hand as I said, "Hi, Tommy. Do you remember me?"

He hesitated a moment as he studied my face, then said, "Lorraine, Lorraine Patterson, right?"

"Well, yeah! Have I really changed that much?" *Maybe I didn't put enough makeup on to cover my wrinkles. Have I aged that much?*

"Oh, I mean no. You have matured into a beautiful woman." He paused again. "I've thought about you so many times. How have you been?"

"It's been a rocky road, Tommy, but I make the best of it. How about you? Looks like you've done all right for yourself."

"Oh, yes. God has been so good to me! I'm curious. What brought you here tonight?"

"Well, I'm very interested in spiritual things and prophecy. I saw the article in the paper so I decided to come. Besides, I saw your name. I wasn't sure if it was you or not, but here I am."

"Did you enjoy the lecture?"

"Yes, but some of it went over my head. I was surprised that it was on prophecies of the Bible. I've gone to seminars on prophecies, but they're on topics like Nostradamus." I cocked my head. "You know, Tommy, you really looked good up there tonight. You are a terrific speaker. And you know something? You are even more handsome than when we dated in high school. You must take care of yourself."

"Just good, clean living and God's help. But I don't know about being a good speaker, Lorraine, if you say you couldn't understand what I was trying to say."

"No, I didn't mean that. It wasn't you! For one thing, I was late getting here. I have to admit, I was thinking back to all the good times we once shared. I'm sorry I let my mind wander so much, but what I did hear, you were great! Perhaps you could fill me in on what I missed? I'm free for the rest of the night."

"It's kind of late tonight. How about meeting me tomorrow, here at the hotel at noon?"

"I'd love to! What's your room number?"

"Excuse me? Oh, no, I didn't mean that. I thought you could meet me at the hotel's dining room tomorrow."

"Yeah, sure. I didn't mean anything inappropriate. It's just that I feel so close to you. After all, you did ask me to marry you once, remember?"

"Of course I do, but that was a long time ago. We were kids."

The next morning I got Kathy up early to tell her all about seeing Tommy. "Oh, Kat, he is so handsome now—and successful. He had the auditorium full."

"So what was his lecture about?"

"It wasn't anything we are interested in. It was Bible prophecy."

"No!"

"Yes, but I still want to see him. I still have that special feeling for him. Maybe I can get a second chance with him."

"Is he happily married?"

"I didn't ask. I'm just trying to figure out if I can rekindle the love he used to have for me."

I selected a tight-fitting pink suit that had a very short skirt. Whenever I could show off my long, shapely legs, I did it. Of course, I had to top it off with three-inch heels. Then I asked Kathy, "Not too shabby for a mother with a fifteen-year-old son, right?"

"Heck, no, girl! You still have all the right curves in the right places."

"I only hope that it's not top provocative for the proper Mr. Thomas Perkins." I laughed.

"So, if it is, girl, you'll just have to lead him astray."

⌘ ⌘ ⌘

"Oh, Lord, if only you would let me go back to the time that Tommy first kissed me. I wouldn't have friends like Amy. I would be a better person, doing good works. I would keep Your Ten Commandments."

"YOU CANNOT BE SAVED BY DOING GOOD WORKS. YOU COULD NOT KEEP ALL OF THE TEN COMMANDMENTS. NO ONE CAN. YOU ARE SAVED BY GRACE. I GAVE THE LAW TO SHOW MAN HOW I WANTED HIM TO LIVE. THE LAW IS AN ESSENCE OF ME, RIGHTEOUSNESS. I GAVE YOU THE LAW SO YOU COULD RECOGNIZE WHAT SIN IS. IT IS A GUIDE FOR YOU TO LIVE BY. A DEBT HAD TO BE PAID FOR SIN. THAT IS WHY I WAS CRUCIFIED ON THE CROSS. I WAS SACRIFICED ON THE CROSS TO PAY YOUR DEBT, SO YOU COULD BE BLAMELESS BEFORE GOD."

32

When I arrived at the hotel's dining room, I was greeted by a hostess. She asked, "Will that be a table for one, or are there more joining you?"

"Actually, I'm meeting a gentleman. Perhaps he's here already."

"May I have his name, Miss?"

"Yes, it's Tommy! I mean, Thomas Perkins."

"Oh, yes. Right this way. They are waiting for you." *What is that stupid girl talking about? They? There's only one, and it's my Tommy.*

When the hostess brought me to the table, there was another person sitting with Tommy. I thought maybe she was one of his fans. I didn't care who she was. I just wanted her to leave!

Tommy noticed me and stood up. "Lorraine, I'm glad you could make it. I'd like to introduce you to Laura, my wife."

My heart sunk. *She looks a lot younger than me. Huh, that's funny. In a strange, uncanny way she looks like me. Except she's really plain looking. Same hair color, even though it's piled on top of her head. She's even got my blue eyes. It's almost like looking into a mirror, except she dresses so conservatively and could use more makeup. She doesn't seem to have any wrinkles like I do.*

"Hi, Laura. Tommy didn't mention that he had a wife."

"I'm sorry, Lorraine. We didn't get much time to talk last night. It's good that we'll be able to catch up today."

"Thomas, didn't you show her pictures of our children?"

"No, Laura, we only talked a short time."

"That surprises me. He's so proud of our kids that he's always quick to get their pictures out."

"Well, yes, matter of fact I am." He reached in his pocket and took out his wallet. "This is Thomas, Jr. He's ten, and this is Esther, she's eight."

"Lovely, children. Laura, you must have married young, I wouldn't have thought you would have children that old."

"Thank you! That's very kind of you, but actually I'm the same age as Thomas. We married right after college. How about you, Lorraine? Are you married?"

"No, not anymore, but I have two kids also. I don't have pictures with me, but just like you, I have a son and daughter."

Laura hesitated, then smiled. "There's nothing more fulfilling then kids, right, Lorraine?"

"Absolutely! I don't know what I'd do if it weren't for my Scott. He's my rock. We're more like friends than mother and son. In fact, when we go someplace together, people think we're just friends. I don't mind because it makes me feel young. He likes it when I let him be the 'man of the family.' He helps me take care of my daughter Linda a lot."

Laura's smile dropped. "Oh really, how nice for you." She put her smile back on. "I really feel blessed with our children. They both love the Lord. They are really good children."

"That's because of their God-fearing mother," Tommy added. "I give her most of the credit. As an evangelist, I'm on the road so much that Laura has had to do most of the childrearing by herself."

"That's not true, dear, you play a huge part in our lives. You have given us a wonderful foundation. You have followed God's Word to the letter on how you should bring up your children."

Tom smiled. "What has worked for us is that Laura has been a wonderful Christian wife. Because we do it God's way, Laura and I are always in agreement on how to discipline our children. God lays out all the instructions that we need in the Bible, so we can live our lives righteously. He tells each of us what role we are to have in the family. It's all laid out; all anyone has to do is read it in the Bible."

As I watched Laura and Tom, I could see the love in their eyes for each other. For a minute, I wondered if they even knew that anyone else was there but them. I was burning up with jealousy. I wanted what Laura had. I wanted that happy, contented love that I could see they shared. I don't know why I felt so much ownership toward Tom, but I did. Maybe it was the old memories I was in love with. Or perhaps it was because I never had a love as deep as theirs.

When Tom finally tore his attention away from his wife, he must have realized that I felt like a fifth wheel. So he started up a conversation with me again. "Lorraine, last night you mentioned you have been interested in prophecy lately?"

"Yes, I've been searching to find some peace in my life. I have had so many tragedies recently."

"I'm sorry to hear that. Sometimes it helps to talk about it."

I poured my heart out to him while Laura listened on. I told him about when I got pregnant with Scotty, Greg's abuse, my divorce, and lots of dead-end relationships. I broke into tears as I told him about my father committing suicide and Mother going insane.

"Oh, my, you certainly will be in our prayers. I am really sorry for your struggles."

We ordered our meal. After it was served, Tom said a prayer. I was very uncomfortable bowing my head in a public place, but I felt compelled to do it. When Tom remembered me in the prayer, I was touched.

While we ate, I said cheerfully to Tom, "You know, lately I've been getting more and more spiritual."

"Great, Lorraine. During hard times it's so important to be surrounded by God's people who can give you support. Have you been attending a church?"

"No, not really. I go to seminars and get together with friends for spiritual discussions. I have a personal spirituality that comes from within, so I can get in touch with my higher being. Our small group works on developing our unlimited human potential."

I wasn't sure if I liked the disapproving look that Tom and Laura gave each other. Sure, it wasn't from their God, but at least I was trying to be a better person.

"What exactly have you been taught at those meetings, Lorraine?"

"Our concept of a god is that it is in everything: the moon, the sun, and the very universe. Humans are the top intelligent beings. As the top intelligent beings, we have to control our own destiny."

"It sounds to me," Tom said, "that you are becoming involved in the New Age Movement. Is that a fair observation?"

"Yeah, Tommy. They call it the 'New Age.'"

"Oh, my dear, oldest friend, they are deceiving you! There is only one true God! The God, our Father, who is the creator of you and the entire universe! The 'New Age' religion has been around for a long time. It's been called by different names, but it all comes from the root of Satan. He now is using the name 'New Age Movement' to usher in a time just before the end of the Age."

Laura said, "That's right, Lorraine, the stage is now set for the end of this Age to take place. The conditions are right for it. The Bible describes what condition our world will be in at that time. The condition of the world is now ready!"

"Yes," Tom spoke. "In Daniel chapter 12 it tells us that knowledge shall increase. Look around at the incredible technological explosion in this century. Knowledge now has a doubling of global information every twenty-two months, which keeps growing. It's awesome!

"It was prophesied that before Christ came back, the Jews must return to Israel. Also that they have control of Jerusalem. After almost two thousand years these events were initiated in 1948! Israel became a nation after the Six-Day War of 1967. Is that not awesome, or what! I get chills thinking about it. Prophecy happening in our own modern history."

"Yes, it's wonderful!" Laura spoke up. "The Bible also speaks of how bad morals will be near the end of the age. You have to admit, Lorraine, that there has been a worldwide decay in our culture. Look at the music and films that are out there. They are full of lust, hate, violence, sex, and are Satanic oriented. Your 'New Age Movement' is part of it."

Tom said, "If you ever get a chance, Lorraine, read Matthew chapter 24. It's a great prophetic chapter. It tells about false religions like the 'New Age Movement. Through a religion like that, the Antichrist will come. They are preparing people's hearts and minds for the Antichrist to take over, which happens after the Rapture. When he comes to power, he will appear to the world as their savior, because he will give them a false belief in peace. Halfway through that seven-year period of the Tribulation, he will reveal himself and will cause persecution and chaos to the Jews and the Christians who were saved after the Rapture. He will cause people to take his mark and worship him. In Revelation 13:18 it tells us that the Antichrist's mark is called the 'Mark of the Beast' and its number is 666. No one will be able to buy or sell without that mark. Also many will be beheaded for God's sake during that time. You can find that in Revelation, chapter 13. The Bible says that if anyone takes the mark of the beast or worships his image, they'll face eternal punishment in the 'Lake of Fire'!"

"I remember that from our Teen Meet, Tom."

He smiled. "We had a good discussion about it afterwards at our soda shop where we always stopped after the meeting."

"Tommy," I said with hesitation. "I've done a lot of things I'm not really too proud of. Is there any chance I could still go to heaven?"

Tom gazed kindly at me. "Of course you have a good chance to go to heaven, Lorraine. Everyone, no matter how bad they have sinned, can ask Jesus into their hearts, confess their sins, and repent of them. It is making a decision to follow the Lord, to give your heart to the Savior. Would you like to make that commitment now? To let Jesus come into your heart? Would you like me to help you pray?"

I squirmed in my seat. "I just can't right now. I'm not ready. I want to, but I don't want to change my style of living. To tell the truth, I work as a bartender in a topless bar. I like to party. I kind of live on the fast track, if you know what I mean."

"Yes, Lorraine, I hear what you are saying. All you need to do is give your heart to Jesus just as you are, and He will make you a new person!"

"I get it, but maybe I don't want to be a different person right now. When I get older, or find a good guy, then I can become converted, but not now."

"I'll be praying for you, that your heart will soften by the Holy Spirit's help. There are no guarantees how long any of us will be on this earth. You never know when your life will be taken from you. Christ could come tomorrow. In Matthew 24:14 it says the Gospel will be preached in all the world as a witness to all to nations, and then the end will come. Do you know how close that prophecy is from being fulfilled? Oh, Lorraine, Jesus could come at any moment! He will come out of heaven with a shout 'COME HITHER!.' Then all His saints from all corners of the world will go to meet our Lord Jesus in the clouds. Every two thousand years a great prophecy has been fulfilled. Two thousand years after God created the earth, there was a world flood. Remember Noah and the Ark?"

"Yes."

"Two thousand years after the flood, Christ came to earth to die for our sins. Now it has been approximately two thousand years later. Our calendars were somewhat different, so we don't know the exact year. What prophetic event do you suppose will take place at any time?"

"Christ coming back."

"BINGO! Yes! Christians are anxiously looking for the Rapture of the Body of Christ's Church at any moment."

"Tommy, I don't want to be rude, but I really should be going.

Laura, it was nice meeting you. I sincerely hope you and Tom have a very happy life together."

"Sure, Lorraine. I always get so wound up when I start talking about my favorite subject that time just gets away from me." He reached down for his briefcase and pulled out a book. "Please, take this book as a gift from us. It's very interesting. Once you start reading, you won't be able to put it down. It's written by two awesome writers, Tim LaHaye and Jerry B. Jenkins. This book is titled *Left Behind*. It's the first novel in the exciting series. It's fictional but based on the prophetic verses in the Bible. It leads you up to events that occur right before and after the Rapture, the seven years of Tribulation, and straight through to the glorious appearing of Jesus. They even take you through the Millennium. Believe me, it is exciting. When you get one book done, you can't wait to get the next one. This book will give you a lot of answers."

"Thank you, Tommy…and Laura. I'm not sure when I can get at it, but I'll read it sometime."

"Don't wait too long." Tom gave me a hug good-bye as I fought back tears. I felt like I was leaving a part of myself behind as I walked out of the door.

⌘⌘⌘

I was trembling as I stood before the Lord Jesus at the Great White Throne Judgment. I said in a soft, defeated way, "I came so close to accepting you as my Savior that day. Why, oh why, was I so blind?"

"MY HOLY SPIRIT WAS WORKING SO HARD TO CONVINCE YOU TO RECEIVE ME. THOMAS' HEART WAS BURDENED AND TROUBLED FOR YOUR SOUL. YES, YOU WERE CLOSE TO ACCEPTING ME INTO YOUR HEART, BUT YOU WOULD NOT LET GO OF YOUR SINS AND REPENT. HENCE, I HAVE BLOTTED YOUR NAME FROM THE BOOK OF LIFE."

33

Scotty was beginning to grow away from me as he lived his own sinful life. His closest friend was Danny, and they had been best friends for over a year. Danny hung out at our apartment more than he did his own. He really liked me, said I was a cool mom. Danny said that his parents nagged him all the time. I liked the kid a lot. He was kind of a rebel like Scotty and me.

The boys were being harassed so much by gang members in the neighborhood that they thought they needed to join one just to survive. Scotty knew that Freddy, the guy he bought drugs from, was involved with one of the toughest gangs in the city, the Devil's Advocates. So after their drug deal, Scott asked, "Hey, man, what's the chances that I can get into the Devil's Advocates?"

Freddy gave a laugh. "What makes you think you have the right stuff, boy?"

"And what makes you think I don't?"

"Well, for one thing, I haven't seen any of your graves, or anything that shows you're bad enough to be one of us."

"That's because I haven't killed anyone yet, and I don't want to unless I have to. So far I've been lucky. I've only had to break a couple of heads, because of deals gone bad. My buddy, Danny, and I have been out here with no protection dealing, so we need the gang to back us up."

"So what makes you think we would even let a couple of punks like you in?"

"Because you need us! We could move more drugs, make your business expand. Plus, look at me. I'm a big dude; so is Danny. We know how to fight, Freddy!"

"What kind of weapons do you carry?"

"We each have a couple switchblades."

"No guns?"

"We're not afraid to carry them!"

"The Devil's Advocates is a very secretive gang. No one leaves the gang alive. Is that a problem?"

Scotty chucked a little. "You're kidding right? Man, I'd be proud to be one of the Devil's Advocates. There's no way I'd ever want out! I know Danny feels the same way."

"There's a tough initiation. If you pass it, you're in! If you don't, you're dead. Now do you want to join, or not?"

"How challenging is it?"

"You have to be tough and give your complete allegiance. That's all there is to it. Nothing you can't do...if you want to."

"I'm in, but I need to tell Danny the stipulations. I've got to make sure he's willing to agree. I'll meet you back here tomorrow, same time, and let you know, okay?"

They touched their knuckles together, and Freddy said, "Tomorrow, bro."

Scott was shaking inside and hoped Freddy wasn't aware of it. Could he pull off whatever this initiation was, or not? He went straight to Danny's house and explained everything to him. At first he was scared and didn't want anything to do with it. Scott told him he was scared, too, but was willing to do anything to be in the protection of a gang with the tough reputation that the Devil's Advocates had. Danny wouldn't have done it, but he knew if he didn't, they could no longer be friends.

The boys went the next night to meet with Freddy and swore their allegiance to him and the Devil's Advocates. Freddy gave them an address and told them that there would be directives when they got there.

It was a dark, cold night, and the address took them to an even rougher part of the city than where they were from. "There it is, Scotty! That's the building."

"Yeah, that's the right number. What a creepy, dingy old building. Look—the name of the store is Aquarius."

"Yeah, I wonder what they sell in there?"

"Well, dude, I guess the only way to find out is to open the door and go in." Scott slowly turned the knob and attached bells gave the warning that someone was entering the small storefront.

They didn't see anyone when they first went in—only weird things like chicken feet hanging on the wall. There was also a collection of books for sale, and it seemed they were all about witchcraft and the occult.

Danny looked at Scotty with a scared expression. "Come on, man, let's get out of here before it's too late!"

Scott grabbed him. "Dude, it's all ready too late! We gave Freddy our pledge. Like he said, the only way out now is our death!"

Then from the back room walked an old woman with a sheer scarf wrapped around her head. In an old crackly voice she asked, "Can I help you boys with something?"

In a shaky voice Scotty answered, "No, I mean yeah. Freddy sent us here. He said there would be someone here to give us further directions."

"Ah, yes," said the mysterious old woman. "Follow me. Freddy has been waiting for you two." She walked over to a door and opened it. There was a staircase that led down. The boys peered into the darkness as the old lady gave them further instructions. "Go down these steps, and you will find a secret passageway. There will be a guide to help you after that."

The boys crept slowly down the squeaky, dark steps. At the bottom it was as dark as midnight; they couldn't see a thing. Danny held on to Scott's shirttail, and Scott stretched his arms out to find something to touch as he walked around in complete darkness. After a bit he felt the wall. He walked in front of it, pushing the palms of his hands into the wall. He was looking for an opening or a special way that might swing around, anything.

After what seemed to the boys as hours, Scotty's hands opened a door, and it swung open to a dim light. At that point a man appeared from out of the darkness. "We thought that you would never make it, welcome, and follow."

The air was full of smoke as they approached the group this man was leading them to. The boys saw shadows of flames dancing on the walls as they drew closer. Then they saw a large group of people all wearing red robes and hoods. They were chanting. The boys wanted to run, but they felt trapped. Their guide ordered them to join the circle. They stood there stunned at the realization they were in a satanic ritual.

The man who seemed to be in charge of the group raised his arms and lowered them, as everyone sat down Indian style. He then began to distribute pills to the right of him. Each person passed them down until each was holding a pill, including Scott and Danny.

When they each had one, the leader said, "Let's all participate together." Everyone in the group swallowed the pill in their hands. Then the leader said, "You are dismissed."

When the circle broke up, some of the members congregated in small groups. Others went their own way. Scotty and Danny went and sat down in a corner of the dusty, dingy basement. When they came off their trip from the pill, Scott said to Danny, "Man, that was some pill. I wonder what drug that was? I sure had a horrifying trip."

Danny stared at Scotty with a scared stiff look. "Did you see him, Scotty? Did you see him?"

"Calm down, bro. See who?"

"Satan! That's who, Scotty, Satan!"

"Say what? Man, you were on some trip. It was a bad trip, but I sure didn't see some devil. Besides, I don't believe in all that garbage. I thought you didn't, either. You're kidding, right?"

"No, I swear on my life, man! I didn't believe in that stuff, but I do now. I swear, I really did see him. I was face to face with the devil, Scotty!"

"How do you know? What did he look like?"

"It wasn't like all the pictures of a devil; it was different."

"What did he look like?"

"Not like I've pictured him. He was short and had a potbelly. He was a bright orange red color. He had small horns and eyes like a cat. Oh yeah, he did have a tail like the pictures. He was skipping along to music that was in the background. I believe the lyrics of the songs I was hearing were worshiping him. Like a satanic band. When he noticed me staring at him, he turned his head and looked at me. He was really ugly."

"Come on, Dan, you're making this all up."

"No, man, I swear, I'm telling the truth. It scared me half to death!"

Freddy walked up to the two boys. "Well, guys, you passed the first test. Are you all right with it?"

Scotty spoke up, "Yeah, I guess. I sure wasn't expecting a satanic ritual. This thing you guys did tonight sure seemed real, but I don't really believe in a devil."

Freddy narrowed his eyes. "Satan is as real as you are! He is our master. If you will obey him and worship him, he will give you more power than you could ever imagine. You will now be required to come to this ritual once a month. You will see your powers grow."

"Man, I believe in him," Danny told Freddy. "After taking that pill I was given, I saw him. I did; I really saw Satan!"

Freddy got a crazed look and said to Danny, "That's wonderful, my man! Sometimes that happens to specially blessed people when they take LSD. That means he has honored you, letting you see him. You are in his favor."

"Freddy, have you seen him, too?"

"Not many people are fortunate enough to see him, but yes, I have. I've been honored to see him. Like me, you are one of his chosen. Your powers can be unlimited! Now all you need to do is to bow down and worship him. And if you obey him, you will have eternal power with our god forever!"

"How do I get those powers?" Scotty asked.

"Because of your friend's faith in Satan, and your willingness to receive his powers, the two of you are invited to our utmost secret meeting next week. There you will really see Satan's power rule. Perhaps you will even see him for yourself, Scotty."

⌘ ⌘ ⌘

"Oh, no," I screamed at The Great White Throne Judgment, "I must go back, Lord! Don't you see? It's my fault that Scotty got tangled up in Satanism. He had asked me about God, and I never took the time to talk to him about you. I wasn't even sure if I believed in you or not. Please, Jesus, let me go back to that time so I can keep him away from the devil, please!"

"AS I TOLD YOU BEFORE, THERE IS NO RETURN FROM THE JUDGMENT. I GAVE YOU MANY OPPORTUNITIES TO COME TO ME, BUT YOU REFUSED. IF YOU HAD COME TO ME, YOU WOULD HAVE GIVEN YOUR CHILDREN THE RIGHT FOUNDATION OF LIFE. FOR IT SAYS IN THE HOLY SCRIPTURES:

TRAIN UP A CHILD IN THE WAY HE SHOULD GO, AND WHEN HE IS OLD, HE WILL NOT DEPART FROM IT.[24]

DO NOT WITHHOLD CORRECTION FROM A CHILD, FOR IF YOU BEAT HIM WITH A ROD, HE WILL NOT DIE. YOU SHALL BEAT HIM WITH A ROD, AND DELIVER HIS SOUL FROM HELL.[25]

"YOU LEFT YOUR CHILDREN TO FEND FOR THEMSELVES WHILE YOU

PARTOOK IN THE WORLD'S WILD PLEASURES. INSTEAD OF GIVING THEM GOOD MORAL GUIDELINES AND TRAINING, YOU GAVE IN TO THEM. YOU COULD NOT CONTROL THEM. 'THE ROD AND REBUKE GIVE WISDOM, BUT A CHILD LEFT TO HIMSELF BRINGS SHAME TO HIS MOTHER. WHEN THE WICKED ARE MULTIPLIED, TRANSGRESSION INCREASES; BUT THE RIGHTEOUS WILL SEE THEIR FALL. CORRECT YOUR SON, AND HE WILL GIVE YOU REST; YES, HE WILL GIVE DELIGHT TO YOUR SOUL.'"[26]

34

Scotty and Danny got even more involved in the occult.

The night of the next ritual had come. Scotty was nervous and scared, but he and Danny had gone too far now to put it behind them.

The boys walked back into the witchcraft store where Freddy was waiting for them. Freddy slapped each of them on the back. "You guys made it; you're in! The high priest has given his permission for you to join us in the most sacred room. Follow me."

Freddy led them down the dark steps, through the secret passageway, and past the room where they were before. There Freddy touched a button on the wall, and another hidden door opened. There, as before, a large group was standing around a ring of fire.

Scott whispered to Danny, "This place reminds me of an old dungeon. And that sickening smell makes me want to puke my guts out."

A woman dressed in a red robe handed each boy a robe like hers. Then she ordered, "Take off your shoes and put this robe on before you join the others. You will be walking on sacred ground."

They did as the woman said and then joined the others. As they did, they noticed an altar in the center ring of the fire.

An older man stepped forward. "I am the high priest of this Holy ground. Tonight we are welcoming into our midst two new honorary members, Scott Patterson and Dan Hill. Let us precede. Who brings forth the offering tonight?"

One of the occult members stepped forward with a young cat. "I do, high priest. I come bearing an offering to our god this night."

The man handed the priest the kitten, and the priest said a chant over it. When he was finished. the priest laid the kitten on the altar. The occult member stabbed him with their sacred dagger. The man shook and threw his arms up high above his head as he screamed, "I have renewed power! Great power, thanks be to Satan." Then he knelt down, kissing the dirty cement floor in front of him. Flames came shooting out from behind the altar, which signified Satan's approval of the sacrifice.

In the weeks to follow Scott and Danny went to several of the sacrificial rituals. They saw all kinds of animals slain in the name of Satan. The more they went, the more they were convinced that Satan was really there giving them power.

Then one night the high priest pointed at Dan. "You! You, Dan Hill, are chosen to bring the sacrifice to our next ritual. Be sure the animal you surrender to our god is a virgin, or our god will be angry."

At the next meeting Danny did as the high priest had ordered him to do. Scott watched as his best friend placed a rabbit on the altar, which was encircled in a ring of fire. The priest spoke his chant, and then Dan raised the special ceremonial knife high in the air, plunging it down into the rabbit's heart. Danny screamed as blood squirted up in his face, "I've got the power! I feel the power surging into my body!" He fell to the ground in satanic worship. The whole group joined in the celebration, as the magical Satan flame ignited.

When Danny left the meeting that night he felt invincible. He felt that he indeed had an overwhelming power within him. Scott was impressed and a bit envious of his friend. He felt anxious and wanted to participate himself. He wanted to be able to possess the same powers that Dan had seemingly achieved.

At the following meeting the high priest said, "Halloween will be here in two months on October 31st, the last day of the Celtic calendar. Originally it was a holiday honoring the dead. Halloween was referred to as All Hallows Eve and dates back over two thousand years. Its culture is traced back to the Druids, a Celtic culture in Ireland, Britain, and Northern Europe. Roots lay in the feast of Samhain, which was annually celebrated on October 31st to honor the dead. Often sacrifices over a huge bonfire were made to Samhain, the Lord of the dead, in order to satisfy him.

"Dead souls roam all over the earth during this time of year. That is why we celebrate our god's day on the night before Halloween. It is called the devil's night. At that time our god is honored with nothing less than a human virgin sacrifice.

This year's honor will be given to one of our newest members, Dan Hill. He has proven his loyalty and faithfulness to our god! Dan was allowed to see Satan at his first visit with us. Satan was well pleased with him. Also, he has proven his allegiance when he sacrificed an animal at the altar."

Scott and Danny stood frozen in the circle of fire, wondering how they had gotten in so deep. Now the high priest was asking one of them to commit a murder.

Scott went home that night filled with fear. He didn't know what he was going to do, but he couldn't go back to that devil worshiping again. He also had to stay away from his best friend, Danny. It was evident Danny was in well over his head. The main thing was to avoid Freddy and the rest of the occult members.

Scott became as subdued as Linda, hanging out in his room as much as possible. He even quit school, in fear one of the members would see him.

Two months later Loraine's family read in the paper that Daniel Hill's body was retrieved from the harbor. There was a full investigation, but the authorities didn't come up with any suspects.

⌘ ⌘ ⌘

I stood before the Judgment seat and cried out, "Surely, Lord, you can't blame me for my son being mixed up in that heinous occult, can you? I never for one moment suspected Scotty to be involved in something like that! Why was he so foolish, Lord? How could he let himself get messed up with the occult?"

"AS THE HOLY SCRIPTURES READ: 'BE SOBER, BE VIGILANT; BECAUSE YOUR ADVERSARY THE DEVIL WALKS ABOUT LIKE A ROARING LION, SEEKING WHOM HE MAY DEVOUR.'[27] PEOPLE CHOOSE TO FOLLOW THE DEVIL BECAUSE OF VARIOUS REASONS. HE USES THESE REASONS TO BRING TEMPTATION TO YOU.

"YOUR FATHER WAS TEMPTED BY THE DEVIL BECAUSE HE WANTED RICHES AND POWER. YOU WERE TEMPTED BECAUSE YOU WANTED TO BE POPULAR AND ENJOY ALL THE PERVERSE PLEASURES OF THE WORLD. SCOTT AND DANNY WANTED POWER SO THEY COULD PROTECT THEMSELVES against the gangs in the street. The reason doesn't matter to the devil, just as long as he is able to tempt you into selling your soul to him.

"Scott and Danny were even more involved with the devil than most, but the result is the same. Either you choose to follow Me, or you let the devil deceive you into temptation.

"When I walked this earth, the devil tried to tempt even Me. It is written in the Bible that I was led by the Spirit into the wilderness to be tempted by the devil. And when I had fasted forty days and forty nights, afterward I was hungry. Now when the tempter came to Me, he said, 'If You are the Son of God, command that these stones become bread.'

"But I answered, 'It is written, Man shall not live by bread alone, but every word that proceeds from the mouth of God.

"Then the devil took Me up into the holy city, set Me on the pinnacle of the temple, and said to Me, 'If You are the Son of God, throw Yourself down. For it is written: He shall give His angels charge over you, and in their hands they shall bear you up, lest you dash your foot against a stone.'

"I said to him, 'It is written again, You shall not tempt the Lord your God.'

"Again, the devil took Me up on an exceedingly high mountain, and showed Me all the kingdoms of the world and their glory. And he said to Me, 'All these things I give You if You will fall down and worship me.'

"Then I said to him, 'Away with you, Satan! For it is written, You shall worship the Lord your God, and Him only you shalll serve.' Then the devil left Me, and behold, Angels came and ministered to Me."[28]

"'Therefore submit to God. Resist the devil and he will flee from you.'"[29]

35

While bartending one night, a tall, handsome man came into the club and sat at the bar. Most of the guys were all alike, but this dark-haired, distinguished-looking guy was different somehow. Unlike most of the guys who hang out at girlie bars, Kevin was a very shy, quiet man. Nevertheless, it was obvious he couldn't keep his eyes off me. I didn't care; I was used to men staring at me. With the low-cut, tight dress that was my uniform, I outshined all of the dancers in the place. My boss always said he didn't know who the guys came to see—me or the strippers.

Kevin looked at me differently than most men did. He talked to me with respect—not like the others, who treated me like a play bunny. We did talk a lot. He told me he was a sales manager for a large company out of Ohio, and that he was here on business for an extended time.

Kevin became a regular customer at the bar. He was there every night. He never noticed when the dancers were on the floor; he only had eyes for me.

After a couple months of Kevin coming into the bar, it was obvious with the rest of the employees and the regulars that he had a mad crush on me. It was evident I enjoyed his company too. It was a pleasure to talk with him, because he was the only guy at the bar who didn't treat me like a sex object. I really was impressed with him.

Annie, another bartender, said to him, "Hey, Kevin, why don't you ask Lorraine out? Everyone in here can tell you are totally infatuated with the woman!"

The waitress who was picking up her drinks at the bar said, "You two would make a perfect match. You're both drop-dead good-looking, both the same coloring. It looks like a match made in heaven. Come on, Kevin, ask the lady out to dinner."

Kevin's face got red as he looked at me. "Lorraine, would you go out to dinner with me?"

There was no way I could turn him down. I knew it took a lot for Kevin to muster up the courage to ask me. So I answered, "Sure, Kevin, I'd love to go out with you."

That was the beginning of a major love affair for Kevin and me. I even stopped going out with other guys, because I was totally in love with him.

For the next two months we were practically inseparable. Never before had I ever had a more sizzling, passionate love affair than I had with Kevin Potannette! Then the time came I had been dreading. Kevin's business dealings in the city were wrapping up. He soon would be gone. One evening over dinner he asked me, "Lorraine, why don't you give up this rat race and come live with me? I live in a quiet little town. My neighborhood is very nice, with lots of trees. Do you like flower gardens?"

"Oh, yes!"

"Then you'd love it there. I have a really big, beautiful flower garden in my backyard. The front yard is nice too…all sorts of trees and shrubbery."

"Oh, Kevin, it sounds heavenly!"

"Do I sense a but in there somewhere?"

"Well, I mentioned that I had two kids, right?"

"Yeah. I don't really see a problem with that. I love little kids."

"They're not so little, Kevin. Linda is twelve, and my son, Scott, is sixteen."

"Wow, I had no idea you had kids that old! How old are you, if I may ask?"

"I'm thirty-three. I hope that doesn't scare you away."

"I really thought you were at least ten years younger. Man, that's hard to believe! Well, you got me by three years, but that's okay. It doesn't bother me, if it doesn't you."

"Of course not, darling. Only there still is a problem. Linda gets really upset when I live with a guy. She is terrified of men. She's had some bad experiences."

"That's awful. I'm so sorry for her. I'm sure in time I could get her to trust me, Lorraine. I'm really good with my nieces and nephews."

"Then there's Scotty. He likes being the man of the family. When I'm living with a man, he really resents it. Besides, he's a city boy. I'm sure he would give me trouble about leaving. However, he has been really nervous lately. Stays in his room a lot, which isn't like my son. I believe he might have a big monkey on his back, or something. The more I think about it, maybe getting away would be good for him."

"Hey, sweetheart, these are all things that we can work out. Would you like me to go talk to the kids for you?"

"Thanks, honey, but I think it would be better if I did it alone."

The next morning was Saturday, and the kids were both sleeping in their beds. I hollered out, "Hey, you sleepy heads, up and at 'em!"

They stumbled out of their rooms. Scotty had a big frown as he said, "What the heck is going on? It's nine o'clock in the morning! Why are you up so early?"

"You guys, I have some really, really good news."

Scott looked disgusted. "You won the Lottery?"

"No silly! How would you kids like to get out of this dirty old city?"

"Yeah, winning the Lottery might be easier."

"No, Scott, I'm serious."

"Hey, Lorraine, it ain't going to happen. We could never afford to get out of the projects, let alone the city."

"Yes, Scott, there is a way. My boyfriend has got this really nice home in a small town in Ohio. It sounds so lovely, with flowers and trees all over the yard."

"You promised, Mom," Linda whined. "You promised me you wouldn't bring any of your creepy boyfriends home anymore."

"Yes, honey, I know I promised, but Kevin—that's my boyfriend—he's different. He's a real nice guy. I know you will like him."

"That's what you said about the last creep. I swear, Ma, I can't take any more of your boyfriends. I'll run away first!"

I put my arms around my daughter. "Listen, honey, Kevin's not like the rest, I promise. He is a very compassionate man and loves kids."

Eyes full of tears Linda said, "Like Rex and Gary? They liked kids real well, remember?"

Rex was one of many men that I had lived with, and Gary was my ex-husband. I held my head down in shame. "I'm so sorry about that. No, he doesn't like kids like that, honest. If you guys will just give Kevin a chance, I know he will give us a good life. I really care for this man a lot. I'm in love with him! Kevin is a way out of these slums. Most of my ex-boyfriends moved in with us. They were content living with us in the projects. Kevin's different. He has his own home, with a big yard full of flowers. It could mean a whole new life for us. I wouldn't have to work in bars anymore. I could stay home and be a mother to you guys. Doesn't that sound great?"

Linda still had tears in her eyes. "Yes, but what if he turns out to be mean?"

"Then we'll pack up and hit the road! Any place has to be better than here. Besides, you told me how petrified you were about starting high school this fall. You're afraid to walk home from school because of all the shootings."

Linda's eyes filled up again. "The high school is so big. The halls are packed full of kids, and a lot of them carry knives in school. I'm so scared!"

I held her tighter in my arms. "That's why it is so important to move while we have the opportunity. In a small town you can walk down the sidewalks or go to the park without worrying that something bad will happen to you. The schools are smaller and less crowded. Come on, sweetie, say you'll give it a try!"

" I don't know. What do you think, Scott? Do you think we should?"

"I don't know, Sis. I don't know if I could handle a small town. All I've ever known has been the city. I don't know any other life but these wicked streets. Maybe I'll stay behind. I can support myself, no problem."

"I'm not going unless Scotty does," Linda said in a determined way.

"Come on, you guys, give me a break here. I love the guy! This is my—I mean our—only chance for a real happy family. Come on, Scotty, you of all people should want to get out of town. You and Danny were so close. Don't tell me that the thugs who killed him won't come looking for you. I know the business you've been in; it's a very dangerous enterprise, my son."

He flinched. "Point well taken. What do you think, Squirt? Should we give this a try? If this guy as much as looks at you wrong, he's dead! Nobody is going to hurt my little sister again!"

Before the week had ended, Kevin was helping us load up a U-haul that he had rented, and we were headed for Ohio. Hours later we rolled into a town that looked like it was out of a Rockwell painting. It was autumn, and the leaves had peaked to radiant reds and brilliant yellows.

When we pulled into a paved driveway with an attached three-stall garage, I was flabbergasted at the huge ranch home Kevin was offering us.

I gave Kevin a big hug when the motor stopped. Tears flowed. "Is this it?" I said with excitement in my voice. "Is this really your home?"

"Yeah, are you disappointed?"

"Disappointed? Are you crazy? This home is like a dream come true. It's absolutely beautiful! And it's so big. I've been living in cracker-box apartments since I was sixteen. This is fantastic!"

The kids couldn't even speak they were so overwhelmed.

Kevin unlocked the door, opened it, and grabbed me up in his arms, carrying me over the threshold. The kids thought that was cool. Kevin put me down and gave us all a grand tour of our luxurious new home. The kids were thrilled over their spacious bedrooms. It wasn't as grand as the mansion I grew up in, but it seemed even better to me. I wanted to fill it with love...nothing like the cold home I was raised in.

As the months zoomed by, I could even see an improvement in the kids. Linda actually liked school and was making friends. Scotty was getting acquainted with some of the town's teens. He even started dating a cute little blond. As for me, I couldn't be happier. The only drug I was doing now was marijuana, and I only did that once in a while with Kevin. Scotty and Linda even acted like they enjoyed the small-town atmosphere. Finally, life was looking good for my family.

One afternoon while I was happily singing and doing my housework, I was startled by a noise. I relaxed when I looked up and only Linda was standing at the door. "Wow, you scared me," I said to her. "Is it time for school to be out already?"

With a singing, teasing voice Linda said, "Yeah, Mother! School gets out every day at the same time."

"Oh, I guess it does, doesn't it? I enjoy keeping this beautiful house clean so much that I lose track of time."

Linda started giggling. "Hey lady, have you seen my mother around here lately? She looks a lot like you, but she hates housework. At least she did."

"You little stinker," I kidded back. "I'm just so content here. Kevin has made me so happy."

"I sure can see a change in you, Mom. It's like you are a whole different person. I believe Kevin has made a difference in our family."

"Yes, dear, he has. You are doing so good in school now. By the way, did you pass your algebra test today?"

"Yes, I aced it!"

"No! Get out of here. That's my girl!"

"Mother, I couldn't have done it without your help."

"My help? What do you mean? I couldn't have done it without Kevin helping me figuring it out a couple of times. It's been a long time since high school."

"Yeah, I know he was a big help too, but just you caring makes all the difference in the world. Before you never seemed to care if I got good grades or not."

"I know, honey, and I'm sorry. Life was so hectic for me back then. Now I have time to be the mother that you and Scott deserve. Kevin has made my life complete. This past year has been the happiest time of my entire life! I'm almost afraid to go to sleep. I might wake up and find out that it's all a big dream."

"You sure were right about him, Mom. Kevin really is a great guy. He treats me like he's my father. I've never had someone like that before."

"I've got to start dinner. Want to help?"

"Sure, I love helping you cook. You sure are a lot more fun these days, Mom."

"So are you! It is so good to see you more outgoing and happy."

"You know, I'm really happy here. I feel like we are all a family. There's only one thing missing."

"What's that, dear?"

"It would feel even more like a family if you and Kevin got married."

"That would be wonderful, but he hasn't asked."

"Well, this isn't the old days. Why don't you ask him?"

"That's funny. I had a visitor soon after we moved in. It was a Mrs. Roothberry from across the street. She told me that she saw Mr. Potannette carry me over the threshold when we moved in. She wanted to come over to congratulate us and welcome us into the neighborhood."

Linda giggled. "She thought that you and Kevin were married?"

"Yes! I believe I shocked her when I told her we weren't. I guess living together isn't something they do that much in a hick town." I laughed. "She got real embarrassed and told me that it wasn't her place to judge. Anyway, she invited us to church. I guess she thought that I better get my soul saved."

"You got to be kidding! She actually invited you to church?"

"Not just me, the whole family. Don't look so shocked, young lady. It might not be a bad idea. I went to church when I was around your age. In fact, I was quite involved in a teen group. I even dated the nicest boy in the class."

"But, Mom, I remember once when I asked you about God, you told me that there wasn't any God."

"That was when I was very bitter, Linda. How could I believe in a God when my life was so bad? But now, talking with the neighbor has rekindled my memories of when I went to church. I remember learning about The Great White Throne Judgment. I'm sure if there's a God, he's turned his back on me long ago. I'm not even sure if I believe in God. However, I think it might be good for this family to give church a try sometime. What do you think?"

"Hey, if you want to go, Mom, I'll go with you."

Just then Scotty walked into the house. Linda said to him, "Mom wants us to go to church sometime. What do you think?"

Scotty looked a little disgusted but agreed to go if Linda and I really wanted him to. He asked me, "Has Kevin ever gone to church?"

"I haven't the slightest idea! We never talked about that topic."

That evening I outdid myself and cooked a mouthwatering dinner. As we all sat down, Scotty smiled and said to me, "Smells and looks delicious, Mom." Hearing the word *Mom* coming out of my son's mouth for the first time felt like music. I was feeling like a mother, really for the first time. Scott told Kevin, "She sure has come a long way in her cooking skills, since we moved in with you. Before, a good dinner was a couple cans of soup or a frozen pizza." Everyone laughed.

"Hey, Scott, cut me a break here. I worked a lot of hours to support you kids."

"Yeah, and a lot of partying too," Scott answered back.

"And too many boyfriends," Linda chimed in.

"All right, that's enough, kids. Kevin doesn't care to hear all about your mother's past indiscretions."

"I'm not perfect either, kids. I was just very fortunate that with all the men pursuing your mother, she chose to be with me."

"Oh, darling, you are so sweet! Well, the bottom line, Mr. Kevin Potannette, is that you have made a wonderful influence not only on me, but on this whole family."

When we finished our delightful dinner, Scott jumped up. "Here, Mom, let me give you hand with the dishes."

I gave out a quick chuckle. "Quick, Linda, go get the camcorder! This is a first; we need to capture it on film!"

Everybody laughed.

Scott got this funny little smirk. "Funny, Mom. If you want help, I'd suggest you cut the humor and savor the moment." We playfully laughed, and Scott gave me a big hug.

It was a great feeling as Scott and I were alone in the kitchen doing the dishes. I felt closer to my son than I ever had. We talked about all sorts of things. I told him how impressed I was because he wanted to help me with dishes. He said, "It ain't a big deal. It's just that I've really been proud of you lately. You have changed so much. Even the way you keep house! You actually like doing house work now. Besides, I thought doing dishes together would give me a private time to talk to you."

"What is it, Scott? Is something wrong!"

"Oh, no, Ma, something's right! I just wanted to tell you that I think you made a really good decision when you decided to move in with Kevin. I really like the guy. For the first time in my life, I like the guy you are with."

"I am so happy to hear that, son!"

"Yeah, it's neat; he seems like a real dad to me. I've never had that before. He treats me like a man, but also like his son. I wouldn't let this one get away, Ma. Maybe you ought to think about getting a ring on your finger."

"Funny you say that. Linda just told me about the same thing earlier. To tell the truth, Scott, I'd love to marry him."

Later that evening as we laid in each other's arms by the fireplace, I remembered the conversations I'd had with my kids. They had actually encouraged me to make our situation permanent: to get married!

I looked up into Kevin's eyes. "I love you, Kevin Potannette!"

"I love you too, Lorraine."

"You know, the kids were both telling me tonight how much they like you. That is a big honor. They could never stand any of my boyfriends before. You are very special to all of us."

"Babe, you're all special to me, too."

"Have you ever considered us getting married?"

Kevin hesitated for a few seconds, then said, "Lorraine, honey, I care very deeply for you, but I can't make that commitment right now. It's too soon, wouldn't you say? I need more time!"

I couldn't hold back the tears, and I yelled at him, "More time? We have been living together for almost a year. If you don't know by now if you want me, then something is wrong! Is it me? The kids? What is it?"

"No, baby, it's not you or your kids. It's me, okay? I have a problem that has nothing to do with you. It's something I have to work out before I can commit to anyone."

"What is it, Kevin? You and I can talk about anything. You know that you can tell me anything, baby. Just be honest with me."

Kevin pushed me aside and got up. He went to the window and stared out of it as if he wanted to be somewhere else. "I can't," he finally said. "I just can't talk about it now. You've got to be patient with me, Lorraine. I'll tell you, but I can't right now, okay?"

"Fine!" I left him to stew and went to bed. I barely talked to him for a week.

Then I started to notice that he wasn't feeling good. After that, he began burning up with fever. Kevin was reluctant to go to the hospital, but because of my insistence he finally went. The emergency doctor admitted him. I spent most of the next two weeks sitting next to Kevin in his hospital bed. After several days the doctors came up with the diagnosis. When they gave us the news, I felt like a knife had been thrust into my heart. Kevin and I were both devastated! I stayed for a while and talked to him, but then I had to leave. I couldn't stand being in that hospital room one minute longer with the man I loved. I left and went home.

Linda was scared to death when she came home from school. She heard loud crashing coming from the living room. She walked in and saw me throwing everything I could get my hands on. I was screaming and crying as I destroyed everything I could. The room was a disaster zone.

"Mother! Stop! What's the matter?" Linda cried.

I was in such a rage I barely knew my daughter was in the room and continued throwing things. Linda ran outside and waited for Scott to get home.

Luckily, Scott got home soon. Linda filled him in on the state I was in. He rushed into the living room. "Ma! What the heck is wrong with you? Stop it! Calm down!"

I wouldn't stop, so Scott grabbed me and wrestled me down on the floor. Finally I gave up the struggle and laid on the floor crying. Scott got up and went over to the couch and sat at one end of it. He said to me, "Get up, Mom, and come lay your head down on my lap."

I did as my son said and went and lay down on the sofa, resting my head in my son's lap. Scotty always knew how to calm me down. I was able to doze off as Scotty's soothing fingers brushed my hair back away from my tearful face.

Half asleep I heard Scott say to Linda, "Something bad must have happened to Kevin at the hospital today. Nothing else could make her lose it like this."

"You don't think Kevin could have died, do you?"

"No! Don't say that, Linda. Kevin's not that sick."

After lying there with my eyes closed for a while I opened them. Linda noticed and said in a soft voice, "Mom, are you feeling better now? Can you talk to us and tell us what's the matter? Kevin didn't die, did he?"

"Linda!" Scott scolded.

"No, no, Scotty, that's okay. I know you kids are concerned about Kevin. And no, Kevin isn't dead. However, it is only a matter of time."

Scott's eyes opened wide. "No! Not Kevin."

Linda started crying. In between sobs she asked, "What's wrong with him, Mom?"

"Kevin has been really sick lately because he has pneumonia. What's so horrible is that he got it from being weak from having the AIDS virus!" I broke down crying again. "He has AIDS. Kevin has AIDS!"

"AIDS?" Scott looked stunned. "No, Ma, are they sure?"

"Yes. That's why it took so long. They have taken all the necessary tests, and they're positive it's AIDS!"

Puzzled, Scott said, "But how does a guy like Kevin get infected with that horrible sickness? He doesn't seem like much of a skirt chaser. Ma, you have got to get tested right away!"

"Yes, Son, I know. I was so angry at him when I found out about it, I wanted answers. Kevin finally admitted to me that he was bisexual. He told me he had broken off all his homosexual affairs when he met me. He had been affected by the virus without him even knowing. He also admitted he still was in love with his last partner and lately had been tossed between him and me. He told me he loved me, but he wanted me to get in touch with his male friend. That's fine with me. He can have him. I sure don't want anything more to do with him!

"I'm so scared you may have the virus, Mom," Linda cried.

I fought back tears. "Me too, sweetheart. I am so scared of that dreadful disease. I don't want to die either!"

Scott put his arms around me, and I cried like a baby.

⌘⌘⌘

I could still feel the hurt and betrayal that Kevin put me through as I had watched all this from The Great White Throne Judgment. I questioned Jesus, "Why do you make gay men so handsome, and why did you make them gay in the first place? Just so they could break women's hearts?"

"Homosexuals were not born gay. Being gay is when someone commits acts of sin that are unbridled lust to satisfy their godless sexual appetite. In the Bible it is written in the Book of Genesis that I destroyed the cities of Sodom and Gomorrah because their perverted sexual sins were very grave. Out of both cities I found only one man by the name of Lot who was worthy to be saved.

"Two male angels were sent to warn him and help deliver his family out of the city. When the angels were in Lot's house, the men of Sodom—Sodomites, both young and old—surrounded the house and shouted to Lot, 'Bring out those men to us so we can rape them.'

"Lot begged them not to do this evil thing and in exchange offered them his two virgin daughters instead to do with as they pleased. But they were angry and tried to force their way into the house to get the men. The angels were able to push them away and blocked the door, and temporarily blinded the men of Sodom.

"The angels told Lot that he and his family were to flee the city because they were going to destroy it completely. The stench

OF THE PLACE HAD REACHED TO HEAVEN, AND GOD SENT THEM TO DESTROY IT. HOMOSEXUALITY IS ABSOLUTELY FORBIDDEN, FOR IT IS AN ENORMOUS SIN.[30]

"GOD SHOWS HIS ANGER FROM HEAVEN AGAINST ALL SINFUL, EVIL MEN WHO PUSH AWAY THE TRUTH FROM THEM. FOR THE TRUTH ABOUT GOD IS KNOWN TO THEM INSTINCTIVELY. GOD HAS PUT THIS KNOWLEDGE IN THEIR HEARTS. SINCE EARLIEST TIMES MEN HAVE SEEN THE EARTH AND SKY AND ALL GOD MADE AND HAVE KNOWN OF HIS EXISTENCE AND GREAT ETERNAL POWER. SO THEY WILL HAVE NO EXCUSE WHEN THEY STAND BEFORE GOD AT JUDGMENT DAY.

"AFTER A WHILE THEY BEGAN TO THINK UP SILLY IDEAS OF WHAT GOD WAS LIKE AND WHAT HE WANTED THEM TO DO. THE RESULT WAS THAT THEIR FOOLISH MINDS BECAME DARK AND CONFUSED. INSTEAD OF WORSHIPPING THE GLORIOUS EVERLASTING GOD, THEY TOOK WOOD AND STONE AND MADE IDOLS FOR THEMSELVES.

"SO GOD LET THEM GO AHEAD INTO EVERY SORT OF SEXUAL SIN, AND DO WHATEVER THEY WANTED TO DO—YES, VILE AND SINFUL THINGS WITH EACH OTHER'S BODIES.

"THAT IS WHY GOD LET GO OF THEM AND LET THEM DO ALL THESE EVIL THINGS, SO THAT EVEN THEIR WOMEN TURNED AGAINST GOD'S NATURAL PLAN FOR THEM AND INDULGED IN SEXUAL SIN WITH EACH OTHER. AND THE MEN, INSTEAD OF HAVING A NORMAL SEX RELATIONSHIP WITH WOMEN, BURNED WITH LUST FOR EACH OTHER, MEN DOING SHAMEFUL THINGS WITH OTHER MEN AND, AS A RESULT, GETTING PAID WITHIN THEIR OWN SOULS WITH THE PENALTY THEY SO RICHLY DESERVED.[31]

"DON'T YOU KNOW THAT THOSE DOING SUCH THINGS HAVE NO SHARE IN THE KINGDOM OF GOD? DON'T FOOL YOURSELVES. THOSE WHO LIVE IMMORAL LIVES, WHO ARE IDOL WORSHIPERS, ADULTERERS, OR HOMOSEXUALS WILL HAVE NO SHARE IN HIS KINGDOM. NEITHER WILL THIEVES OR GREEDY PEOPLE, DRUNKARDS, SLANDERERS, OR ROBBERS.[32]

36

The next day I was out desperately looking for a job. I couldn't stay in Kevin's house one minute longer than I had to. Bruce (his lover), was at the hospital by Kevin's side, so he didn't need me anymore. I drove to the nearest, largest city I could find, which was Cleveland. I had never been there before, so I stopped into a gas station and asked where the hot spots were located.

All I knew how to do was to bartend. I had no choice. I couldn't change my occupation at this point of my life. If I did, I would only be able to earn minimum wage. I knew I could make the most money at an exotic dance club, so that's where I went. The second place I went, I got hired.

The manager of the bar handed me a uniform and said, "Here, doll, it's a bit skimpy but brings in good tips, and the fringe benefits aren't bad, if you're into that type of thing."

"Okay, thanks. By the way, do you know where I can get a reasonable three-bedroom apartment around here?"

"Yeah, there's a few in the neighborhood. They're dumps, but you're still going to pay through the nose for a three bedroom."

I drove to the addresses my new employer had given me. He was right—they were dumpy. But I rented one anyway.

To say the least, the kids were very disappointed when we stood in the doorway with our suitcases in our hands. It was a letdown after living in Kevin's beautiful home for almost a year.

As the months moved on, all three of our lives soon began to spiral downhill, like they had before Kevin came into our lives. Again I became embedded in the pleasures of the world. Scott went back to drug trafficking. Linda isolated herself in her room, missing a lot of school. I was barely aware of what was going on with my children; my own life was too far off-track to notice. I had become very bitter, especially with men. Now I only went out with guys to have fun, or for what I could get from them. There was no more fantasy about finding Mr. Right and falling passionately in love.

One evening I overheard Scott talking about this fantastic party that was coming up. It was going to be at the Demarkho's mansion (one of Cleveland's wealthiest families). Scott's buddy Jack Demarkho's parents were away on a business trip, so their son planned a small party.

I begged Scott to let me go along with him. Of course, Scotty was not thrilled about taking his mother with him to a party.

I teased, "Come on, Scotty, no one will know I'm your mom. I might be pushing forty, but I still get carded at bars. I'll dress like a teeny bopper. No one will know the difference."

Finally I wore Scotty down. "All right, Lorraine, you can go, but you're on your own," he told me. "I can't be hanging out with you. I plan on doing some big business at that party tonight. There's going to be a lot of rich kids there."

"Sure, Scott, you know I'm not bashful. I just need a way in, that's all. I love parties! Hey, how about taking Linda along with us?"

"No! That's going too far. This kind of a party is not a place for a fourteen-year-old, anti-social girl like Linda."

"That's the point, Scott. We need to help her get out and have some fun! It's not natural for a girl her age to lock herself up in her bedroom all the time. She needs to get out and make friends. My heart bleeds for her, Scotty. I remember how I felt when I was a kid like her. I don't want Linda to feel that way. Come on, Scott. You won't even know she's there. I'll look after her."

"All right, all right! You win! Now get off my back. We'll make a family affair out of it. Just stay away from me once we get there, okay?"

It was the Saturday night of the party, and Scott drove us up the long paved drive to the Demarkhos' house. The home was a beautiful three-story estate nestled in tall pine trees. On a normal evening it was the scene of serenity and tranquility, but that was not the case that night. Cars were parked all over the immaculate landscape, and smoking, drinking teens filled the grounds. Some were even falling down drunk, and it was only nine o'clock when we arrived. We were parked about a hundred yards from the mansion, but we could hear the boom of the music.

We sat in the car for a few minutes assessing the situation. Scott looked at me. "Man, this is some gigantic party! My buddy Jack never was expecting a turnout like this. His parents are going to kill him if they find out. Okay, girls, are you ready to party?"

I jumped out of the passenger side of the car (Scott always drove when we went anywhere). "Let's party!"

"Come on, Linda, get moving," Scott prodded. "We should have been here an hour ago."

Linda just sat in the back seat with her arms folded with a big frown. "I told you guys I didn't want to go to this silly party. I hate parties!"

"Oh, come on, you've never been to a party before," I said. "You'll have fun, baby girl! Trust your mom. Would I ever lie to you? Don't answer that." I laughed. You'll have fun meeting some new kids. I bet the boys will be lined up, asking you to dance. Come on, honey, it'll be fun!"

"I won't know anybody there."

"Sure you do, Squirt!," Scott reassured his sister. You've met a couple of my buds. They've been over to our apartment. You remember Jack, don't you? If I remember correctly, you had a crush on him, right?"

"Did not!"

"Yes, you did," Scott teased.

"I just said I thought he was cute, that's all. Your friends are too old for me."

"Jack is only sixteen, and he acts fourteen. I don't think that the dude has even had a date with a girl."

"It really doesn't matter anyway. A rich, good-looking boy like Jack won't give me the time of day. I'm fat, and we're poor."

I thought this was a good time for a mother to step in. "Okay, Scott, stop teasing your sister, and let's just go in. Come on, Linda, quit acting like a baby and get out of the car. I want to party! Besides, you are adorable."

Linda got out of the car, and we walked up to the house. The mansion had huge double doors, much like the home I was raised in. All three of us were overwhelmed at the home's beauty. I gasped in envy. "To think I actually lived in a splendid home like this. How I'd kill to get a place like this now."

As we walked into the crowded entry hall, one of Scott's friends spotted him. "Yo, dude, over here."

"Sorry, girls," Scott said, "I've got to meet up with Eddie. We've got a big deal going down. Lorraine, you and Linda will be okay, right?"

No party was ever intimidating to me, so I answered, "Sure, Scotty, go on. Linda and I are going to have fun, right, baby?"

Linda frowned. "Yeah, sure. Whatever."

Linda found a chair in a corner, and I went straight to the party's trash can. That's a new, large garbage can, where people bring bottles of booze and dump it in the mix. It also had various fruits cut up in it. I poured out two large glasses full and took one over to Linda. "Here, baby, try this."

"That's got booze in it, Ma!"

I whispered, "Linda, at a party like this, call me Lorraine. And that is good stuff! Yeah, it's got some booze in it, but it's got a lot of fruit and juice in it, too. I could drink something like that all night and hardly feel it." I was too immature to think I was a seasoned drinker. My young daughter had only sips of my drinks when we were sitting around at home.

Linda took a sip. "Okay, Lorraine, I guess it's not too bad."

"Trust me, you'll feel like dancing when you get that down."

I barely had the words out of my mouth when a guy came over and asked me to dance. I became quite popular on the dance floor. There wasn't anything shy about me, and I was there to have a good time. It was like I was a teenager at Greg's basement bar again. I danced and danced, never thinking about my bashful, insecure daughter sitting in a corner.

Time was dragging for Linda as she sat there a couple of hours by herself. When she was about half asleep, Jack Demarkho walked up and said, "It's Linda, right? Scott's little sister?"

"Yes, hi, Jack, this is really a big party."

"Yeah, but I never invited all these kids. My parents will kill me if they see one thing out of place. It's already a mess in the house and on the grounds. I hope I can get it all cleaned up by the time my parents get home tomorrow. But enough of my problems. I saw you sitting here all alone and thought you might want some company."

"Well, yeah, but you're the host; you don't have to babysit me."

"Hey, maybe I'd like to dance with you. What do you say?"

"I've never danced before. I'd step on your feet."

Jack laughed. "I'll take my chances."

Jack and Linda were dancing to a slow song, so they were able to talk a little. "You know, Linda," Jack said, "I thought you were cute ever since I met you at your place, when Scott introduced us."

"Really?"

"Well, yeah. I wanted to ask you out, but I know how protective your brother is of you."

After the dance Jack asked Linda if she wanted a drink from the trash can. She agreed, and in the next hour she and Jack danced and drank the exotic fruit blend. I noticed her a couple of times dancing, so I thought she was fine and was having a good time. It was such a large crowd, it was impossible to keep track of her all the time. I was hot and needed some fresh air, so I stepped outside for a while with one of the guys I was dancing with.

When I walked back into the house, there was a huge fight going on. The guy I was with asked somebody what started it. A poker game, another guy told us. Someone had yelled "Cheater!" and the table was flipped over, with cards and drinks flying everywhere.

I could see the Demarkhos' beautiful china and figurines smashed and scattered all over the floor, along with broken furniture.

I screamed for Linda, and she didn't answer. I shoved and pushed my way through the crowd, looking for my kids. I had to find them so I could get them out before the cops got there!

After pushing through the crowd, I spotted Scott. He was lying on the floor, out cold. I was scared to death. I slapped his face gently a few times trying to get him to come to. Finally he opened his eyes and moaned.

"Are you all right, son?"

He slowly lifted his head. He had a swollen eye and a bloody lip. "Yeah, Ma, I'm okay. Just give me a hand up, and I'll be fine."

"Scotty, I can't find Linda."

"Linda isn't with you? When was the last time you saw her?"

"I don't know for sure. It's been awhile; we both were dancing. In this crowd, Scott, I couldn't keep my eyes on her all the time. I stepped outside for a few minutes for a breath of air, and when I walked back in everything was chaotic. It could have been an hour since I last saw her, I don't know! All I know right now is we have to find her before the cops get here."

Scott and I frantically made our way through the crowd calling for Linda. Finally someone Scott knew pointed toward the staircase and hollered, "Scott! Your sister is on the top step of the staircase with Jack."

We looked up the long winding staircase and there she was with Jack holding on to her. Scott yelled, "I'm going to kill him!"

"No Scotty," I cried. "The main thing right now is to get her down and out of here before the cops come!"

Linda's hair was all messed up, and her clothing was all twisted and wrinkled. She looked like a zombie, leaning against Jack at the top of the steps.

Jack looked scared as he saw us staring up at them. Then his eyes wandered around his devastated, once beautiful great room. He could see it was trashed. There were even a few still fighting. I could see his thoughts. He wanted to die. He could only imagine what his parents were going to do to him, but for now he had to deal with the immense anger he was seeing in our faces. He knew he was in big trouble.

I rushed up the stairs with Scott right behind me. I screamed at Jack, "What have you done to my baby?"

Scott's fist was doubled as he yelled, "You're dead!"

"Never mind that right now, Scotty, we have to get Linda out of here before the cops come."

"Yeah, Ma, you're right, Here—I'll grab this arm, and you grab hold of the other."

"Let me help you, Scott," Jack pleaded.

"Just stay out of our way! My ma and me will get my sister out of here. You've done too much already. Just keep your filthy hands off my sister!"

Even though Linda remained in a zombie state, we were able to drag her down the steps and out of the house. When we got outdoors, Scott picked her up and carried her the hundred yards to where our car was parked.

Scott and I argued for a time, as to which one was sober enough to drive. Scott won out like he normally did. "Lorraine, I can handle a car better than you. You're high on alcohol. I've only been doing pot. My mind is sharper than yours, trust me."

I was exhausted, so I relinquished the control and jumped into the passenger side of the car, laying my head back on the seat.

We were down the road about a mile when we saw the blue lights of police cars and heard their sirens as they passed by. "Wow, Lorraine, we got out of there just in time. Looks like our lucky night."

"Yeah, Scotty! All but our little Linda, who's out in the back seat. I hope she will be okay." I laid my head back against the back of the seat again. "I'm just going to rest my eyes a little. Holler if you get sleepy."

It was a long drive home, and Scott was in pain. He was pretty much out of it when he pulled onto the expressway for the final part of the long drive home. Unfortunately, he pulled onto the wrong ramp and was driving on the wrong side of the expressway. There wasn't any traffic when we first got on the highway, so in no time at all, Scotty started to nod off to sleep.

I woke up just as I saw headlights coming directly toward us. I screamed, "Scotty! They're going to hit us!" Then I saw blinding headlights and heard the terrifying clash of steel....

⌘ ⌘ ⌘

Falling down on my knees in front of the Lord Jesus at the Judgment I cried out, "Please, God, let me go back and help my kids! I know it's too late for me, but they're just kids. It's my fault that they don't know you. I have to warn them. I was a terrible, selfish, sinful mother. It isn't their fault!"

"YES, LORRAINE, YOU WERE AN UNFIT MOTHER, BUT THE HOLY SPIRIT GAVE EACH OF YOUR CHILDREN AN OPPORTUNITY TO CHOOSE IF THEY WANTED TO SERVE ME, OR TO SERVE THE DEVIL. BOTH WERE BEYOND THE AGE OF ACCOUNTABILITY. THEREFORE ONLY THEY COULD HAVE DECIDED TO GIVE THEIR HEARTS AND LIVES TO ME.

"LORRAINE, YOU DID GIVE YOUR CHILDREN A BAD FOUNDATION. THE CORRECT FOUNDATION IS WRITTEN IN THE BIBLE IN LUKE CHAPTER 6. THERE I LAID DOWN INSTRUCTIONS THAT LEAD PARENTS TO LAYING A GOOD FOUNDATION FOR THEIR CHILDREN AND THEIR HOUSEHOLD. IF YOU DO NOT LAY A GOOD FOUNDATION, YOUR HOUSE WILL COLLAPSE. THAT IS EXACTLY WHAT HAPPENED TO YOUR HOUSE. EVEN SO, ULTIMATELY EACH PERSON HAS TO MAKE THAT DECISION FOR THEMSELVES."

"Please, Lord," I begged once more, "let me go back and tell my kids now what is waiting for them if they don't listen to your call. I will never be that unfit mother again. I'll stop going out drinking and doing drugs!

How stupid I was to practice that New Age junk. I was absolutely nothing without you. I realize now that you are my creator, the only Divine Living God. I'll never put another god before you again!"

"THE DEVIL AND HIS ANGELS KNOW THAT, TOO. UNLESS YOU CHOOSE ME FOR YOUR SAVIOR, YOU SHALL NOT BE SAVED."

"I know I can't be saved now, Lord, but my kids need to know before it's too late. I need to tell them about this eternal hell. Please let me tell them!"

"AS I'VE TOLD YOU BEFORE, THIS IS THE GREAT WHITE THRONE JUDGMENT; THERE IS NO RETURN. TURN, LORRAINE, LOOK. IT WAS YOU. YOU WERE YOUR CHILDREN'S LAST CHANCE ALSO."

As I turned, I could see my precious Linda and Scott being led to me. As they drew closer, I could see the torment on their faces, the hurt and blame in their eyes toward me. I cried out to them, "I'm sorry!"

"THEIR NAMES ARE NOT WRITTEN IN THE BOOK OF LIFE. THEY WILL BE CAST INTO THE LAKE OF FIRE, WHERE THERE WILL BE WEEPING AND GNASHING OF TEETH FOR ALL ETERNITY."

37

As I was twisting and moaning, I faintly heard a voice saying, "Please, sweetheart, wake up. Come back to me." Struggling to open my eyes, I could see a blurred vision of a man in front of me. My eyes opened further and I cried out, "Tommy, Tommy."

"Yes, my darling, I'm right here!" Tears were flowing down his face, and he laughed a little under his breath. "You haven't called me that in years. I thought I lost you, my darling."

In confusion I whispered, "What are you doing here? Did God let you come to save me?"

"Of course I'm here, honey. I haven't left the hospital since our accident."

"Our wha...what? Hospital? I thought I died? That I was being thrown into the Lake of Fire along with my kids!"

"Lorraine, honey, calm down. You can't get so excited. You've just come out of a three-day coma."

"Oh! I'm not in hell?"

"Of course not, silly. You're my angel, and you're going to be just fine."

In a panic I said, "The kids...are the kids okay?"

"Sure, honey."

"They weren't hurt in the accident?"

"No! My poor baby. You still are confused, aren't you? It was just you and me in the car. You were taking me to the airport, remember?"

I struggled to focus. "Oh, yes. I remember now."

"You wouldn't believe all the prayers that have been going out for you. Not only have the kids and I been praying over you night and day, but our church members have been faithfully holding prayer vigils for you, too. God answers prayers! Praise His name!"

"You can say that again," I said in a relieved voice.

"Let me call down to the cafeteria and let Linda and Scott know that you are back with us again."

In no time my precious kids came rushing into my room and sat by my side. "Oh, Mother, I love you so much," Linda told me. "I was so scared that you wouldn't make it, but we prayed for you; and look, God answered our prayers. I don't know what I would ever do without you, Mom!"

Scotty took me by the hand. "How are you feeling?"

"I'm feeling very sleepy, but very happy that I'm alive here with my precious family. You kids look older!"

Scott laughed. "We're not really any older, Mom. You have only been out for three days. I'm still in my second year of Bible seminary, and Linda is still a senior in high school."

"Oh, yes, Lorraine," Thomas added. "You should be very proud of our daughter. She has decided to go to a Bible College next fall."

"Linda, sweetie, that's wonderful!"

I frowned. "Now I remember what happened. You had a 3 a.m. flight. I was driving you to the airport so you could catch a flight to attend a conference. The last thing I remember were those awful, bright headlights coming toward us. I remember screaming, 'They're going to hit us!' That was the last thing I remember until now."

Thomas shuddered. "It happened out of nowhere! We were driving down the expressway, when all of a sudden this car comes barreling toward us. It hit us head on."

"Were you hurt?"

"Not really. A few minor bumps and a bloody lip, nothing major. The car hit more on your side. I wish I could have taken the blunt for you. You mean so much to me. I couldn't do anything; it happened so fast. When I held you, I thought you were dead! While you were in surgery, your heart stopped for five minutes. The doctors thought they had lost you."

Tears welled up in my eyes as the previous days leading up to the accident started unfolding before my eyes. I said to my kids, "Come here, you guys." I gave them a big hug. "Do you know how much I love you? You and your father are my whole world."

I was having a problem holding back my emotions so I asked, "Kids, would you mind giving your father and I some private time? We need to talk."

Scott stood. "Sure, Mom! You must be really tired after all you've been through. I've got my car here, and it's getting late. I'll drive Linda home tonight. We'll see you first thing in the morning."

"Yeah, Mom, you need your rest. So do we! We haven't slept in our beds since you've been in here."

The kids both gave me hugs and kisses. They told me they loved me, then left. When I saw them leave, the flood of tears I'd been holding back burst like a mighty dam. Thomas held me close while comforting me until I was cried out. "I'm sorry, Thomas, I'm so sorry!"

"Honey, don't be sorry. You have gone through a traumatic ordeal. Of course you would have all this bottled up in you. I'm glad to see you can let it all out."

"Oh, there is much more that I have to get out. Much more that I need to get off my chest!"

"I'm here for you, darling. You know you can tell me anything, don't you?"

"Yes, my love, I know. However, what I have to say is going to be very painful. Not only for me telling you, but to you as you listen. It's as if God has given me a mirror to look into, where I could see my dark side. Thomas, do you believe all people have a dark side?"

"Of course, darling! In the flesh we all have a dark side. When we allow Jesus to come into our hearts and accept His gift of salvation, His grace is sufficient to help us overcome the darkness."

"But there are temptations! Thomas, I have been to my dark side because of temptation."

"Lorraine, the Bible tells us to flee from temptation."

"I know, but I allowed myself to be tempted and God stopped me before I got to my darkest side."

"What are you talking about?"

"I don't know where to start…"

"At the beginning."

"First of all, I need to say you are my anchor, my one true love. You have actually saved my life!"

"As you are mine, and I love you dearly. But why do you say I saved your life?"

"You did, my love, you did! Remember when we were young and my friend Christina invited me to the church's Teen Meet club? That's when we first met, remember?"

"Of course I do! That club was a big part of our growing-up years.

When I met you for the first time, I fell for you. I was just a kid. I never even dated a girl before. I thought you were the most beautiful creation that God had ever made on this earth!"

I smiled. "Well, you weren't as handsome back then as you are now, but you were the nicest boy I had ever met. You know what kind of a background I came from. Wealthy parents who were only concerned about their public appearances. My parents and I weren't Christians when I met you, but thank God that by going to that Christian club, I was able to be saved. I loved that church and became active in it. I sure loved being a Sunday school teacher."

"It took a long time for your folks to be converted, but by your loving Christian faith and examples, they finally became saved too."

"That was your doing! You were very patient and kind when you tried to talk to them about the Lord. It was your persistence that got them to visit our church."

"Maybe, but it was the Holy Spirit who convicted their hearts that day."

"Amen to that!"

"It was so neat that after that our parents became best friends, and we all attended church together. Those are pleasant memories."

"Yes, they are!" I said mischievously. "Do you remember when we had that hayride where you kissed me for the first time?"

"Like I could forget it!"

We laughed. "Yes, but do you remember that same night when I told you and Christina that I had met a new girl at school, and she asked me to go to a dance with her."

"Oh, yes! Christina got so mad at you that night because you wouldn't listen to her about how wild that particular girl was."

"I always thought she was mad at me because she had a crush on you."

"No! Remember, she wasn't mad at you anymore when you made the decision not to go out with…a…Amy, that was her name. You were so determined you wanted to be friends with her, even though you were so different. You were a Christian, and she had one of the worst reputations around. Thank God you finally took our advice and waited until you found Christian friends at your new school. Then you surprised me and started that Christian club at school. I was so proud of you."

"Yeah, the new school! My parents were so unfair about making me go to another school. They thought the worst about our friendship. We were just real good friends, but Mother didn't trust me. I thought we were only friends, too. At that time I didn't even know you cared for me in a romantic way."

"They didn't know any better. They were trying the best they could."

"Thomas, remember my senior prom?"

"Of course I do. I was there with the most beautiful girl, not to mention the queen of the prom. You were so beautiful and radiant that night, not only in looks, but deep within that Christian soul of yours. That was the night I knew I had to have you as my wife someday."

"I love you so much! By the way, I knew a year before that, that I wanted to be your wife."

Thomas laughed. "Okay, you were always a little smarter than me. We sure did have a wonderful courtship, didn't we?"

"Yeah, but not long enough! If my parents wouldn't have interfered, we could have gone to high school together."

"It upset me too, honey, but maybe it was for the best. We were so young and in love. If we had been together more when we were so young, maybe we would have yielded to temptation. At least we were able to go to the same college. We were more mature and could handle our emotions better then."

"Yeah, I suppose you're right."

"Sure, I'm right. Things for us didn't turn out too bad, did they?"

"Well, I didn't become a lawyer like my dad wanted, but he was proud of me when I became a teacher. My parents think the world of you, Thomas. After all, if it wasn't for you, they might not have been saved. I shudder to think what would have happened to them or me, if it wasn't for you and of course the Lord in my life."

Then my tears began to fall once again. I buried my head in my husband's chest and cried.

"Darling, what's the matter! Are you in pain? I'll call the nurse!"

"No, no, Thomas, wait! I'm in pain, but not physical. It is my soul and heart that is aching. When I think of what I might have thrown away, it kills me! I don't want to lose you, my darling!"

Thomas held me close and tried to soothe me. He brushed my long strands of hair from my tearful face with his fingertips. He whispered in my ear, "Sweetie, it can't be that bad. There's nothing my godly wife could do to make me leave her. We all have sinned and come short of the glory of God. You also know that Jesus died on the cross and will forgive your sins."

"Yes, Thomas. I know that Jesus will forgive me if I ask and repent of my sins. And I will; I promise, I will. I know He will forgive me, but I don't know if you can."

"Where's all this going? You're getting me worried."

"Let me start from the beginning. Since you received your new appointment two years ago, things have really changed in my life. Before you took the appointment, I didn't let you know how I felt about it. I was being a submissive wife, as the Bible says. There was no way I was happy about our move. I loved our church family there; it was home to us."

"Lorraine, why didn't you say something? I thought you were happy about us going to a larger church. It had been our goal to advance, to have a larger congregation, a bigger and better home for our family. Sure, I miss the people from our old church, but there are some great people at this one also."

"Our old church was small. We knew each family on a personal basis. Remember the Jacobs? They brought us fresh eggs every week. Whenever the neighbors butchered, we always got a good portion of their beef, pork, or chickens."

"Yeah, honey. We didn't have much money and the parsonage was small, but we always had plenty of food on our table, bless their hearts."

"Thomas, you and I were really happy back then. We were at that church from the time we got married. When we had our kids, the congregation all loved them. I never was in need of a babysitter while I was teaching. Which is another thing I've resented! I was finally doing what I loved, teaching. Now that's all over."

"But, honey, I thought you loved having such a big part in the church. You still teach, but now you lead the woman's Bible study. You teach Sunday school class, counsel teens, and are involved in AWANA. I thought you were happy and fulfilled with all that."

"I'm so ashamed! My heart hasn't been into it. There was a cloud of resentment hanging over me. Remember the day you got the invitation to come to this church?"

"Of course, I was thrilled! I thought you were also."

"You came into the house glowing that day with a dozen red roses. You told me you had a really great surprise for me. That's when you told me about the invitation to the new church."

"Yes, I was very happy. It was what I had been working so hard to achieve. The new position had excellent pay, insurance, and the most beautiful home for my family. I thought you would be thrilled. I had no idea."

"Then you told me my career in education was paying off. That I could be a big asset to you in our new church. I thought it had paid off already for me; I loved teaching elementary school."

"Lorraine, if you didn't want to move, why didn't you say something?"

"Because I couldn't tell you! You were so happy about it, I couldn't burst your bubble. I was so happy and contented there. I loved my life just the way it was. However, I knew how much it meant to you, so I couldn't say a word. Remember what you are always saying, 'Wives are to be submissive to their husbands'?"

"Yes, but the Bible also says, 'Men, love your wife as Christ loves His Church.' Honey, I love you so much. I wouldn't have taken this commission if I knew that you felt so strongly about this. Yes, ultimately I make the finally decisions for our family, but on a major issue I'm always open to discuss it with you. In fact, I implore you to share your ideas with me. Sometimes you sway my thinking. We are partners!"

"That's why I couldn't tell you! I knew how much you wanted it. I told myself I'd be able to adapt to a new life, but unfortunately, I never did. I went through the motions of being happy about it. I guess I could have won an academy award for my performance. Even though my heart was back at our little church and my teaching job, I went about my new tasks with as much zeal as I could muster up. It was overwhelming at times. The congregation was so big that it didn't seem possible to know any of them personally, not like at the old church. There wasn't that friendliness of a small church. I really missed that."

"I'm so sorry that I was so absorbed in church business that I didn't see what my wife was going through."

"You can't blame yourself. You're a very dedicated pastor. You're always there for anyone who needs you. We both have been busy, going different directions. What I miss the most is the close intimacy we had before. When we do have a few minutes to share, it's always about church business or the kids. I actually started resenting you because of it. I'm ashamed to say, I was even getting jealous of you with other women."

"Jealous of me with other women? Why?"

"I guess from the lack of intimacy we shared. When you counseled women, especially divorced women, I was always afraid you would give in to temptation. I was feeling inadequate and insecure as a woman."

"Sweetheart, please forgive me for making you feel that way! Didn't you realize that whenever I met with any woman that I made sure one of my assistant pastors was always with me? Not because I would be tempted, but to protect myself and the church from any allegations? Honey, I could never cheat on you!"

I lost it again and started crying. "Darling, I don't deserve a godly man like you. I can't keep it in any longer. I have to confess to you! I have done something unforgivable. I'll understand if you don't want anything more to do with me. I don't deserve your love anymore."

"Lorraine, you're beginning to scare me! What have you done that is so bad?"

"Last month, when you sent me out to buy a new bedroom suite, that is when it all started. This is a poor excuse, but the night before I went to the store, you had been out until ten o'clock counseling a very attractive and recently divorced woman. My jealous mind was imagining all sorts of things.

"When I arrived at the store, a young, handsome salesman greeted me at the door. When I told him what I was there for, he directed me to the bedroom section of the store. From the start he was very attentive and a bit flirtatious. He had me lay down on a bed to find the special feel. As I laid there a second enjoying the comfort of the bed, he sat down next to me. He said to me, 'You look like an angel lying there with your beautiful long black hair flowing about. The contrast of your black hair against that blue suit makes your gorgeous blue eyes stand out and sparkle.'"

"You do look beautiful in that blue suit, but he was out of line talking to you that way."

"Yes, I know. He said it in a very seductive voice. Thomas, forgive me, but I have to admit that his flattery made me feel alive. It had been a long time since I had a compliment like that from a man. Now this guy, not much older than my son, was finding me attractive."

"You shouldn't have to be told. You are by far the most beautiful woman I've ever seen! On second thought, I should have been telling you that more often. I'm sorry. If I would have given you the attention you deserve, you probably would have been insulted by his boldness."

"You're right. I should have walked out of there, but I didn't. It was awkward for me, and I could tell my face was red."

"That's disgusting. I've heard enough! That young man has stepped over his boundaries. I'm going to have a talk with his manager."

"No, please, it was partially my fault. I have to admit I was enjoying being flirted with, and he could tell. I was going along with it. It's my fault! I don't know what came over me."

"The old devil himself, that's who! You were yielding to temptation, Lorraine. He was a good salesman, all right. Looking at the bill on the set, he must have done a good job of seducing you into buying the most expensive bedroom outfit on the floor."

"You're probably right about that, but he wasn't only trying to seduce me for my cash."

"And what does that mean!"

"I'm so ashamed, but you need to know why I did what I did. At least you deserve the honest truth. The bad part is that I was enjoying this dangerous game the salesman and I were playing. I even flirted back with him. It made me feel glamorous, like the stars on soap operas."

"You aren't watching that trash, are you?"

"Yeah. You are gone so much and the kids are gone most of the time. I started watching them, and now I think I've become addicted to them."

"Aren't the characters always involved in extramarital affairs?"

"You're right, Thomas. They made my life feel boring, unloved. That's when I started fantasizing about having a love affair. Those stupid shows led me into temptation!"

"That's right! They did! So, I guess you were living through one of your fantasies when you and that gigolo were flirting back and forth, right?"

"Yes, you are right. The next few days that passed, I couldn't get him off my mind. I was fantasizing about him. I'm so sorry!"

"I hope that was the last of it."

"It's appalling, but no. I'm so ashamed. When the men delivered our new furniture, one of them handed me a note and a red rose. The note was a thank you for purchasing a new bedroom suite. It also came with an invitation from Todd to meet him at Al Plato's for lunch the next day."

"That jerk! You mean he had the audacity to ask you out? Tell me, Lorraine, you didn't accept!"

I started crying again and in-between the sobs answered, "Yes! I am so sorry. I tried to rationalize it. Just a friendly, innocent lunch, nothing to it. But deep down I knew there was nothing innocent about this lunch. I wrestled with my conscience for the rest of the day and into the next morning. I found myself dressing for the lunch date."

"How ignorant can you be? The Bible says that if you lust in your heart after another, it is the same as if you already committed the sin. Lorraine, that would make you an adulteress in your heart!"

"I know, I know. But at that point I was only thinking about his company, not anything else. I felt flattered that he wanted to take me out for lunch. I really thought it was an innocent lunch. However, there was a gnawing in my soul. I felt like there was an angelic war going on around me. I could almost see God's angels going to battle, trying to keep me from temptation, while the devil's demons were trying to get me into trouble. I know it must have been some conflict, because I had plenty of conflict within my soul."

"I hope you listened to the Holy Spirit telling you not to go?"

In a defeated way I said, "I'm sorry, but the devil won the battle. If I had been walking closer to the Lord, none of this would have happened. I should have put on the full armor of God. But I didn't."

"So, you are telling me that you went?"

It killed me to see the hurt in my saintly husband's eyes. "Yes," I cried out. "Oh, how sorry I am! Thomas, darling, I wouldn't have hurt you for anything. If I could only take it back, I would."

"But you can't. What's done is done! Is there more?"

In a weak voice I answered, "I'm afraid so." I went on to explain, "I meet him at Al Plato's, which is a very lovely, expensive restaurant."

Thomas looked at me disgustedly. "I wouldn't know. I don't frequent places that sell alcoholic beverages. I thought my wife didn't either!"

"I didn't realize that until we ordered. The restaurant was dimly lit. It took awhile to adjust my eyes, while the host directed us to a table in a corner."

Thomas gave me a painful look. "A den of iniquity, and a table conducive to cheating lovers. How convenient!"

"Believe it or not, I was thinking about how nice it would have been if it had been you there with me, not him. I was very uncomfortable. I wanted to run out, but was too embarrassed to do so. When the waiter came to our table, Todd told him to bring a certain bottle of wine. He didn't give me a chance to say anything. The waiter brought it back to our table and poured wine into the crystal wine glasses in front of us."

Thomas stared at me in shock. "I hope you didn't drink any. Did you?"

"At first I wasn't going to, but I felt kind of barbaric. What would a little wine hurt? Besides, I was a little curious. You know I've never tasted it before. I justified myself by thinking about Jesus making wine at the wedding supper. If Jesus made wine, He must have approved of it."

"That was no excuse. You know that the wine in the Bible Jesus made was not fermented!"

"Yes, I guess so. I was trying to justify my actions. The problem was that I really liked the taste of it. It was enhancing to my meal, so it went down easy. The second glass went down faster."

Thomas got up from my bed and started pacing. He stopped and met my eyes. "So what now? You must have been drunk, seeing you aren't used to drinking!"

"You're right. I was feeling it. I felt myself loosening up. I became giggly. Todd said I had a bubbly personality. We talked and laughed. Then I was shocked as Todd put his arm around me and started to kiss me."

"Well, what did you expect? You probably wanted to be kissed!"

"First I told him to stop. I pushed him away and told him that I was married. He didn't care. He said he noticed my wedding ring in the store. I felt totally ashamed as I told him that I was married to a minister, and a minister's wife does not act that way."

"Did that end the indiscretion? Did that stop him cold?"

"No, he wasn't going to let anything stop him. He told me that when he was intrigued with a woman, he does his homework. He already knew I was a pastor's wife. He said it made me more exciting and challenging."

"Why, that God-less moron!"

"He tried to kiss me again, and I told him that it was time for me to go, that I had to get home and pack my husband's suitcase for a weekend conference."

"Why would you let him know I would be away for the weekend?"

"I wasn't thinking clearly because of the wine. Todd kept insisting that I meet him for dinner while you were gone. I kept saying no; but after the third glass of wine I gave in and said yes."

That's when Thomas lost it completely. He broke down and started to cry. My heart was breaking for him and for our twenty-three-year marriage.

"Thomas, please, come here." He sat on the edge of my bed, we embraced, and both cried until there were no more tears left.

Finally I was able to speak again. "When I sobered up I was so ashamed, but I still was planning on meeting Todd that evening. Maybe I thought that it was a way of helping me cope with the jealousy in my head, or that I was so obsessed in my fantasies. I don't know, but for some insane reason I was planning to go."

"Never in my wildest dreams did I think that my wife, who I thought was a righteous wife, was plotting to deceive me, to cheat on me!"

"You have got to believe me, I don't think I would have let it go that far! I really don't think I could have cheated on you. Besides, while on the way to the airport, God intervened by causing the accident. Don't you see? He showed me what my life could have been like, if I continued living a sinful life. He gave me a second chance at The Great White Throne Judgment!"

"What are you rambling about, Lorraine? There will be no second chance at that Judgment. It's the final judgment after Christ's Millennium on earth. That's when all of Satan's children will be thrown into the Lake of Fire forever, and ever!" Sarcastically he added, "Where the adulteresses will go!"

"Yes, Thomas, I know it now. It's all so very clear to me. God gave me a second chance! I could have committed the biggest mistake of my life, had it not been for God's intervention. I am so thankful He caused us to be in that traffic accident. Praise God, He showed me how I could have destroyed my life. Even if I lose you, my darling, the most important person in my life, I will still dedicate my life to serving God. From now on, I'm going to keep my life so full of God that there will be no more room for the devil. My only regret about the accident is the people in the other car. Were they hurt?"

"Lorraine, there were three people in the other car—a mother and her two teenage kids. The boy was driving on the wrong side of the expressway and hit us head on. There were drugs and alcohol involved. They were all killed."

"Oh, no, how terrible! Just like in my vision! That poor, poor family. When I was in a coma, God showed me what my life would have been like if I wouldn't have listened to you back when we were kids. Thomas, you helped me to find the Lord. I will always be grateful to you for that. He showed me how absolutely horrifying my life would have been if I would have gotten involved with Amy."

I continued telling Thomas the whole vision that I was shown by God at the Great White Throne Judgment.

Thomas quietly said, "What a horrible tragedy that would have been for not only you, but your parents as well. I'm so grateful you opened your heart to the Holy Spirit back then."

"Me, too. But now, after all these years, I have strayed. I became out of fellowship with the Lord, and I ended up in that accident. I'm so ashamed." I looked up into Thomas's eyes and pleaded, "Please, my darling, forgive me. I love you more than anything on God's earth. But if you can't forgive me, I can understand it. But I beg of you, give me a second chance like God did. I'm so thankful He opened my eyes. It took a terrible accident, but now I can see."

Thomas answered back in a low voice, "The important thing is that you get your heart right with the Lord, and ask His forgiveness."

"You are absolutely right, my darling! Will you pray with me while I ask God to forgive me?"

With tears sliding down his face, Thomas whispered, "Yes." He took my hand, and I prayed.

"Dear God, please forgive me for sinning so greatly against You and the wonderful Christian man You have given me. I am so sorry for falling from Your wonderful grace and mercy. Forgive me for all the selfish feelings I've had. Forgive me for wandering so far away from Your sweet fellowship. You were always there for me, but I wasn't there for You. Forgive me for not having enough faith or love in my heart for You. For if I had, I would have had enough love for others.

"If my husband can find it in his heart to forgive me, I will forever be grateful. Please help him to forgive me! If he is willing to give me a second chance, help me get to know and love all of my brothers and sisters in our large congregation.

"And please, precious Lord, forgive me for having adulterous feelings in my heart. Help me to resist temptation from now on. And again I pray, let my wonderful husband find it in his heart to forgive me.

"I pray, my Dear Savior, for the family involved in the accident. I hope and pray that even though they were in a drunken condition, their souls were not lost. It's not my place to judge their hearts, I know You are the only one who can do that. I can only pray that they are not headed to hell, like I was in my vision. How tragic it is when a young life is cut short, not knowing You as their personal Savior. I also pray that their loved ones have You as their personal Savior. It is so comforting to be able to lay our burdens down at Your feet at a sorrowful times like that.

"Thank You, Lord Jesus, for literally stopping me from committing the worst sin of my life! The accident was life-saving for me. Your Holy Spirit made me stop and realize what an awful mistake I was about to make. A decision that could have ruined the rest of my life…maybe even my eternity! In myself I know it would be almost impossible to live without my husband, but with You I know I can if I have to.

"Dear Almighty God, I don't believe I really accepted You in my heart the way I should have. Now I want to give You all of my heart. I want to rededicate my life to You. I pray I will do your will. Please help me now to be Your obedient child from this day forward. I surrender completely to You. I'm nothing without You. I know that all things are possible for You. I want to live the rest of my life serving You. Please guide and direct all my decisions. I pray that my heart will be full of your goodness, so there will never be enough room for the devil again! I found out, Lord, that I'm human. Even a pastor's wife can fall short of the glory of God. Thank You for letting me see right from wrong, darkness from the light. Thank You so much, my heavenly Father, for your unconditional forgiveness. I ask this all, in Jesus Christ's Holy name, amen!"

When the prayer ended, Thomas buried his head into the edge of my bed and cried. I reached out to him. "Darling, I love you so much. Do you think you can find it in your heart to forgive me? I know that God has forgiven me. I've heard you say many times in your sermons that we are to forgive others as God has forgiven us. I only hope and pray that you will be able to forgive me, too…."

A Note from the Author

Throughout my story, Lorraine, the main character, makes many bad choices that lead her to The Great White Throne Judgment, where she and Jesus converse about the major decisions in her life. Many of Jesus' words are taken from the Bible, and He applies them to the temptations of life and struggles that many of us go through.

I wrote *Journey to The Great White Throne Judgment* to show that God is always with us. His Holy Spirit knocks on our heart's door until we answer: whether it be for Him, or against Him. And with every choice, there is a consequence. Revelation 3:19-21 says: "As many as I love, I rebuke and chasten. Therefore be zealous and repent. Behold, I stand at the door and knock. If anyone hears My voice and opens the door, I will come into him and dine with him, and he with Me. To him who overcomes I will grant to sit with Me on My throne, as I also overcame and sat down with My Father on His throne. Through His Lamb, God has given us the gift of grace, to help us resist temptation."

In the story, Lorraine and her children are offered salvation through the death and resurrection of our precious Lord Jesus. In addition, I couldn't write a story without including my favorite subject: Bible prophecy. In fact, I've devoted part of a chapter to the End Time Prophecy.

My prayer is that this story will touch the hearts of faithful Christians, the unsaved, and those who are out of fellowship with God. If one Christian is drawn closer to God by reading this story, what a wonderful blessing that would be. If only one person is saved, it will be worth the years I've put into writing the story. Finally, if one Christian who was out of fellowship with God repents by reading my words, it also would be worth it. For with repentance, they will be back in the service of the Lord.

Notes

[1] Inspired by 2 Corinthians 6:14
[2] Luke 11:4
[3] Matthew 7:17
[4] John 3:3
[5] Matthew 7:1-5
[6] Hebrews 13:4
[7] Ephesians 5:25, 28
[8] Matthew 5:16
[9] John 15:12
[10] Hebrews 13:1
[11] Matthew 25:31-40
[12] Matthew 7:13-14
[13] Mark 10:14
[14] Proverbs 16:18
[15] Matthew 5:32
[16] Psalm 5:4-6
[17] Proverbs 31:30
[18] Colossians 3:12-14, *The Living Bible*
[19] Ephesians 4:31-32, *The Living Bible*
[20] 1 John 2:18
[21] 1 John 2:22-23, *The Living Bible*
[22] 2 John 7, 10-11
[23] Exodus 20:2-4; 34:14
[24] Proverbs 22:6
[25] Proverbs 23:13-14
[26] Proverbs 29:15-17
[27] 1 Peter 5:8
[28] Matthew 4:1-11
[29] James 4:7
[30] Leviticus 18:22, *The Living Bible*
[31] Romans 1:18-27, *The Living Bible*
[32] 1 Corinthians 6:9-10, *The Living Bible*

About the Author

JUDY KAY SCOTT, who has a B.A. in Business Administration, has worked in the field of marketing and also pursued a career in education. After retiring, she had more time to write. When God gave her the inspiration to write this story several years ago, she was shocked! Even though she had been saved as a child, she was, at that time, out of fellowship with the Lord. She wondered how God could possibly use a person like her.

During those early years she put the task God had given her on the shelf, while continuing a busy lifestyle. Throughout the years, as her faith in the Lord continued to grow stronger in the Lord, the Holy Spirit kept convicting her to write more until she couldn't stop until she was finished. There was no doubt in her mind that this story had to be a spiritual intervention by God. "I believed that God wanted to send a wakeup call to the world through my writing…perhaps even to myself. It was only through God that I was able to write the story. God only needs a willing vessel, and He will do the rest."

Judy and her husband, Russell, live in his hometown of South Haven, Michigan. They are members of The Anchor Baptist Church.

To email the author: **judykayscott63@hotmail.com**

www.oaktara.com